Because It's Christmas

Center Point
Large Print

Books are
produced in the
United States
using U.S.-based
materials

Books are printed
using a revolutionary
new process called
THINKtech™ that
lowers energy usage
by 70% and increases
overall quality

Books are
durable and
flexible
because of
smythe-sewing

Paper is
sourced using
environmentally
responsible
foresting methods
and the
paper is acid-free

Also by Katherine Spencer and available from
Center Point Large Print:

The Way Home
Songs of Christmas
Harbor of the Heart
All Is Bright
Together for Christmas

**This Large Print Book carries the
Seal of Approval of N.A.V.H.**

Thomas Kinkade's Cape Light

Because It's Christmas

Katherine Spencer

CENTER POINT LARGE PRINT
THORNDIKE, MAINE

This Center Point Large Print edition
is published in the year 2017 by arrangement with
The Berkley Publishing Group,
an imprint of Penguin Publishing Group,
a division of Penguin Random House LLC.

The text of this Large Print edition is unabridged.
In other aspects, this book may vary from the original
edition. Printed in the United States of America on
permanent paper. Set in 16-point Times New Roman type.

ISBN: 978-1-68324-617-6

Library of Congress Cataloging-in-Publication Data

Names: Spencer, Katherine, 1955- author.
Title: Because it's Christmas : Thomas Kinkade's cape light /
    Katherine Spencer.
Other titles: Because it is Christmas
Description: Center Point large print edition. | Thorndike, Maine :
    Center Point Large Print, 2017.
Identifiers: LCCN 2017041666 | ISBN 9781683246176
    (hardcover : alk. paper)
Subjects: LCSH: Cape Light (Imaginary place)— Fiction. |
    City and town life—New England—Fiction. | Large type books. |
    Christmas stories. | GSAFD: Christian fiction. | Love stories.
Classification: LCC PS3553.A489115 B43 2017 | DDC 813/.54—dc23
LC record available at https://lccn.loc.gov/2017041666

To my family—with love always

Dear Reader

Every year my daughter sends me a list of items she'd like to find under the Christmas tree. This tradition has probably evolved from the days of writing letters to Santa. Maybe I don't mind because for so many years I was studying those crayoned lists and doing Santa's shopping. Also, I truly enjoy giving everyone on my list something they really want, valuing accuracy above the surprise factor. Some will say that takes the fun out of gift buying and giving. They might even say I'm lazy. These are usually the same people who roam the mall and Internet tirelessly, searching for those unrequested but hopefully perfect presents. I do admire them.

After writing this latest Cape Light story, I've been wondering which category Heaven falls into: Answering our prayers exactly, down to the item number, color, and size? Or delivering a blessing that's absolutely perfect, though we may never have asked for or even imagined it?

As Christmas draws near, Sophie Potter, Emily Warwick, and Zoey Bates each doubt the wishes closest to their hearts will be fulfilled. All Sophie wants is to remain in her home and spend the rest of her days on her beloved orchard. But her children believe she can no longer live alone, despite the unexpected arrival and companionship of her grandson James.

Emily has lost the election to Charlie Bates. Determined to turn the page, she takes up new hobbies and puts her family first. Secretly, she misses the satisfaction she found guiding the citizens of Cape Light. Must she choose one way or the other? Her Christmas wish is to find some other path. One that makes everyone, including herself, happy.

Zoey has been working hard at college and at the diner her family owns. As the fall semester ends, a wonderful career opportunity moves into her sights, and a special relationship grows with James Potter. But family responsibilities come first. Zoey must put her dreams aside, and James must carry through with his plans. Cape Light is only a short stop in his travels. Or so they both believe.

But Sophie, Emily, and Zoey discover that Heaven has read their "wish lists" very carefully and found each of them the perfect gift for Christmas. Maybe not exactly what they asked for or imagined, but something even better.

I hope you find a few perfect surprises under the tree, too.

Wishing you and everyone you hold dear a wonderful holiday season and a happy, healthy New Year.

Katherine Spencer

Chapter One

"FLOUR, BUTTER, SUGAR. YOU DON'T NEED much more than that." Sophie Potter confided the recipe for her delectable piecrust in an unusually serious tone. "Easy, right?"

"Very easy." Zoey Bates nodded, noticing a dash of flour across Sophie's cheek that was a perfect match to the wispy bun at the back of her head.

They were both elbow-deep in ingredients while neat rows of pans on the long wooden table waited to be filled with apple, pumpkin, or pecan. Zoey would deliver most of the pies to church tomorrow, to be tucked into boxes and baskets of Thanksgiving meals and sent out to families facing difficult times.

Sophie would bring one of each to the Potters' family gathering at her daughter Evelyn's house. And Zoey would take one or two home for her family's holiday dinner, too.

"I bet my dad is going to say, 'Why aren't you ever interested in *my* cooking lessons?'" Zoey imitated her father's voice perfectly. "He always wants to teach me stuff at the diner. But I know he gets most of the cakes and pies from a big commercial bakery. Even though the menu says 'homemade.' "

Sophie laughed and swept a knife edge over a heaping cup of flour to level it. "I'm sure your father can teach you a lot about cooking, too. My girls didn't have any patience to learn from me, either. Now they teach me a thing or two. Evelyn barely agreed to let me bring dessert for Thanksgiving. She'd have me sitting in an easy chair all day, watching TV. Or something equally useless. I didn't dare tell her I was baking for the church baskets."

Sophie's daughter Evelyn lived in town with her family and was still a member of the church she had been raised in, the stone church on the village green, where Zoey's family also attended.

"She'll probably hear about it on Sunday. If she hasn't already. You know how Reverend Ben thanks everybody at the service."

"By then the pies will be long baked and eaten. She won't be able to put up too much of a fuss." Sophie wore a mischievous grin as she mixed the dry ingredients. "You can add a dash of cinnamon and nutmeg, to give it some backbone. But not too much."

Sophie slipped on her glasses before carefully tilting each shaker. She added the spices to the first bowl, then held them out to Zoey. "Here, you try."

Zoey was dicing butter with a special hand tool, as instructed, and felt comfortable with that job. Spices seemed much trickier. "Maybe you should do it. I don't want to ruin the dough."

"Nonsense. How can you learn? Cooking is a lot like life, honey. You're going to make mistakes, but most can be fixed. Start with a light touch, and you'll do fine."

Zoey took the shaker and followed Sophie's advice, sprinkling carefully.

"Perfect." Sophie mixed more flour, and Zoey continued with the butter.

"How many people will be at your daughter's house?"

Sophie squinted a moment. "Let's see . . . With my grandson's fiancée and my nephew's baby, at least twenty-five. We'll need two big tables—and two turkeys—for sure."

The Potter family tree spread far and wide, and Zoey was not familiar with all of Sophie's relatives; just those who lived in and around Cape Light. She did know others by their photographs, which covered nearly every table, ledge, and wall of the old house.

"That's a lot. Even with the Tulleys and Grandma Dooley, we'll only be eight."

"A small gathering is nice. You can have a real conversation at the table. When the Potter clan gets together, it's mayhem."

"We're not that many people, but it's never that

13

quiet. Not if there's a football game on." Zoey was thinking about her two stepbrothers and her father. Loud when they were happy and their team was winning, and loud if the game was going the other way.

Zoey had not grown up in the Bates household. She had been taken in by Lucy and Charlie Bates about five years ago, when she ran away from a foster home and ended up in the Clam Box one rainy, cold winter night. With barely a dollar in her pocket and nowhere to go, she was so sick with the flu, she could hardly stand. Kindhearted Lucy persuaded Zoey to come home with her and Charlie, and what began as a one-night respite from her hard, chaotic life evolved into Zoey finding the loving family and real home she had never known. Lucy and Charlie had adopted her, and Zoey now thought of them as her real parents, and even called them Mom and Dad.

Sophie shook her head. "Football. If they're not watching it, they're all outside, tackling each other. I tried keeping the game off one year. You would think I'd changed the menu to peanut butter and jelly sandwiches."

Sophie rubbed flour on the rolling pin, a good deal of it powdering her soft arms. "Not my call to make this year. I'm not the hostess." She sighed and suddenly looked serious. "This isn't the first time I'm not having the family for Thanksgiving, but for some reason, it feels like it. Other times, it was my choice to let Evelyn or Una take a turn. This year, they all said they wouldn't allow it. That's what makes it different. I'm afraid they're going to try to take Christmas away from me, too."

Zoey met Sophie's glance and found a defeated look. Defeated and frightened. As if the new rules her children had set down about holiday entertaining warned of bigger battles to come.

"They're worried about you, Sophie. They don't want you to run yourself down and get sick again, like last winter."

"Oh, that bug was a fluke. I was never sick a day in my life before that. I'm still working outside in all types of weather."

The declaration had been true for decades, but was actually not as accurate now. "You were in the hospital for weeks and needed a nurse here every day when you got home."

Zoey remembered the Sunday announcements in church last February; Reverend Ben asking for prayers for Sophie, who was in the hospital with double pneumonia, even in critical condition at one point. But through the grace of God and her own strong will, Sophie had survived. She had required nursing care at home for months, and visits from friends and neighbors as well. That was when Zoey had begun visiting Sophie, first as a member of the church's Care and Concern group and, soon after, as a real friend. Now Zoey cherished Sophie as more than a friend. Her connection to Sophie felt like family.

Zoey did have Grandma Dooley, Lucy's mother, who had been delighted to finally have a granddaughter to shop for. But they weren't nearly as close as she and Sophie, who was so much fun to talk to and made her feel ten feet tall for the smallest accomplishment. An unlikely friend for a college student, it was true, but Zoey often thought of Sophie as her "real" grandmother, though she had never said it aloud.

"It was rough sledding for a while," Sophie finally admitted. "But I bounced back, a hundred percent. Even the doctor says so. Thank goodness I talked them into letting me come home instead of shipping me off to one of those cookie-cutter assisted living places. Bet they wouldn't let me keep Mac in a place like that."

At the sound of his name, Sophie's dog, Macintosh, who was curled up in his dog bed in a corner of the kitchen, lifted his soft, furry head and met Sophie's glance with an alert look.

"It's all right, Mac. I'm not going anywhere without you," Sophie promised. Comforted by her tone, the border-collie mix settled down and closed his eyes again.

Mac was the perfect dog for Sophie, Zoey thought. Medium-sized, with a shaggy, brown and white coat, he was still nimble enough to steal food off the counter in a flash, yet he had the steady, affectionate temperament of a Labrador. Zoey couldn't imagine Sophie's house without him.

Sophie continued kneading the dough with surprising strength for a woman her age. "Or they'd have me move in with Evelyn. It's hard to say if Mac's included in that long-standing invitation, either. My kids want me to sell this place, no secret there. But I'm not leaving this house on my own two feet. They know that, too."

Zoey hated the idea of Sophie selling the orchard, but she could understand how Sophie's family felt. Zoey worried about Sophie, too, and knew that Sophie had resisted hiring help, claiming she had all her friends and family to help her. Especially friends from the church.

Zoey would have liked to visit Sophie even more than she did, but it was difficult juggling her schedule, with college classes and studying and working at the diner in town that her family owned. She also volunteered at an after-school center for children. Never mind fitting in a social life; even hanging out with girlfriends was a treat these days. Never mind finding a boyfriend, either. She did manage to visit Sophie at least once or twice a week, though she knew that wasn't nearly enough to ensure her safety.

"It was easier when Miranda and Eric were here. You weren't alone so much," Zoey reminded her.

"That's true. But they have their own lives. I was grateful for the years Miranda did stay," Sophie added. "She got a great opportunity in North Carolina, working for a big jewelry firm. I would never have wanted her to give that up. But I can't see why the rest of them want me to give up something I love," she reasoned. "Evelyn already talked me into giving up the Christmas Fair. She doesn't want me to be in charge again this year. I agreed after all her pestering. Now what am I supposed to do with myself over the holidays? Sit in the corner and twiddle my thumbs?"

"Of course not." Zoey was surprised to hear about the fair. Sophie had always been the chairperson of the church's biggest fund-raiser. The fair had been Sophie's idea, over thirty years ago. Giving it up was a big compromise with her daughter. It sounded as if her children were serious this time.

"Miranda was a godsend. My kids were trying to make me move out back then, too, after my dear Gus died."

Zoey already knew the story of how Miranda came to live on the orchard. Unable to gain much traction in her acting career, Sophie's granddaughter Miranda came to visit one winter to rest and regroup, soon after Sophie's husband, Gus, had passed away. Miranda had always loved making jewelry, and Cape Light turned out to be a perfect place to develop her craft—and the perfect place to meet the love of her life, Eric Copeland. After they married, they stayed on to help Sophie run the orchard while pursuing their own careers and raising a family.

But the couple had moved over a year ago, leaving Sophie to manage a staff of seasonal workers on her own. Problems arose that she could no longer handle. Her children, especially her son, Bart, were often called on to step in.

"Maybe you can figure out some solution, Sophie, some plan your kids will agree to. You never know. Anything can happen."

"Can the good Lord send me another miracle like Miranda? Only He knows for sure. I've been praying on it. You can count on that."

"I'll say a prayer, too," Zoey promised.

"Thanks, honey. I know you will." Sophie's bright blue eyes met Zoey's with a warm look. "I'm also praying that the subject doesn't come up at Thanksgiving dinner. I don't want to spoil the party. I'm hoping it will be too hectic for any serious talk."

Sophie had poured a big bowl of flour into the first bowl of butter and tossed in a few spoonfuls of ice water, and was now kneading a ball of pale yellow dough with all the pent-up emotion the conversation had inspired.

"They think they're going to lay down the law and not allow me to have my Christmas party this year. But I'm set on that. And I'll get my way," Sophie promised.

"I hope so," Zoey said sincerely. "I'll be happy to help you."

"Thanks, honey. I'm going to take you up on that." Sophie pushed and patted the dough. "Okay, you've seen how it's done. Now you take that other bowl of flour and knead some. I'm going to mix the pumpkin filling. Don't handle it too much. It will get tough," she warned as she pushed a bowl in Zoey's direction.

"Start with a light touch?" Zoey replied with a grin.

Sophie nodded, looking pleased. "That's right. A light touch will do it. Most of the time."

"OH, DEAR. THIS DOESN'T LOOK RIGHT AT all, does it?" Wearing big red kitchen mitts that looked like lobster claws, Emily Warwick carefully carried a pumpkin pie from the oven out to the dining room.

Her daughter Jane sat at the dining room table, concentrating on a textbook and piles of notes, highlighted and underlined. She lifted her head to watch her mother set the pie on a trivet on the sideboard. The corners of her mouth twitched

20

with a smile. "It's not so bad, Mom," she carefully answered.

"It's okay, you can laugh." Emily shrugged, smiling now, too.

"It might be okay if you scrape the burnt part of the crust a little. Is it done in the middle?"

"I was wondering about that myself. But if I poke it again, it will look even more hideous." Emily glanced back at Jane, and they both laughed. "I only have three more in the oven. They look even worse."

"You tried. That's what counts. Sorry I had to bug out on you."

"You have a test. That's more important." Emily glanced at Jane's textbook, Earth Science, opened to a complicated cross-section diagram of a volcano that made her head spin.

Jane had been talking about the midterm for weeks. Emily knew she should have remembered that before volunteering to bake for the church. She had thought she would do it with her daughter, but had ended up baking, quite unsuccessfully, alone.

"At least we have the brownies you made after school. Those are perfect," Emily said. "I'll buy some pies tomorrow at Willoughby's. That will solve it."

"Good plan," Jane agreed with a sly grin.

"How's the studying coming? Ready to taste test the brownies?" Emily asked hopefully.

"I think I can take a break for that." Jane stacked her textbooks and notes, then cleared a space on the table.

Emily returned from the kitchen with two brownies and two glasses of milk. "Hmm. These are good—as good as the bakery's," she said. "I don't know how you learned to cook like this. Your aunt Jessica? I got Grandma's genes for culinary arts."

Jane's eyes went wide. "Give yourself *some* credit, Mom. Grandma doesn't try at all."

"True. But she opts out on principle." Emily's reply was partly sardonic and partly serious. Her mother, Lillian Warwick Elliot, who had been raised in a wealthy Boston family, still felt cooking and most domestic arts were far below her, and barely deigned to heat a can of soup.

Emily had always wanted to learn how to cook, but never had the time. Until now. Cooking classes were definitely on her list. But at the very top was spending more time with Jane. That was an even more important part of her life, and she had shortchanged it lately.

Practically every woman she knew felt torn between her job and her home life, especially when it came to giving their children enough time and attention. But the question struck Emily deeper than most. She had another daughter, Sara, who was grown and married, living in

Boston and working as a reporter. Sara had been born just days after the death of Emily's first husband. Now it seemed another lifetime—Emily and Tim Sutton had eloped just as Emily was due to leave for college. Nine months later, Tim was dead and she was the mother of a newborn. With her life in turmoil and her judgment clouded by grief, Emily had been persuaded by her mother to give up her baby for adoption. It was a decision she always regretted.

Emily had made many attempts to find Sara, without success. But through some miracle—and answered prayers—when she was in her early twenties, Sara came to Cape Light and found Emily. After a rocky start, they formed loving bonds, and Emily quickly learned the knack of mothering an adult child. But Emily had deeply regretted missing out on raising Sara and watching her grow, sharing all the special moments of her childhood and adolescence.

Emily and her second husband, Dan, adopted Jane eleven years ago, when she was an infant. With grown children from his first marriage, Dan didn't want to start another family. But Emily had longed for a baby with all her heart, and Heaven had found a way to bring Jane into their lives. Dan soon realized that they had been blessed, and he couldn't love Jane more if he tried. Emily felt blessed with this second chance to cherish and enjoy all the moments of motherhood she had forfeited with Sara.

But had she really valued that blessing and honored that vow? Emily often wondered about that. Her job as mayor of Cape Light had been so demanding, it was always a juggling act. Now here she was, finally free to carry out that promise to her younger daughter and herself. Though, so far, it was not as easy as she had expected.

Jane sniffed the air, then glanced at the kitchen. "Mom . . . didn't you take the rest of the pies out?"

Emily turned quickly. "Oh, blast . . ." She grabbed the mitts and ran to the stove. A black thread seeped from the oven door, and as she pulled it open, a large black cloud floated out, which she fanned with her hand.

"Are they on fire? Should I call Dad?" Jane sounded alarmed.

"It's okay, honey. Got it under control," Emily replied, though she wasn't entirely sure that was true. "Just open the back door and the windows, so the smoke alarm doesn't go off." Holding her breath, she reached into the oven and took out the charred pies.

Jane had wisely turned on the oven fan before running off to the door and windows. She returned to the kitchen and stared down at the products of her mother's labor. "It's just a timing thing, Mom. You'll get the hang of it."

Emily laughed and coughed, then dropped a kiss on her daughter's head. "If you say so. I'm trying."

An hour later, Emily was still cleaning the kitchen. Jane had finished studying and gone to bed. *I'm not only a bad cook but a messy one,* Emily reflected. She scanned the room, sponge in hand, for any splatters of pumpkin or flour she may have missed.

"What happened in here? Did the pot closet explode again?" Dan stood in the kitchen doorway and gazed around in wonder. His glance fell on the pies—*If you could even call them that,* Emily thought.

"You were baking. I should have guessed. I thought the chimney backed up."

"Very funny." Emily tried to sound insulted, but she couldn't help laughing.

"Were those for our Thanksgiving party?"

"Of course not. I already ordered dessert from the bakery. They were supposed to be for church. For the Thanksgiving baskets they're giving out."

"Oh, I see." Emily couldn't tell if Dan was still puzzled by this fit of domesticity—or if he was thinking the results did not bode well for Thursday. The entire family was coming for dinner this year, and Emily was in charge of the kitchen.

"It does make me a little nervous about

cooking for our party," she admitted. "But I'm not actually cooking much. Jessica is bringing a few starters and sides, and I'm getting a lot from Willoughby's."

"Don't worry, Em. It's going to be fine. Jane and I will help you." He touched her arm. "It's just a turkey, honey, not brain surgery."

"I know. But I've been doing a little research on the Internet, and there are a surprising number of theories about the way to roast a turkey. Slow, low-heat, or high? Deboned? Stuffed? Or even upside down? Then there's the whole question of brining . . ."

Emily showed him the thick folder on the kitchen counter where she had been collecting articles and recipes.

Dan's smile grew even wider. "I say keep it simple. Don't make yourself crazy. You ran this town for over fifteen years. I'm sure you can pull a turkey dinner together."

"It's just that I haven't taken on a family holiday since . . . Well, I can't remember the last time. I always had the excuse that I was too busy. I feel like I forgot how to do it. If I ever knew in the first place," she admitted. "But I'm getting organized. I found some good ideas for making a centerpiece and interesting table settings."

"That's just what I mean. Let's buy a bouquet of flowers and stick it in a vase. *Simple.*" Dan paused. "Sometimes, you're like a cannon pointed at a mosquito, sweetheart."

Emily stared back at him. "I'm not sure if that's a compliment or . . . not."

"It's a compliment. Most of the time."

"I know, I have one speed. But I'm not used to doing this yet, Dan, all of this at-home stuff. Not as a full-time job." She glanced around at the jumbled kitchen and the misshapen pies.

Dan's look softened. "I know it's hard for you, a real sea change. But just relax. No one is judging you. No one is peeking through the window, trying to get a photo for the *Cape Light Messenger*." Dan framed an imaginary headline with his hands. " 'Mayor Warwick Incinerates Church Pies.' "

Emily laughed. "*Former* Mayor Warwick. If I was still mayor, I wouldn't have volunteered."

"It hasn't been that long. Not even two weeks, right?"

Emily glanced at the clock. "Two weeks exactly. Three minutes from now. It was midnight when we heard the news, remember?"

Dan nodded, looking serious again. "I do. And you took it very well. Like a champion."

The news was that Charlie Bates had narrowly—but definitely—won the election for mayor. Now, after more than fifteen years and eight terms in the post, Emily no longer held that title. Hearing that news was one of the most difficult moments of her life. The memory was still sharp and painful.

"Thanks, honey. But I don't remember feeling like a champion. For a moment, I thought I might throw up. At least I didn't cry. I mean, not in public."

Hearing the news, Emily had felt as if some unseen hand had landed a heavy blow straight into her heart. She had lost her breath for a moment and couldn't even stand. But, somehow putting her political self on automatic, she had managed a quick recovery and said all the right things that night to her supporters and to the local media. It was a blur in her memory, though she had watched her performance later on the TV news.

"This whole transition will take time," Dan said. "You're doing great. Remember when I handed the newspaper over to Lindsay?" Dan had stepped down as publisher and owner of the *Cape Light Messenger* and put his daughter in charge—just around the time that Dan and Emily's romance had begun. "I was looking forward to being free of the daily grind for so long. I couldn't wait to jump on my boat and sail into the sunset. But when the time came I felt so confused, I was practically walking into walls."

"With a giant cast on your leg, as I recall. From that fall rigging the new sails. You thought you'd make a quick getaway. But God had other plans for you."

Dan laughed and placed his hands on Emily's shoulders. "For us, I'd say. He made me stick around until I finally noticed the most beautiful, intelligent, and accomplished woman in the world was right under my nose."

"It didn't take *too* long." Emily rolled her eyes, and Dan laughed again. "I know what you're trying to say, but that was different. You wanted to leave your job. I didn't. Though I had been thinking of stepping down soon. But not by losing to Charlie Bates."

"I know, Em. I know it still hurts." Dan pulled her close in a warm hug. "All I'm trying to say is, be patient with yourself. You don't have to be perfect at everything you try to do, and you don't have to volunteer for every project that comes along because you're afraid of being bored or unproductive."

"I guess it's my way of dealing with this. And I did think Jane and I could have some fun. I forgot she was booked up tonight, literally. She's getting older. She's so busy with her own life now, I need to be more mindful of her schedule."

"It's almost as complicated as yours used to be."

"The tables have turned," Emily agreed, though it stung a bit to realize that, too.

Jane's after-school hours, filled with music

lessons, sports teams, and study groups, had always seemed like a good arrangement to Emily when she was busy in her office, sometimes late into the night. Dan was in charge of the home front, fitting his writing career around their daughter's many commitments. Now it was Emily's turn.

"I thought the upside of leaving Village Hall would be spending more time with her. But so far, that hasn't happened," Emily admitted.

"That will come, too," Dan advised. "Meanwhile, please don't book yourself up with a million random commitments and causes. I'm going to get you a T-shirt for Christmas that says, 'Stop Me from Volunteering.'"

"That would be great. I'll wear it, I promise. But I also want cooking lessons. And I'd like to start learning a language, too. Maybe Spanish?"

"Good idea. We should study a language together. That will come in handy when we travel." He picked up a dishcloth and began to dry the pile of pans and mixing bowls on the drain board. Emily got back to work, wiping down the counters and stove.

"Right now, I think you should take a break—a break from volunteering, and everything. No one will blame you for taking some time to clear your head. You've earned it."

"I know. But I'm glad the holidays are coming. It's a great distraction—doing all this holiday prep and entertaining. Maybe by the New Year, I'll figure out something useful to do. Part-time, I mean; nothing too intense. I do want to spend a lot more time with you and Janie. That's on the top of my list."

"You're always on the top of my list, Emily." Their eyes met in a loving smile. "I know it wasn't the way you wanted to leave office, but now that it's happened, I have to admit, I'm happy to have my wife back. I love having you around, more than you know. And I can't wait until we do all those amazing things we've always talked about—all the trips and adventures. I think we should take a ski trip in Vermont this winter, over Presidents' Day weekend, and then take a bigger trip when Jane has spring break."

"That would be great. Any ideas?"

"Remember how you always say you'd like to go someplace exotic, on one of those eco-tourism trips? I was reading a travel magazine today, and I saw an article about it—places in Costa Rica and even the Galápagos Islands. There are inns in the rainforest, built on stilts, with all these exotic birds and monkeys just roaming around. And we can scuba dive and see giant sea turtles . . ."

Emily smiled, watching her husband get carried away with his descriptions. She wasn't sure if he was imitating an exotic bird or a giant turtle. It didn't really matter; his enthusiasm was contagious. Dan loved to experience different cultures and foreign places—one of the many things Emily had always loved about him.

"That sounds wonderful. Jane would love it, too."

"I think she will. We'll have a great time. That's something to look forward to, right?"

"Absolutely."

"Here's an idea," Dan said, a mischievous look in his eye. "This time, we plan the trip *together*. Instead of you just showing up at the airport and grabbing your ticket and itinerary."

"Oh dear, is that what I do?"

"Well . . . more or less. I've given you a pass all these years. But I think it would be more fun if we both work on it."

"I do, too." Emily touched his cheek. She could see it meant a lot to him. "No more volunteering. I have plenty to do here."

"And it's perfectly fine if you do nothing at all," he reminded her. "We love you the same. Even more."

Emily smiled and felt a bit teary. Dan could always read her like a book. It never failed to amaze her. "Thank you, sweetheart. I love you, too. More than you know."

She had never been more sure of that.

SOPHIE'S HOUSE WAS FILLED WITH A SWEET, buttery scent as Zoey washed the last of the large mixing bowls. She breathed in the cinnamon-spice aroma like a rare perfume. Sophie was in the next room, talking on the phone to her daughter, Evelyn, reviewing their Thanksgiving menu for the umpteenth time.

Sophie thrived on holiday anticipation. Zoey hoped Sophie's children would let her have Christmas at the orchard again this year. Even more than that, Zoey hoped they didn't force Sophie to leave the orchard altogether.

Zoey stared out the big kitchen window and noticed that it was snowing. When did that start? She hadn't heard any forecasts for snow tonight, but that was the weather in this part of New England—unpredictable.

Fat, heavy flakes had piled around the window frame and coated the landscape with a soft white blanket. The orchard looked lovely, the bare branches draped in white lace.

It would be so hard for Sophie to leave here, Zoey thought. *Hard for me, too, to know I could never come back to visit her. To cook and bake, or help with some household chore. Or just have a cup of tea and listen to her stories.*

She wiped her hands on a towel and glanced around the kitchen. She loved the view of the orchard framed by the window over the sink, and the big farm table, a dozen pie pans long tonight. She loved the worn pots that hung from a rack above the stove, like a crazy wind chime, and the open shelves stacked with mismatched china and oddly shaped glasses, with Sophie's prized collection of teapots on the very top.

Sophie's walk-in pantry was almost as big as Zoey's bedroom, filled with jars of honey, jam and preserves made with fruit from the orchard, and vegetables from her garden. Sophie had kept bees most of her life and was known throughout New England as a gifted "bee charmer." She had given up that hobby a few years ago, but people still said the honey from Potter Orchard was the very richest tasting because Sophie's bees were so content.

But Sophie herself was the real reason Zoey loved coming to the orchard. And she loved the stories that Sophie told—how she inherited the orchard and ran it on her own when she was so young, almost the same age Zoey was right now.

Amazing in that day, Zoey thought, when women were barely allowed to work outside of their homes and never allowed to be the boss of anything. Sophie had been an independent, "liberated" woman before the label existed. Sophie knew she was different from other people; she marched to her own drummer. Zoey felt that way, too. Maybe that's why Sophie really listened and took her seriously— unlike her father or even her mother, at times. That's what she loved about Sophie.

"You cleaned up all by yourself? You didn't have to do that." Sophie's tone was partly scolding but mostly pleased. "It's hard to get Evelyn off the phone when she's all wound up. You'd think she was entertaining two hundred people instead of twenty-five."

"I think twenty-five is plenty. I'd be wired."

"Don't be a fretful hostess, Zoey. Promise me? Always remember to enjoy your own parties. Just put the food out and turn up the music. Everyone does fine. Now, I think we should taste those pies and make sure they'll meet with my daughter's approval. What do they call that—product testing?"

"Good idea." Zoey was sure the pies were perfect, but she was dying for a bite.

"I'll set up the teapot and you put the kettle on. There's a lot of snow out there. It snuck up on us." Sophie glanced out the window to take in the white winter scene. "I don't think you should drive. You call your mom and tell her you're going to stay the night."

"Thanks. I think I will." The orchard was not far from Zoey's house, but on the Beach Road at night in bad weather, she would be crawling in her little hatchback, and the trip would take forever.

Zoey set the honey jar and a pitcher of milk on the table as Sophie brought over the teapot. Three slices of pie sat between their places at the table—apple, pumpkin, and pecan. Zoey couldn't wait to taste each one of them.

Sophie sat down first. "Feels good to get off my feet. We've earned our reward, dear."

Zoey was about to agree when a banging noise filled the room. Someone was knocking on the back door. Mac had settled under the table, waiting for tasty crumbs to rain down, but he now ran to the door, barking wildly, reminding everyone of his formidable skills as Sophie's protector. The two women stared at each other.

"Expecting anyone?" Zoey asked.

"No, I'm not. Who could it be in this weather?"

Sophie began to get up, but Zoey touched her arm. "You sit. I'll get it." Before Sophie could reply, she ran over to the door. The knocking had escalated into a pounding sound.

"All right, I'm coming." Zoey held Mac's collar with one hand and unlatched the door with the other, then turned the knob. But the door was stuck, frozen with the snow and cold. This door was finicky, she recalled. She pulled on the knob again with all her might. It didn't budge at first, then suddenly flew open.

A snow-covered form stumbled inside, falling right into her arms. She raised her hands and pushed back. She could tell it was a man, and a big backpack on his shoulders set him off balance. But she couldn't tell much else.

His coat collar was turned up, his head covered

by a baseball cap, and a thick scarf was wrapped around his face so that only his eyes showed.

Mac took a few steps back and growled low in his throat. Zoey stepped back as well and held the dog's collar again. The man tried to pull his scarf away, but it was tied, and his hands looked stiff with cold.

Sophie had jumped to her feet, and she quickly walked toward them. "What in heaven's name! . . . Who are you?"

Chapter Two

THE SCARF FINALLY LOOSENED, AND THE man tugged off his hat. Zoey was surprised to see that he was young, about her age. And very good-looking.

"Grandma, it's *me* . . . James."

"James?" Sophie sounded suspicious of this declaration and walked closer, but her wariness quickly melted to delight. "For heaven's sake . . . where did you come from? You look like the Abominable Snowman. Did you walk all the way from New York?"

Before he could answer, Sophie tugged her unexpected visitor into the kitchen and pushed him down in a chair. "Take off those wet clothes. You're going to catch a cold. Get some towels, Zoey, then fill a pail with hot water for his feet. He's soaking wet."

"Grandma, please. I'm okay. It's just a little snow."

Zoey hoped he was really okay, but felt a chill just watching him unbutton his jacket. She ran to the laundry room, glancing back just for a moment. Thick, reddish-brown hair stood out around his head, and dark blue eyes watched her from beneath thick brows. His cheeks were apple red, like those of a boy in a painting by a Dutch master.

That's James? The most recent photo Sophie had of that grandson showed a boy of about nine or ten, with a scrunched-up face and a mouth full of braces. His looks had sure improved, Zoey thought, her pulse still racing.

Racing back to the kitchen, she caught sight of her reflection in the hall mirror. She took a moment to smooth her long, dark ponytail and tuck her shirt into her jeans, then gave up. *You look like a deep-sea troll and smell like pumpkin pulp. Deal with it.*

When she returned with the towels, James was standing with his back to her. He had taken off his coat and draped it on a chair, and had removed his boots and socks as well. She couldn't help noticing his broad shoulders, outlined by his damp denim shirt.

Sophie stood at the counter, fixing tea with lemon and honey—using not one of the dainty china cups they had been using but the biggest mug in her cupboard.

"Here are the towels." Zoey handed them over and he smiled—a very likable grin that made deep dimples appear in his cheeks. His teeth were very straight and white. *Those braces worked out fine,* she wanted to say. But, of course, she didn't.

"I think you need to soak your feet in some hot water," Sophie said. "Zoey will make a pail for you."

"Don't be silly. I'm fine." He rubbed his head roughly with the towel, then draped it around his shoulders. "I couldn't find a cab at the bus station so I hitched a ride. But they had to let me off at the crossroad."

"You walked all that way? And up the road to the house, too?" Sophie wasn't really asking him to confirm this, just murmuring to herself. "You should have called. I would have picked you up."

"Picked me up? Dad said you aren't driving anymore."

"I don't. Not really. Only for emergencies." Sophie quickly covered her tracks, her expression suddenly sincere.

Zoey glanced at Sophie and then down at the table, trying not to laugh. Sophie had promised her children that she would stop driving, but had never sold her beloved old truck, Bella, reasoning that a truck was needed at the orchard, even if she didn't drive it.

Zoey knew Sophie still took Bella out on short rides, redefining the meaning of emergency. Like, going to church or visiting friends in the village. Zoey tried to chauffeur her as much as she could, but Sophie could be crafty when she had her mind set.

James laughed and patted his grandmother's hand. "You're not fooling me, Grandma." He glanced over at Zoey. "She drives whenever she feels like it, doesn't she?"

Before Zoey could reply, Sophie jumped in. "Don't put Zoey on the spot. That's not polite. Speaking of manners, I've forgotten mine. James, this is my friend Zoey Bates. Zoey, this is my grandson James Potter. He's Bart's son; Miranda's younger brother."

Zoey had already guessed where James sat on the family tree. James offered his hand, and she briefly shook it.

"She helped me make all these pies, and now she's stuck here for the night."

"Believe me, it's a good night to stay put. And good to meet you, Zoey."

"Nice to meet you. That was quite an entrance . . . Are you an actor?" Zoey wasn't sure why she asked him that. It had just popped into her head. He was certainly good-looking and charming enough to be onstage.

He laughed. "It's even worse. I'm a writer."

"Really? What do you write?"

"Different things—book reviews, short stories. I've had a few pieces published this year. I'm working on a novel right now."

Zoey nodded. She didn't know what to say. She was studying art, but didn't consider herself a real artist yet. She had never sold her work or exhibited in a gallery outside of the college she attended.

Sophie peered at her grandson. "Did you eat anything today? You look hungry."

"I had a sandwich on the bus. But I wouldn't mind some pie." He smiled, eyeing the three slices on the table.

Sophie laughed. "Help yourself." She gave him an extra fork, and he selected the pumpkin. Zoey took the apple, and Sophie, the pecan.

"Well, what do you think?" Sophie asked after a moment.

"Only the best apple pie I ever had in my life," Zoey said, which was true.

"Potter Orchard apples. Doesn't get better than that," Sophie agreed.

"The pumpkin is . . . ambrosia, the nectar of the gods, Grandma. My taste buds are doing backflips."

Sophie laughed. "You've got to be a writer, honey. Your head is full of fine words." She took another taste of her pie, and they sat quietly for a moment, savoring the treat. "So, how's it going in the city, James? Is everything all right?"

James looked up at her briefly and nodded. "Absolutely. I just had some extra time and was planning to go up to Connecticut today. I thought I'd come straight up here instead and visit you. I was writing something the other day about my childhood and all the summer visits to the orchard, staying here with you and Grandpa and the cousins. It was like . . . Apple Camp or something."

"Apple Camp?" Sophie smiled. "I like that. Those were wonderful days; some of the best of my life. You kids could be a handful, but I wouldn't trade those times for anything."

"I wouldn't either, Grandma."

Zoey sat, eating her pie. She knew it wasn't smart to make snap judgments about people—especially about a guy you met five minutes ago. But she already liked James Potter. She could see—or at least, thought she could see—that he was a thoughtful, sensitive person. Funny, too. Important ingredients for a writer, she thought. She wondered if he was a good one.

"As long as your father knows you're here and won't be worried, I think it was very sweet of you to surprise me," Sophie told her grandson. "We can talk more tomorrow. And you can drive me to Evelyn's on Thanksgiving Day," she added. Her bold wink made both Zoey and James smile.

"That's a deal, Grandma. Don't worry, your secret is safe with me."

"And with me," Zoey added, exchanging a brief glance with James.

Sophie had finished and pushed her empty dish aside. "I don't know about you two, but I'm going to wrap these pies and get to bed."

"I'll help you," Zoey offered.

"I'll help, too." James came to his feet and picked up the dirty dishes and cups, balancing the pile on his arm with an expert flair. Zoey didn't doubt his claim that he was a writer. But she did wonder if he was earning his living as a waiter, too.

They quickly packed the pies, putting most of them in boxes for Zoey to bring to church.

"Time for bed, everyone," Sophie announced. "Zoey, you take the room upstairs, next to mine. James, you can sleep in the little bedroom down here. The sheets are clean, and there's an extra quilt in the closet. There are also some dry clothes in that chest that should fit you."

"Thanks, Grandma. I'll be fine."

"Sleep tight, dear." Sophie gave him a hug. "I'm glad you came to see me."

"I'm glad I did, too. Good night, Zoey. Nice to have met you."

Zoey glanced over her shoulder as she followed Sophie down the hallway. "Good night . . . nice to meet you, too." The way he watched as she walked away made Zoey feel self-conscious.

Zoey focused on Sophie, helping her up the stairs. Her older friend had been going full steam all night, but now it was apparent that the baking had not been that easy for her.

They parted at Sophie's bedroom. "Good night, dear. You know where everything is. I'll see you in the morning. And we have a strong young man here to shovel us out." Sophie's tone was a gleeful whisper. "See? God provides."

Zoey just smiled. She was used to shoveling snow and digging her own car out. But she still found Sophie's perspective amusing; Sophie rarely missed a chance to remind Zoey of the heavenly hand she believed watched over everyone.

Before Zoey slipped off to sleep, she remembered her promise, but wasn't quite sure how to start off a prayer for her friend.

Well, God, I promised Sophie I'd say a prayer for her, so here goes. I know that more than anything, she wants to have her Christmas gathering here this year. And more than that, to stay in her house, on her land, until her very last days, even though her children don't want her to do either of those things. I know this might be a tough one to manage. And it might be best for Sophie if she doesn't get her wish. But maybe there's some way things can work out for her? Some way we just can't see and you can? If anyone deserves a favor, you know it's Sophie.

Also, thanks for sending James to shovel. I do need to get into the village early tomorrow, come to think of it.

WHEN ZOEY WOKE THE NEXT MORNING, IT took a moment for her to remember that she had stayed over at Sophie's house. The soft, hazy

46

light that filled the bedroom reminded her that it had snowed the night before.

She picked up her phone from the bedside table and checked the time. She had overslept and missed the alarm. How had that happened? She had to rush now. There were no classes today, the day before Thanksgiving, thank goodness. But she had to drop off the pies at church and then race home to shower and change and get over to the diner in time for her shift. Ever since her father had been elected mayor, she had to work more hours at the diner, and he was even nuttier about her coming and going *exactly* on time. *You'd think I was in the army or something.*

Charlie always said he was teaching her valuable lessons that would help her in the "real world"—how to be responsible and mature, how to be a good employee. "Someday you'll thank me," he promised. But that wasn't happening anytime soon, as far as Zoey could see.

She splashed her face with water and combed her hair. She had a dark blue pullover in her backpack and pulled it on, stashing the pumpkin-stained T-shirt in her pack. She was glad in a way to be in a rush and not have much time to spend with James. She still looked like a troll—a tired one who needed her hair washed. And what was the point? He was definitely cute. And cool. But he was older than she was, and he lived in New York City. And a guy like that had to have a girlfriend somewhere. More than one, probably.

Five minutes later, when she walked into the kitchen, James sat at the table, sipping a mug of coffee. Sophie stood at the stove, an apron over her long pink bathrobe. Mac stood right beside her, waiting for a morning treat. Zoey saw scrambled eggs and bacon on a platter on the table, which was set for three. She also smelled toast and something even tastier—coffee cake. How early had Sophie gotten up to cook?

"Help yourself to coffee, Zoey. Scrambled eggs okay? I can make a few over easy for you. Oh, and there's coffee cake, fresh out of the oven."

"It all looks delicious. But I'm in a rush. I have to get to work." Zoey sipped her coffee at the counter. She knew if she sat down, she would be tempted to eat some of the tantalizing breakfast and would get to the diner even later.

"That's all right, dear. I understand. But you take something with you. Some coffee cake, okay?"

Before Zoey could answer, Sophie was cutting a wedge of cake and wrapping it for her to go.

James had left the table but now returned, wearing his jacket, scarf, and boots. And carrying a straw broom. "The snow isn't very high. I think you can get out easily. I'll brush off your car."

Zoey was surprised by the offer, despite Sophie's prediction. She hurried to slip on her parka and grab her backpack. "That's all right. I can do it." She tried to take the broom from him, but he held on tight. She tugged a second and felt silly, watching him slowly smile. "Really," she said, "you don't have to leave your breakfast."

"I have plenty of time for breakfast. I have nothing else to do all day. And right after that, I'm sure my grandmother will want to make me lunch." He glanced over his shoulder at Sophie, who laughed to herself. "And after that, but not too long after . . . she'll be cooking dinner. In fact"—he tilted his head at a charming angle, as if a fascinating insight had just struck him— "I'll be eating here *around* the clock. And you would be doing me a great favor to let me burn some calories by cleaning the snow off your car."

Zoey could not argue, not after that recitation. She could barely answer at all, staring into his bold, blue gaze.

"All right. When you put it that way," she mumbled. She gave Sophie a quick hug and wished her a happy Thanksgiving, then slung her backpack over her shoulder and grabbed one of the boxes packed with pies.

"I'll get the other box," James offered as he opened the back door.

"Thanks." She swept past him. *Is he going to make another Shakespearean speech about that?* She hoped not.

They marched to her car, which was parked

a short distance from the house, their steps crunching in the snow. Zoey didn't like to talk a lot in the morning, and she felt intimidated by James as well. Though she hated to admit it.

They set the boxes in the trunk. Then James walked to the front of the car and brushed snow off the windshield and hood with the broom. "Why don't you get in and start the heat? I can handle this."

Zoey started the car and turned on the defroster. She found her snow brush on the backseat and started working on the outside of the car, too. The smaller brush wasn't as effective as the broom, but the snow was very light.

Once the back windows were done, she checked the roof. She could almost hear her father: "It's dangerous to leave snow on the car roof, Zoey. It can slide down on the windshield and blind you while you're driving, and you can end up in an accident."

Even though she rolled her eyes at these disaster warnings from her parents, she did remember them. She jumped up on tiptoe and gave the snow a big swipe with the brush, reaching as far as her arm would stretch.

"Hey . . . what was that?" James popped up like a gopher from a hole. He had been brushing the back of the car, and she hadn't noticed him there. Now he was covered from head to toe.

She didn't want to laugh, but it was hard not

to. "Oh, my gosh . . . you look almost as bad as you did last night. What is it with you? Can't you stay frost-free for a few hours?"

"Cute." He wasn't wearing his hat and shook his head like a big dog, snow flying everywhere. "It's not so bad. The snow isn't even cold. See?"

The next thing she knew, a cloud of snow was flying her way, courtesy of one swift, neat stroke with the broom.

Zoey sputtered, wiping snow from her face and eyes. She wanted to yell at him, then had to laugh. "Nice move. For a city boy."

The snow she had wiped from her face was still in her hand, and she quickly packed it—then hurled a tight little snowball straight at him.

"Gotcha!" She couldn't suppress her glee as her frosty missile smacked his shoulder.

"Correction . . . I grew up in the wilds of Connecticut. We have snowballs there, too."

He fired one back in an instant, popping out from behind the car and ducking down again.

Zoey squealed and spun, trying to get out of the way, but it caught her directly on her nose. She raised her hands to her face. "Ouch, that hurt! No fair," she moaned. She turned her back, pretending to be hurt, even though it only stung a little. "I think you broke my nose," she mumbled against her gloves.

James rushed from the other side of the car, slipping and sliding in the snow. "I'm so sorry!

I didn't mean to throw it that hard. Here, let me see. Are you bleeding?"

He sounded so worried, Zoey had a momentary pang of conscience. Still, he started it, she reasoned, and she could not resist turning slowly and meeting his concerned expression with another heaping handful.

"Only kidding," she said with a shrug as he coughed and sputtered under this latest assault.

"You little weasel. I'll get you for that." His words were harsh, but he was laughing. At least he was a good sport.

She brushed herself off, jumped behind the wheel, then slammed the door. She rolled the window down a crack. "Thanks for helping me clean the car," she said sweetly. "By the way, I have three brothers. I know this stuff."

"Now she tells me."

"Next time, I'll give you fair warning." Zoey suddenly felt repentant for her sneaky maneuvers.

"It's all right. All's fair in love and snowball fights."

"I don't know about the first part, but I do agree with the second."

"Obviously." He smiled at her, a warm smile that made her feel a bit weak at the knees. "Hope to see you again, Zoey. When there isn't any snow around," he teased.

"Sure, see you," Zoey replied with a brief wave. His parting words surprised her. She didn't know how or when she would see him again anytime soon. He was only visiting for Thanksgiving and was probably leaving tomorrow night, or, at the most, over the weekend.

He was just trying to be nice. He didn't mean anything by it, she decided. She steered her car down the bumpy, snow-covered lane that ran from Sophie's house to the main road. In the rearview mirror, she could still see James watching her drive away—to make sure she didn't get stuck in a drift?

When she reached the road, she glanced back. But he was gone. As she fixed her gaze on the road ahead, Zoey could still see him clearly, in her mind's eye, and knew it would take a while for the image to fade.

SOPHIE HAD WHISKED THE PLATE OF EGGS and bacon into the oven so the food wouldn't get cold, but as soon as James came through the back door, she quickly set it on the table. He took off his jacket and boots and sat in his place again.

"Did Zoey get off all right?"

"No problem."

She poured more coffee in his mug and then sat in her own seat and filled her plate with bacon and eggs. "She's a dear girl. Puts her heart into everything she puts her hand to. She helps me a lot around here. I'm not sure what I would do without her."

"I'm glad you have help around here, Grandma. And companionship. Zoey has a good sense of humor, I noticed."

Sophie had watched the snow fight from the window. Zoey had gotten the best of her grandson, using her brains instead of her brawn. Sophie smiled; some things did not change.

"She's also very smart and creative," Sophie said. "She's studying to be an art therapist. Did she mention that?"

James looked interested and a bit surprised. "We didn't get to it. I can see the arty side. But she doesn't look . . . I don't know . . . serious enough or something to be a psychologist."

"Oh, she's got a serious side. She's a deep girl. She's been through things." James looked curious to hear more, but Zoey's past was not hers to tell. "So, are you going back to the city Thursday night, or heading back to Connecticut with your dad?"

"I'm not sure. I'll have to check work and see what my schedule is."

Sophie nodded. "Still working at the same café? What was it called again?"

"Bistro Cassis. The tips are good," James added with a shrug.

"No shame in hard work while you get your writing off the ground. Isn't that the plan?"

James nodded, but avoided meeting her gaze. She could always tell when one of her children—

or grandchildren—wasn't telling her the truth. Or even shading the story.

"What is it, James? Did you lose your job?"

He finally looked up at her. "What gave you that idea?"

Answering a question with a question. Dead giveaway. Sophie knew her guess had hit its mark.

"I know you love me, honey. But when you take a six-hour bus ride and then walk three miles in the snow to visit, something's up. You could have hopped on a train in Grand Central and been at your father's house in less than half that time. Dry as toast in the bargain."

He didn't answer, just stared straight ahead, his cheeks growing red.

"I might be old, but I can still do simple math, and it doesn't add up."

James sighed and cast her a wry smile. "Yes, I lost my job. I had an argument with the boss and he fired me. My roommate moved out a few days later, and since I needed to save money anyway, I sublet the apartment. I've been couch-surfing ever since. That got old fast. I ran out of couches, and I still haven't found a new job."

"I see." Sophie had suspected it was something like that. "How about your parents? Won't they help you? All kids have tight spots like this, here and there."

"Tell that to my dad. If he ever had a 'tight

spot,' he doesn't remember it." James sighed and pushed back his plate. "He has helped me, a few times. But he said he won't do it again—not unless I give up on writing and work for one of his friends. Selling insurance or something. I'd rather take poison."

Sophie shook her head. "Don't even say that." The boy had a flair for drama. "What about your mom? Maybe she'll help you."

"She's sympathetic, but always says I have to talk to him."

"Can't you just try—one more time?" Sophie knew her son, Bart, could dig in his heels when he thought he was right, but he wasn't heartless. He was probably worried about James, who still seemed a little lost two years after graduating college. It was only natural for his father to be concerned. And once Bart thought he had a solution to a problem, he didn't have much patience for considering there might be another way. He always thought he knew best. Especially with his children.

"You've only been out of school . . . two years?"

"A year and a half," James corrected her. "That isn't very long to get a writing career going. Some people take decades. Not that I plan on taking that long," he quickly added.

Sophie had to smile. Young people never think success will take long. Which was good, in a way, she reflected. "Of course not. But it's not the same as other careers. I understand."

"I'm glad somebody does. Tell that to Dad. I'm getting published—in a few places, at least. Editors like my writing; readers, too. Things are going pretty well," James insisted. "But nothing short of the front page of the *New York Times* will impress Dad. All he can say is 'Stop playing around. You have to get serious, James.'"

Unfortunately, Sophie could hear her son saying just that.

"What does he call serious?" Sophie asked curiously.

"Going to law school. Or taking some mind-numbing job in a bank or a brokerage house. Anyplace like that. Where you hand over your brain and become a mindless clone. He has a lot of well-connected friends and wants me to go on interviews. I'm dreading facing him tomorrow. Once he finds out I've lost my apartment and my job—"

"You're *in between* jobs, that's all." Sophie met his glance and saw he appreciated her interpretation.

"Even that explanation won't go over well. You won't tell him, will you?"

"It's your news to tell, dear. But I won't lie if he asks me. I don't want to get in between you and your father, but you're welcome to stay here

57

until you can figure out what you want to do. At least through the holidays."

"Thank you, Grandma. Honest." His expression was a portrait of relief.

"Not at all. It's my pleasure. I have my own battles going on now with your father . . . and your aunts. They're trying to persuade me—more like force me, truth be told—to give up this place. But I'm not going without a fight."

James looked concerned. "I hope they don't make you leave. But I do think you need more help. That's where I come in. I'm going to start by shoveling snow and fixing that back door."

"I'm impressed. Quite a to-do list already." Sophie leaned back and laughed, pleased at her grandson's ambition.

"What did you think, Grandma? I would just lie around all day and eat your cooking? I might try to find a job in town, too. Even if it's just for a few weeks, that will be something. I'm definitely not going back to Connecticut, but I don't want to go back to New York, either. Not right now."

"Really?" Sophie was surprised. She thought James loved the big city. "Where do you want to go? Cross-country or something like that?"

"I want to travel. But outside of the U.S. There's a website that posts work on farms all over the world. It's called Worldwide Agricultural Volunteers—WAVE for short. You can find a farming job with room and board in some interesting country and work there awhile. Then, when you're ready, you go to a new place."

"That sounds very adventurous."

"I did it one summer during college. It was awesome. It's what a real writer would do—have adventures, see the world, meet all kinds of people, and have something to write about. Not just give up at the first speed bump."

Sophie was impressed by her grandson's spirit and persistence. And secretly pleased that he wasn't giving in to his caring but strong-willed father.

"That's a good plan, James," she said. "If I can help you without crossing your father, I will. In the meantime, let's stick together at the Thanksgiving dinner tomorrow. Sounds like we'll *both* be thrown into the lion's den."

Sophie rolled her eyes, and her grandson laughed. Though, in her heart, she wasn't really joking.

Chapter Three

EVERYTHING IS DELICIOUS, EMILY. THE turkey came out perfectly. And I love that centerpiece. Did you really make it?"

Emily appreciated her sister, Jessica's, praise. Jessica knew Emily was domestically challenged and was trying her best to be encouraging. She was also very grateful that Emily had taken on Thanksgiving this year. She had been promoted at the bank and had almost no spare time now, though Emily was fairly certain Jess and Sam would still want to have the family over for Christmas Eve, as they usually did.

"I hedged my bets with the roasting. Draped it with cheesecloth *and* used a foil tent," Emily admitted. "Jane and I made the centerpiece. We just copied a picture in a magazine."

Her mother, Lillian, glared at them. "Very festive," she grumbled. "Keep fiddling with mini-pumpkins and pinecones while Rome burns. That's just dandy."

Emily decided to ignore the remark, a veiled reference to the goings-on in Village Hall. Which she was not part of any longer. Despite the fact that she had been voted out of office, her mother persisted in acting as if Emily had deserted her post. Or had perhaps been ousted by some sinister scheme and was now in exile, planning her return. Or should have been.

Dan, who never had high tolerance for his mother-in-law's critiques, was clearly annoyed. "Fiddling while Rome burns? What's that supposed to mean?"

Before Lillian could reply, Emily said, "More sweet potatoes, anyone? These are delicious, Jess."

Jessica forced a smile, her gaze darting warily from Lillian to Dan. "Gee . . . thanks."

"I'll have some more." Jessica's husband, Sam, held out his dish. "They came out great, honey."

"I'll have some as well, thank you." Ezra Elliot, Lillian's husband, glanced at his wife. "Some very fine food at this celebration. We appreciate all the work that went into this meal. Don't we, Lillian?"

Lillian shrugged. "Hats off to the cooks. I hope every family in town is sitting down to such a fine dinner. How does that old saying go—the condemned man ate a hearty meal?"

Dan had begun eating again, but now sat back in his chair, ignoring Emily's desperate look. "Honestly, do you need to hijack our entire Thanksgiving dinner with these grim conundrums?"

Lillian gazed back at him. "It's no riddle. You all know what I'm talking about. How can we sit here so complacently, chatting about pumpkin displays and Brussels sprouts, when the election of Charlie Bates as mayor has sounded a death knell to the village? And I don't see anyone trying to do a thing about it." Lillian stared at Emily, a spark of challenge in her eyes. As if Emily were the obvious choice to spring into action.

Emily shook her head. "Mother, really. Let's not talk about this now, all right?"

"Charlie was elected, fair and square," Dan stated firmly. "I can't imagine what you expect anyone to do. I don't think there's anything to talk about, now or later. Or ever."

Emily knew he was being protective. But after all these years, he still didn't understand that confronting her mother head-on was like waving a red flag in front of a bull.

"Fight him," Lillian replied sharply. "That's what can be done. Fight him on this zoning issue."

"Lily, please," Ezra cut in. "Can't you let us eat our dinner in peace? Thankful for *all* that we do enjoy—instead of spinning gloomy disaster scenarios?" Ezra waved his arms in the air and made a face, making his grandchildren laugh. "Believe me, the world won't come to an end because Charlie Bates was elected mayor."

Well said, Emily thought. Though Lillian did

not look pleased to be laughed at. Another red flag.

"I will not pipe down. And I'm surprised at you, Dan, of all people. You spend your days glorifying local history in those books you write. But you don't care a whit if the very soul of this village—its historic character—is wiped out? If the streets are filled with condo developments and strip malls?"

Dan stared straight ahead, his mouth in a tight line. Emily could see he was angry but trying to hold his temper.

Sam spoke up. "This will all blow over. I don't think most people want the zoning changed. Charlie just had a lucky night. You didn't lose by much, Em."

Lillian gave her other son-in-law a look. Everyone knew Sam's sunny disposition and perennial optimism annoyed her like a skin rash. "Emily should have asked for a recount. I told her that a hundred times."

"I decided it was best not to drag out the situation. As Dan said, Charlie won, fair and square. It's out of my hands now, Mother."

Emily had campaigned on the side of zoning that would preserve the open spaces and farmland beyond the village center. Charlie was in favor of changing the zoning to allow for more development—housing developments, condos, and even commercial real estate.

Emily had assumed—wrongly perhaps—that most people in town wouldn't want the village to change in such a harsh way, and that she would win the election handily. But Charlie had argued that change would bring more young residents to the town and more revenue for schools and village improvements. In the end, he had managed to get more of his supporters to the polls, and she had not.

"Since there seems no avoiding it, let's set the record straight," Dan said finally. "Emily ran a great campaign and made a very graceful exit. She has nothing to feel ashamed about. But she's done with politics now, and she's the last person who should be held responsible for the fate of the zoning laws. She's championed these causes long enough, Lillian."

Lillian frowned, as if she had just tasted something sour. "So you say. But I haven't heard that from my daughter yet. Will you stand back and watch that witless wonder ruin this town? You ran on this issue, Emily. You seemed sincere. Or was that all just empty campaign talk? I heard that a group is organizing to oppose new zoning. You can fight Charlie. And you can run again. People will remember whether you stood up for what you believe in—or hung back on the sidelines, baking yams."

Emily sighed. Only Lillian could make "baking yams" sound so disreputable. "I'm taking a break from politics, Mother," she explained patiently. "Just like Dan said. I'm going to sit this one out. Maybe *you* should join the group if you feel that strongly."

"There's an idea." Ezra glanced at Emily, looking pleased at how she had turned the tables. "What do you think of that, Lily?"

Lillian snapped her napkin across her lap and sat up straight in her chair. "I've already signed on. I'm not just a talker, like some people around here."

Emily was surprised to hear that and wondered if it was true. Her mother had volunteered quite a bit when she was younger, but except for the board of the Historical Society, she didn't take part in committee work anymore. *She's just baiting me,* Emily decided. *But I'm not going to bite.*

"You've always been a woman of action, dear," Ezra replied smoothly. "Now that we have that sticky wicket out of the way, let's move on to more cheerful topics. Do I spy an apple pie on the sideboard? Or did Charlie Bates ruin that tradition for us, too?"

Everyone laughed except for Lillian. But she couldn't help smiling a little as she poked her husband with her elbow.

Thank goodness that Ezra is in the family, Emily thought, offering up an extra Thanksgiving prayer. *Where would we be without him?*

• • •

BY THE TIME ZOEY SAT DOWN TO HER family's Thanksgiving dinner, she had been facing turkey and the traditional side dishes all day, working at the diner with Charlie from noon until five. Her older adoptive brother, C.J., had gotten home from college late the night before and stayed home to help set up for their own feast. Zoey's younger adoptive brother, Jamie, had come along to bus tables, but it had still been a hectic shift. The number of customers who showed up for the Clam Box "Thanksgiving Dinner Special" had surprised her.

To Charlie's credit, he had created a cheerful atmosphere, with pots of brightly colored mums and pumpkins on the counter and tables. Many of the customers who arrived looked as if they lived alone or weren't able to cook for themselves.

Her father was actually doing a good deed, Zoey decided, though she wasn't sure he realized it. Or maybe he did? The price for the three-course meal was surprisingly low. "Everyone ought to have some turkey on Thanksgiving," he had been grumbling all day. "Who else is going to serve it to them if I don't?" Charlie might be gruff and stubborn, but he had a good heart.

Zoey was glad when they locked up and went home. Her mom's dinner was much more appealing and far tastier than the one at the diner. Lucy was a very good cook, though she let Charlie have all of the glory.

"Charlie, are you done carving?" Lucy called back as she and Zoey carried side dishes out of the kitchen. "I don't want the rest of the food to get cold."

"Hold your horses. I know my way around a turkey by now. I can't go any faster. There's an art to this, Lucy."

Zoey and her mother shared a secret smile. "Okay. But we're waiting. Speed it up, Picasso."

Tucker Tulley, her father's best friend since childhood, chuckled softly, and so did his wife, Fran. Their children were a bit older than Zoey and her brothers and were busy with their own lives. But they would all be home for Christmas, Fran had been telling everyone. "I can hardly wait," she said.

"I can. The house isn't big enough to hold all of us anymore." Tucker rolled his eyes, but Zoey knew that Tucker was happy as a clam when his children visited.

"There's a beautiful colonial on Ivy Lane that just came on the market," Fran said. "Plenty of bedrooms and motivated sellers." Fran was in real estate, and always campaigning for a new house.

"I'm very thankful for the house we have now," Tucker said. "And thankful to see Charlie finally bringing in that turkey."

Her father bustled into the room, carrying the big platter, an apron over his dress shirt and tie. "I picked out a beautiful bird for you this year. It came out perfectly, if I do say so myself."

Zoey knew that Lucy had cooked everything and should have gotten some credit. "Everything looks delicious, Mom," she said. "Nice carving, Dad," she added.

"Thank you, Zoey. Help yourself, everybody," Charlie said.

"While we're passing around the food, I think it would be nice if we each shared something we're truly thankful for this year," her mother added.

Zoey heard her brother C.J. softly groan. She glanced at him, and they both laughed.

Charlie's eyes darted to his oldest son. "C.J., why don't you start?"

"I better think about it, Dad," Charlie Junior said quickly. "Why don't you come back to me?"

"I'm going to think about it, too, Dad," Jamie said.

Lucy's mother, Grandma Dooley, sat at the head of the table, opposite Charlie. She was in her seventies and looked like an older version of Lucy, with a slim build and red hair that had mostly gone white. "I'll start," she said, bailing out her grandsons. "I think when you're older you're likely to appreciate little things. Just getting up in the morning seems like a blessing,"

69

she added with a laugh. "I'm thankful for many things—my health and my friendships. But mainly for my family. I love you all," she said simply. "And I'm just happy to share another Thanksgiving at this table."

"Thanks, Mom. We love you, too." Lucy smiled, her eyes a little misty.

"I'm thankful that our children will all be with us at Christmas," Fran offered, "and that our family is growing. Michael's wife is expecting. We're going to be grandparents."

"What wonderful news! We're so happy for you." Lucy leaned forward in her chair. "When's the baby coming?"

"In April. We have plenty of time to prepare . . . and look for a bigger house." Fran glanced at Tucker again, but he focused on spooning cranberry sauce on his plate.

"You're going to be a grandpa, Tucker? That makes me feel old, my friend," Charlie said.

"Maybe so, but I can hardly wait. You being elected mayor made me feel old, so I guess we're even."

Her father laughed. "That's what I'm thankful for this year. In case anyone has a doubt. It took me long enough, but I finally did it." He paused a moment and sighed, as if he had run a long race and just crossed the finish line, Zoey thought. When he looked up again, he fixed his gaze on Zoey and her brothers. "I hope the young people here take a lesson from that. You don't always get what you want at the first try."

"Very true." Tucker nodded.

As Zoey expected, when it was her mother's turn, Lucy was most thankful for her family and for being able to enjoy their dinner together. "When you work in a hospital, you realize not everyone is this lucky or has a real family."

Zoey agreed. Even if she could forget her younger years—bouncing around foster homes—working at the diner today was proof enough that there were a lot of lonely people out there. She thought of her younger brother, Kevin. They had been separated in the foster system but always kept in contact. Kevin had also been adopted by a loving family, a short time after Zoey had been taken in by Lucy and Charlie. He had lived a short distance away and they had seen each other often, until recently, when his adoptive family moved to Minnesota. Zoey missed him, especially at holidays. But they kept in touch with FaceTime and Skype, and most of all, she knew he was growing up in a happy, safe home. And enjoying a Thanksgiving dinner today, just like this one.

"Zoey, would you like to take a turn?" Lucy prompted.

Zoey felt everyone staring at her. She knew most people thought she was brash and would say just about anything. But inside, she often felt very shy.

"Let's see ... I guess I'm thankful that I finally found something I really want to do when I finish school—work as an art therapist. A job that won't even feel like work to me," she added.

Lucy had been very encouraging, as always, of Zoey's college major and career plans; Charlie, less so. He didn't have a high opinion of her studying psychology, or art. He thought both were frivolous pursuits and never missed a chance to poke fun at therapy, especially one that involved "arts and crafts."

Zoey ignored his objections. He could be narrow-minded about things he didn't understand.

Lucy reached over and gently touched her hand. "Zoey volunteers at a youth center in Salem. It's part of a psychology course, and she's doing some wonderful work there. We're very proud of her."

"I'm glad for you, honey," Grandma said. "But what does an art therapist do ... if you don't mind my asking?"

"That's okay, Grandma. A lot of people don't know. Basically, you're a psychologist who helps patients work out their issues using drawings or paintings, as well as talking. The center where I volunteer works with children who can't express their feelings well with words," she added. "This method really helps them."

"That makes sense to me," Tucker said. "You're lucky to find something that you can put your whole heart into." He met her glance with a warm look of approval. "I guess you'll need to go to graduate school for a degree in a field like that."

"Whoa there, Tucker." Charlie held up a hand. "One tuition bill at a time. She isn't even done with four years yet. And we've got Jamie coming through the chute soon, too."

Jamie was sixteen, a sophomore in high school. C.J. was a year older than Zoey and attending the University of Vermont on a lacrosse scholarship, which made her parents very proud.

Zoey didn't want to worry about graduate school. She planned to work hard and get good grades. Maybe she would get a scholarship when the time came. She had applied for an internship at the center during her winter break. It would give her hands-on experience in the field, and would help with recommendations later. Zoey really hoped she'd get it, though she hadn't even been called in for an interview yet.

"Good gravy, Lucy," Charlie said as they started eating. "And the stuffing is very tasty, better than mine. Then again, I'm cooking for the masses. It's hard to include the fine touches."

"You do a good job. I bet a lot of people in

town would go without a turkey dinner today if you didn't keep the Clam Box open," Lucy said.

"I agree," Zoey added.

Charlie looked surprised at the compliments. "Thank you, ladies. I had second thoughts about staying open again this year on the holiday. But I don't want anyone to think I'm getting too full of myself because I'm mayor. I felt it was my duty, in a way."

"You've got a lot of love and loyalty for this town, Charlie. That's why you were elected," Tucker said. "How's it going at Village Hall? How do you like being in the hot seat?"

"So far, so good," her father reported happily. "I think Cape Light was ready for a change. I'm not going to sit here and criticize Emily Warwick—"

"I hope not," her mother cut in. "The election is long over, and it *is* Thanksgiving."

"I know, Lucy. Don't worry. But we're among friends here. Let's just say a new broom sweeps clean. And there's a lot to sweep after Emily's umpteen years in office."

A new broom? Charlie was full of corny mottos, spouting them night and day. Zoey had no idea what half of them were supposed to mean.

"Speaking of brooms, how do you manage running the diner *and* being mayor? You must run up and down Main Street all day," Fran said.

"Tell me about it. I'm ready for the Boston Marathon. It hasn't been easy, burning the candle at both ends."

Another one. Zoey rolled her eyes, though she knew that was true; Charlie ran in and out of the diner all day and had almost doubled her hours over the last two weeks. She hadn't made a fuss so far but wasn't sure how much longer she could put up with it. She had her own life to take care of. He didn't seem to understand that.

"You need a manager, Charlie," her mother said. "I thought you were going to promote Trudy."

"I'm trying. But Trudy says she doesn't want the job. Can you believe that? I'm still working on her."

Zoey could believe it. Trudy, a longtime employee, probably thought the job was more bother than it was worth. Trudy knew her father well—his good points and his not-so-good points.

"Zoey's been a big help," he continued. "She's really stepped up. She can help me even more during her winter break."

Zoey nearly dropped her fork. "I can't work full-time during the winter break," she said quickly. "I might get an internship at the center. That's a full-time job. And even if I don't get the internship, I promised them at least twenty hours a week in January, as a volunteer."

Charlie nodded and spooned more mashed potatoes onto his plate. "We'll see, honey. We don't have to talk about it now."

Zoey felt Lucy's arm slip around her shoulders. "We'll work it out, honey. Don't worry about it now."

Zoey nodded and sat back in her chair. Her mom would stick up for her; Zoey felt sure of that. Lucy understood that working at the center was important for Zoey's future. She couldn't act all dedicated and then disappear for two months. What kind of impression would that make?

Luckily, Tucker quickly changed the subject, asking her brothers if they had been watching the Patriots. What a question. That was like asking if they liked to breathe or eat food. They both started talking at once, trying to outdo each other, spouting statistics and recounting each play.

Zoey felt relieved to be out of the spotlight. It wasn't right to argue about this with her parents now and ruin a holiday dinner. But no way was she spending winter break at the diner.

Excuse me? It's my life, and I have some say, Zoey answered back silently. She was happy that her father was finally mayor. That was what he had wanted his entire life. But why was it suddenly her problem? *No way am I going to be stuck in the diner all that time. Dad is crazy if he believes that.*

THE HOLIDAY GATHERING AT EVELYN'S HOUSE went smoothly, thanks to the careful planning of Sophie's daughters. Their large family sat at two long tables that were beautifully set. Beyond Sophie's predictions, three turkeys were needed for their feast.

Evelyn was terrified of running out of white meat. "And I hate when there aren't any leftovers. That's what Thanksgiving is all about—turkey sandwiches and turkey hash."

"And turkey chili," Sophie's younger daughter, Una, added as the women bustled around the kitchen after the meal, cleaning up and putting the food away. The men were in the family room, watching football. Every last one of them, Sophie noticed. She knew it wasn't the modern way, but it was still the Potter way, unlikely to change in her lifetime.

She was in charge of putting out the desserts while Evelyn's daughter, Amelia, washed pots and pans, and the others ran about, drying and putting things away.

"Those pies look delicious, Grandma," Amelia said. "Did you bake all three?"

Sophie proudly lifted her head. "Yes, I did. I baked twelve pies all told. A friend and I did it together," she added. "We gave most to the church for their Thanksgiving baskets."

Her daughters exchanged a look. "That's wonderful, Mom," Evelyn said in her most diplomatic tone. "But at your age—twelve pies? You must have been exhausted. Leave it to the young people now. Give someone else at church a chance to do good deeds."

The others laughed, and Sophie did, too. But her silent alarm sounded. She could smell where this conversation was going.

"It was no trouble. I enjoyed it. And I wasn't tired at all. I made the cranberry relish, the string beans, and the butternut squash soup the day after," she reminded them.

It was true, too. Though James had helped her in the kitchen yesterday.

The coffee was almost ready, and the pleasant aroma filled the air. "The pies look delicious," Evelyn said finally. "We've got some rice pudding, cranberry-orange cake, and brownies for the little ones." She placed those dishes on the table, too.

"So many good cooks in this family. Aren't we lucky," Sophie said.

"It's not luck, Mom. You get the credit for that." Una stepped over and put her arm around Sophie's shoulders. "You taught us everything we know."

Sophie smiled at the compliment. "I taught you the basics. But you two outdo me now with your fancy recipes. Like those turnips cooked with curry. Very tasty," Sophie added, praising their adventurous efforts.

Evelyn laughed. "We're not trying to outdo you, Mom. But it's nice to try a few new dishes. We don't have to eat the same thing every year."

"I've already started working on the Christmas menu. I have a few surprises up my sleeve, too," Una said gleefully.

Sophie pinned her younger daughter with a stare. "That sounds like fun, dear. You bring whatever you like. I'm not like Evelyn. You don't have to clear every covered dish with Homeland Security."

Sophie was trying hard to make light of the subject. But the way Una glanced at Evelyn was making her nervous.

"Well, Mom . . . Evelyn and I want to talk to you about Christmas. We thought that since she had Thanksgiving, I'd have the family for Christmas. It seems only fair. We know that you love having us all over," she quickly added, "but honestly, we both feel . . . and Bart, too . . . that it's too much for you now. Way too much work and stress."

"We would all worry about you, Mom, trying to hold a big party like that." Evelyn put a hand on Sophie's shoulder. "You're not up to it. So please don't argue with us."

"I'm not going to argue," Sophie said calmly.

"I'm telling you all, point-blank, I'm having Christmas at my house. Just like I always do. If you don't want to come, well, that's your business."

"Oh, Mom, don't be like that," Una said. "Please don't be so stubborn. All the parents of my friends have passed the big holidays on to their children, and a lot are much younger than you."

Sophie shrugged. "To each his own. Maybe they don't enjoy it. But I do. I see no reason why I can't have you all this year, like I always do. Didn't I just bake a dozen pies without batting an eye? What do I need to do to prove I'm well again—jog home in the snow?"

Her son, Bart, walked into the kitchen, obviously lured by the smell of coffee and the dessert table. "Who's running home in the snow? What are you arguing about in here anyway?"

"Evelyn and I decided that I should have Christmas this year. Remember, we told you?" Una's tone was nervous, Sophie noticed. Maybe there was a chink in their armor.

Bart nodded but avoided Sophie's gaze. "Oh right . . . I remember now," he mumbled.

So he's in on this, too? Surprise, surprise.

"Mom doesn't agree. She not being realistic," Evelyn added. Sophie knew her older daughter was very practical, a trait that served her well most of the time. Being "unrealistic" was one of the most severe criticisms Evelyn could level at anyone.

But there are plenty of times when you should be impractical and unrealistic, Sophie knew. When you should bend a bit, like a birch tree. Evelyn, bless her heart, was more like a mighty oak.

Bart stared down at his mother. "I guess I agree. It's high time you passed the holiday-making to the younger generation. We're not even that young anymore." He laughed, glancing at his sisters.

Sophie knew that was true. But they had no idea how young they seemed to her, still in their forties and fifties. She would give a lot to be that age again. Beyond that, they would always be her children. Her babies.

"Very true. But you never know, this could be my last year in that house. I have my heart set on celebrating Christmas there, like we always do. Like we did when your father was alive. He was crazy about Christmas. That was the high point of his entire year," she reminded them.

She could see the expressions on their faces soften. *Thank you, Gus,* she said silently. *I knew you would help me sort this out.*

"Oh, Mom. You don't have to make us teary now," Una said.

"Sorry, dear. Not at all my intention," Sophie said honestly. "But it's true."

"What's this about it being your last year in the house?" Bart leaned against the counter, a mug of coffee in hand. "Does this mean you're ready to sell the place?"

Sophie had expected this question to come up today. But the dinner conversation had gone so smoothly, she had let her guard down and felt unprepared.

"I didn't say that, son. Don't go putting words in my mouth. I only meant you never know what the good Lord has in store. This could be my last slice of pumpkin pie, for all we know." She smiled and continued to cut the pies, though her hands trembled a bit.

"I hope not, Mom," Evelyn said. "But that's our point. You're not getting any younger. We really don't want you to go through another winter like last year, stuck all alone in that house. Even if your health is perfect."

Before Sophie could reply, Bart said, "We've been waiting for your answer on this question, Mom. Waiting since last winter," he reminded her. "You know what we think you should do. In fact, we've been talking about it, and we'd like you to put the place on the market right after the holidays, sometime in January."

"So, you have your own timetable, whether I'm ready or not. Is that what you're telling me?"

"Not exactly," Evelyn said with a sympathetic look. "It's your house and ultimately your decision. But we have to be reasonable. We want you to be reasonable, too. If this winter is anything like the last, it won't be safe for you to be there all alone. Even with visitors and help from the church group."

"Surely you must see that? You were snowed in several times," Bart reminded her.

"We could hardly take care of you, and we were worried sick. And it's already started snowing," Una pointed out. "Maybe you should move in with me, and we'll make Christmas together— at my house?" she suggested in a more cheerful, cajoling tone.

Sophie swept a glance around the room. Her children stared at her, waiting for her answer. The way they did years ago, waiting for permission to stay up late for a favorite TV show, or to ride their bikes to the beach to go swimming on their own.

"My, my. Time changes everything doesn't it?" she said softly, mainly to herself.

"Yes, Mom. It does, whether we like it or not." Evelyn's tone was low but firm. They meant business this time.

Sophie took a breath and brushed a few crumbs from her hands. "I know you all mean well, trying to push me along, out of love and concern. But put yourself in my shoes. An apple doesn't fall from the tree until it's ripe. That's how I feel. I'm just not ready to go."

"Oh, Mom . . . please." Bart sighed and closed his eyes. She could tell he was trying to hold on to his patience.

"You're not an apple, Mom," Evelyn reminded her sternly.

Under any other circumstance, Sophie would have laughed. Instead, she felt stuck, trying to think of some reply.

James walked in, his focus fixed on the desserts, like a bee heading for a rosebush. He picked up a paper plate and began piling on his selections.

"So, Grandma is not an apple. Did you recently notice that? Or have you been considering the possibility for a while?" He glanced at his aunt, looking amused by the conversation.

"We're in the middle of something, James," his father said. "A serious discussion."

"Sorry to interrupt." He glanced at his father and then at his grandmother. She could tell her grandson knew what the serious topic was. James took a fork and sat down at the table next to Sophie. He began eating, as if minding his own business. But she felt as if a loyal watchdog had suddenly appeared and planted himself at her side.

"We know you don't feel ready now, but will you ever?" Evelyn asked.

"Someday I might," Sophie offered honestly. "I'm not sure yet what I should do. Until then, I'm staying put. At least until the new year. I mean it, too," she added, in case there could be any question.

Her children exchanged looks. She sensed she had gained the edge. *Thank you, Lord. Let's close it now, okay?* she asked silently.

"I guess it can wait a month or so," Bart said. "But in the meantime, you have to have some help in the house. Live-in help. And don't say you don't like that idea either, Mom. I won't sleep a wink if you don't agree to that at least."

"Yes, dear. I understand. I've already got that covered. I will have someone with me day and night, and all the help I need." She turned to her grandson, pleased by the surprised looks on the faces of her children. "James is going to stay with me until the new year. Isn't that good news?"

Her daughters looked over at Bart, but he shrugged in a helpless gesture. "James, is that true?"

"Yes, it is. Grandma and I talked it over yesterday. Things weren't working out with my roommate, and I decided to take a break from New York. Too many distractions from my writing."

Sophie knew that wasn't the entire story. Her son seemed to sense that, too, judging from his expression. She had thought that by now, James would have told his father what was going on in his life. Obviously not.

But it wasn't her place to set the record straight.

She would encourage James to be honest with his father. That was the important thing.

"Why don't you regroup in Darien? It's quiet there, too. And much closer to the city and your friends," Bart reminded his son.

"Very true. Too close. Too tempting. Besides, Grandma can use some help and some company. Isn't that what you've been talking about?"

"I think it's very good of you to stay at the orchard right now, James," said Evelyn.

"It certainly solves our problem. For now anyway," Una added.

Sophie sighed. Was she suddenly a problem to be solved? She held her tongue, knowing it was not wise to rile up tempers. Not while she seemed to be winning this battle.

Bart glanced at his sisters, who seemed relieved to hear James's plan. "If that's what you want to do, James, and it's all right with your grandmother—"

"Delighted to have him." Sophie met her grandson's bright gaze. "The nicest surprise I've had in ages."

"I guess it's settled, then. For now," Bart said. "We can wait until the holidays are over, if that's what you need, Mother. But not much longer. I don't mean to sound harsh, but it's for your own good."

"Let's talk again after Christmas," Evelyn suggested.

"Which can be at your house. If you let us all help," Una added.

"Agreed. Thank you, children, for being so reasonable. I'm sealing this bargain with a slice of pie. Anyone care to join me?"

"I'll have another," James said. "I think I'll try apple this time." Sophie met her grandson's bright blue eyes and they shared a secret glance. Somehow, they had outfoxed the hounds. For now.

She didn't mean to be stubborn, but she believed she would know when it was time to leave her house and her trees. It was impossible to explain. But in her heart, she would just know.

Chapter Four

EMILY ALWAYS ENJOYED CHURCH ON THE first Sunday of Advent. The sanctuary wasn't decked out in all its Christmas finery yet, but there were plenty of touches to set the mood—a centerpiece of pine boughs on the altar, a wreath hanging behind the pulpit, and the large blue Advent candles that would be lit one by one as Christmas drew near.

"Oh drat . . . that candle prayer. I hope it doesn't slow down the service," her mother muttered.

Emily sat between Dan and her mother. Jane was still at a sleepover, and Ezra, who was coming down with a cold, had decided to stay home. Emily had taken her own car to pick up her mother, expecting that they would run errands after the service. Dan had to head in a different direction to pick Jane up after her party.

Emily and her mother had reached church a few minutes late. Dan had saved them seats toward the back of the sanctuary, which was easiest for Lillian, who walked with a cane, but was the last place she liked to sit.

"They say a few short prayers and light the candle," Emily whispered back. "It doesn't take long at all."

"Who's that family? I don't know them," Lillian replied.

"Jeff and Carrie Carlson, and their son, Noah. Jeff has been in the church a long time. Carrie and her son joined about a year ago."

"I remember him. A doctor of some kind? He lost his wife a few years back," Lillian recalled. "I see he found another."

"They're newlyweds, married in September," Emily said. Had they met at church? Emily didn't think so. Carrie's son, Noah, had brought them together in some way, but she couldn't recall the story.

"Well, I don't know them," Lillian mumbled.

Then you should introduce yourself at coffee hour, Emily was about to reply, but Dan gave them a look.

The Carlsons had stepped up to the candles. They took turns reciting the Advent prayers. Noah did very well for a little boy. He read in a loud voice without stumbling at all.

The warm looks the couple exchanged, the way Jeff put his arm around Carrie's shoulders, and how they both helped Noah light the candle, spoke of loving bonds that made Emily's heart glad. Jeff had told Emily that after he lost his wife, he never imagined finding anyone he could love as much. But he had suddenly found two people who meant more to him than anything.

If Carrie's flowing dress and the way Jeff guided her down the steps were any sign, Emily guessed that they were expecting a little sister or brother for Noah soon, too.

She glanced at her mother, who sat reading the church bulletin, clearly bored by the ritual. Reverend Ben walked up before the congregation and thanked the Carlsons, then began the weekly announcements.

"Many thanks to everyone who donated food and who cooked and baked for the Thanksgiving baskets this year. The baskets were very bountiful and much appreciated," he said sincerely. "Now it's time to start our Christmas projects, including the annual Christmas Fair. As I mentioned last Sunday, our longtime chairperson, Sophie Potter, is stepping down. We are thankful for her many years of service and for her inspiration that created this event, so long ago." He smiled in Sophie's direction. "How many years ago was that, Sophie? Do you remember?"

"I know you won't believe it, but it's almost forty," she called back. "I love doing it, as you all know. But I need to rest on my laurels now. That's what my children tell me," she added with a laugh. "I'm happy to offer advice and cover my share of the crafts and whatever needs doing."

"I'm sure you will," Reverend Ben said kindly.

"But we need a new chairperson. No one has come forward yet for the job. As you all know, the fair is an important fund-raiser. We count on it to support our church and outreach projects. There will be a meeting for everyone interested in working on the fair right after the service. Perhaps we can elect a new chairperson today?"

He gazed around the congregation. Emily felt her arm stir. She always loved the fair. What if Reverend Ben didn't find anyone? It would be a shame if the church had to abandon that event. It was an important moneymaker, and she had plenty of experience managing people . . .

She felt Dan lean against her, not that hard or in an obvious way. But enough to keep her arm in place. "Don't you dare," he whispered with a hint of amusement. "Someone else will step up. I promise."

"You're right. I wasn't thinking."

Lillian leaned over. "Quiet, please. I can't hear a thing back here in no-man's-land."

"Sorry, Mother," Emily said automatically, but her mind was on her new life. *Maybe I'll help a little,* she told herself, *but I'm not going to run a thing. Not for a long time.*

ZOEY HAD COME TO CHURCH WITH HER mother and her brother Jamie. C.J. had a ride back to school today and might even be gone by now. Charlie had left the house early, off to the diner by dawn. She was going to work there after the service, when the lunch shift started. She didn't mind that much; it was never as frantic as Sunday morning breakfast.

She had spotted James sitting next to Sophie a few rows ahead. She was sure James hadn't noticed her. But when the service ended, James quickly turned and waved, and Zoey waved back.

She wasn't sure if he meant hello or good-bye. Did he want her to walk over and talk? Feeling shy, she decided not to and ducked out a side door, then headed for the diner.

She walked quickly across the green. A strong breeze off the harbor lifted her hair and cooled her warm cheeks. So, he had noticed her. That made her happy. *At least I look better today than when we met. And I don't smell of pumpkin.*

She was usually pretty cool about attention from guys. She attracted her share. But something about James Potter intimidated her. He was older, for one thing, and lived in New York. Zoey had only been there once, on a class trip in middle school. Lucy always promised they would go for a girls' weekend someday, to shop and visit museums. So far, they hadn't made it.

Zoey knew she seemed arty and edgy for Cape Light. She had been a bit wild in high school and still had a blue bracelet tattoo around her wrist and a few extra piercings in her ear. She liked to dress in thrift-shop, bohemian style, too. But she guessed that James met a lot of girls like that, truly hip girls who were actresses, painters, or writers. *He'll never be interested in me. I must seem hopelessly quaint, stuck out here in the middle of nowhere.*

Okay, I have a tiny crush on him, she admitted to herself. *Who wouldn't? But he'll be returning to New York any minute. He was probably waving good-bye. I'm surprised he's stayed this long.*

"ANY SPECIAL REASON YOU DIDN'T WANT to stay for coffee hour today, Mother?" Emily snapped her seat belt, curious about her mother's rush to leave church. Lillian had forgone her usual chat with Reverend Ben, including her weekly review of his sermon. She had even skipped socializing in Fellowship Hall, where she enjoyed giving her opinion on a range of subjects and gathering bits of gossip like a lint brush.

"We can stop at the market and the drugstore on the way home. I'm sure you need a few things." Emily glanced at her mother as they headed down Main Street. "Unless you think Ezra needs you?"

"Ezra will be fine. He's a doctor. He should be able to take care of himself for a few hours. He doesn't need me to watch him nap." Her mother turned to her. "I don't need any groceries. But you could take me somewhere. To a meeting. And stay with me until it's done, of course. I won't have a ride home otherwise."

"A meeting? What group is this?" If her mother was going to attend any meetings today, Emily thought it would have been back at the church, one of the committees forming for Christmas projects.

"The open-space group. They're meeting today at the Elks Lodge. We'll be just in time." Lillian pulled out a flyer from her purse and waved it at Emily. Of course, Emily couldn't read it while driving, but she got the main idea from the large headline on top. A knot of dread twisted in her stomach. Of all the underhanded tricks . . .

"You told me to get involved," Lillian reminded her before she could protest. "Practically dared me, I recall. I hear there's going to be a very large turnout. Should be quite interesting."

Emily shook her head. "Mother, this tactic is beyond transparent. Beyond even your usual manipulation. You realize that, don't you?"

Lillian feigned an innocent, even injured, look. "I have no idea what you're talking about. Ezra has a cold. You saw him. Otherwise, he would have driven me. That's what I planned. I suppose you can just drop me there. I might find someone to give me a lift back to town, or call a taxi. Either way, I mean to put my shoulder to the wheel, Emily. Not just spout a lot of fine words about the situation."

Her tone made Emily sigh. Her mother knew very well that Emily would never drop her off and drive away. The Elks Lodge was quite a few miles outside of the village. It would be hard to get a taxi to go out there.

"I'll stay and wait for you, but I'm not participating. I'm sitting this one out," Emily reminded her mother.

"You've made yourself perfectly clear. No need to get huffy. You can stay in the car if you like, check your email. But I guess you don't get nearly as much anymore, since you lost the election. That must leave a lot of time free."

"Yes, it does." Emily forced a smile but didn't say more.

A short time later, they pulled into the parking lot of the Elks Lodge. There were more cars than Emily had expected, and she hoped she could stay under the radar, but her hopes were short-lived.

"Mayor Warwick! So glad you could come." A woman at the door beamed as she handed them agendas.

I should have worn a floppy hat and sunglasses. I'll have to remember to keep some in the car.

"Just call me Emily, please. I'm a private citizen now."

"But concerned about this issue, as we well know," a man nearby replied. He stood at a table, handing out copies of news articles about the issue. Emily recognized him—Martin Becker, a history teacher at the high school. She also recognized the headlines, some trumpeting the arguments against new zoning she had made during her campaign.

Emily smiled back and moved her mother along.

"You should have no qualms about keeping your title. Don't they still call former presidents 'Mr. President'?"

"Mother, don't be absurd. This isn't Washington, D.C."

Emily quickly chose seats for them at the back of the room but, of course, her mother preferred to sit up front. "I can't hear a thing otherwise. You know that," she insisted, pushing ahead to the front of the room.

"All right, you sit up there if you like. I'll see you later," Emily countered, determined to keep her distance from this situation, both figuratively and literally.

Lillian looked cross as Emily walked away, but didn't argue.

Emily settled in a distant spot and reviewed the agenda. She was still annoyed about the way her mother had tricked her into coming, but was secretly interested to see what would go on. Could the group organize and block Charlie Bates and the pro-zoning crew? She hoped so. She worried about the future of the village; all of its historic charm and character was at stake. Everything that made Cape Light . . . well, Cape Light.

Martin Becker and Marion Ross, the woman who had greeted everyone at the door, were up front, running the meeting. They sat at a long table, along with three others. Martin Becker introduced himself.

He seemed intelligent and serious. An argyle vest under a tweed jacket gave him an academic air, along with wire-rim glasses and gray brush-cut hair.

"Thank you all for coming. I hope that you're all ready and willing to fight the changes in the zoning laws that our new mayor supports. We believe these changes will ruin our town's charming, unique character. They will also bring down our property values and harm the wildlife that now thrives in this area.

"The question is, how can we block the group that is determined to push through these changes? Unfortunately, they have the new mayor on their side, as well as most of the town council. This issue is at the top of their to-do list. We do not have much time to organize and fight it. We have to strike back fast and efficiently."

Emily knew this was true. A number of tactics came to mind, but she was determined not to speak. She waited to see what others would suggest.

A few hands went up in the audience, and suggestions were offered—from collecting signatures to holding back on real estate taxes. Not bad ideas, Emily thought, but not time-effective.

"Maybe we should dump some fake tea in the harbor . . . as a protest," one man said. "I bet we would get some news coverage." Probably, Emily thought, though she doubted the theatrics would do anything to block the zoning changes.

A woman in the front row stood up. Emily recognized Grace Hegman, who owned Bramble Antiques Shop. "I'm sorry to seem uninformed, but can you please explain how Mayor Bates and the town council can change the zoning? Don't the village residents have to vote on a question this important?"

"That's true," Martin said. "A vote of all residents must be called. But with their majority, they'll easily pass a call for a vote. And likely set a date within a month or two—before we can get the real facts out to everyone who might vote against the change once they know the true consequences. If the vote were held today, Mayor Bates and his group would likely win. Otherwise Bates wouldn't have been elected."

Emily felt her face flush with embarrassment. When she lost the election, it had been more than a personal defeat. She had let the town down. She had left them unprotected from this disastrous possibility.

Martin suddenly realized his faux pas and looked embarrassed. "Sorry, Mayor Warwick. Former mayor, I mean," he mumbled into the microphone. "No slight intended. You had my vote and, I'd guess, the votes of many others in this room."

Everyone turned to look at her, and Emily forced a smile. "No need for a show of hands. I trust you," she called out, making everyone laugh. "Just to clarify, what Mr. Becker said is true. That's the way it will likely go in Village Hall. Starting with the next council meeting on December fifth, I expect this issue will be discussed. The council will decide then to call a vote on zoning changes that will allow more commercial building."

"Yes, that's right, first Monday of every month. I was just getting to that," Martin Becker quickly added. "The meeting is Monday, December fifth, at six thirty in Village Hall, open to everyone. We need a big turnout and need to voice our opposition. Any other suggestions, Mayor Warwick?"

Everyone looked her way again. Emily felt put on the spot, which was exactly what she had *not* wanted to happen. Her mother caught her eye, smiling and nodding, looking very pleased that her plan had worked out after all.

"Should we get T-shirts and signs made?" one woman asked. "I think that makes a big impression. You can really see how many people are united in the same cause. Red, maybe? With white letters—SOS. 'Save Our Open Spaces.' "

It wasn't exactly an acronym. There was an

extra *O* in there, Emily noticed. But she didn't bother to point that out.

"That's an idea," she replied, "but you probably want to focus on a fact sheet. Before the meeting, get it into the hands of as many people as you can and urge them to come to the Village Hall meeting. The flyer should state the points against this idea, plain and simple. It takes a long time for information like this to penetrate and sway opinions. You have to make a real push there."

A job my campaign didn't do all that well, she nearly added.

"Excellent points," Martin said. "We need to have volunteers out every day—at the train station, the post office, and the markets—handing out fact sheets and explaining our position. We'll have a sign-up sheet at this table right after the meeting."

A hand popped up, and Martin recognized a new speaker. Emily quietly sighed. *So much for sitting here like a fly on the wall. You were a very noisy one,* she scolded herself.

Now she had the problem of stepping back—gracefully or awkwardly. She would be disappointing everyone here who thought she was jumping into this effort with them, heart and soul.

Would it be so bad to take part? Just a little?

Dan won't like it. He won't even like knowing

that I came here today. But I can blame my mother.

When the meeting ended, Emily managed to snag Lillian and escort her out of the building without anyone stopping them to talk.

Once in the car, Emily felt herself fuming. She took a moment to collect her patience as she carefully steered out of the parking lot.

"I thought it went very well. You gave them some good advice," Lillian said. "Why bother with T-shirts? Silly window dressing. We need to get the word out, get more citizens on board. That's the only way to beat Bates and his crowd." When Emily didn't answer, she added, "I'm glad to see you've come to your senses. I knew you'd never be able to watch from the sidelines, Emily. It's not your style."

Emily gripped the steering wheel hard to keep from raising her voice. "I know you think you've tricked me into joining this group. But you're wrong. I offered a few remarks to help out. Mainly because everyone was staring at me."

"Tish-tosh. You know you enjoyed it. You could have stepped up and taken the microphone from that Bentley fellow and—"

"Becker. His name is Martin Becker."

"Whatever. You could have stepped into his place, and no one would have objected. In fact, I think even he would have been pleased. Will you let them down now? They think you're signed on to fight the good fight. You certainly made that impression. Some part of you at least must want to join in."

"I'm not going back, so don't try this again," Emily said smoothly. "It won't work twice."

"It was a straightforward request, not subterfuge in the least. I resent your accusation. It's most unfair," Lillian complained.

They drove silently for a few minutes, her mother's head turned toward her window in a stiff pose as she stared out at the tall marsh grass that bordered the Beach Road. Mostly brown this time of year, the thick patches of reeds stretched for miles, swaying gently in the wind, breaking here and there to reveal a pool of water or muddy flats.

A flock of birds rose from the brush and swooped gracefully across the clear sky. Emily's gaze followed them, her heart growing lighter at the sight.

Her mother heaved a heavy sigh. "Suit yourself, Emily. You always do. But don't be surprised if by the time you're ready to come back to politics—and I have no doubt that day will arrive—you'll find an outlet mall on this very road, and the nesting grounds for the osprey and snapping turtles and all those fine, delicate creatures out there will be covered with condo units. This is an important moment. Mark my words, people will remember what you do, and don't do, right now."

Emily did not reply, though she knew there was more than a grain of truth in her mother's goading. But she also knew that Lillian had drawn a great deal of pride and status from being the mother of the mayor. She clearly felt a great loss to her own identity with Emily's defeat. If her daughter couldn't be mayor right now, at least she could lead the charge against Charlie Bates.

But what sense would it make to confront her mother about that and open yet another can of worms? Emily was sure her mother would deny those motives, the same way she denied tricking Emily into attending the meeting.

Emily pulled into her mother's driveway. "I'll help you to the door," she said.

Lillian got out of the car, leaning heavily on her cane. "I'm fine. I've kept you away from . . . well, from whatever you'd rather do today . . . for too long. I can see that."

Emily was about to fire back a tart reply, her patience fraying totally, when she spotted Ezra coming down the walk to meet them. "Here's Ezra. He'll help you in," she said simply. "Good-bye, Mother. Enjoy the rest of your day."

Lillian straightened her spine. "I shall. I'm going to make some calls and get some people from church over to the next meeting. I'm with the rabble-rousers now. You know, I've changed my mind. I hope they *do* give out red T-shirts. I'll be proud to wear one."

Emily smiled at the very idea. She had never seen her mother wearing a T-shirt, much less one with a slogan on it. Perhaps if it was made of cashmere or satin? That might work.

"I'm going to the next meeting on Wednesday. If you don't want to drive me, and Ezra is unable, I'll call a cab," Lillian said.

"You should plan on that," Emily agreed. "I'll be busy. Jane has a volleyball game that day. I promised I'd watch her play."

Her mother tilted her head back, looking stung. "Yes, very important. Good luck to you both." She turned and headed to the door, her cane steadying slow steps.

Ezra stood halfway down the walk, waiting for his wife. He waved, and Emily waved back. Normally, she would go inside and say hello, but today she felt relieved to back out of the driveway and head straight home. The meeting had been only an hour, maybe less. But Emily felt as if she'd been out with her mother for days on end.

"SLOW TODAY, ESPECIALLY FOR A SUNDAY afternoon. I guess everyone's home, eating their turkey leftovers," Charlie said. He wore his reading glasses balanced on the tip of his nose, his gaze fixed on a letter that was typed on Village Hall stationery.

"Maybe we should close early, Dad," Zoey suggested. "I have a ton of studying and papers to work on. Finals are coming soon."

Zoey had noticed that her father had his own pile of homework, stacks of folders and papers he carried around with him, ever since he had started as mayor. He often left them on the counter or in some other inconvenient spot. It was a miracle that his official documents did not end up splattered with ketchup or drowned in coffee.

But what he had said at their Thanksgiving dinner was true. It was hard for him to run the diner and Village Hall, too. He was either flipping burgers or flipping the pages of a building inspector's report.

"We'll see how it goes," he replied in the vague way parents always did. He slipped the letter in a folder and let his glasses hang on the cord around his neck. "Wipe down all the menus and refill the napkin holders, will you, Zoey?" He turned his head and squinted at the busboy. "Scotty, you come back into the kitchen with me once you've emptied that rack. I've got another job for you."

Zoey had already wiped the menus. Charlie had obviously forgotten. Though the order was a good sign. They might close early, after all. She gathered up the menus, along with the napkin holders.

She had been hoping to read a few pages from a textbook she had stashed near the cash register. No luck with that plan. Her father didn't like to see any of his employees idle for even a minute. The mere possibility really got under his skin, even though he stole plenty of downtime now to keep up with his village duties.

She was in the midst of jamming a wad of napkins into a particularly stubborn holder when a customer walked in. Zoey looked up and nearly sprayed napkins all over the diner, but saved herself from complete mortification just in time.

James Potter met her surprised expression and smiled. "Hey, Zoey. You work here?"

"I do," she said lightly. "Sit down anywhere. I'll get a menu." He was alone. Where was Sophie? And why wasn't he on a train or a bus headed to New York by now?

He smiled again, then chose a table near the window. He hung his thick leather jacket on the back of a chair and took a small notebook and his phone out of one of the pockets before he sat down. He wore a nubby gray sweater that was a bit worn but looked just right on him. His thick hair was windblown, and he smoothed it back with his hand.

Zoey walked to the other side of the counter to grab a menu and a glass of ice water. She snuck a tube of lip gloss from her pocket and swiped some on. Not that all the makeup in the world could do anything to hide her geeky uniform—complete with a ruffled apron and the ugly black sneakers she had to wear for kitchen work.

I looked so cute in church, in my black skirt and boots. Why can't I ever run into this guy when I look half decent?

She set the menu and water in front of him. "There are some specials on the board. Not that anything we serve is actually special," she added quietly.

He laughed. "At least that's honest."

"Why would you eat here when you can have Sophie's cooking?"

"My grandmother has been in one meeting after another after church today. I've been wandering around town, and now I'm hungry enough to eat this menu."

"That's about the level of our cuisine. Don't say I didn't warn you."

"Fair enough." He glanced at the menu a moment. "How about a hamburger, medium, with lettuce, tomato, and fries?"

"Good choice. Anything to drink?"

"Just coffee. Black is fine."

Zoey marked his order on her pad. "I should have guessed. Isn't that the way writers always drink coffee?"

He smiled, amused by her observation. "Not

always. I don't stay up all night, drinking coffee and chain-smoking, if that's what you think." His smile widened, and dimples appeared in his cheeks. He really was killer cute; she tried not to stare.

"No offense. But I haven't thought that much about it," she replied with a small smile, then feared her nose was going to start growing like Pinocchio's. "I'll put your order in."

"Great, thanks." He didn't seem offended by her quip. He opened his notebook and took out a pen and a pair of glasses. The square, black frames suddenly made him look very intellectual.

He does look like a real writer. And I haven't even served the black coffee yet, she thought wryly.

A short time later, Zoey returned with his food. James was scribbling wildly in his notebook and didn't notice her. "The ketchup is on the table. Can I get you anything else—more coffee?"

He looked up, then down at the food, as if he had just woken from a nap. She could see that he had been off in his own world, not purposely being rude.

"That was fast. Thanks." He met her gaze and pulled off his glasses, then took a huge bite of the burger. "This isn't so bad," he mumbled around the mouthful. "How long do church meetings last? My grandmother is the only person in the world without a cell phone."

Zoey checked her watch. "The first probably didn't start until at least half past eleven, after coffee hour. The second meeting probably started around twelve thirty, or even one?"

He looked relieved and ate a French fry. "Thanks. I guess I don't have to choke this down, after all."

"You'd better not. I don't know the Heimlich maneuver, and it takes a long time to read that poster." She was teasing. She knew all types of first-aid procedures, but had never needed to use them. She certainly didn't want to start on James. "More coffee?" she asked.

"I'm good. I keep forgetting I'm not in the city. No reason to stay up all night. I've been sleeping like a baby at my grandmother's house. It's so peaceful out there, it's like a Zen retreat or something."

Zoey smiled. She felt the same about Sophie's house and the orchard. "A Zen retreat with apples."

"Exactly."

She liked the way he laughed at her jokes. She watched James inhale more fries, her tray balanced on her hip. "I thought you'd be on your way back to New York by now."

He shook his head, his blue eyes disconcertingly wide. "I'm staying with my grandmother for a few weeks. Through the holidays. She needs the help, and I can use a break from the city."

"Oh, wow . . . that's good!" Zoey blurted out. Then she quickly tried to backtrack. "I mean, it works out well for both of you. I sort of worry about Sophie being alone out there."

She felt her face turning red. So much for acting cool. No matter what she had said to cover up her flub, he knew now she liked him.

Good job, Zoey. That would have been lame even if you were still in middle school.

"I think it's going to work out fine. This village is more interesting than I remembered." He met her gaze again and smiled. Was he really flirting with her? Zoey gave herself a mental shake. *Get a grip. You have to be imagining that.*

Usually, she would have walked away by now, letting a customer take his time with his meal. For some reason, she felt a sudden, uncontrollable urge to rush him along.

"I guess you're in a hurry to pick up your grandmother. Here's your check." She had added the total and quickly tore off the slip and placed it facedown on his table.

James sat back and stared at her. "Thanks."

"You're welcome." She turned and walked away, feeling his eyes on her.

Back at the counter, she attacked the napkin dispensers again and forced herself not to look at him. He had his notebook open and seemed oblivious once more to his surroundings, lifting the last of his French fries mechanically to his mouth.

If he's staying here a few weeks, does that mean he doesn't have a steady relationship in New York? But maybe his girlfriend is going to visit him here. That wouldn't be too hard.

After a few moments, she saw him stand and put some bills on the table. He slipped on his jacket and headed for the door. "So long, Zoey. I'll see you around."

"Sure. See you." She nodded and looked back at the napkins, her very important work.

The door closed. Zoey sighed with relief. So, James Potter wasn't disappearing to New York this weekend. She wasn't sure if that was good news or bad. She already had a little crush on him and got the feeling he liked her, too.

But she could also see that James knew he was attractive and liked to flirt. She guessed he had girls falling all over him. *I shouldn't take him seriously.*

Her attraction seemed just as pointless now as it had when she thought he was on his way back to Manhattan. Maybe even more.

Even if he doesn't have a steady girlfriend, he would never be interested in me. And he's only staying for a few weeks. It's not as if he's moving here. Another reason not to think too much about him.

Zoey strolled over to pick up the check on

James's table and take away the dirty dishes. He had left her a generous tip.

Which I don't exactly deserve. Along with the check and the money, she found another slip of paper, folded in half. It looked like it must have been torn from his notebook. She opened it and read:

"Not all those who wander are lost."
—J. R. R. Tolkien

Glad I wandered in here today and saw you.   —J.

Zoey was surprised . . . and pleased. She quickly read the note a second time and felt herself blush. *Maybe he does like me—a little? Or he's a terrible flirt. Maybe both things are true,* she realized with a smile. *I guess now I'll have time to find out.*

She tucked the note in the pocket of her uniform and practically skipped to the register with the table check. Just as she was putting the money in the drawer, a huge crash in the kitchen made her jump. She slammed the register drawer and ran toward the kitchen.

"Dad, is everything okay back there?"

The kitchen doors flew open and Scotty ran out. He pulled on a fleece jacket with one hand and pulled off his apron with the other, then tossed the apron on the counter and headed for the door. "Bye, Zoey. Good luck. Your father is crazy. I hope you know that."

Zoey turned to watch his speedy exit, but didn't reply.

She knew Charlie had his difficult moments. But another part of her—a larger part—bristled with indignation at the insult.

She pushed through the doors to find her father standing in a pile of broken pottery. A broom and a dustpan in hand, he didn't seem to know where to start. It looked as if the dishwasher had exploded, but of course, that was not the problem.

"Dad . . . what a mess. What happened?"

"That damn fool kid . . . I told him not to overload that shelving. The bolt came loose from the wall, and I didn't have a chance to fix it yet. Did he listen to me? No, sir. Why listen to me? I'm only the boss around here."

Zoey bent to pick up a piece of a broken plate near her foot, but Charlie shouted at her, "Gloves, Zoey! Heavy ones. Use your head. I don't need a trip to the emergency room today on top of everything."

Good point, she thought, *though he could have said it in a nicer way.* She pulled on some work gloves she found near the utility closet and brought over another broom and trash bag.

"To top it off, the darn kid quits on me. Jumps right over the mess and out the door. Like a scared rabbit." Her father's voice got progressively louder. "Does he think he's going to come back next week, looking for his paycheck? I'm deducting every dish, cup, and saucer. He's going to end up owing me money."

Unlike some other restaurants, Charlie didn't usually charge the help for items that were broken while serving. It's not as if the Clam Box served on fine china and crystal. But she knew some restaurants did charge the help, and this situation was extreme. Though on the other hand, was it really Scott's fault that her father had not fixed the bolt?

"It's too bad you didn't get to fix the shelf, Dad," Zoey said finally. "Anybody could have overloaded it."

" 'Anybody' didn't do it. He did. After I warned him." Charlie dumped a scoop of broken glass into the trash barrel. "I can't do everything around here and run the town, too. That's the problem, Zoey. Flip the burgers, fix the bolts, open up, close down. Et cetera and so on . . ."

Zoey could tell he was approaching some meltdown moment. She didn't know what to say. She picked up a few more pieces of broken pottery and tossed them into the pail, too.

"Problem is, I need a manager, someone who knows the diner and can watch over it for me."

"That's a good idea. You should find someone. Did Trudy ever get back to you?"

"She doesn't want to do it. She's made up her mind. I can't persuade her."

"That's too bad." Trudy had been working at the diner as long as Zoey could remember. She wouldn't need any time to be trained.

"It is too bad," her father said. "That's why I need you to step up. As soon as your term is done, I need you to work here during your school break and handle things. I'll give you a nice raise."

Zoey dropped the bits of broken glass in her hand and stared at him. "I told you I can't work here full-time during my break. I've applied for an internship at the center where I volunteer. If I get it, it starts right after Christmas. Even if I don't, I promised them I'd come in extra hours in January, at least twenty hours a week."

Charlie shook his head. "I know, but this is real work I need you to do. Not volunteer stuff. I can't do two jobs at once, honey. It's just not humanly possible."

Zoey felt so upset and angry, she thought she was going to cry. "My stuff is important, too. I'm really happy that you're finally mayor. I know you really wanted that for a long time. But why does that have to mess up my entire life?"

"Mess up your life?" Charlie looked amused now, leaning on his broom and rolling his eyes. "How am I messing up your entire life? You have more than a month off from school and absolutely nothing to do. A lot of college kids are scrabbling for jobs right now, trying to make a little money over their vacation."

"Then put an ad in the newspaper or post it online. You can hire one of them," she retorted.

He squinted at her. "Don't sass me, young lady. You know what I mean. I've already hired you. I'm expanding your responsibilities and your hours. It's not like I'm asking you to do this for free."

Zoey took a breath and tried another tack. "I know I don't get paid at the center. But I need the experience and good recommendations from the people I work with there for my résumé. If I suddenly disappear for two months, they won't think I have a serious commitment."

Her father didn't answer right away, and for a moment she thought she had swayed him.

"I don't know what to do about that," he finally said. "I think you ought to talk to them, tell them you have a family emergency and you have to take a break for a few weeks. It's not a lie, Zoey. This is important. I don't mean for it all to fall on you. But C.J. has to go back to school right after Christmas, to make up some course he needs during intercession. Or I'd have him in here, too. Though I have to add, I wouldn't trust him to run things around here the way I trust you."

Zoey knew her father thought that was a huge compliment. She did feel a bit proud of his trust in her, but she also wished her brother was here to share the job. C.J. worked in the diner as much as she did when he was home from school, and she missed having him around. At least they had some fun together.

"I'm sorry, honey," Charlie said, "but this is more important than your volunteer work right now. We've got a situation here that's urgent."

"But, Dad—"

He shook his head. "Case closed. I'm not talking about this anymore. Now you go out front and turn the sign. We're closing early today."

Zoey pulled off the gloves and pushed through the kitchen doors. She felt her eyes blur with tears of anger and frustration.

Stuck in this diner her entire winter break? No internship. Not even volunteer hours? And what about a social life or any fun things she might want to do during time off from school? It sounded as if her father expected her to sleep in the pantry or something.

She flipped the sign on the door to SORRY, WE'RE CLOSED. SEE YOU SOON! Then she locked the door and started the rest of the routine—the closing-up chores that she knew by heart.

There had to be some way out of this. Some way to change her father's mind. She wondered if her mother knew about this plan. Zoey doubted it.

Mom will speak up for me, Zoey told herself. *She knows I can't be stuck in the diner for my whole winter break. It's great that Dad got to be mayor. Whoopee for him. But why does that mean my entire life has to be screwed up? It's just totally and completely unfair.*

Chapter Five

"CAREFUL ON THESE POTHOLES, HONEY. I'D rather we didn't bust an axle," Sophie gently warned her grandson. "This truck is so old, no one will be able to find the part."

"Good point, Grandma." James didn't own a car and hadn't been driving at all in the city, so he didn't mind driving slowly today. The truck handled like a small armored tank; he had no idea how his grandmother drove it on her own.

It was nearly two p.m., and they were just getting back from the village. Though Sophie had given up running the church Christmas Fair, she had stayed on after the Sunday service to give her successor detailed instructions.

"You ought to get this private road paved, Grandma."

"I know. I never got around to it. I suppose if I ever want to sell the place, it would be a good idea. You don't want prospective buyers to get their teeth shaken loose before they even see the place."

"Why not? That would definitely put them off," he pointed out.

Sophie laughed. "Good idea. Every time your father suggests it, I'll just put him off. Tell him it gives the place a real country feel."

As they rounded a bend in the lane, another car came into view. It was parked alongside the house, and James recognized it immediately—a sleek BMW sedan with a Connecticut license plate. "Looks like you'll get a chance to tell my dad right now."

His grandmother peered out the windshield. "I'll be. That is his car, isn't it? Sneaky to park on the side of the house like that. I didn't even see it."

"Dad isn't exactly sneaky. But he likes to have an edge. A surprise ambush is definitely his style." James came around to the passenger side and helped his grandmother down from her seat. It was a bit of a hop to the ground, but she was surprisingly nimble for an old person.

She stood by the truck a moment, yanked down her knitted hat, and tucked a few strands of hair under the edge.

"Are you all right, Grandma? Need to catch your breath?"

She shook her head. "Not at all. Just straightening myself out to face your father. It can't be a good sign, him coming all the way out here alone. It might be nothing, but"—she swiped some lipstick across her small mouth and dropped the tube back in her bag, then took her grandson's arm—"I think we should be prepared."

James nodded. He felt the same. Just the sight of the sedan made his stomach knot.

As they walked up to the house, the side door swung open. James's father stood there, smiling. Mac jumped up and did a little dance around his grandmother. James imagined the dog was confused, waiting alone with the surprise visitor.

"There you are. I thought you'd never get back. I tried your cell phone, James. Didn't you see my messages?"

"Sorry, the battery died. I couldn't charge it in the truck."

Bart glanced at the old red pickup. "It's surprising that engine still turns over. Charging a phone might have killed the battery."

"Don't talk that way about Bella. She might hear you." Sophie walked past him and took off her heavy coat and muffler but, for some reason, left her hat on. James guessed she thought it made her look more dignified—or perhaps even regal? The hand-crocheted hat did have a bit of a crown shape to it, and some tiny pearls sewn on as well.

"The truck has a name?" Bart followed his mother into the kitchen. "I suppose you've named the trees, too."

Sophie smiled. "Of course I have. I could pick out each one blindfolded, too. Why do you think they've given us such wonderful-tasting fruit all these years? That's no accident, son." She had flipped Mac a biscuit, and he trotted back to his dog bed and crunched on it happily. Then she turned to the sink and started filling the kettle.

"I'll make some tea. Would you like to have dinner with us, Bart? I'm just heating some left-overs Evelyn gave me."

"Thanks, but I've got to get on the road. I had some business in Boston the last two days. I just stopped by to say hello before I head home."

Cape Light was almost two hours north of Boston. Not exactly the most direct route back to Connecticut, James knew.

"Very thoughtful of you, son. But you didn't have to go out of your way like that," his grand-mother said.

"I want to make sure the house is ready for the winter," his father replied. "I think you ought to chop more wood and put insulation tape around all the windows. And the basement door. I can feel a draft from here."

"Good idea. I'll make a note," Sophie replied, though she made no move to write it down.

"Buy plenty of Ice Melt and some sand for that private road. We need to get it paved soon, Mom. It's treacherous."

The kettle hissed, and Sophie turned to lower the heat. "James and I were just talking about that road. You do need to take it slow, but it gives the place a real country feeling. People visiting the orchard for pick-your-own just love that." She glanced at James with a mischievous grin.

"I know you like things a certain way, Mom. You're used to the clutter and the inconveniences. But we need to keep this place up. By the time you're finally ready to sell, it will be a falling-down wreck. I was just upstairs. Some of those rooms look like walk-in closets, and every one of them could use a coat of paint."

"Things do accumulate. I can't argue with that." Sophie carried the teapot to the table and set out three mugs, though James had never once seen his father drink tea.

Sophie sat at the table, and, finally, Bart did, too, taking a chair across from James. "Have you had the chimney cleaned lately?" Sophie nodded, mixing a spoonful of honey into her cup. "How about the gutters? Did you ever call the number I gave you?"

"I just get up there with a broom or a big metal spoon and scoop the leaves out around the end of fall, when it's all come down. I can't see paying anyone to do that."

"You climbed a ladder? By *yourself?*"

Sophie shrugged. "It's not a very tall one. If I lost my balance I'd just end up in the hydrangeas. They're big and soft enough to break even *your* fall."

"Good to know," his father replied. He closed

his eyes and rubbed his hand over his face, a gesture James knew signaled that he was trying very hard not to lose his patience.

"Are you all right, Bart?" Sophie asked. "You're not getting one of your headaches, are you? I'm not sure you should drive if that's going on."

"It's not a headache. I'm fine." He opened his eyes, looking in control again. "I'll make a list of what needs to be attended to around here and make some calls for you next week."

"All right. Why don't you try Sam Morgan? He might be in between big jobs. He's a very nice fellow," Sophie added.

"Okay, I will." James couldn't tell what his father was thinking; his expression was unreadable. He suddenly turned and looked at James. "Why aren't you going back to the city? I don't really understand."

James knew he was in the hot seat now. Grandma's turn was over.

"Oh, I don't know. There are too many distractions there for my writing, and I wasn't getting along with my roommate."

His father didn't answer for a moment. "You lost your job. Is that it?"

James sighed and stared down at the table. "Well . . . I did. But that really wasn't all of it. I—"

"I knew it," his father cut in.

"It wasn't just that," James insisted. "I could have found another one."

"Sure, another job waiting tables in some dumpy restaurant. I don't doubt that for a minute. When are you going to get serious about your future, James? You wanted some time after you graduated to try out this writing business. Okay, we gave you time. But it's been almost two years. Time enough for you to stop fooling around."

"I'm not fooling around, Dad. I'm writing every day. I've had articles and short stories published." James didn't mean to raise his voice, but he couldn't help it. "I've sent them to you. Did you even read them?"

His father sighed again. "Of course I did. That isn't the point. It's all very nice, but it doesn't pay the rent if you still need to scrape by waiting tables. You need a real job, with a career track. Or even graduate school. I can get you hooked up in five minutes with twenty interviews." His father picked up his phone and waved it around. "There are young men your age who would jump through flaming hoops to get some of the interviews and training programs I can get for you in a heartbeat, James. Be realistic."

James stood up from his chair. "I'm not a circus animal. You can't just crack the whip and see me jump."

"That's not what I meant, and you know it. You can't hide out up here for the rest of your life,

127

behind your grandmother." Bart cast an accusing stare in his mother's direction.

She made an innocent face, and shrugged. "I invited him to stay here for the holidays. He needs to get his bearings. I don't think there's anything wrong with that."

Bart didn't answer but turned back to James. "And what are you going to do after you get your bearings? Run into the woods and build a cabin, like Henry David Thoreau?"

His father must have learned about Thoreau in school, eons ago, but James was surprised he remembered anything like that, especially since Thoreau was a writer.

"It worked out pretty well for Henry," James replied. "But I plan to travel. I'm going to find jobs in other countries on that website WAVE. Remember when I did that one summer in college?"

"Your mother and I thought of that as summer camp for a twenty-year-old. We didn't intend for you to make a career of it."

"Right, you'd rather I wasted away in a cubicle all day, in some mind-numbing job. I want to see the world, Dad. I want to experience other cultures and meet all kinds of people. I want to have something worthwhile to write about."

James watched his father's color rise. He had pale, sandy hair, thinning on top, and there was no way for him to hide his stress and anger.

"Be serious a moment. Be realistic. All those years of college, all the tuition—what was that for? So you can work on a farm in some backward place where they don't even have running water? You won't last a week. You never even liked to mow the lawn."

James didn't answer. He sat back, his arms folded over his chest. His father didn't understand. He never would. He had never wanted to do anything with his life beyond being a trust attorney. That was his choice. He was very good at it and seemed to like it. James didn't think any less of his father for his choices. But why couldn't he realize not everyone wanted to take the well-traveled path? Not everyone was ambitious for the same kind of success?

His father tried again. "I understand if law school or investments don't grab you. I get that. It's not your style. What about social media or public relations? Or advertising? You might like that. You can write all you want in your spare time. I'll find a nice apartment for you in the city, all your own. Anywhere you like," he added, sweetening the bait.

James took a deep breath. He was not tempted. He would never sell his soul for an apartment. His father should know better than that. "Sorry, Dad. I know you don't understand, but this is my plan. I'm sticking with it."

Bart shook his head. "Your plan, huh? Where

do you expect to get the money? Will you pick an airline ticket off one of those apple trees out there?"

James ignored his father's sarcasm. "I'm going to look for a job in town."

"Really? Well, better not rush to pack your bag. This could take a while. You'll be lucky to get the minimum wage out here." His father suddenly pinned his grandmother with a stare. "You're not going to give him money, are you?"

"Who, me? Never crossed my mind," she insisted, though James doubted that. "But since James is staying, maybe he should try his hand on that list of repairs. I mean, if he wants to."

"Great idea. I can paint and use a hammer. I was going to fix a few things around here anyway. You don't have to pay me, Grandma."

"Nonsense. We have to pay someone, and it's hard to find a good repairman for small jobs. Especially this time of the year."

Before his father could weigh in on the idea, James quickly replied, "Great, it's a deal. And I won't charge nearly as much as a real carpenter or a painter would."

His father's glance swept from James to his mother and back again. "No need for me to put my two cents in here. I can see that. It's getting late. I'd better go." He picked up his muffler and hat from a chair.

He walked over to Sophie and kissed her cheek.

"Good-bye, Mother. Take care of yourself. And please don't overdo it."

"Don't worry, son. I have James to keep an eye on me."

His father pinned James with a look as he stood at the door.

"I know you think you've gotten your way. But this isn't over, James, not by a long shot."

James wasn't sure what to say. "We can talk more sometime, Dad, if you want."

His father nodded curtly, pulling on his hat. "We will, I promise you." His pulled on the door, but it didn't open right away, adding a comical touch to his angry exit. James kept a straight face until his father managed to get outside and close the door behind him.

Sophie hid a small smile behind her hand. "Oh dear. He was madder than a wet hen, wasn't he? He got like that sometimes when he was a boy. He could get all fired up. There was no talking to him. But then, a little while later, he would settle down and forget all about whatever was bothering him."

James sat back and sighed. "I don't know, Grandma. I doubt he's going to settle down and forget about this. You heard him. I don't think he's going to let it go so easily."

"Maybe not," Sophie conceded. "But the best way to convince someone that you mean business is to do what you said you were going to do. All the fine words in the world don't add up to one single act."

"Good advice. The first thing I'm going to do is fix that door." He got up from the table and set off for the toolbox. "I promised you Tuesday night I'd take care of it."

"So you did," Sophie recalled with a smile. "Thank you, James. I'll mark it off our list."

SOPHIE WOKE ON MONDAY MORNING AND glanced at the clock. It was still early; sunlight had barely seeped below the edge of her bedroom curtains. She rolled over and closed her eyes again. Mac was curled at her feet, a warm mass weighing down the quilt at the bottom of the bed. He was content to sleep in, too.

She had been an early riser all her life, up with dawn, good weather and bad. But in her later years, especially since the pneumonia, she sometimes found herself sleeping in until Mac's cold nose nudged her cheek. It wasn't as if she had that much to do. Especially when the orchard was in a quiet season.

She had nearly drifted off again when she suddenly smelled coffee. Coffee? How could that be?

She sat up and remembered—James. He must be up, even though it was barely seven. *There's a surprise. There will be coffee all ready for me when I go downstairs this morning.*

That was enough incentive to make her push the covers back and search for her slippers and robe. The drowsy dog woke and yawned, then reluctantly jumped off the bed and trotted downstairs behind her.

"Morning, Grandma," James said as she entered the kitchen. "I hope I didn't wake you up, banging around down here."

"Didn't hear a thing. I did smell the coffee. That got me moving." She walked to the stove and filled a big mug.

James sat at the table, dressed in jeans and a flannel shirt, his hair still damp from a shower. He was writing in a notebook and barely looked up. "I woke up with an idea for a story. I like to get things down while they're fresh in my head."

"You work. I need to be with my own thoughts, too, for a while."

Sophie walked to the back door and let the dog out. James had done a good job fixing it. It opened smooth as butter. She pulled the collar of her bathrobe close against the chill morning air and gazed at the trees. A frosty mist had settled on the land like a magical cloud. It would probably burn off soon, if the forecast was right. It looked so delicate and mystical now. Sophie wished she had a camera and could take a photograph.

I might need a picture like that someday, if my children have their way and make me leave here.

She smiled out at the trees a moment, greeting

them each by name in her mind. As she turned to go in, Mac came scurrying back and ran inside. "Good dog, Mac. Time for your breakfast," Sophie quietly crooned, mindful of James still writing.

By the time she had given Macintosh his kibble and sat at the table with her mug, James had closed his notebook and put it aside. He smiled at her. "What's on the agenda today? I'm at your service."

"Like a genie in a bottle, aren't you? I forgot how nice it is to have someone in the house," she said honestly. "Visits from friends and family just aren't the same."

"No, I guess not."

She knew he didn't really understand. Not at his age. Her children had grown up and gone their own way, as it should be. Her dear husband had passed on, too. The house had once been a noisy place, full of life. But it had grown very quiet with just her and Mac. The kind of quiet people her age knew too well. It was nice to have someone to plan the day with. Or cook for. A young man like James was her ideal customer.

"I think we ought to start upstairs," she replied after considering his question. "Your father is right. Those rooms need cleaning out and painting. I've been meaning to sort out that old stuff. I bet we can bring most of it to a charity or a shelter."

"Sounds like a good plan," he said cheerfully. He looked down at his perfectly flat stomach and gave it a gentle pat. "I don't need breakfast after that big dinner last night."

"Those measly leftovers?" Sophie scoffed. "That was nothing. It's not healthy to miss breakfast. I'll fix oatmeal."

"Okay, oatmeal. A small bowl. I knew I wasn't going to get away with skipping a meal around here."

Sophie laughed and headed for the stove. "Honey, if you want to get along with your new roommate, you'd better forget about that idea right now."

A short time later they were upstairs, trying to sort out the boxes and assorted items in the large bedroom at the front of the house.

"Best to tackle the worst first," Sophie said, leading the way. James hadn't been in the room in a long time. Probably since he was a boy and would stay over in the summer with his cousins, or visit with his family on a holiday.

"This room definitely needs paint, Grandma. That brown spot on the ceiling doesn't look good," he added, noticing a possible leak from . . . somewhere.

"First things first. Let's start on the boxes and make three piles—keep it, donate it, throw it out. We may need to drive the trash to the dump. I noticed in the local paper the trash collectors are unhappy about their new contract and are 'slowing down service.' Whatever that means."

James wasn't sure, either. "I guess we'll have to see. I can bring it to the dump in your truck. That's no problem."

There was a vast assortment of items collected in the room. James felt overwhelmed as his grandmother dived in, tossing books, clothes, and knickknacks in all directions.

"Look at this picture album. People just don't save photographs like they used to. It's all stuck in their telephones or computers," she murmured, turning the brittle pages.

James glanced over her shoulder and saw a black-and-white photo of a young woman posed next to an apple tree. She wore a simple white blouse with a long sash tie at the neck, in the style of the 1940s or 1950s. Her skirt fell just below her knee, billowing out in the breeze. Her long hair was pinned up on one side, the waves framing her pretty face. Her arm was lifted, touching a branch of the tree, which was filled with white blossoms. She almost looked as if she were sitting in a cloud.

"What a beautiful photo. Is that you, Grandma? Wow . . . you were a knockout."

His grandmother lifted her chin and smiled. "You think so? That photo was taken right before I met your grandfather. I was an old maid. That's what people called me, anyway. My fiancé had died in the war, and I didn't think I'd meet anyone to fall in love with and marry after that."

"But then Grandpa came along," James finished for her.

"He did, thank heaven. The good Lord sent your grandpa to me. One sunny day, I was up on a ladder, picking apples. And my brother brought your grandfather home for a visit. They were army pals. I looked down and saw him. He was so handsome, I almost lost my step and fell into his arms."

James smiled at the story, though he had heard it many times before. His grandmother turned the page and there was his grandfather Gus, wearing an Army uniform that hung loose on his tall, rangy body. His dark hair was slicked back, his eyes bright. He had been very handsome, and had remained so in his later years, when James knew him.

"Look at this one. Now, this is old. I ought to enlarge it and hang it up somewhere." Sophie pointed at a sepia-toned photo, a family portrait formally posed in a studio. Dark velvet curtains framed the family in fancy clothes, the many children and the father carefully positioned, with everyone standing except the mother, who sat on a chair with a high back, a toddler on her knee.

"That's my mother, Mary, and my dad, Jim. You were named after him," Sophie added.

"Yes, I know. But I don't think Dad has any pictures of him. I've always wondered what he looked like."

"There aren't too many. He was a shy man, never liked photographs. I don't know how my mother got him to sit for this one. Those boys are my brothers, and that little curly-headed girl on my mother's knee is me. Can you believe it?"

"You were cute," James said.

"Wasn't I?" His grandmother sounded as if she couldn't believe that she'd ever been that young. "We weren't exactly poor, but not wealthy, either. Those aren't our clothes, though. They were rented out for the portrait. Some women even rented their wedding dresses in those days," she confided with a laugh.

James thought that was interesting. "Did your parents grow up around here? How did they start the orchard?"

"My mother's family lived in Salem. Her father had a big clothing store there. They were fairly well-to-do. She met my father at a church social. They liked each other right away. He was from Ireland, recently landed. He was working for a cousin out here, in Cape Light, who owned a poultry farm. The courting wasn't easy. He didn't own a car. But they managed. Obviously," she added with a smile.

"Sounds very romantic. But how did they end up out here?"

"When they married, my grandfather persuaded them to settle in Salem. He rented a nice house for them and gave my father a job in his store. My father tried it, but he didn't like being a salesman, and he didn't care anything about clothes."

"He had to be his own person, march to a different drummer," James guessed.

"That's right." Sophie smiled. "That must be where you get it from."

"So, what did he do? Go back to the poultry farm?"

Sophie laughed. "Good lord, no. My mother couldn't stand that idea. But they both loved Cape Light."

James could easily imagine it. "It must have been beautiful here back then."

"Yes, but much more remote. Harder to get to without the big highways and train service extended to this point."

"So how did your parents jump from chickens to apples?"

"Lucky for my mother, this orchard and house came up for sale. Bank foreclosure—it was nineteen thirty, the start of the Depression. But her father still had money. He bought this property for a song. He loved his daughter, and he approved of apples. He knew my folks would never be millionaires, but they'd do well if they worked hard, took care of the land and the trees, and managed their business properly. He helped

139

my father with that," she added. "My father, to his credit, paid him back every penny. My grandfather respected that."

James slipped the photo from the plastic sheet that covered it. "I could take this someplace and have it enlarged and framed for you, Grandma. Maybe I should make a few copies. You can give them out at Christmas, to the family—to my father and aunts?"

Sophie beamed. "What a nice idea. Is it much trouble for you?"

"Not at all. But I'd like to look at this album more. Maybe I can do something with the pictures so that they aren't stuck in a box somewhere. I'd like to know more about the family's history, too. I love all your stories."

His grandmother patted his shoulder as she came to her feet again. "I thought you might. You've got more than a touch of the poet in your soul, dear."

As James put the album in a safe place, he noticed a photo on the floor. Sophie had noticed it, too. "Pick that up, will you, dear? Let me see. That one looks more recent . . ."

He handed her the photo. It was clearly more recent. A color photo, though not all that modern, with its bright yellow and red tones. A little boy in a baseball uniform, about to swing his bat, a gap showing in his smile where a tooth was missing.

"That's your father. Didn't you recognize him?"

James shook his head. "That's big, bad Bart? That skinny little twerp?"

Sophie laughed. "One and the same. He thought he was headed for the major leagues at that age. He wasn't very good at baseball, but he loved it, and we encouraged him, Grandpa and me."

"Good to know he wasn't always that realistic about his career goals, either," James said, still stinging from the previous night's showdown.

"He also wanted to be an astronaut." She gazed at the photo a moment. "He was a good boy, always had a kind heart, and was protective of his sisters. Though he could be mischievous. Nothing terrible," she added. "He was a little scoundrel; always made us laugh."

"Sorry, Grandma, I find that hard to believe," James said honestly. His father was still kind and protective of the people he loved. But he didn't have much of a sense of humor or even flexibility.

"He hasn't changed that much," she insisted. "When you have words with him, try to remember this picture. It might help."

James thought that was interesting advice. "Okay, I'll try. But you probably should, too."

His grandmother looked up at him. "You got me there. Maybe you should make copies of that one, too," she added with a laugh.

James gathered a pile of clothes his grand-mother had tossed in the donation pile and shoveled them into a large black plastic bag. "Are you really leaving here, Grandma?"

He heard her sigh. "I don't know. In my heart, I don't feel as if I am. I just can't picture it. But lately, it does feel like I'm being swept away on a riptide. I'm trying to fight it, but it's just too strong to swim against."

James heard the sad, defeated sound in her voice. "I don't want to do this repair work if it's going to help my dad and aunts push you out. I can find a job somewhere else. I think I need two jobs anyway, to earn the amount of money I need."

"That's good of you to say, dear. But it won't make a difference either way. The cleaning out and repairs need to be done, whether I stay or not. I can't let the place fall down around me. Maybe my time here has come to an end. 'To everything there is a season, and a time for every purpose under the heaven . . .' You know that Scripture, don't you?"

"Yes, I do." James didn't know too much Scripture, but he was familiar with those famous lines.

"Maybe I just have to get my mind . . . and my heart . . . around those words. It's very hard, going through all this old stuff. It doesn't make the question any clearer," Sophie confessed, gazing around. She looked confused and suddenly tired, he thought. "All I can say is, life goes by awful fast. You don't feel that way when you're young. But at my stage, when you look back, it seems like a movie that was running on fast-forward the whole time. Years and years went by in a heartbeat. Inside, I hardly feel any different at all."

James gazed at her with sympathy but couldn't help smiling, too. "That's a good way to describe it . . . Can I use that line in a story sometime?"

She laughed, surprised and suddenly cheerful. "I'd be honored. I never thought I ever said anything worth writing down." She glanced at her watch. "What do you say—ready for lunch?"

"Sure. Let's take a break." He could tell she was ready to leave this room and her memories. And determined to serve him three squares a day.

AFTER LUNCH, JAMES BEGAN TO CARRY THE trash out from the room they were cleaning. It was a long walk from the upstairs bedroom down through the kitchen and out the side door to the truck. On the second trip, he piled the boxes high—higher than he could see—and Sophie scurried to the door to open it for him.

"Be careful. You're going to fall like that," she warned.

"I'm okay, Grandma. Just point me toward the truck." He could see a little, around the edge of the cartons. But as he swung out of the house and headed for the driveway, he smacked into something solid—that gave out a high-pitched squeal.

"Oh, my gosh. I didn't see you there . . . I'm so sorry."

The boxes tumbled down, the contents spilling all over the drive—old shoes, broken toys, a woman's wide-brimmed hat covered with dusty cloth flowers, and a water-stained roll of Happy Birthday wrapping paper that unfurled like a flag.

At the same time, Zoey dropped the paper bag she had been carrying, and a collection of pie tins poured out and rattled to the ground, rolling around like pinballs until they each spun to a stop.

James stared at Zoey, and she stared back.

"Instant yard sale?" she asked in a small voice. James grinned, and they both started laughing.

"One man's junk is another man's treasure." James began picking up the fallen debris, and Zoey bent down to help him.

"I should have seen you coming. I was in a daze or something." She had actually been so anxious at the possibility of seeing him, she'd been totally distracted, worrying about her hair and her outfit and what she would say. *So now you just look like a complete klutz. Good job.*

"I piled the boxes too high. It was my fault," he said.

Zoey didn't reply. The guys she knew rarely admitted it when they messed up, and never so easily. *That's refreshing,* she wanted to say.

"No harm done," he added, tossing a worn-out sneaker into one of the cartons. "How about those pie tins? Need any help chasing them down?"

"I can manage." Zoey had to go around the truck to get the last tin, which had rolled underneath and come out the other side. Despite her claim that she could handle it, James had come around the truck and they met face-to-face, practically knocking each other over. Zoey slipped a bit on the gravel, but he grabbed her arms just in time. She stared up at him. She could feel his breath and, for some odd reason, couldn't pull her gaze away from his. His face was so close. Was he going to kiss her?

Mac came racing around the truck. He picked up a pie tin in his mouth, circled them quickly, and dashed off toward the barn, gravel flying out from under his paws.

James laughed, stepping back from her. "What in the world was that—Space Dog?"

"Looks like he beat us both to that one. He must think it's a game. He wants us to chase him."

"That dog needs a Frisbee. There must be at least one in this pile of junk. I'll check before I go to the dump."

"Are you helping Sophie clean out closets?"

"I'm helping her clean out everything. And

145

paint and do some other repairs. I fixed the door. It isn't stuck anymore," he reported proudly.

"Really? I didn't know writers could be handy, too." She was teasing him a little. But it was also true. She was surprised he knew his way around a toolbox.

"My dad taught me. He knows carpentry, how to paint, and all that. My grandfather taught him. Running the orchard, he had to do his own repair work most of the time."

Zoey nodded. "That makes sense."

"My father hates to do any of that stuff now. He always hires someone. But I like it. It makes me feel productive, and it's a good way to earn money," he added, tossing a box into the truck bed.

"So you're going to work on Sophie's house while you're staying here?"

"Yes, it all worked out. She needed to hire a handyman and here I was, just hanging out. I would do it for free, but she insists on paying me. And I really need the money. For my trip," he added, tossing another carton in the truck.

"What trip is that?" Did she miss something the last time she spoke to him? She didn't remember him mentioning that he planned to travel.

James glanced at her and smiled. "Oh, sorry. I told my grandmother, but I guess you weren't around. I'll be leaving right after the holidays. I'm not sure where yet. Someplace really interesting—South America, maybe? There's this website called WAVE where you can find agricultural jobs all over the world. You apply and are matched up with a farm. I did it in college over a summer. I went to Spain. It was a great experience."

"It does sound great." Zoey had always wanted to take a trip like that, just backpacking around and going to different countries with no set schedule. Even a semester abroad would have been great. But her parents couldn't afford it. "How much money do you need to save?"

"At least two thousand dollars, for my airfare and expenses until I start working. I don't have much time. I'd like to leave right after New Year's. I'm going to look for another job in town, too, but at least I can save everything while I'm staying with my grandmother."

"I'd love to travel like that someday, too. Maybe after I graduate. I guess you'll see all kinds of interesting things to write about and meet all sorts of people."

"I hope so," he said cheerfully, tossing another box in the pickup. It fell with a soft thud on top of the others. "My grandmother told me that you're an art major?"

"I have a double major, art and psychology. I'm studying to be an art therapist. I'll have to go to grad school, too."

He looked impressed. "What an interesting

career choice. When I was a little kid I had a lot of nightmares. My parents brought me to a shrink, and she made me draw pictures."

Zoey smiled. "I want to work with children, too. I volunteer right now in a center where the counselors work with kids. I'm getting good experience there."

"See, I guessed right off you were the type. Artistic . . . but smart and kind," he added. His blue gaze met hers, and she felt herself starting to blush.

Zoey stepped back, hugging the bag of pie tins. "Why were you having nightmares? Did you ever find out?"

He shrugged. "Too many Harry Potter books. My mother kept telling me it was just a story, but I was sure that we were secretly related. Like he was a lost twin, and nobody wanted to tell me the truth."

Zoey laughed. "Did you get teased in school for having the same last name?"

"A little," he said. "But that only convinced me more. They say children with high IQs have very active imaginations."

"Yes, I've read studies about that."

"Did you read Harry Potter books when you were little?"

"I did," Zoey replied. "Hermione was my favorite. I always wished I could have her for a best friend."

"I liked Hermione, too. I had a crush on her," he admitted. "I never understood why Harry didn't." He smiled. "Now that you mention it, you look a little like her."

He was flirting again. She tried to ignore it, but that was hard.

"Did you grow up in Cape Light?" he asked.

Zoey had guessed that question was coming, but she never liked answering it. It was too complicated. "Not really. But I like it here. It's a nice place to live. For now, I mean."

She heard her phone buzz, signaling a text. She thought it was rude when people pulled out their phones in the middle of a conversation, but this time, she felt saved by the interruption. "I'm sorry, I have to see who this is."

"That's all right. I don't mind." James tossed two more cartons onto the pile. Even though it was cold outside, he wore an open flannel shirt with a T-shirt underneath. The shirt flew open each time he tossed the boxes, and Zoey couldn't help noticing his strong chest.

The text was from her dad, who needed her at the diner earlier than her scheduled shift. She quickly texted him an okay.

"My dad. I have to get to work. He needs me there early," Zoey explained as she slipped the phone into her pocket. "Can you give the pie tins to your grandmother? Oh . . . I forgot they fell. I'll take them home and wash them first."

James pulled the bag from her hand. "No problem. Got this covered. You sound like you're busy enough, running to work, to school. Volunteering," he added. "Do you ever just hang out?"

She wasn't sure why he was asking. Did he think she was some sort of totally serious, stressed-out person, rushing around like a lunatic all the time?

"Sure. I hang out."

"Good to know. Would you like to hang out with me sometime? Like, go to a movie or something?"

Did he just ask me out? Zoey had to take a breath before she answered. "Sure. That would be fun."

"How about Friday night? Have any plans?"

She pretended to think about it a moment, trying not to seem so super available. "I have to work, but I get off at five."

"Great. My grandmother has your number. I'll check in, and we can figure it out."

Zoey nodded, not knowing what to say. She was afraid that she would do or say something terrifically dumb. She glanced at her watch without even seeing it. "Got to go. Good luck with the cleanup."

"Thanks. I need it. My grandmother's a real pack rat. Everything she ever owned has some sort of sentimental value."

"Yeah, I know. But that's what makes her so special."

His expression softened. "Very true. So long, Hermione . . . I mean, Zoey."

"So long, Potter," she called over her shoulder as she walked to her car. "Hope nothing too scary pops out of the closets. But I'm sure you can handle it."

She heard him laugh and saw him wave as she started down the drive.

A date with James? Really? Does he actually like me, or is he just bored to death up here?

Steady, Zoey. You don't want to drive into an apple tree. You have plenty of time to think about this later . . . at the boring old Clam Box.

Chapter Six

ON WEDNESDAY AFTERNOON, EMILY pulled up to Emerson Middle School and parked near the gym. She was already a few minutes late for Jane's game, but hoped it hadn't started on time. There was usually some delay, waiting for refs or the opposing team to arrive.

She ran down the hallway to the gym, not really noticing how quiet the school was. The gym was surprisingly empty—except for two boys playing basketball at the far end of the shiny wooden floor, the sound of the ball and their shouts echoing in the big space.

"Can you help me?" Emily called. "Isn't there a girls' volleyball game here today?"

The boys stopped and glanced at her. One continued bouncing the ball. "I don't think so."

"I think they're away today," the taller boy said. "There's a schedule on the bulletin board," he added, shooting a hook shot over his friend's head.

"Hey, man, that doesn't count," the shorter boy protested.

"Yeah, it does." He grabbed the rebound and stuffed in another.

Emily shouted back a word of thanks but knew they didn't hear her. She ran back out to the hall and checked the bulletin board near the door, filled with schedules for all the school teams.

Finally, she found it: *Wed. 11/30 Girls Volley-ball: Away. Simpson Middle School—Beverly.*

She ran back out to her car, jumped in, and drove out of the lot, heading for Route 1A. She wasn't sure she remembered the way to Simpson Middle School. *The talking gadget on your phone, Emily. No-brainer . . .*

She pulled over to the side, set her phone to direct her—even though the robotic voice drove her crazy—and pulled back out on the road.

"Turn left in five hundred feet, at the next light," the voice said.

"Will do, thanks." *Am I the only person in the world who talks back to that thing?* She could only blame her mother for teaching her and her sister to be unfailingly polite at all times.

Emily's phone rang just as she stopped for a red light. She quickly glanced at the screen—her mother again. Emily didn't have to listen to the message. She knew it was another last-minute pitch to get her to the open-space meeting, though Emily had made it perfectly clear that if her mother wanted to go, she needed to arrange her own ride. But it was more than transportation that Lillian was after. Emily knew that, too.

"Proceed on Route 1A, two miles to Hitchcock Lane." *Two more miles. Not so bad.* Emily remembered now that the school was right after that turn. She drove quickly but carefully the rest of the way and arrived a few minutes later. It wasn't hard to find the gym, and she sighed with relief, hearing the sound of a game going on as she jogged the rest of the way to the open doors and quickly found a seat in the bleachers.

She felt as breathless and sweaty as the players on the court and quickly slipped off her jacket. The whistle sounded and parents cheered. Simpson had just scored. The score looked close. Where was Jane? Emily scanned the court but didn't see her.

Then she spotted her daughter on the bench. Jane looked as though she had been out on the court already; she was chugging from a water bottle, her bangs plastered to her forehead.

Oh drat. For once the coach started her and I missed it?

Emily felt like kicking herself. She tried to catch Jane's eye, but her daughter was focused on her team, jumping up and cheering as a friend spiked the ball so hard it bounced off the floor and into the stands.

Emily cheered, too. "Number Five! Way to go!"

The woman next to her beamed. "That's my

daughter, Number Five, Tara Bartow," she said proudly.

"She's very good," Emily replied. "I'm here for Number Nine, Jane Forbes. She's on the bench now, but it looks like she played for a while."

"Yes, she scored three points in the first quarter," Tara's mother reported. "She's terrific."

Emily felt her heart drop. "I'm so sorry I missed it. I went to the wrong school and . . . well, maybe she'll be put in again."

"Hope so." The woman gave her a curious look. "Hey, aren't you Emily Warwick, the mayor?"

Emily smiled but shook her head. "Former mayor."

"Oh, that's right. I thought I recognized you. Well, your granddaughter is a super player. Now you have time to cheer her on."

Emily felt the smile on her face freeze. "She's my daughter. But that's my plan. Thanks."

The other woman's face flushed with embarrassment. Emily was grateful when a loud cheer from the stands distracted both of them. The opposing team had scored, and now they were ahead by three points. Before the two teams could set up again, the whistle sounded for halftime. Jane's coach called his girls into a huddle near the bench.

Emily gazed around, wondering if she knew any of the other parents. They all looked so young. *I don't look that old for my age, do I?*

She wondered if she should consider a new hairdo.

Poor Dan was the one who got the grandfather tag, ever since Jane had been a baby. His hair had gone prematurely gray in his early forties.

The woman on her other side chatted with her neighbor. They seemed to be good friends, deep in a serious conversation.

"—but I told them I just can't do it right now. Maybe when Max is done with kindergarten."

"I'd like to go more, too. But I'm in the same boat with the twins. Audrey is having trouble with reading. I've got to stay on top of that," the other mother added. "So much after-school stuff. At least I started the Crock-Pot this morning. I barely have time to figure out dinner."

Emily hadn't given a thought to dinner. Dan usually cooked dinner; he made simple meals, but he was quite good at it. She had made some noises about taking over, but hadn't started yet.

Though she had gone through all these stages with Jane, she didn't feel as if she had much in common with these parents—even if she could manage to break into a conversation.

A woman on the bleacher below sat with needles and yarn, stitching away at a feverish pace. *Maybe I should learn how to knit. It would give me something productive to do over the winter.*

The whistle blew and the teams came back on the court. Emily was excited to see Jane take a front-line position.

The plays were fast, the girls on both teams agile and strong. Emily jumped up and down in her seat as Jane made two huge spikes, the second totally confounding a player on the other side; the poor girl fell to her knees, trying to reach it in time. Luckily, they all wore knee and elbow pads.

The second half of the game flew by, with Jane on the court twice. When the final whistle blew, Emerson Middle School was behind by two points. A narrow loss but well played, Emily thought. She was no stranger to that outcome.

She joined the wave of parents heading down to the court to meet the players. She gave Jane a big hug. "You were awesome, honey. What a spike! I'm going to call you Hammer at home."

Jane looked pleased at her praise, and a little embarrassed, too. She was at that age. "Thanks, Mom. Too bad we lost."

"Not by much. You all played really well. Do you have a lot of homework? I thought we could get ice cream or something. You must be starved."

Jane had been a picky eater as a little girl, but now she could eat a large lunch, another full meal after school, and still have an appetite for dinner. And she just got taller and thinner.

"I have to go back to school on the bus with my team, remember?"

"Sure. That's right. I'll meet you there."

Emily had gone to so few games that she had forgotten the routine. *But I'm going to remember from now on. I'm going to put the schedule in my phone and be at every game.*

"I'm going home with another girl on the team—Tara Bartow? Guess I forgot to send you a text. We're doing a project at school together, and we need to work on it tonight."

"What's the project?"

"It's a debate for history class. It's not due for a few weeks, but we need to figure out a question and take sides and all that."

Emily felt excited at the news. "That's something I can help you with. Maybe your friend should come to our house."

Jane looked uncomfortable at the suggestion. "It's all sort of planned. Another girl is coming, too. It's too late to change it, Mom. But thanks."

"I see." Emily suddenly realized that Jane wasn't used to offering their house for after-school meetings. Usually, Emily wasn't home and Dan was writing and needed quiet.

"Sounds like you'll have more meetings about this. Next time, everyone can come to our house. Maybe I can help a little. I've been in a few debates."

Jane had watched Emily debate in the last two

159

elections and grinned at the understatement. "Sure, you can help us next time. I'd better go. Everyone is getting on the bus."

Emily nodded and kissed her forehead. Jane slung her pack over her shoulder and ran to catch up with her friends. Emily watched, feeling wistful. And a little deflated.

We're all in a period of transition now. Not just me, she reminded herself as she headed for her car. *I can hardly blame Jane for not volunteering our house or asking me for help. She's not used to the fact that I'm totally available for her and not stuck in an office until late at night.*

I need to be patient. It will take her a while to get used to all this. But not too long, I hope.

EMILY GOT HOME TO FIND DAN IN THE kitchen, taking a fragrant roast chicken out of the oven. "How was the game?" he asked.

"Emerson lost but fought valiantly. Your daughter has a mean spike. I never realized she was so tough."

"Oh, Jane has a competitive streak. Not always visible, but definitely there. I wonder who she takes after," he said with a sly smile.

"Yes, I wonder." Emily knew that she, too, could be competitive when necessary. "I like to see her jump in and do battle with a team. But I didn't really have anyone to talk to," she admitted. "One mom thought I was Janie's grandmother." Emily rolled her eyes. "Time for that expensive eye cream?"

"A lot of people marry young around here," Dan pointed out. "You wouldn't feel so out of place as an older mom if we lived in Boston."

"I know. I should be used to it by now, being an older-than-average mom. Maybe I should get bangs next time I get my hair cut? They say it takes ten years off."

Dan laughed and put his hand on her cheek. "Honey, you look fine. You're just not used to hanging out with the after-school sports group. Just don't talk about politics or religion. You'll be fine."

"How about Crock-Pots? That seemed to be a hot topic . . . Do we have one?" She bit down on a raw string bean and gazed around the kitchen.

"Somewhere. I've never used it. Hey, there's something you can work on, mastering the art of Crock-Pot cooking. That would let me out of kitchen detail every night, too."

"Good idea. I'll look for some videos online." She was half joking, but half serious, too. She saw plates stacked on the counter and began setting the table.

"Where's Jane? Did she run up for a shower?"

"She went home with a friend. They have a school project to work on. The history class is having a debate."

"A debate? That's right up your alley."

"I noticed. And I plan to help them. Next time," she clarified. The phone rang, and Emily glanced at the number but didn't pick it up.

"Who's that? Don't you want to answer it?"

"Not right now. It's just my mother. I know what she's calling about."

They heard Lillian's voice on the answering machine. "Emily, are you there? I tried your cell phone. You didn't answer. I'd like to speak with you. I went to the meeting and I have some news. It's important."

Dan turned to look at her. Emily was folding napkins and placing forks and knives at each place.

"What's that all about? What meeting? Something at church?"

"No . . . something else. Some group she wants me to—"

The phone rang again. A name flashed on the caller ID—Martin Becker, the chairman of the open-space group. Had she left her home number with them? She didn't think so.

"Your mother again? I think you should get it, Em. She'll give us no peace." Dan was carving the chicken, his hands too slippery to grab the phone.

"It's not her. Let me just listen a minute . . ."

"Hello, Emily. This is Martin, from SOS. Sorry you missed today's meeting. Your mother said it was okay to call. We decided on a strategy, and we need to be ready for the village meeting next Monday evening. We could really use your input on this. We have so many questions and so little time. If you could get back to me soon, I'd greatly appreciate it."

Dan turned, holding his carving knife and fork in the air like a surgeon. "What's SOS? And what sort of meeting is this? I thought you said you weren't going to—"

"I know what I said. I was really trying to stick to it, too. But last Sunday, Mother tricked me into going to a meeting for a group that's fighting the new zoning proposal. I thought I was taking her food shopping after church, but she made me bring her there instead. And I couldn't just leave her there. Sitting in the car seemed childish, too." She paused. "I know I broke my promise, but I hope you're not mad at me?"

"Of course not. I know how Lillian is. And I know this issue is important to you. You were very vocal about it during your campaign, and I know that wasn't just talk."

"I really do care, Dan. It was encouraging to see how many people joined the group. But I don't want it to look as if I'm purposely trying to undermine Charlie—as if I'm a sore loser, out to embarrass him. That's not it at all."

"I know it's not," he assured her. "But it is a slippery slope. If you get involved, some people will see it that way."

"I sat way at the back and didn't even intend to talk," Emily explained. "But some of the ideas people offered would just be a waste of time. I know how zoning gets changed and the ways to block it. I couldn't help giving a little advice."

Dan stood at the sink, washing his hands. "Sounds like they need it." He turned to face her again, drying his hands with a towel. "I just don't want to see you get swept up in another . . . town tornado. Something like this can eat up all your time again, Em. *Our* time."

"I know. I don't want that either, believe me. We're going to have a really nice Christmas. And plan our trip. I'm just going to help them prepare for the council meeting next Monday night. After that, they're on their own. I'm not going to lead a charge down Main Street. Been there, done that."

Dan smiled and rested his hands on her shoulders. "Good plan. I think everyone in this house has been there and done that."

Emily was glad they had talked this out. She had meant to tell Dan that she had gone to the meeting, but somehow, it had ended up a secret. It was a relief that he knew and wasn't upset that she had broken her promise. Not broken it—bent it, just a bit? Just until the council meeting at Village Hall Monday night. *The trick of life is to set limits,* she advised herself.

Dan had set the platter of chicken on the table, and Emily brought over bowls of green beans and noodles. "This looks delicious. Thanks for cooking. My turn tomorrow night."

"You're welcome. And I was hoping you'd say that," he admitted with a grin.

Another promise she had made to her family. She was going to keep it, too. "I may surprise you," Emily replied.

Dan smiled and kissed her. "You always do."

"THERE ARE THE USUAL PRESCRIPTIONS, AND some new drug the doctor wants me to take for my stomach acid," Emily's mother told her on Friday afternoon. "The drugstore said it would be ready today, but it's not that important. These doctors are rabid to write out prescriptions. They get fancy dinners and vacations from drug companies. Did you know that? I saw it on the news, a special report."

"I never accepted so much as a ballpoint pen from a drug salesman," Ezra shouted from the living room. Emily didn't even realize he'd been listening.

"Of course not, dear. You would never stoop so low," Lillian shouted back. "I mean these young doctors, the type we see."

Emily wondered who her mother could be talking about. Lillian and Ezra's youngest physician had to be over fifty. But she didn't contradict her. She had been at the house almost an hour and was eager to leave. Her mother claimed she had caught Ezra's cold and couldn't go out today, so Emily had offered to help. During the many years she had been mayor, she had managed to run over to Providence Street at random breaks in her day or while driving to or from meetings. She had always shared the care of her mother with her sister. But with Jessica's recent promotion and Emily out of a job, the visits and errands were falling her way.

She really didn't mind. Jessica had shouldered most of it for a long time, and it was her turn to step up. She also had her own errands to cover and wanted to be done in time to pick up Jane at school.

"So it's the drugstore, the library, and these items at the market?" Emily met her mother's glance, trying to keep her on track.

"That's right . . . and mail these bills for me, please?" Lillian passed Emily a handful of envelopes. "And I need you to give out a few of these around town. For the open spacers. I promised I would give them out by today."

Her mother picked up a sheaf of papers from the kitchen counter and held them out to her. Emily could see they were flyers advertising the group's mission and the council's meeting on Monday night.

"Mother, are you serious? I'm not walking down Main Street handing out flyers. Don't be ridiculous."

"I don't see why not. What are you ashamed of?"

"I'm not ashamed of anything. I just don't have time to knock on doors and talk people into taking flyers. Did you really volunteer to do that?"

"Yes, I did. I'm very persuasive when I put my mind to it," her mother said proudly. "But I don't feel well enough to march around all afternoon out there. And you can do it so much faster than I can."

That was true. A lot faster, and with far less danger of falling and breaking a hip.

"Why don't you call Martin and tell him the truth? You've got a cold and can't do it. I'm sure he can find someone else."

"The flyers should have been up days ago. How would that look? So irresponsible." When Emily didn't answer, Lillian added, "Is this so much to ask? Aren't people going to see you at the meeting Monday night with the group? Don't you plan on coming? Or will you sneak in and sit at the back again—incognito?"

"Of course I'm coming," Emily said, though she did plan on keeping a low profile. She knew the newspaper might try to play up her role in the group opposing Charlie. She could only imagine what reporters would infer.

Lillian sighed and sat in a kitchen chair. "Just skip it. I'll get dressed later when I feel a bit stronger and give it a go. I can make it to a few stores. If I get dizzy again, I'll stop. I promise."

Emily knew it was an act. Her mother had not mentioned anything about feeling dizzy before this. Still, she felt her resolve melting. "All right, no need to put on a long face. Give me those." Emily reluctantly took the flyers and stuck them in her bag. "I'll see what I can do."

Lillian shrugged, looking suddenly bright and energetic again. "That's all I've ever asked of you, Emily, that you try your best."

A few minutes later, Emily parked at the harbor and stuck the flyers into her big purse. It was a bright day and not too cold, for December. She walked across the green, deciding to stop at Willoughby's Bakery first. She had noticed the Christmas decorations on Main Street but hadn't seen the ones in the village square yet. She passed the big tree, feeling a little wistful. This was the first year in over fifteen that she hadn't presided over the annual tree lighting—announcing Santa's arrival on his fire truck, tossing candy canes and chocolates to all the children. It was hard to believe she would never lead that event again.

But I had a good run, she reminded herself. *And the only thing you can depend on in life is change.* Emily tossed her scarf around her neck and lifted her chin. Time to get cracking on the flyer assignment. Willoughby's should be an easy sell.

Molly Willoughby was family—her brother Sam was married to Jessica—and she greeted Emily with a hug. She had already heard of the open-space group and quickly agreed to hang the sign in the front window.

"Leave some at the counter. We'll hand them out for you. The last thing this town needs is a bunch of ugly condos and big-box stores." Molly had a way of cutting to the point that Emily loved.

"I know you're the busiest person in the world, but it would help so much if you came to the meeting Monday night," Emily said. "People listen to you and respect your opinion."

Molly laughed. "You make it sound like I should run for mayor next. I have a million things to do, but if you think it's important, I'll try to come."

"It is important. Your opinion would make a big impression on people, believe me."

Emily went into the pharmacy next. She needed to pick up her mother's medications. While Frank Dillard checked on the prescriptions, she showed him the flyer. "This is about the council meeting next Monday night, Frank. Can I hang it up on your bulletin board?"

"I'm sorry, Emily. Lost dogs and cats, people renting apartments, or selling cars—that sort of thing is fine. But we can't take sides on political issues. We have to keep the store a welcoming environment for everyone."

"I'm not asking you to take sides, Frank. It's just information. Won't you read it and then decide?"

He ignored the sheet and her question. "Here are your mother's prescriptions. Give her my best."

Emily thanked him and headed toward the Beanery, a coffee shop and café. They already had two flyers in their windows. No question what side Felicity Bean and her husband, Jonathan, were on. Emily dropped off extras to hand out.

Bowman Realty was next on the street. Emily's longtime friend Betty Bowman had stepped away from her realty business years ago to become Molly Willoughby's partner, finding the bakery and café more interesting than buying and selling houses. But she still held an interest in the firm that carried her name.

Fran Tulley, who had worked there for nearly twenty years, held the reins now. Emily liked Fran, but she knew the Tulleys were best friends with Charlie and Lucy Bates. She doubted the flyer would get far with Fran as gatekeeper.

Fran greeted her cheerfully and glanced at the notice, then put it aside on her desk. "Sure, you can leave it. I'll read it later. How's everything,

Emily? How are you adjusting to civilian life?"

"It's a change, but a good one. I'm keeping busy."

Fran smiled. "Yes, I can see. You're a busy bee, as usual. It's hard to sit still and not get involved in things, I'll bet." Her smile was friendly but her tone held an ironic edge.

"Thanks, Fran," Emily said, deciding to ignore any hidden meanings in Fran's words. "I'll see you around."

"Busy bee, my foot," she grumbled, heading to the next store, which was Krueger's Hardware and Variety Store. Fran was a piece of cake next to George Krueger. A huge supporter of Charlie's campaign, he still had a "Vote for Bates" poster in the window.

Are you really going in here? You must know it's pointless.

Before she could decide, George Krueger walked up behind her. "Hello, Emily. Going in or coming out?"

She turned and met his glance. He was holding a brown paper bag, which she guessed was his lunch, from the Clam Box. "Just . . . window shopping." She had been staring in the window, trying to decide, so that wasn't a total lie.

"I'd be happy to help you inside. It's a little chilly out today."

"Yes, it is. I'd better get going. Have a good day."

"You as well," he replied with a curious look.

She continued down the street but was not too far away when she heard him call after her. "You dropped something, Emily."

George Krueger held up one of the flyers and waved it, a sour expression on his face.

Emily turned but didn't walk back. "You can keep that. It's about the council meeting Monday night. Hang it in your window," she suggested, knowing he would do no such thing.

"I know all about it. Thank you very much."

His tone had been tart, but Emily acted as if she hadn't noticed. "Good. See you then."

She glanced over her shoulder, and he caught her eye, crunching the flyer into a ball before going inside his store.

CHARLIE HAD SHUT OFF THE RINGER ON HIS cell phone, but it buzzed insistently. He glanced at the screen to check the number. It wasn't Zoey or Trudy with some diner disaster to report. Just George Krueger, down at the hardware store. What did he want? Charlie let voice mail pick up and turned his attention back to the weekly Friday meeting. His new staff circled the table in the conference room that adjoined his office in Village Hall. They all looked grim and nervous.

The pressure was on with Monday's council meeting only three days away now. They didn't seem to understand how crucial this meeting was for him. Or were they just pretending that they didn't?

"So you're telling me you can't get a complete budget for the roadwork project ready by Monday, Ed? Or you just don't want to?" Charlie stared at Ed Shaw, head of the town's public works department. Ed was a young man, in his early thirties, with an engineering degree and plenty of other certifications. What Charlie called "college smart"—no common sense and as slow as molasses in January.

"I don't drag my heels," Ed said evenly. "This report takes time to research and cost out."

"I'm not asking for a price down to the penny. Can't you even estimate?" Charlie pressed him. "How long does it take to crunch a bunch of numbers on a calculator?"

"Pull a figure out of thin air, you mean? That would be bogus and irresponsible. We haven't inspected half the roads yet."

"I don't know why not. You've known since the first day I walked into this office that road repair is a top priority—at the top of the agenda for the council meeting Monday night. You have the whole weekend to work on it. I need a budget for roadwork, snow removal, and a new contract with K&B Carting. Is that a surprise to all of you?"

A small voice in Charlie's head—Lucy's, maybe?—reminded him that raising his voice was a bad idea. But he couldn't stop himself, and he quickly noticed he was shouting at a circle of stunned faces.

Ed Shaw came to his feet. "I'm not a waiter in your diner, Charlie. I don't know what you think goes into compiling a budget for a project like this, but it's not like a customer asking for his check."

"It's not brain surgery, either," Charlie told him. "If you walk out of this meeting, consider yourself fired. And don't expect any recommendations out of me, either."

The others shifted uneasily in their seats.

"You can't fire me. I resign. Mayor Warwick was always happy with my work. I can get a recommendation from her, no problem." Ed picked up his laptop. "It was certainly different when she was in charge," he added, marching out of the meeting room.

Charlie watched his staff exchange glances. Was this the beginning of a mutiny? Were they all still loyal to Emily Warwick and just waiting to walk out? Or maybe they *were* dragging their heels, trying to make him look like an incompetent fool?

Well, he was not about to back down. "Anyone else feels that way, there's the door. Things are different now. I'm the no-excuses mayor, and we're going to run this town on a lean, mean budget. Not like your old boss."

Joe Newland, a building inspector, cleared his throat. But no one made a motion to leave. Charlie felt relieved. Then his secretary, Miriam, stood up.

"I'd better go, too. I'm sorry, but this isn't working out for me," she said. "I tried, but . . . I'm really sorry." Head down, clutching a yellow legal pad to her chest, she scurried out the open door.

Charlie heard muffled laughter. He wasn't laughing, not one bit. He could find another secretary sooner or later, but he needed Shaw to work over the weekend and get the figures ready for the meeting. What a time to walk out on him.

Florence Simpson, the newly elected town clerk who had run on his ticket, opened her own pad to a fresh page. "I'll take the minutes, Charlie. Why don't we continue? We have a lot more to cover."

"That's right. We do. Back to work. We need to figure out those trash collectors. What's the latest, Karl?" he asked, turning the floor over to the town attorney, Karl Nelson, who had been negotiating with the company.

Charlie forced himself to focus on the attorney's report. The bitter taste of Shaw quitting and Miriam deserting the ship, too, lingered. For goodness' sake, wasn't this job hard enough without having to deal with all these touchy personalities? In time, he would weed out the deadwood and get his own people in here. *Right now, you have to make do,* he reminded himself. *You have to pull this group together, and look sharp by Monday night. Even if you have to camp out in this office all weekend to do it.*

AFTER HER LITTLE RUN-IN WITH GEORGE Krueger, Emily stopped at the Bramble and had a far more encouraging chat with Grace Hegman, who owned the antiques shop. Grace had a quiet but reassuring way about her and gave Emily a cup of hot tea that took the chill off. Browsing the lovely shop, Emily even found a few Christmas gifts. Though it felt odd to be shopping so early . . . early for *her.*

Grace's father, Digger, came down from their apartment upstairs and chatted with her, too. As Emily had expected, the old seaman was strongly opposed to more building, or altering the village in any way.

"I'm coming to the next meeting. I want a front-row seat. Gracie says the excitement is bad for my heart, but what's the sense of having a heart if you don't listen when it speaks to you?"

"Very true. I'm going to remember that," Emily agreed.

Digger—who had often claimed he could hear clams whispering under the sand and could communicate with fish beneath the waves of the sea—had a poetic way of expressing himself, one that went straight to the core of things, Emily always thought.

The Bramble marked the end of the shops on that side of the street, and Emily crossed to visit an art gallery and a toy store. Her last stops, she decided. It was getting late, and she had to pick up Janie soon.

As she headed for the Firefly Gallery, the distinct aroma of burgers and French fries wafted toward her. The Clam Box. How could she have forgotten? It was right next to the toy shop. The idea of offering her flyers there made her smile. She imagined being chased out with a broom—or something worse.

Lost in the amusing, imagined scene, she nearly missed Charlie Bates, headed straight toward her. Head down, hands deep in his jacket pockets, his expression was grim as he marched briskly along.

Had he noticed her? She wasn't sure. He was staring at the sidewalk, deep in thought. She could have easily passed by, but that seemed churlish, as if she held a grudge. Which she didn't.

"Hello, Charlie. How's it going?"

He looked up, his expression friendly at first, then sour when he realized it was her. "Just fine. Like a well-oiled machine. How about you? How's civilian life, Emily?"

"So far, so good. I enjoy being a private citizen again."

He looked surprised. "Really? That's not what I hear. I hear you're going door-to-door stirring up trouble for me."

Emily wasn't surprised. Somebody—probably George Krueger—had alerted Charlie to her walk down Main Street.

"You want to derail my meeting Monday night, don't you? You just can't stand to see someone else run the show. Well, it's not going to happen. No way, no how."

Emily held on to her temper, though it wasn't easy. Charlie was misinformed—and a bit paranoid, as usual.

"That's not my intention at all. I campaigned on this side of the question, in case you've forgotten."

"Guess what?" Charlie replied. "The election is over. I don't have to debate with you anymore. The voters picked me. Maybe *you've* forgotten *that*." Charlie smiled at her smugly, then turned to go. But someone called out to him and he turned around again.

"What's with the trash collectors, Charlie? Any progress on that yet?"

Nina Barnes, the owner of the Toy Barn, emerged from her shop and walked toward them, black trash bags dangling from each hand. "The truck only stopped once last week. I'm tired of driving to the dump."

"I know it's been tough, Nina. I'm in the same

boat at the diner," he reminded her. "But they're asking too much. I can bargain them down, but it's going to take time. We're hiring some outside help. They're starting on Monday," he promised.

"All right. But don't take too long."

"I understand completely."

"Do you? Christmas is coming, Charlie. I don't have time for this, too."

"No worries. I'll get it straightened out," Charlie promised.

Nina nodded and glanced at Emily. "Nice to see you, Emily. Stop by sometime. We can catch up."

"I'd like that." Emily was itching to hand Nina a flyer. She had a feeling the toy shop owner would side with the open-space group. But she decided not to start that conversation in front of Charlie.

As Nina tossed the bags in her car and pulled away, Charlie's smile melted. "I've got to go. I've got two businesses to run now," he added, as if to say, *You have none.* "Enjoy the rest of your walk, Emily."

"Thanks. I will."

She crossed the street again and headed for her car, instantly regretting her sarcastic tone. How had their conversation gone so sour so quickly?

That wasn't at all what I intended. I could help him with K&B Carting. I know how difficult they can be, and I know a few tricks for getting around them. But of course, he won't take my advice.

Do I really want to stir up trouble against Charlie? Am I fooling myself, thinking I'm just concerned about this issue and it has nothing to do with losing the election?

Emily hated to face it, but suddenly she wasn't sure if her motives in this fight were so lily white after all.

Chapter Seven

CHARLIE SWEPT INTO THE DINER AND headed straight for the kitchen. He pulled off his jacket and slipped on an apron in one efficient, well-practiced motion. Trading barbs with Emily Warwick on the street had been bad enough. But did she have to hang around and gloat while Nina Barnes griped about the trash problem? Just his luck to have some unhappy shopkeeper read him the riot act in front of Her Highness. That must have made her day.

Meanwhile, his day was going from bad to worse to a complete crash-and-burn scenario. At least people listened to him at the diner. He didn't have to deal with a lot of back talk.

Tim, the lunch shift cook, was eager to go and had texted twice. So was Trudy, who sat at a back table, counting her tips. He spotted Zoey at a table by the window, taking an order, but she tagged after him and caught up just past the swinging doors.

"Hey, Dad. I thought you were coming back at two."

"Got held up in the office. But it looks like

you've been holding down the fort today. It takes a load off my mind to know you're down here watching over things, Zoey. You know I always say it, but it's true."

Zoey clipped her order on the wheel, then gave him that smile, like she didn't really believe him. "You don't *always* say it, Dad. You hardly say it at all."

"I don't? Well, I'm thinking it. All the time. What do you kids say? You're the bomb?"

Zoey rolled her eyes. "Thanks. By the way, nobody says that anymore," she added in a fake whisper.

He nodded, checking the prep area, the stainless steel tubs of garnish the waitstaff added to the dishes before they went out. "Low on pickle spears, honey, and lemon wedges. Some more red onion wouldn't hurt, either."

Zoey made a face. "I hate red onion. I bet it destroys the ozone layer. Red onion is contributing to global warming."

Charlie laughed. "I don't think so. Just keep the wrapping over it. Life isn't a rose garden, you know."

"I know, Dad." Her singsong tone amused him today for some reason.

"Hey, before you do that, I've got some good news and some bad news. Which do you want first?"

Zoey eyed him warily. "Good news, I guess."

"I hired a new busboy. He starts tomorrow. And we still have Lyle on the schedule," he said, mentioning another staffer who bussed and helped in the kitchen.

"That is good news." She looked genuinely happy, and Charlie felt relieved.

"What's the bad news?" She winced, as if bracing herself. Charlie felt guilty already.

"Come on now, honey, it's not that bad. It's just that I can't stay here late tonight, like I thought. I have to get back to Village Hall for another meeting tonight—about that stalled contract. So I need you to close up."

Before he could say more, Zoey's high-pitched squeal made him raise his hands to cover his ears. How in the world did teenage girls do that?

"Da-a-d! You've got to be kidding! I can't stay tonight. I have a date. I told you this morning, remember?"

Charlie didn't doubt it. She probably had told him, but it had gone in one ear and out the other. He had so many more important things on his mind right now.

"I'm sorry. It must have slipped my mind. I'll make it up to you, honey, I will. But this is really important. It's crucial. I have the big council meeting on Monday night. My first time on the chopping block—the whole town will be there. I can't go in without good news about the contract. I just can't."

She sighed, her shoulders sagging. Tim hit the bell behind the counter. "Order up, Zoey . . . Charlie, when are you jumping in here? I've got to get home."

"Keep your shirt on, man. I'm coming," he grumbled without glancing back. Zoey looked like she was going to cry. He hoped not. It killed him when she cried—especially if he was the one who upset her.

"Daddy, *please.* Do I really have to stay?"

He felt bad now, hearing that plaintive tone. He knew how important a date was at that age. Zoey didn't go out that much, either. She wasn't the party type, like some kids he heard about. He was proud of her for sticking with her studies and doing so well in school.

"Honey, I'm sorry . . . but yeah. You do." Before she could answer back he said, "Who is this guy? Do I know him?"

She shook her head, chin down. "He's not from around here. Just visiting for a few weeks, with his family."

"I see. Well . . . if he likes you that much, he'll ask you out again. Don't worry. It's good to play hard to get. You ought to make a boy ask you out at least two or three times before you say yes. Boys like that, believe me."

She rolled her eyes and grabbed a plate that held a cheeseburger deluxe. "Yeah, maybe back in the eighteen hundreds, when you were a kid.

Maybe I should wave a fan in front of my face and act like I have fainting spells."

He knew she was sassing him, but sometimes she was so funny, he couldn't help laughing. "Hey, I'm not kidding. Back in the eighteen eighties, I must have asked your mother out about ten times before she said yes. I knew she was the one. I didn't give up."

Zoey sighed. "Lucky for her." She stood over the garnish bar and added the appropriate extras—a pickle spear and the dreaded red onion slice, wrinkling her nose like a rabbit.

He patted her shoulder. "Don't worry. This boy will ask you out again. Or he's a dumbbell and you're well rid of him."

She headed out to the dining room. "I hope you figure out that contract thing. Those trash collectors are ruining my life."

"You and me both, kiddo." Charlie shook his head as the kitchen doors swung closed behind her.

Nothing easy about this day, he reflected. *Everywhere I turn, drama and more drama. I feel like I'm fighting a wildfire, running from one spot to the other with a water pistol.*

Two more years of being mayor? I'm not sure I can make it.

BETWEEN THE KITCHEN DOORS AND HER customer's table, Zoey somehow conjured a

185

smile. She set down the burger deluxe platter with extra pickle and red onion. "Can I get you anything else?" she asked.

"All set for now, thank you." The customer, a woman about her mother's age who worked in the bank down the street, came in a few times a week for a late lunch. She usually read a book while she ate and was already engrossed. Zoey checked the author's name. She didn't recognize it, but that didn't mean much. She didn't read many novels these days—mostly just textbooks.

Maybe someday I'll look down and see James Potter's name on the cover, she thought. *I can tell everyone I almost had a date with him. That will be a great story for my grandchildren.*

Back at the counter, she slipped out her cell phone and checked for his number. They had been in touch over the week and had made plans to see a movie in Newburyport and have sushi after.

Zoey hated to break their date. She had really been looking forward to it, and had even planned her outfit down to the earrings.

What if James didn't believe her or felt insulted? What if he didn't even care that much?

She did not need dating advice from her father—even though what he said was true. Some guys did seem to like it if you didn't seem so available. But she didn't think James was like that. She certainly wasn't going to wait for him to ask her out ten times more before she agreed. Once seemed like hitting the lottery.

She chickened out on calling and sent a text:

> Sorry but I can't go out tonight. My dad just said I have to stay and close up.

She hit send and waited. Should she add a frowny face? That seemed too much. She didn't want him to think she was that disappointed. Though she was.

Should she say more? Like, "Hope we can do it another time"? As in, *Can we reschedule now? I'm available tomorrow night. And the night after that . . .*

That seemed too obvious. And a little pushy.

His answer was already coming back and appeared on the screen:

> Bummer. Another time, I guess. Catch you soon.

Zoey sat back. He didn't seem that concerned about it. That made her feel even worse.

I guess it wasn't a big deal for him. He's just bored. He would have asked out any girl his age who could fog a mirror.

Forget about James. He's sweet, but he's out of your league. And leaving for a trek around the world in a few weeks. Duh? Not exactly steady boyfriend material.

As Sophie would say, *Things happen for a reason.*

ZOEY WAS DETERMINED TO SLEEP IN SATUR-day morning. She had drawn her curtains tight the night before and made sure her phone alarm was off. She was tired from last night's long shift at the diner and feeling blue about missing her date. And she had stayed up late, watching a dumb romantic comedy she'd seen a hundred times before.

It felt like the middle of the night when someone gently shook her shoulder. "Zoey? You need to get up now. Sorry, honey." Her mom stood beside the bed, her expression sympathetic.

"Get up? What time is it?" Zoey rolled over to check the bedside clock. It was barely seven. "No way." She rolled over with her back to her mother. "I don't have to be at the center until this afternoon. I want to sleep some more."

"I know, sweetie." She felt Lucy sit on the edge of the bed. "But we have to go down to the diner and do breakfast. Trudy and Tim opened, but they need help. Dad didn't get back from his meeting until three o'clock this morning, and he can't move." Her mother sighed and gently pushed Zoey's hair back from her face. "I'm sorry, sweetie, but we've got to do it. So shake those pretty legs."

Zoey finally opened her eyes. "But I'm scheduled to work at the center this afternoon. I can't cancel on the center, Mom. They're counting on me."

"Just do the breakfast rush with me, Zoey, and you can go. I have the day off, and I'll work until Dad comes in." Lucy stood up and headed for the door. "We all need to pull together now, sweetheart. We have to pitch in and help your father until he sorts things out at Village Hall."

Zoey didn't answer. She knew there was no negotiating. At least she didn't have to work all day. It was good of Lucy to stay and let her go, considering that Lucy's nursing job was intense; she worked at least forty hours a week and often worked overtime, and she probably had her own long list of things she wanted to do on a rare day off.

I'll have to thank her later. When I'm conscious.

THE DINER WAS A WILD SCENE WITH ONLY Trudy on the floor waiting tables. Tim, the backup cook, kept running out of the kitchen, trying to cover the counter customers.

Lucy turned to Zoey briefly as they came in, fresh recruits into the battle zone. "Keep your head down, honey. It's a madhouse in here."

They quickly stashed their coats, pulled on aprons, and grabbed their order pads. Lucy took the tables at the back of the room, where impatient customers waved madly to flag her down. Zoey headed for the booths at the front, moving from table to table, scribbling down orders that she hoped Tim could decode.

"And can I have some more coffee please, miss?" A customer held out her mug.

But before Zoey could reply, a hand holding a coffeepot magically appeared and filled the cup.

"Thanks," the woman said, giving her menu back to Zoey.

Zoey turned, expecting to see Lucy, or maybe Trudy. But it was James, standing a few steps back from the table and grinning at her. He wore a white shirt and black pants and carried a big empty tray.

"What are you doing here?" She tried to keep her voice down, but couldn't hide her shock.

"I'm the new busboy. Your dad hired me yesterday."

"I get that part," she said tartly. "Why didn't you tell me?" She headed off to the kitchen to put the orders in, and he followed.

"I should have told you yesterday. But I thought it would be fun to surprise you."

"Was it?" She tried to sound annoyed, but was actually really happy.

"Yeah, it was." His wide grin underscored his

reply. "That's why I didn't ask if you were free tonight when you changed our plans. I knew I had to work here."

Zoey was glad to hear that. Luckily, her back was turned toward him as he followed her through the swinging doors to the kitchen, so he couldn't see how happy she was. Maybe Charlie did have a point about acting a little hard to get. "I see," she said simply. She clipped the orders to the metal wheel at the service window.

"Are you working all day, too?"

"Just for breakfast. I'm going to the children's center this afternoon." She glanced at him. He looked unhappy to hear she was leaving so soon.

A plate of eggs and home fries appeared at the window. "Order up!" Tim shouted. Zoey checked the table number.

"How about Sunday? For our date, I mean."

The question surprised her. So he did want to see her. Her first impulse was to do a cartwheel across the kitchen. Then she realized she had to say no—again. *Why is my life such a total disaster?*

"I'm sorry . . . I really want to, but I have finals next week and a ton of papers due. I really have to study."

He looked disappointed but as if he understood. "No worries. I get it. We'll go out when the semester is over and celebrate."

Zoey smiled again, then heard Trudy call out

from the kitchen door, "Hey, new guy—get out there and clear those tables." Trudy stared at James, looking very annoyed as she carried in a tub of dirty dishes. She dumped it near the dishwasher, then held the empty tub out to him. "I can't seat people at dirty tables. And you can't stand around all day flirting."

James ran over, grabbed the tub, and headed out to the dining room. Zoey felt her cheeks redden. She placed another plate of eggs and toast on her tray and headed out to the dining room. But not even Trudy's dark look and mortifying comments could tamp down Zoey's bright mood. As Sophie would say, *You never know what's going to happen when you get up in the morning. Expect the best and that's what you'll find.*

Funny how working extra hours at the diner didn't seem like a jail sentence anymore. It didn't seem so bad at all.

"ARE YOU SURE YOU HAVE TO GO? CAN'T someone else drive your mother and Ezra over?" Dan stared up at Emily, his fork hovering over a bowl of chili with all the trimmings.

Emily had pulled out the Crock-Pot over the weekend and, by Monday, had been armed with enough recipes to cook with it for the rest of the year. She started with chili, which was simple enough even for her. Dan and Jane seemed to like it, though there had not been enough time for

Emily to eat with them—not if she was going to get to the meeting at Village Hall on time.

Jane was still eating, too; her expression told Emily she agreed with her father.

"I'm sorry. It's too late to find them a ride and, frankly, I'm curious to see what happens." Emily grabbed her coat and purse from the rack near the side door. It was already six. She barely had time to pick up the seniors and get over to Village Hall by half past.

"All right, whatever." Dan shook his head and took another bite of his dinner.

She knew Dan thought she was back to her old ways, but part of her was sincerely reluctant to go. She had gone to some trouble to plan a nice family dinner and had even made baked apples for dessert. "I won't be back late," she said, tugging on her jacket.

Jane looked up at her. "Are we still going to practice for my debate?" Emily had forgotten that plan, but caught herself. "Absolutely. I'll be home in an hour," she promised, dropping a quick kiss on Jane's hair. "See you later," she said, avoiding Dan's gaze as she headed out the door.

By the time she guided her mother and Ezra into the meeting room at Village Hall, nearly every seat was filled.

"Just my luck. I hate to sit in the back," Lillian grumbled.

"A hot ticket. I had no idea," Ezra said.

Emily had been hoping to sit in the back and found three seats in a distant corner. She had told Dan the truth; she was curious to see what went on tonight but had no intention of getting involved. *You handed out those flyers and gave them some good pointers on drafting their counterproposal. You've done your part,* she reminded herself.

Charlie sat in the middle of a long table at the front of the room, flanked by the town council. They talked quietly together, Charlie with his hand over his microphone.

A podium with a microphone was set up in front. It looked exactly like one of her meetings, except that Charlie held a gavel. Emily didn't like being so formal and rarely had trouble keeping order or getting the crowd's attention. She wasn't surprised by the accessory. It suited his personality.

"Good evening, everybody. Thanks for coming out tonight and taking part in running our beautiful village," Charlie began cheerfully. "First item on the agenda—K&B Carting Company, contract negotiations." His gaze swept over the audience. "Is this settled yet? No, not yet. But trust me when I say that we have been working night and day to come to terms with this company. For reasons I won't go into here, this company thinks we're soft and willing to give

194

them whatever terms they ask. That may have been true in the past, but it's a different ball game now. We have to show them we're not pushovers anymore. Even if it takes a little longer to get the job done right."

Emily felt her mother's pointy elbow dig into her side. "You know who he's talking about, don't you, you soft old pushover?"

Emily ignored her and did her best to ignore Charlie's thinly veiled criticism. He made her regime sound like a candy store for town contractors. Of course he had to make some excuse, and it was easy to blame this situation on her. For now, at least.

"The handout shows you what they're asking and what we want to pay. And the difference is substantial. The floor is open for comments. Two minutes per speaker," he warned.

Nina Barnes was the first to the microphone. "What's the sense of having free parking if shoppers have to climb over trash bags to get to my store? I just want to see this settled, the sooner the better. We don't have to make some big showdown out of this, Charlie."

A chorus of agreement rose up in the audience. Charlie banged the gavel. "Order, please. If you want to talk, line up at the microphone."

Tucker Tulley was up next. "I think we should stay the course, like Charlie says. If all the firms that do business with the town ask for more money, that's going to raise our taxes."

"Just my point. Thank you, Officer Tulley," Charlie said.

"*Officer* Tulley? They've only known each other since kindergarten," Lillian said.

"Longer than that. I delivered them both within days. They were in the infant ward, side by side," Ezra corrected her.

"That must have been a sight," Lillian murmured.

Audience members asked questions—how long was the new contract and could the town call in a professional mediator?—and all the council members had their say.

"I propose the council take a vote on whether to accept the K&B offer or stand tough," said Karl Nelson, the town attorney.

"I second the motion," added Art Hecht, who owned Hecht Insurance and had always been one of Charlie's supporters.

Emily wasn't surprised to see the vote fall in Charlie's favor.

"It's still the honeymoon phase. They haven't gotten tired of him yet," Lillian said with a shrug.

Charlie banged his gavel. "Motion carried. The town will continue negotiations with K&B and hold the line. Item two: New zoning. A draft of the revised zoning is in the handouts. As I've said, I feel certain this change will have a big payoff for Cape Light—mainly increased revenue to repair our roads, improve our schools, and create more housing for young families and seniors. We'll open the floor to comments, with a two-minute limit per speaker."

"He's quite pleased with himself," Lillian grumbled. "But I think the wind will be blown out of his sails pretty soon."

"We can hope," Ezra quietly agreed.

Emily wasn't sure. Charlie seemed to be steering the ship of state with a steady hand so far.

George Krueger jumped up and took the microphone. "Mr. Mayor, I have a petition here signed by over a thousand residents who support the new zoning proposal. This is something long needed in this town. We can no longer pretend we're living in some bygone day. We may as well rename our town 'Cape Light Historic Restoration Village.' "

His quip brought laughter from the pro-zoning group.

Lillian sniffed. "An obvious plant from the Bates camp."

"Krueger couldn't possibly have thought up that line," Ezra agreed.

Perhaps, Emily thought. She had to admit that Charlie's side was effective. A string of supporters for the new zoning spoke in detail and at length.

Finally, someone from the open-space group

shouted out, "Time limit, Charlie? I thought you said two minutes per speaker?"

"Right you are. Thank you. Next speaker please?"

Martin Becker was next in line, presenting his petition of over a thousand signatures. "These citizens strongly oppose any change in the zoning, especially in the outlying areas of the village, the marshes and farmland. This area is home to an abundance of wildlife. Any sort of development will pose a great threat to these beautiful natural habitats, which are—"

"Thank you, Mr. Becker. Your time is up. Please step away and let the next citizen speak."

"I haven't finished my statement," Martin protested. "If you'll just allow me a few—"

"That's the rule, Mr. Becker. Time is up. I'm just trying to keep this meeting fair and let everyone have their say." Charlie banged the gavel and waved his hand, indicating Martin Becker should move along.

"Silence and censor the opposition, a traditional mode of dictators." Lillian didn't even bother to lower her voice.

Grace Hegman was next. She gently leaned toward the microphone. "I allot my time to Mr. Becker," she said in her whispery voice.

"Hear! Hear! I second that. Nice move, Gracie." Grace's father, Digger, applauded.

Charlie leaned into his microphone. "You can't

second what she said. It isn't a motion. And you can't give your time to someone else, Grace. That's not allowed, either."

"But we've always done it that way." She turned around and looked at the audience, tucking a wisp of her gray hair behind her ear. "Haven't we?" she asked in an innocent tone.

"That's right, Grace. We've always been allowed to give time to another speaker. You can't rewrite the rules, Charlie."

Molly Willoughby had come to her feet, very certain about the question.

Charlie covered the mike a moment and conferred with the council. He returned and spoke in a more conciliatory tone. "That was true when my predecessor was in office. But we're following *real* parliamentary procedure now, not some mishmash version. This is the right way to do things, believe me."

"I like the way we did it in Mayor Warwick's day. No one was cut off midsentence," Felicity Bean said.

"You ought to put away your rule book and get off your high horse, Charlie," someone else shouted out.

"All right, simmer down!" Charlie tapped his gavel.

Emily stood up. She had not wanted to say anything, but she had been in that hot seat, and it was painful to watch Charlie flounder.

"What Charlie just said is true. We were not following correct procedure by giving each other time to speak." She heard her mother groan, but ignored her. "It was just the way the meetings had been run, back through Mayor Pritchard's day," she added, mentioning her predecessor.

Charlie looked surprised but quickly followed up. "See, the former mayor agrees with me."

Martin Becker took hold of the microphone again. "Typical of Emily, to be honest and straightforward. And typical of you, Charlie, to change the rules in the middle of the game. I remember when you were fighting the parking meters on Main Street. Your group gave you all of their time, and you held the floor for over an hour."

"Touché, Becker. Well done!" Lillian called out.

Emily had forgotten that famous filibuster. It was actually one of many Charlie had staged during his long career opposing her.

"That was then, this is now. You shouldn't have let me have the floor that long. See where it got you?" Charlie laughed, trying to lighten the mood. "As I was saying, Grace, if you don't have anything to add, please step aside and let the next in line have their turn."

Sam Morgan stood up. "I'd still like to hear the rest of what Mr. Becker has to say. Isn't that the point of these meetings?"

Martin Becker stood at his seat and spoke in a voice loud enough for all to hear. "Thank you, Sam. I was going to add that the environmental impact of this development would be—"

Karl Nelson, the town attorney, took the microphone from Charlie. "Didn't you hear the mayor? Your time is done. The council must insist on order in this meeting."

"Simmer down, everybody!" Charlie yelled. He could hardly be heard over the arguments that had broken out all over the room.

"I've seen enough of Mayor Mad Hatter for one night," Lillian said as she and Ezra got to their feet. "Let's head for the door before the rush." Emily grabbed her coat and purse and then her mother's arm as they swiftly left the room.

Ezra and Lillian had a lot to say on the ride home. "I have to get out to these public forums more often," Ezra said, sounding very energized. "It's better than television."

"Anything is better than television," Lillian replied. "I was surprised you tossed him a lifeline, Emily."

"The man is his own worst enemy. It's his pugnacious attitude," Ezra replied. "That's what gets him into trouble. He's smart enough, in a rough-around-the-edges way. But he has no bedside manner."

"I still don't know how he got elected," Lillian said.

Emily was relieved to see they had reached Providence Street and quickly pulled into the driveway. Her mother was on the verge of calling for a recount—or an impeachment.

Ezra got out of the backseat and helped Lillian from the car. "I'll take it from here, dear. Good night," he called to Emily.

"Good night, Ezra. Good night, Mother," she called back.

She rolled up her window and headed home, feeling drained and unsettled. The meeting had only made the situation worse, heating up antagonism. It was exactly the wrong way to solve the problem.

She walked wearily to the house, hoping Dan had cleaned the kitchen. She was ready for a cup of tea and a good book, then realized how late it was.

Jane's project. I promised her we were going to practice.

It was my idea in the first place.

She pulled her phone from her pocket and saw that Jane had sent her a text at nine o'clock, but she had shut her phone off in the meeting. It was already nine thirty.

"Hello? Where is everyone?" Emily came in the front door and looked around the house. Neither Jane nor Dan were in the family room, or the kitchen, though the TV was on, set to the History channel, of course.

"We're upstairs," Dan called back. He stood at the top of the staircase and stared down at her. "I'm helping Jane with her opening statement for the debate."

She could tell by his tone he was annoyed but trying not to show it. Emily took the stairs two at a time.

"I didn't forget. The meeting turned into a madhouse. How's it going, honey?" She brushed past Dan, who stood near the door of Jane's bedroom. Jane was at her desk, frowning over her laptop.

Jane finally turned to her mother. "I'm not sure. It's too wordy or something."

Emily sat on the edge of the bed and gave Jane her full attention. "We can fix that, don't worry. Let's hear what you have so far."

Dan met her gaze, then slipped out of the room. He did have every right to be annoyed. She had promised Jane she would be home over two hours ago. The meeting had been such a kangaroo court, anyone would have gotten distracted. *But you're stretching yourself too thin again, Emily. You've done your part for the open spacers. You have more important things to focus on.*

"THEY'VE GOT ME TARRED AND FEATHERED, Tucker. What do you expect from a newspaper that's run by Emily Warwick's daughter-in-law?" Charlie tossed the Tuesday morning edition of the *Cape Light Messenger* on the counter.

Tucker Tulley stirred his coffee. "It's not favorable. No doubt about it."

" 'Mayor Bates's Debut: Town Meeting Meltdown.' " Charlie read the headline aloud. "And it gets worse. The inside is full of stories and interviews with residents, and there's even an editorial. Didn't anything else happen in this town yesterday?"

"It's one meeting, Charlie. Try to get the big picture. You're just getting out of the gate."

"Out of the gate and flat on my face, two yards down the track." Charlie focused on the grill, pushing the sizzling bacon to one side, then turning two fried eggs. "Maybe they're right. What do I know about being mayor? Maybe I should stick to dishing out chowder and clam rolls."

"You must know something about being mayor. People voted you in," Tucker reminded him.

"And last night those same voters turned on me like a pack of starving coyotes. You saw it. I tried to keep the peace and not lose my cool, but no one would listen."

"You're spinning too many plates at once. If you don't mind a little restaurant humor." Tucker laughed at his own quip, but Charlie didn't. "You should settle with K&B. Show people you can take action and resolve a big problem. Maybe it's not worth it to hold out."

Charlie served Tucker his usual breakfast: two

fried eggs, bacon, and toast. "I hate to look soft after everything I said. But maybe we can reach terms I can live with."

"That's the way, Charlie. You've got to compromise."

"In some situations. Not with those open spacers. They're going for the jugular. Did you see who their ringleader is now? Emily Warwick. Becker is just a front. She's pulling the strings."

"I don't know. She was pretty quiet last night. She even stuck up for you a little."

"That was just a trick," Charlie said. "I know for a fact she's in that gang. It's a revenge thing. She can't stand to see me in office."

Tucker spread butter on his toast and took a bite. "Emily Warwick was against zoning changes during the campaign. It's not as if she never mentioned it. Besides, Charlie, you're mayor now. You have to focus on the problems and fix them. That's the way to win confidence and trust. Never mind about Emily. She's old news. A lot of people voted for you. We're counting on you to step up and prove we made the right choice."

Charlie met Tucker's glance. He felt touched. "I won't let you down, Tucker. I won't let anyone down. But it's impossible to run the diner and be a good mayor, too. I've got to get out from behind this counter and focus on Village Hall."

Tucker wiped his mouth with a napkin and

brushed a few crumbs from his uniform. "I saw that coming. Why don't you put an ad in the paper for a manager and maybe another cook?"

"I would, but I'm strapped for cash right now. That campaign cost a lot, and I've got tuition bills to cover, too. Trudy doesn't want the job. She's told me flat out. At least I have Zoey. She can cover for me as soon as the semester ends. She'll do a good job, too," he added. "She looks a little kooky with her hairdos and way-out clothes, but she's a smart girl, very responsible."

"I know she is. But how does she feel about the promotion?"

Charlie felt color rise in his face. He cleared Tucker's empty dish and wiped the counter. "I've brought it up, but she just squawks. You know teenagers. She'll fall in line eventually."

Tucker put his police hat on. "If you say so."

Charlie could tell by Tucker's tone that he didn't think it would be so simple. He crossed his arms over his chest. "I'm her father. She has to do what I say."

Tucker laughed as he headed for the door. "Right. Get back to me on that one."

CHARLIE CLOSED THE DINER AT NINE THAT night. When he got home, he was glad to see Zoey's car in the driveway. Best to get this news off his chest right away.

The living room and dining room were dark, but

he followed the light and laughter coming from the family room in the back of the house. Lucy and Zoey were already in pajamas, watching TV together, sipping hot cocoa and eating popcorn.

"I can't believe she said that! Did you see Briana's face?" Zoey bounced on the chair cushions. "Wait . . . I'm going to play it over. Let me just rewind."

"Oh, yes, let's see that one again." Lucy was still laughing as she greeted him. "Hi, honey. Was the diner busy?"

"Quiet night. A few couples out Christmas shopping. What's going on here? Looks like a slumber party."

He had brought a pile of folders in from his truck, paperwork from Village Hall that he had to look over before he went to sleep. He dropped them on the end table and sat on the sofa next to Lucy.

"We're celebrating," Lucy explained. "Zoey had her last final exam today and just sent in her last term paper."

Charlie was glad to hear that, for more reasons than the relieved look on his daughter's face. He took a handful of popcorn from the bowl. "That's good news. So the semester is officially over?"

Zoey wore a rare, wide smile. "That's right. And I just got an email from the youth center. They want to interview me for the internship.

They're only talking to three students, so my chances of getting it are really good."

Charlie felt his heart sink but forced a smile. Lucy was beaming with pride. "Isn't that good news?" she said. "There were at least fifty students who applied, and now Zoey is one of three!"

Charlie nodded. "Just getting called in to talk is a feather in your cap. If you don't get this, another chance like this will come along. You'll see."

Zoey had practically been dancing around with happiness but now stood still in the middle of the room. She looked at him curiously.

The picture on the TV screen was frozen—two women in evening gowns and a lot of smeared makeup were in the middle of some sort of fight. That silly housewife reality show they liked to watch, mostly to make fun of it. Everyone was going to need a laugh in a minute or two, he reflected.

Lucy turned to him. He knew that look. Her antenna was up. "Zoey might get this one. We ought to think positively."

Charlie rubbed his hands together, trying to find the right words. "The thing is, I need Zoey to work in the diner during her school vacation. Full-time. I need her to manage the place so I can focus on being mayor. We talked about it a little, honey, remember?"

Zoey's eyes were glistening with tears. "I can't work at the diner full-time, Dad! I already told you. The internship is full-time."

"I know, I know . . . but other opportunities like this will come along for you, honey." Charlie felt awful. He hated to see her cry, but he needed her to understand. "Listen, I only have this one chance to be mayor. I don't see how I can do it otherwise. I just can't find a manager on such short notice and train them and what have you."

He turned to Lucy. She had to back him up. "You saw what happened at the meeting last night, Lucy. They nearly ate me alive."

Lucy looked upset, too. "That meeting was rough," she agreed, but she didn't say more.

"Dad, *please*. I don't want to work in the diner every single day of my life. Even if I don't get the internship, I promised the center I'd do more hours there. It will be good for my résumé and good experience for me."

Charlie tried to keep his tone calm. "I understand what you're saying. But you've got time for that, Zoey, all the time in the world, even though you can't see it that way." He could tell she wasn't listening to him, but kept going. "My situation is different. It's like . . . like the house is on fire. I've got to take care of it right away. Starting tomorrow."

"Tomorrow? I'm not on the schedule tomorrow," she corrected him in a tart tone.

209

"Well, I am, as the manager. But I'm off the roster now, and you're being called up from the minors." He knew she didn't understand that baseball terminology but didn't stop to explain. "I'm sorry, honey. This is the only way. You've got to step up and help the family. Do you like seeing your father made into the laughingstock of the entire village?"

From Zoey's expression, he realized that had not been a good question to ask her at this moment.

"Of course not," Lucy cut in. She put her arm around Zoey's shoulders. "I didn't realize it was such a crisis for you, Charlie. I guess the meeting last night was an eye-opener."

She turned to Zoey. "I do think, all things considered, your father can use our help right now. You know how long he's waited to be mayor. He deserves a chance to do a good job now. I'll help at the diner when I can and take fewer hours at the hospital next month. C.J. will be home again at Christmas, at least for a week or so. He can help, too. We'll work it out, honey. It won't be so bad."

Zoey still looked forlorn, on the verge of tears. But at least Lucy had calmed her down a little.

"That's right. It won't be so bad," Charlie repeated. "I'm giving you a nice raise—plenty of extra money for clothes shopping. That part is good, right?"

"There's nothing good about this. But I guess I don't have any choice, do I?" Zoey's gaze bounced from her father to her mother and back again.

Lucy looked upset, too. He could tell she wasn't going to field this one for him.

"No, honey. I'm sorry. You don't," he finally replied.

Lucy rubbed Zoey's shoulder. "Want to watch the rest of the show?"

"I'm tired. I'm going to bed."

Lucy didn't seem surprised. "Okay. Good night, honey."

"Good night, sweetheart," Charlie chimed in.

Zoey left the room and headed upstairs, her dark head hanging to her chest.

Charlie stuffed more popcorn in his mouth, though he wasn't hungry. He watched Lucy walk around the room, clearing up the empty mugs and magazines. Picking up an empty bowl, he followed her into the kitchen.

"Do you think she'll ever forgive me? Maybe when she's forty-something and has teenagers of her own?" he asked quietly. "I feel awful forcing her into this. But I don't know what else to do."

"I know. She's disappointed. She's been working hard to get that internship. Maybe she won't even go for the interview now."

"I hope not. What's the point?" Charlie hoped Zoey would decide not to go. If she was picked, he would have to go through this wringer all over again. "Hey, I'm not heartless. I know this is tough for her, but that's the way life is sometimes. Plans don't always work out."

"True enough." Lucy was fixing the coffee-maker for the morning pot. "But I think she had enough of those lessons before she came to live with us," Lucy added quietly. "I was hoping we could show her the other side of that coin."

Charlie didn't answer. He knew what Lucy said was true.

Lucy said good night and went upstairs, leaving him alone with his thoughts and the paperwork from Village Hall. And a sour feeling in the pit of his stomach.

Well, I got my way tonight, he reflected. *But at a high cost. A mighty high cost.*

Chapter Eight

ZOEY'S ALARM WENT OFF AT HALF PAST six on Wednesday morning. She remembered that she didn't have school and shut it off, gratefully sinking back into her pillow. *No, another voice said, jogging her awake again. You have to go to the diner—instead of sleeping in and doing whatever you please the first day of winter break.*

A few minutes later, she heard a tap on the door. "Zoey, are you up?" her dad asked.

"Yes!" she called back. She barely spared him a word more as she came downstairs on time and they drove through the quiet side streets toward the village.

When they reached the diner, Tim was already at work, cooking bacon and home fries and mixing pancake batter.

Her father went into the kitchen to talk to him. Tim didn't know Zoey was going to be the new manager, and Charlie had to explain the sudden change and give him a checklist he had written out and all sorts of other instructions that Tim probably already knew. Zoey got along well with Tim. She was sure they would work out any problems easily.

She stowed her jacket and purse, then checked the dining room to make sure the tables were properly set. A list of specials for the day, written in Tim's hand on a white sheet of paper, sat near the register, and Zoey started working on the chalkboard. She had to search for the box of colored chalk she had bought, and finally found it on a shelf under the cups.

Her father came out of the kitchen. "Use the plain, white chalk, and none of those fancy curlicues, please."

"I'm the manager now. I get to decide if the specials are written in color or not, curly or block lettering, or even bubble. One job out of a zillion that I actually like here," she mused as she wrote out the words with artistic flair: *Soup of the Day—Hearty Homemade Minestrone.*

Her father took a white sheet of paper from his clipboard. "I made you a checklist, too. All the little things you need to be mindful of as manager."

"Okay, Dad. But I think I know what to do by now."

"Humor me, will you, Zoey?"

Zoey finally looked at the page. Her father had catalogued the tasks involved in running the diner in the tiniest detail: unlock doors, put on lights, shut off lights, lock doors.

She knew he wouldn't feel comfortable about leaving her there until she read it through. Or at least pretended to. After a few moments, she looked back up at him. "Okay, I'll keep this handy so I don't forget anything."

"Good idea. Keep it right here, by the register." He reached into his pocket and laid the big key ring on the counter. "You take this. Put it in a safe place. I don't have duplicates of some of those."

"The Burning Sword of the Masters? You're actually giving that *to me?*"

He squinted at her. "I'm sure you're making fun again, but guess I have to ask, what that's supposed to mean?"

"Just being silly." Zoey shrugged. "It's from a video game. The boys play it all the time. *Battle of the Masters.*"

"Are you mature enough to handle this or not? This isn't one big joke, Zoey."

"I am, Dad. Don't worry." She had gone too far with that last remark. Now he was all nervous again. "I've been doing all that stuff on the list for a long time. You just never paid me for it."

"Now you're getting paid for it, and getting the title, too. I'm counting on you, honey." He reached over and patted her shoulder. "You can take a lot off my back right now if I don't have to worry about this place, too. These last few weeks have just been too much. Too much for me, anyway."

Something about her father's heartfelt tone and vulnerable expression made Zoey forget her annoyance. He was sincerely grateful, and very worried about being able to do his job as mayor.

"Don't worry, I can do this. And I know you're going to be a good mayor, too."

Charlie looked surprised, his eyes suddenly bright. "Thanks, honey. That means a lot to me." He pulled on his Red Sox cap and headed for the door. "Anything comes up, you just call or text."

"I will," she promised for the hundredth time.

The door opened. Zoey expected an early customer, but it was James.

"Look who's here." Charlie paused and checked his watch. "Late again."

"Sorry, Charlie. My grandma's truck wouldn't start, and I hitched a ride."

Zoey was happy to see him but tried not to show it too much. She hadn't gotten a chance to check if he was on the schedule today. There was one bright spot to the day.

"I'm not surprised. Bella has been very moody lately," Zoey said. "I can pick you up if we're on the schedule together."

"No, you can't," Charlie interrupted. "You're the manager, not a taxi service for the staff. You need to be here all the time. They need to find their own transportation."

"You're the manager? Cool." James had pulled off his jacket and was putting on an apron. "Congratulations."

Zoey smiled, feeling the compliment was silly. "It's no big deal, believe me."

Her father seemed ready to argue about that, too, then shook his head. "I'll call you later. Get some Christmas decorations up today, will you? We're the only place in town without holiday cheer. The box is in the basement somewhere."

"Don't worry. By the time you get back, it will look like Santa's Workshop in here."

"Don't overdo it," he called back over his shoulder as he walked out. "We don't want the customers getting dizzy from too many blinking lights. That's not relaxing when you're eating."

The door closed before Zoey could reply, and Charlie finally set off.

"Are you sure he isn't watching on a baby monitor or something?" James whispered.

"I never thought of that. Where would he hide the camera? Maybe in these donuts?" She lifted the glass lid on a cake stand that held a display of donuts and muffins, then looked it over with a serious expression. "Nothing here. Maybe I should check the crumb cake."

James laughed. "Seriously, I don't think your dad likes me very much."

"He's like that with everybody. You just have to get to know him."

"Is he always that . . . intense?"

"Pretty much. Whenever he acts calm, my mom worries he's coming down with something. It's just that he's wanted to be mayor for so long, and he can't believe he's not doing a great job at it."

"That's what I read in the newspaper. People sound pretty unhappy. No offense," James added quickly.

Zoey knew James was just relating what he had read about Monday night's meeting and didn't mean anything by it, but she didn't like hearing anyone criticize her father. Not even James.

"Anybody would get off to a shaky start, trying to deal with all the problems that are going on in the town right now. And trying to run this place. That's why I said I'd help him now that the semester is over. Even though I did have other plans," she added quietly. "I know he can do a great job. If he gets a chance."

"Sure he can," James agreed quickly. "I didn't mean to say he couldn't. A lot of people in town really like your dad and don't blame him at all for the way the meeting went. It's nice of you to help him."

"I didn't exactly have a choice," Zoey admitted. "But he helps me a lot. I mean, we're a family, so we help each other. I'm trying not to make a big deal out of it." *Trying now,* she amended. Last night was another story.

Digger Hegman came in and sat at the counter. Zoey was not surprised to see him. The old fisherman still rose before dawn most days and sat at the harbor awhile, watching the boats and birds. His daughter, Grace, worried about him wandering off, but everyone in town knew his routine and kept their eye on him.

"Hey, Digger. I'll be right there," Zoey said.

Digger raised his hand in greeting. "Hot tea, with lemon and honey. Toast and jam. You know my weakness by now."

Zoey smiled and nodded, then turned back to James. "We'd better get to work. We can decorate later, after the breakfast rush."

"Sounds like a plan." James grabbed some empty water pitchers. "Can I ask you one question before we start? I mean, since you're the manager now and everything?"

Zoey turned to him, feeling very official. "Sure. What's up?"

"Since you're done with school, want to go out this weekend? Whenever we're both off from work, I guess."

Zoey smiled. "Thanks. I would. And since I'm the manager, I'll work out the schedule, too."

James grinned and ducked into the kitchen. Zoey grabbed a menu and headed for her first customer, her smile so wide her face hurt.

She'd never admit it to her dad, but maybe being manager did have some perks.

"LET'S SEE ... WHOSE TURN IS IT?" EMILY gazed at the girls who sat side by side on the couch in the family room, her daughter Jane among them. It had been Emily's idea for Jane to invite her team over for a debate practice, pizza party, and sleepover, and Friday was the perfect night.

With their long hair, braces, and almost identical sweatshirts and jeans, Emily thought they looked like a flock of pretty birds. Smart birds, too. They had been rehearsing for the debate for almost an hour, and she was impressed with how far they had come.

"It's my turn, Mrs. Forbes," said Jane's best friend, Maddie.

"Please argue in support of the statement that the American Revolution was fought for economic reasons." Emily read from the points Jane had prepared for her. "You have three minutes for your opening statement, starting now."

Emily looked at her watch and gave a signal. Maddie stood up, notes in hand, and began. She was almost done when Dan walked in the side door with a stack of pizza boxes. Emily watched the girls instantly respond to the aroma, sniffing the air like hungry puppies.

"Time's up. Good job, Maddie," Emily said. "You spoke very clearly and in a firm voice, not too fast but not too slow. And she didn't have her head down, reading off her notes the whole time, right, girls?"

They nodded in reply. There were a few more points to cover, but Emily couldn't resist the smell of the pizza, either. "Looks like dinner's here. Anyone hungry?" She was teasing, of course.

The girls giggled and jostled each other, heading for the counter, where Dan had set up paper plates, napkins and cups, a green salad, and the essential pizzas.

"Help yourselves. Don't be shy."

Jane hung back in the family room with Emily, helping her pick up papers and textbooks. "Great rehearsal today, Jane. I think you'll all do great next week at the debate."

"Thanks, Mom. And thanks for helping us."

Emily slipped an arm around Jane's shoulders. "Thanks for letting me. I can hardly wait."

The girls descended on the pizza, talking and laughing. Emily stood back at the counter with Dan, eating their own pizza standing up.

"How's it going?" Dan asked.

"Very well. They've got the facts down. We're working on speaking skills now, and a few tricks for counterarguments. They'll be in great shape by next Friday."

"Will we have another pizza party and sleep-over to celebrate?"

"I was thinking of 'Make Your Own Tacos.'

But we're on the same track. Sleepovers are what middle school is all about."

It was a good idea. And Emily wanted Jane to know her home was open to friends as a gathering place, that the fun wasn't always happening at some other girl's house. She knew they had not been good about hosting nights like this, but hoped to catch up quickly.

Her cell phone rang, and she quickly checked the number.

"Who's that? Lillian?" Dan asked.

"Nope. She already called five times today, though. It's Martin Becker. The group is having a meeting tonight. I told him I couldn't come, but he needs some information I promised to research for them."

"Emily, I thought you said that after the Monday night meeting, they were on their own."

"Yes, I know. But something big has come up. And I really have to help them. With some research," she added.

Dan gave her a curious look. "Research into what? Filing a lawsuit against the town?"

"Not a lawsuit. Someone heard that a motion will be pushed through to call for an emergency village-wide vote on changing the zoning. The vote will be held in the middle of the winter when fewer voters are likely to come out, especially older residents."

"Because they're the ones who are most

interested in preserving the town," Dan said, understanding. "That's a tricky maneuver. It could work." He started on a second slice.

"It definitely could work. But I'm almost certain there's a village bylaw that would let the open-space group freeze the zoning laws for twenty-four months. I mentioned it to them, and now they seem to be pinning all their hopes on it. I have to find it and figure out how they can use it."

"You're right. You're probably one of the few people in town who would even know of an obscure bylaw like that. But now that you've remembered, can't they take it from here? Just pass the ball and let someone else run down the field."

Emily could see Dan was concerned about her sinking too deep into this issue when she had promised to just stick a toe in and jump right out. Her cell phone sounded again then, this time with a long text from another open-space group volunteer. Emily started to read it and barely noticed Jane standing right next to her.

"We threw our plates and stuff away. We're going up to my room now, okay?"

"Sure, go ahead," Dan said, before Emily had even looked up from her phone. By the time she had, Jane was walking out of the room.

"It's fine, honey. Don't wait too long to start your movie," Emily called after her.

Dan walked over to the snack bar and began clearing up the leftover pizza.

"I'll wrap this one up," she said, taking a box that had not been opened. Her phone buzzed again, but she ignored it.

"It's all right. I've got this. I'm guessing you need to get to your computer. Before your phone explodes," he added.

"I guess I should. The sooner I get this over with, the better."

Dan had his back turned to her as he loaded the dishwasher and didn't reply. She went into her office, feeling unsettled. She could see he thought she was slipping back into her old routine.

But now that she did see a tactic that might save the open-space group, she couldn't turn her back on them. If she could find that bylaw and figure out how to use it, it would be a game changer.

Dan will appreciate this later, she consoled herself. *He wants this side to win, too. Even though he doesn't seem very happy right now,* she had to admit as she turned on her computer. *Not happy at all.*

JAMES PICKED UP ZOEY AT HER HOUSE AT seven o'clock in his grandmother's truck. Zoey would have been happy to run right out when she saw him pull up, but Lucy insisted that she wait for him to come to the door.

"I've heard a lot about him, and I'd like to meet him," Lucy said.

Zoey sighed and rolled her eyes. She hated to be treated as if she were in high school, but she knew it was no use arguing with her mother about this. She had talked about James a lot. Too much probably.

The doorbell rang. Zoey felt a flutter of nerves but tried to disguise it by acting annoyed with her mother. "All right, let's get this over with. I'm putting my jacket on right now. Just say hello, and we're out of here."

"That's fine. I'll get the door." Lucy opened the door. "You must be James. I'm Mrs. Bates. It's nice to meet you."

James smiled and held out his hand, looking sincerely pleased to meet her. "It's nice to meet you, Mrs. Bates."

Zoey could tell by Lucy's expression that she thought James was cute. He did look very handsome tonight, she thought, in a thick black sweater, a tweed sports jacket, and jeans. A blue scarf, which brought out the color of his eyes, was slung around his neck.

Zoey was glad she had decided to wear a nicer outfit than jeans and a sweater. She had on a black minidress with a swirly print, black tights, and boots.

"How are you enjoying your visit to Cape Light? Zoey told me that you've been living in

New York. It must be a huge change after that."

Great. Remind him how backwoodsy we are out here, Mom. That will help me tons, Zoey fumed.

"Yes, it's a big change but, so far, a good one for me. I thought I would miss the city. But I really don't."

Before her mother could drag out the conversation, Zoey zipped up her leather jacket. "I'm ready. We don't want to be late for the movie."

"Right." James checked his watch. "I think we'll be fine. As long as Bella doesn't act up."

Lucy was already familiar with Sophie's truck and its name. "I hope not. But if you have any trouble, just call me. I'll be in all night."

"Don't worry, we'll be fine." James had opened the door for her, and Zoey glanced over her shoulder as she walked out and gave her mother a small wave. Lucy blew her a little kiss.

In the truck, sitting side by side, Zoey felt suddenly self-conscious. She had spent time with James at the diner and at Sophie's house, but never alone like this. *It's just a date, Zoey. You've been on a zillion dates before. And he's just a guy. So get over it and act like a human.*

"We have plenty of time before the movie," Zoey admitted as James pulled away from the house. "I just said that so my mother wouldn't ask you any more questions. I'm sorry if it felt like she was interrogating you."

"I didn't mind. Your mom seems very nice. I can see her being a nurse," he added.

"She really loves what she does. It's perfect for her. She didn't go to college after high school. She worked in the diner when C.J. and Jamie were young and went back to school about ten years ago. It took her a long time to get her nursing degree, but she finally did."

"Good for her. I guess if you have a real commitment and don't give up, you can do some amazing things in life."

"That's what she always tells me. Though I hope I don't have to wait that long to get going in my career."

"I don't think you will," James said. "You seem very clear on what you want and how to get there."

Zoey was surprised at his observation. How could he know that about her already? They hardly knew each other. "How about you? You seem to be wandering a bit. But maybe you're not lost . . . as the saying goes."

He turned and met her gaze. She smiled at him, feeling her cheeks get a bit warm, and was glad for the darkness in the truck. "I read that in a book somewhere," she added. "No, come to think of it, not a book. A note someone left for me."

He laughed, his eyes back on the road. "One of my favorites. I even have a T-shirt with that saying. I guess I am wandering right now. But I don't feel lost. I know what I want to do with my life—write books. And that's a lot."

"Yes, it is. It's pretty major," Zoey agreed. She wasn't sure how they had gotten into such a serious conversation so quickly. She usually wasn't like this at all on a first date. It felt more like . . . the tenth? James was so easy to talk to. She felt as if she had known him a long time. And that was rare, too.

Still, she felt like it was time for some lighter talk. She didn't want to seem so super serious and freak him out. "I'm glad we're going to a Hitchcock movie tonight. I took a great film study course on him last semester. We had to see all the movies, even the early ones."

"I missed a few of those," he admitted. "*Rear Window* is my favorite. I haven't seen it in a long time."

"That figures. It's about a guy who's always watching people. I guess you identify with Jimmy Stewart?"

James laughed. "Maybe a little. He's stuck in a wheelchair. I don't know what my excuse is."

"It's a great movie, definitely near the top of my list. But my favorite is *Vertigo*. Amazing psychology. The poor detective is totally manipulated. He believes exactly what he's led to believe."

"Poor Jimmy Stewart. Again," James pointed out. "Since you're a psych major, I had a feeling you would like that one best."

"Makes sense, I guess." Zoey shrugged. Maybe he did know her better than she thought.

The theater was crowded, and coming early turned out to be a good thing. She and James chatted more after they found their seats, but once the film started, he was totally focused on the screen. And so was she. She liked that about him. It bugged her when people talked during a movie or poked her at some funny or scary part. She liked to be totally immersed in the film, and, obviously, so did he.

Though, at one point, he slipped his arm around her shoulders. It was a scary moment, when the dog is digging in the garden, and Zoey didn't mind at all.

After the film, they walked down the street to an Indian restaurant Zoey liked. She hoped James liked it, too, and also hoped it helped him see that the area was not as unsophisticated as he may have thought. The cafés in Newburyport offered all sorts of foods, from many cultures—though back in Cape Light one was hard-pressed to find anything more exotic than chowder, clam rolls, or burgers.

"Hmm. This is good." James tasted a bit of the appetizer, a pastry stuffed with a spicy meat mixture. "You know, I was thinking today, I never met anyone with the name Zoey before. I mean, I've heard the name and read it in books. But I don't think I ever had a friend named Zoey."

A friend? Was that all he thought of her? Zoey brushed aside the worry. Maybe he just didn't know what to call their relationship at this point. *At least he thinks of you as a friend,* she told herself.

She also wasn't sure if she should tell him the truth about her name. Where it had really come from.

"It is unusual. That's why I picked it," she finally replied.

"So it's not your real name?"

"It is my real name now," she explained. "But yes, I picked it for myself, back in middle school. My mother named me Elizabeth. I never liked it. I never liked being called Liz or Liza, and definitely not Beth or Betsy."

James smiled and sipped some water. "I can't see you as any of those names, either. But maybe that's because I know you as Zoey."

"Maybe. I just wanted a name that was unusual. And . . . I guess I wanted to put some distance between who I was and my past. I can see that now that I'm older."

He had stopped eating and put his fork down. "Did something happen to you when you were younger?"

Zoey nodded, still not sure how much she wanted to tell him. But now that she had started, it seemed impossible to tell only part of the story. She took a breath and sat back in her seat. "Lucy and Charlie are not my real father and mother. I mean, they feel real to me. But they adopted me about five years ago. That's why I said my real name is Zoey now. It's the name on my adoption certificate. Zoey Bates."

James stared at her wide-eyed. "Wow. I had no idea. I mean, your family seems so close."

So normal, she knew he meant. "We are close. Lucy and Charlie showed me what it's like to be part of a real family, to have parents who care about you. I never knew my real father, and my mother was in and out of our lives. I have a younger brother, Kevin. He used to live around here, but he was adopted by a wonderful family, too, a few years ago. Last year, they moved to Minnesota."

"I see. So you really have three brothers?"

Zoey nodded. "Kevin and I keep in touch over the phone and by Skype. But I'd love to visit him sometime. Anyway, that's pretty much my story. I didn't mean to go on and on," she added, hoping she hadn't bored him. Or worse yet, sounded like a character out of a soap opera.

"You weren't going on and on. I'm really interested to know more, to know all about you," he said. "How did you get connected with Lucy and Charlie? Were they trying to adopt another child?"

Zoey laughed. "No, not at all. I was running away from a foster home and ended up in the diner. My birth mother had died. I didn't have any money or anywhere to go. And I was sick, real sick. I could hardly stand up. Lucy made me come home with her, and she took care of me. I started living there, and after a few bumps in the road, let's say, Lucy and Charlie wanted to adopt me. And I wanted to stay with them and Jamie and C.J."

"Wow, you've had it rough, Zoey." James reached across the table and took her hand. "It's hard for me to believe. You seem so strong and together. Not at all like someone who had such a tough time growing up."

"I was pretty messed up for a while. Angry and all that. But Lucy and Charlie really helped me. I couldn't love them more if they were my real parents. I owe them a lot," she said quietly. "Most of all, they showed me that I could change. I didn't have to be Elizabeth Dugan, in that dark, angry place. I could be Zoey Bates. I could be happy."

"I'm glad you decided to be Zoey Bates. I like her a lot. And I admire her. Greatly." James smiled, and his compliment made her blush again. "Is that why you want to be an art therapist? To help kids who are going through similar things?"

Zoey nodded. "Exactly. I think I'd be good at it, too. At the center where I volunteer, I think I've helped a few kids make some progress. There's an internship there, over the winter break. I have an interview for it on Monday. But I'm probably not going."

She hadn't meant to tell him that. She hadn't meant to tell anyone. But all of her secrets seemed to pour out so easily when James looked at her in his soft, sweet way.

"You're not? But why? You just said how much you love the work. It would be great experience for you."

"I think so, too. It's sort of a long story. I can't work at the center over winter break because I have to work in the diner. Charlie needs a manager so he can run the town. He can't do two jobs at once anymore."

James looked upset by her explanation. "I guess it's hard to run a business and be mayor, too. But that doesn't seem very fair to you."

"I know. But my family really needs my help right now. That's the bottom line here," she said, sorry now that she had brought up the topic. She didn't want to have the same argument with James that she'd had with her parents—with James playing her part.

James sat back, taking a hint from her tone perhaps. "I know it's not my business, but I really think you should go to the interview. Don't cancel it."

"But what's the point? Even if they like me, I can't take the job."

"It will be a good experience for you, if nothing else. And maybe, if you make a good impression, they'll remember you if they need someone later. And you never know, something might happen out of the blue, and you might be able to work there this winter, after all."

Zoey shrugged, still not convinced.

He took her hand again and searched out her gaze with his own. "Just think about it, okay? I'm working at the diner Monday. I'll help you slip out if that's the problem."

That was part of the problem, but now he was taking that excuse away from her, too.

"All right. I'll think about it," she finally agreed.

"Good. That makes me very happy." His tone was sincere. "You're an awesome person, Zoey. I hate to see you hide your light under a bushel."

Zoey grinned. "That sounds like something my dad would say. He's got a lot of old-fashioned expressions."

James laughed. "I don't know where that came from. I've probably been hanging around my grandmother too long."

They enjoyed the rest of their dinner in a lighter mood and decided to walk around the harbor afterward. The streets and shop windows were decorated for Christmas, and the cobblestone lanes and squares seemed magical. So did the feeling of his arm around her shoulders as she asked him more about his own past. He knew so much about her now, it only seemed fair.

James told her how his family had lived in Boston when he was very young and later moved to Connecticut. His parents divorced when he was eleven years old, and his mother now lived in New York. "It was hard for a while," he admitted. "But there was no big drama. My parents made it as easy as possible for me and Miranda."

They had reached the park at the harbor and strolled down the walkway. The water was dark blue, the sky above an even darker shade, dotted by tiny white stars. It looked so beautiful tonight. Zoey tried to memorize the sight so she could use it in her art someday.

"Did you always want to be a writer?" she asked James suddenly.

"I think so. Though I guess I went through the usual stages boys do, wanting to be a pro athlete."

"I'd like to read more of your writing. The piece I read was so good, really interesting and clever." So far, she had only read one of his blog posts, but his talent was clear to her. "Have you had time to write since you came here? You always seem so busy at Sophie's house, and you're working at the diner now, too."

"I've been able to write a lot, usually early in the morning. My grandmother's been telling me family history—about her parents and grandparents. It's given me ideas for some stories that I'm working on now."

Zoey studied the expression in his eyes. "It must be coming out great. You look very . . . inspired." He did look inspired, his eyes bright and a wide smile lighting his face.

"I am inspired. But not by family history right now. I just think I want to kiss you."

Before Zoey could reply, he moved close and surprised her with a kiss. She closed her eyes and kissed him back, holding tight to his broad shoulders. She wasn't sure how long they stood together like that. She felt the world spinning around her. As if the stars in the blue-black sky had drifted down and were spinning inside her head. An absolutely wonderful feeling.

They suddenly heard voices. A big group of teenagers, coming their way. James stepped back, though he kept his arms around her in a loose embrace. "Guess we should head back to Bella now."

Zoey nodded. "Yeah, I guess we should."

"I had a wonderful time tonight. I hope you know that, Zoey. I feel as if . . . well, as if I've known you forever. It's so strange. But in a good way," he quickly added.

"I know what you mean. I feel the same about

you," she admitted. "And now you know my first name was Elizabeth. So you know all my secrets."

James laughed and dropped a kiss on her head. "I'm honored. But I suspect there are a few more hidden up there."

With their arms slung around each other, they walked back to the truck without talking at all. Zoey could rarely recall feeling happier.

EMILY HEARD JANE AND HER FRIENDS HOP down the stairs and take over the kitchen and family room again. Debate practice and pizza feast over, the girls were now in the baking-cupcakes phase of the sleepover. This would be followed by watching a movie and eating the cupcakes. Emily looked in on them as they poured batter into the tins. She trusted Jane in the kitchen more than she trusted herself and knew they didn't need, or want, her supervision. But she still peeked in from time to time, just to make sure the party was going well.

But with all the giggling and chatting—and the loud movie, which seemed to be about gymnastics or cheerleading—Emily ended up putting in earplugs. The noise was so distracting.

She had to wade through pages of tedious, boring legal language in the village constitution and amendments, dating back to the 1800s. But finally, she found the bylaw she had recalled. She read it over to be sure they could use it to block the vote, then printed out copies of the page.

Emily wasn't sure how long she'd been sitting there when she became aware of Dan standing in the doorway. She looked over at him, then pulled out the earplugs so she could hear what he was saying.

"I'm sorry. I had these things in my ears. The girls were getting a little noisy."

"The girls went upstairs over an hour ago. I think they're asleep."

"Really? I thought they were still watching TV." It felt as if Janie had brought her a cupcake just a few minutes ago. The crumpled wrapper was still on her desk, the candy-trimmed treat less than half-eaten. Emily felt a little guilty. She should have checked on them and made sure they had everything they needed before they went to bed. "Are they okay? Why didn't you call me? I would have helped settle them down."

"They're fine. Considering the amount of junk food they ate, I was expecting at least one stomachache."

Emily laughed. "Well, the night isn't over yet."

"We're getting there. Do you have any idea what time it is?"

Emily glanced at the time on her computer. At first she thought it said eleven fifteen, then realized a digit was missing. It was actually a few minutes past one. "Oh my gosh . . . how did it get so late?" She stared at him, honestly surprised.

"The way it usually does, Emily. Once you get hooked by some cause or issue, you zip up to your own planet. You definitely blasted off tonight, and please don't deny it."

"Yes . . . I know. I'm sorry. But I found the bylaw, Dan. Then I got caught up, checking to see if we could really use it and whether it's airtight."

His expression softened. "At least you found it. What is it all about exactly? You never really told me."

"It's very simple, actually. There's a bylaw in the village charter that states if a large enough group of citizens opposes a change to a village law, they can appeal to the county, and the county can then freeze a vote on the change for two years."

"And then what?"

"Well, that two-year freeze creates time for an independent review of the new zoning ideas. So now the open spacers need to give the county a solid reason for why the situation should be studied by an outside group. Impact on the wildlife and environment should be reason enough. But I want to find out if anyone has ever used this tactic before and what the possible pitfalls are."

"That's smart. But isn't there anyone else that can take it from here? There must be a lawyer or someone with good research skills in that group."

"I did think of passing this along. I'm just afraid some other volunteer won't be able to get all the information together as quickly as I can. There's hardly any time at all. I can also call some county officials and sound them out—people who know how these situations work and will talk to me off the record."

When he didn't reply, she said, "Please don't look at me like that. I'm not leading the charge, but I can provide the ammunition. And I want to see it through. I think this strategy can block the effort to overbuild and ruin the town. At least for two years. That should be long enough for people to see reason."

"Maybe," Dan agreed. "Charlie's term as mayor will be over by then."

"Unless he gets reelected or the mayor coming in has the same dumb idea." Emily paused and met her husband's questioning gaze. "I know what you're thinking. But I have no intention of running again—not in two years, not in twenty. No matter what my mother says."

"I believe you. Still, it's good to hear you say it," he admitted. "I just wonder if maybe you do want to jump back in and you don't even realize it." He paused, then finally said, "Is it all for the cause, or partly just to get back at Charlie? I know that's not your nature, but anybody would be tempted, all things considered."

Emily bristled and sat up straight in her chair. "If you can ask me that, then you obviously don't believe me. You, of all people, should know that I'm not doing this for spite."

Dan sighed. "I'm sorry. I shouldn't have put it like that. But you have to admit, from a distance, it does look like you're trying to undermine Charlie. There are a lot of people in town who are going to think you've gotten involved in this issue to undermine him and set yourself up to be reelected."

"I've asked myself that same question," she admitted. "And I'm certain, down to my toes, that this isn't about revenge. I know how it looks and what some people might think. But I learned a long time ago that you can't control what people think or say about you. All you can do is hope that your actions speak louder than anyone's gossip or mistaken judgments. This issue is important to me and to everyone—to Jane and our grandchildren. Even to Charlie's grandchildren, though he certainly doesn't see it that way."

Dan stood by her desk chair and rested his hands on her shoulders. "That is true, Em. And it's something I've always loved about you— you're your own person. I'm sorry for sounding as if I doubted that. I just worry about what's going to happen. You must see that everyone in town links you to the open-space group now.

Many people even think you're their leader. For better or worse, you're going to end up looking responsible for whatever happens. I hope you're ready for that."

She couldn't argue. She had practically been blamed for the melee at Village Hall—just by being there. There was definitely some truth to Dan's words. She just didn't know what to do about it.

Chapter Nine

Y OU'RE UP EARLY. AND YOU LOOK TOO pretty to be heading to the diner." Zoey's mother stood at the kitchen counter in her bathrobe, pouring herself a cup of coffee. "That's a cute outfit, honey."

"Thanks." Zoey was wearing a tunic top she had found in a thrift shop, with big, colorful flowers on a black background. The bell sleeves and neckline were very retro, and it went perfectly with her leggings and boots.

She grabbed a yogurt from the fridge and a bag of frozen blueberries. "I'm working at the diner after church. Sophie's truck wasn't working perfectly Friday night. James had to try the ignition a few times before we could get it started to go home. So I'm giving Sophie a ride to the service."

Lucy sat at the table across from her. "Just Sophie? Or is James going, too?"

"James, too." Zoey had sprinkled the yogurt with granola, chia seeds, frozen blueberries, and cinnamon, then stirred it all up. Her brother C.J. called the mixture Blue Health Glop. But what could you expect from a guy whose favorite breakfast was sausage patties smashed between two Pop-Tarts?

"How was your date? Did you have fun?" Lucy had been up when Zoey came in, but they hadn't talked much.

"It was great. James is really funny. And smart," she added. "And he's a really good writer. He showed me one of his articles the other day. It was published online. I'm going to read some of his fiction, too."

"He sounds like an interesting person. You said he plans to travel—anyplace in particular?"

Zoey glanced up. Lucy was trying to play it cool, but Zoey still picked up a distinct Mom-anxiety-vibe.

"Probably South America, to start. He wants to work on a farm for a while, maybe in Peru or Chile."

"How adventurous. Sounds like something a writer would do. When is he leaving, does he know?"

Zoey spooned up the last drop of her Blue Glop. "Mom, you are so obvious. I know what you're trying to say."

"What am I trying to say?"

"You're worried because I like James and he's not staying here very long."

Lucy shifted, holding her mug with both hands. "I can't say I didn't think of that, honey. You do seem to like this young man, more than I've seen you like anyone lately. He seems very nice and charming. But he is older than you, and he definitely has his plans."

Zoey rolled her eyes. "Two years. That's no big deal. And we've only been on one date. I can't believe you're going off on me like this."

"Okay, one date. But you work together now, and you see him at Sophie's house." Lucy's voice softened. "He's graduated college and he's out in the world. And you're still in school. And he isn't going to be here very long, from the sound of it."

"He's staying through the holidays. He thinks he'll have enough money to leave right after New Year's."

"That's less than a month," her mother pointed out.

Zoey shrugged. She picked up her bowl and mug and set them in the sink. "I know when New Year's is."

Lucy took breakfast ingredients out of the refrigerator—eggs, bread, and orange juice. Jamie would be downstairs soon, hungry enough to eat the kitchen table. Zoey planned to be gone by then.

"I just don't want to see you get involved and then feel bad when he leaves. That's all." Lucy set a frying pan on the stove. "I know I'm interfering. But I wouldn't be a very good mother if I didn't say it. I love you, sweetie. You've had a lot of difficult separations in your life. I don't want to see you get your feelings hurt—if you can help it."

Zoey knew that what Lucy said was true. Her life had been a series of painful separations and losses, until Lucy and Charlie had found her. Zoey sometimes wondered how she was still able to trust people and open up to new relationships. It certainly wasn't as easy for her as it was for most people. But she also knew she had to try. She couldn't hang back, afraid to make connections—or open her heart. What was life all about, anyway, if not that?

"I know what you're trying to say. But it's totally cool. I won't get my feelings hurt. I promise." She stood next to her mother and kissed her cheek. "Okay?"

Lucy slipped her arm around Zoey's waist and gave her a quick squeeze. "Okay . . . but it's not the sort of thing you can promise, sweetheart. I wish it was." Her mother gazed at her with a wistful smile. "See you in church, I guess."

"Sure, see you there."

Zoey headed off for the orchard, relieved to be done with the little heart-to-heart. She knew Lucy meant well, but sometimes she just didn't get it. James was different. He wasn't like other guys.

Still, the warning got under her skin. *Maybe I'm not that good with people moving in and out of my life. But I've worked on that. I've gotten a lot better with it. She should give me some credit.*

And maybe James isn't going to be around for very long. That's fine. I'd regret it more if I don't get to know him. And it seems too late to worry about any of this now.

Zoey pulled up to Sophie's big house and then drove around to the side door. It was easier for Sophie to walk down a step or two there instead of the long flight at the front porch. No matter how strong Sophie claimed to be, Zoey knew that since her illness last winter, Sophie wasn't that sure-footed; now she had to take more care on stairs, or even walking out in the orchard.

Zoey jumped out of the car and knocked on the door. She waited, but no one answered. She knocked again and waited, checking her watch. Maybe they were upstairs, still getting dressed.

Mac ran up to her, wagging his tail. He ambled up the steps and scratched the door, then stared at her as if to say, "We both want in, and you can reach the doorknob."

"All right, if you say so," Zoey said to the dog. She opened the door, calling out as she walked through the mudroom. "Sophie? James? I knocked but nobody heard me."

"We're over here, Zoey. My grandma fell . . ."

Zoey ran toward the sound of his voice and

found them in the foyer, at the foot of the stairs. Sophie was dressed for church but stretched out on the floor, James kneeling by her side.

"Oh my gosh . . . what happened?" Zoey knelt down on Sophie's other side and caught the hand that was offered. Sophie looked pale and scared but forced a smile.

"I just got clumsy, dear. Lost my footing on that bottom step. I need to throw out these old house slippers . . ."

Mac had run to Sophie's aid also, and now nosed his way into the group and licked Sophie's face. She laughed and stroked his muzzle. "Now, now, don't you get worried, too."

James gently tugged the dog's collar and pushed him aside. "Does it hurt anywhere, Grandma? I want to help you up, but I don't think we should move you if you broke a hip or anything like that."

"Did you call for an ambulance?" Zoey asked.

"Ambulance? I don't need an ambulance," Sophie insisted. "I've fallen out of plenty of trees and off ladders. Even off a roof once. This was nothing, just a step. Help me up, both of you. Grab under my arms and give me a boost."

Zoey looked at James. "Should we get her up or call somebody?"

He sighed, looking as confused as she felt. "She insists that nothing hurts. I guess it will be okay."

"Of course it will be okay. Wouldn't I know

by now if my leg or my hip or my big toe was busted? Now come on. I've seen enough of the ceiling. We could use a splash of paint up there, too, by the way."

Reluctantly, and very gently, Zoey and James helped Sophie to a sitting position. "Saints be praised. I thought you were going to leave me there like a giant turtle on her back."

"You're sure nothing hurts, Grandma?" James asked again.

"Give me a minute. Let me get my bearings."

Her upswept hairdo had shifted to one side, quite a few pins and strands dangling. She still looked pale and shaky, Zoey thought, no matter how she tried to hide it.

"I think you need to go to a doctor or a hospital and get checked out," Zoey said. "I know you don't want to, but just to be safe. It's the smart thing to do."

"Why did you go upstairs again? I thought you were ready to leave for church." James sat on the step next to his grandmother and took her pulse, looking grim as he timed it against his watch.

"I forgot my reading glasses. I like to follow along in the Bible when the Scripture is read aloud."

"You should have told me. I would have gotten them," he said.

"I should have a large-print Bible. That would

have solved it completely. I wish someone would get me that for Christmas, instead of more sweaters or knickknacks."

"Oh, so that's the problem. We'll have to tell the doctor you fell because you don't have a large-print Bible?" His tone was half serious and half teasing. "Seriously, Grandma, your pulse is fast. I want to take you to the hospital or an urgent care clinic somewhere. And don't argue about it. We don't have to call an ambulance, but you need to be checked out. If anything is wrong with you, I won't forgive myself. I'm supposed to be taking care of you, not letting you fall down the stairs."

Zoey's heart went out to him. He looked very upset, as if Sophie's fall had been his fault.

"Now, now... what are you supposed to do? Follow me around like Mac and watch my every step? It's my own fault. I should have been holding tighter to the banister. And I need to give up these old slippers, as comfortable as they are..." Sophie's voice trailed off and she sighed. Finally, she nodded. "All right. If you feel that way, we'll go. But it will be a big waste of time. I'd rather go to church."

"I think we have to miss church today," James replied. "And I'm happy to waste my time to make sure you're fine."

"I can take you to a clinic," Zoey offered.

James looked relieved. "That would be great. I

250

was just thinking I should call my aunt Evelyn."

"Evelyn? Don't you dare." Sophie's tone was as sharp as Zoey had ever heard it. "Let's not call Miss Bossy Pants just yet. Then my pulse really will jump the chart."

Sharing a smile, James and Zoey hoisted Sophie up and helped her into the kitchen. Zoey put boots on her feet, and James found her coat. She winced a bit when Zoey slipped her coat on, and Zoey found an ice pack for her left wrist, which seemed to be a little swollen.

A few minutes later they were in Zoey's car, headed for an urgent care clinic that was near the highway. Sophie was in the backseat, her wrist propped up on a pillow.

When they reached the clinic, Zoey pulled up to the front door. James jumped out and came back with a wheelchair. He looked even more worried as they helped Sophie into the chair and wheeled her inside.

"I hope Aunt Evelyn isn't mad at me for not calling her. I'm sure she would want to know that you fell and I took you here, Grandma."

"We'll let her know in due time. No need to make a drama of this," Sophie replied. "I bet I'll be home trimming our tree tonight."

Zoey followed them inside and waited while Sophie told a nurse about her fall and handed over her insurance cards. It was almost eleven, and Zoey was due at the diner at noon. She considered calling Charlie, but decided to call Lucy instead.

"I didn't make it to church after all. Sophie fell and we had to take her to the urgent care clinic. We just got here, and she's talking to a nurse."

"Oh, dear, that isn't good. Is she all right? Did she break anything?"

"I don't think so. She keeps saying nothing hurts. But her wrist might be sprained."

"I hope it's nothing more than that. Poor thing. She must be shaken up. It's hard to take a fall when you're that age."

Zoey had to smile. "She doesn't seem too shaken. We had to talk her into coming here. She can't wait to get home and work on her Christmas tree."

Her mother laughed. "That's Sophie. I hope she goes easy on those doctors. Don't worry about the diner. I'll talk to your father. If he can't get Trudy, I'll go in for a while."

Zoey felt bad that Lucy was covering for her again, especially since Lucy had planned to go shopping today. There were only two weeks left before Christmas.

"Thanks, Mom. I really don't want to just leave Sophie and James here before I know how she is."

"I understand. You stay. And give Sophie a hug from me. I hope it's nothing. Tell her I'll say a prayer, and I'll tell Reverend Ben, too, okay?"

"I will." By the time Zoey ended the call, Sophie was being wheeled out of the admitting area by an orderly. James walked into the waiting area and sat down in the chair next to Zoey.

"They're going to take X-rays and check for a concussion, though I don't think she hit her head. But better safe than sorry," he added.

"Absolutely."

"I nearly freaked when I heard her shout and found her on the floor, right before you came. It was scary," he admitted.

"I know. I got scared when I saw her, too. But I think she'll be fine."

"I hope so." He reached out and took hold of her hand. "Thanks for bringing us, Zoey. I'm just grateful that out of everybody, you're the one here."

His warm look seemed to say much more, and Zoey returned the gentle pressure of his touch. "You don't have to thank me. I'm glad I could help. It was a lucky thing that we were planning to go to church together. You would have had to call an ambulance. Or Evelyn. And Sophie didn't seem to like either of those ideas."

He smiled. "I feel like you were meant to be there this morning, to help us." He shrugged. "I don't know why. I just do."

Zoey didn't know what to say. She met his glance a moment and looked away. They sat quietly for a while, holding hands.

After a bit, James said, "But I did tell my aunt Evelyn. She texted me while Grandma was getting the X-ray. She wanted to know why we weren't in church yet, so I told her what was going on. She should be here any minute. I hope Grandma isn't mad at me, but it was the right thing to do."

"It was," Zoey agreed. "And you can use your aunt's help. Sophie doesn't like to admit it, but she listens to Evelyn."

A nurse came by holding a clipboard. "James Potter?"

James jumped up. "That's me."

"We just examined your grandmother and gave her an EKG. Her blood pressure and heart rate seem fine. We also X-rayed her left wrist, and there are no broken bones, just a mild sprain. But we still need an MRI of her head. So it will be a while longer."

"All right. Thanks for the update. Can I go inside and wait with her?"

"Sure. Just through those doors, you'll see some patient beds, separated by curtains. You can both go back. It's all right," the nurse added, glancing at Zoey.

Zoey followed James and they quickly found Sophie. She was still wearing her dress and sweater, but her feet were bare, her body covered by a thin blanket. The back of the bed was raised so that she could sit up. Her left wrist was wrapped in an elastic bandage and covered with an ice pack.

"There you are. I told the nurse to go and get you," she greeted them. "Can I go home now? Maybe you can ask somebody."

"Not yet, Grandma. They need to give you a few more tests."

"Fiddlesticks. They just like to use all this machinery. How many pictures of my skeleton does the doctor need to see?"

"They want an MRI of your head. To make sure there's no concussion," James explained.

"To make sure I have some brains left. That's the real reason." Sophie sighed and smoothed down the blanket. "I had so much to do today. I've missed the Christmas Fair committee meeting, too. I wanted to start on my crafts. And decorate the tree. I think we can still do the tree later . . . don't you?"

Her glance at James and then Zoey was just as hopeful as a child's. Zoey knew that neither of them had the heart to refuse her. "Maybe tomorrow or another night this week would be best, Grandma," James said gently.

"I think James is right—" Zoey began, but before she could finish her sentence, the curtain was pulled aside with a swishing sound.

"Mom, are you all right? I knew when I didn't see you in church that something must have happened. James said you fell. Why didn't anyone call me?"

"Hello, Evie. Calm down, I'm fine." Sophie stared at James as she answered her daughter. *What's she doing here?* Zoey could almost hear her say aloud.

"Aunt Evelyn sent me a text while you were getting X-rayed," James explained. "I'm sorry we didn't call you sooner, Aunt Evie. We just wanted to get Grandma to a doctor right away. They haven't found anything wrong so far except a sprained wrist."

"I wish you had called an ambulance and gone to the hospital. This is just a clinic. Mom, does your wrist hurt very much?"

"Just a twinge, dear. No need to fret. The doctor said it was just a mild sprain. I'm sure they'll let me go in no time."

"Let's not rush it. We want to be sure you're all right. You never know with a fall." Evelyn leaned over the bed and smoothed the blanket. She looked like Sophie, Zoey reflected. A short woman with fair hair, a round face, and a plump figure. Her skin was smooth and her eyes bright, like her mother's. But she had not inherited Sophie's peaceful, optimistic disposition.

"She had a full physical and a test for her heart. The doctor said everything was fine," James reported.

Evelyn looked over at him. "Where were you

when she fell? Did she have to wait very long for you to come?"

"I was right in the kitchen, waiting for her to come downstairs."

"I know what you're driving at, Evelyn, but this isn't James's fault. He's been keeping a good eye on me. It's just that my slippers are too worn and loose. One of them slipped off my foot as I came down. That's what happened, and poor James can't be blamed because I'm too stubborn to give up my comfortable slippers."

Zoey could see that James felt self-conscious, even a bit embarrassed. He felt bad enough about his grandmother's fall without his aunt rubbing it in.

Evelyn sat back in her chair and set her big purse squarely on her lap. "It's more than the slippers, Mom. It's that big old house and everything that goes with it. I'm not blaming James," she added. "But it just goes to show that even with someone else in the house, it's still not a safe place for you."

"Oh, bother. I knew I'd be hearing that old song sooner or later," Sophie grumbled. "Can't you take a tiny bit of pity on me, Evie? At least wait until I'm out of this bed."

A nurse walked into the room with two orderlies. "We're ready to give you the MRI now, Mrs. Potter."

"Great, let's roll. You folks came just in the

nick of time," Sophie said to the orderlies, who cranked down the back of the bed and secured her in place with a belt.

The nurse smiled, looking amused. "It won't take long. Your family can wait here."

Evelyn stood up and blocked her path. "I'm Mrs. Stotlemeir, Mrs. Potter's daughter. Can I speak to you a minute about my mother?"

James caught Zoey's eye and tilted his head, signaling to follow him out of the cubicle as Sophie's bed was rolled away. They walked back to the waiting area, leaving Evelyn with the nurse.

"I think this is going to take a while," James said. "Maybe even longer, now that Evie is here. She'll drive me back to the orchard. You don't have to wait."

Zoey had wondered about that; she was feeling a bit intrusive now, since she wasn't family. It seemed that Evelyn wanted to discuss serious family matters—even if Sophie and James didn't.

"I guess I will go if you think you're okay. I'll call you later and see how she's doing."

James looked pleased to hear that. "Call anytime. I'm on the schedule tomorrow at the diner. I'll see you before your interview."

Her interview for the internship . . . With all the excitement about Sophie, she had nearly forgotten. Zoey was still wrestling with second thoughts about keeping the appointment, but she smiled and nodded. "It isn't until the afternoon. I guess I will see you."

"Don't worry. Jot down some questions you think they'll ask and figure out your answers. Speak from your heart. I know you'll do really well."

"I'll try."

"They would be lucky to have you, Zoey. I think they already know that." He leaned over and kissed her lips, a fleeting, intense kiss that caught Zoey by surprise. She held on to his shoulders, feeling her knees go weak for a crazy moment. She stepped away from him, not knowing what to say. "Let me know about Sophie," she murmured, then turned and quickly left the clinic, not daring to look back.

As Zoey headed to the village, she felt as if she were driving on a cloud. The road flew by, the bare branches and brush changing to houses and then shops on Main Street. She didn't see any of it, her mind filled with images of James, his smile, his voice, and his touch. She was feeling closer to him every time they were together. He was so caring and concerned about his grandmother, handling the situation in such a mature way. He didn't need to thank her so profusely for helping. She hadn't done much. But that was sweet of him, too, she thought.

James was different from other guys she had known. It had sounded so dumb and simplistic when she'd tried to explain that to Lucy that morning, but she didn't know any other way to say it. She had never known anyone quite like him before.

Was she starting to feel too much for him too quickly? Zoey wasn't sure. But she couldn't help looking forward to seeing him tomorrow. To seeing him more and more.

SOPHIE WAS IN THE KITCHEN MONDAY morning when she heard a knock on the front door. She called out to James, then remembered that he was in the barn, searching for paint and brushes. He had to be at the diner in a few hours and wanted to get some work done around the house before he left.

The knocking sounded again, and she called out, "I'm coming. Just a minute."

Mac ran ahead, barking so much she wasn't sure her visitor had heard a word. But she couldn't shout any louder or move any faster this morning. She felt even achier than she had last night.

Falls were like that; it took a while for all the sore muscles to check in. She had forced herself to get out of bed and get dressed at her usual time, though the aches urged her to sleep late. But if Evelyn or Una came by unannounced, Sophie knew it wouldn't help her case one bit to be found in her bathrobe.

She knew it wasn't either of her daughters visiting now. They always let themselves in. She opened the door a crack and saw Reverend Ben.

"Hello, Sophie." His warm smile crinkled up the corners of his eyes. "I wanted to see how you're doing. I heard you had a fall?"

"I took a tumble, Reverend. No real damage, thank goodness. I think the angels caught me." She smiled and waved him in. "I'm just having a second cup of coffee. Will you sit with me awhile?"

"I'd like that very much." Reverend Ben followed her inside and down the hallway.

"Don't mind the house. We're in the middle of cleaning up and painting. And Christmas decorating on top of that." Macintosh followed them into the kitchen, where he circled the minister's legs, his tail wagging. "Don't let Mac bother you, either. He just wants attention."

"Don't we all." Reverend Ben leaned over and stroked the dog's thick fur, not caring a whit about his black pants. Sophie thought she would offer a lint brush before he left. A minister had to look tidy when he was out and about his business.

"Can I help you with anything?" the reverend asked. "You shouldn't be serving me with a bandage on your wrist."

"I'm fine. It's my left hand. Another blessing," she added. "But you can grab the coffeepot while I bring you a mug."

They sat at the table together, and Reverend Ben poured the coffee. There were muffins left from breakfast, which she offered him. No matter what he said about watching his waistline, he could never resist Sophie's baking.

"My, these are good. Apple cinnamon, my favorite."

Sophie smiled. All of her baked treats were his favorite, but she didn't bother to remind him. "I'll give you a few to take home. James complains I cook too much for him."

"I'm surprised you're able to cook at all. Does your wrist hurt much?"

"Only when I forget and try to use it. I've picked apples and handled three kids under five years old with a dislocated shoulder—or worse. This is nothing. I can still do everything I need to do for Christmas."

"I hope so. But you aren't having your family here for the holiday, are you?"

She knew Reverend Ben didn't mean anything by it, but the way he worded the question irked her all the same. "I don't see why not. It's almost two weeks away. My wrist will be fine by then. Besides, I struck a deal with my children about having my Christmas get-together here, like I always do. My daughters tried to wriggle out of it yesterday, but I made them stick to their promise."

Sophie felt a little worked up just recalling

the conversation. Once Evelyn had brought her home, Una arrived, and both insisted that she couldn't have Christmas after all—despite the deal they all agreed to on Thanksgiving.

"What sort of deal was that?" Reverend Ben sipped his coffee, his eyes curious behind his gold-rimmed glasses.

"My children have been after me to give up this house and the orchard, Reverend. Ever since I was sick last winter, it's just gotten worse and worse."

"Yes, I remember." Reverend Ben had been very attentive to her during her illness, visiting while she was in the hospital and after she came home. Bringing books, flowers, news of the church and village. He had been a good friend and a bright spot during a long, lonely winter.

He had also been privy to visits with her family, and she was sure they had tried to enlist his help in persuading her to their thinking. But the reverend, good friend and fair-minded as he was, had not taken sides. Sophie was grateful to him for that, too.

"Evelyn wouldn't let me have the family here for Thanksgiving," Sophie explained. "She said it was too much work. But I got them to agree I could have Christmas here. In return, I promised to think about putting the place up for sale. The house needs some attention whether I stay or go. That's why James is doing all this painting and repair work. But I'm sure my kids think that's a sign that they're wearing me down. Even though I have no idea what I want to do."

"It's a difficult decision, for everyone," the reverend said gently. "I guess your mishap yesterday brought this all to the surface again."

"Like a big green sea monster rising from the waves." Sophie waved her hands and made a funny face. Reverend Ben laughed, but she could see the understanding in his eyes. "Evelyn wanted me to go home with her after the clinic. Lucky for me, James is here."

"That is fortunate. But how do you feel about selling the property now? Have you given it more thought?"

"Night and day. It's all I can think about. But not even falling down on my bottom has helped me get to the bottom of it. I'm so confused, Reverend. More than I've ever been in my life. On one hand, I'm coming to see their point of view. They do worry so about me, whether I think they ought to or not. They just do. That's only gotten worse, and it's never going to get better. It's starting to feel selfish to stick to my guns like this. Just yesterday at the hospital, Evie said, 'Can't you see we're worried sick about you? Why are you doing this to us?'" Sophie sighed and shook her head. "She looked like she was going to cry. I never thought I was a self-centered mother, but now I'm thinking maybe I am."

Reverend Ben leaned over and patted her hand. "Don't be so hard on yourself, Sophie. You're the least selfish or self-centered person I've ever met. Your children have your welfare at heart, no question. But you have your own needs and concerns, as well. You've lived here your entire life, from the moment you came into the world."

"Right in that back bedroom," Sophie said with a proud smile. "My mother was late for everything. She left it too long to get to the hospital." She laughed, and Reverend Ben did, too. But once the mirthful moment passed, she felt a wave of doubt come over her again. "I'm just so confused, Reverend. Do you have any suggestions for me? You're probably the one person I'd really listen to."

Reverend Ben smiled kindly, his eyes bright. "That's quite a compliment, coming from you, Sophie. But I'm sorry, I have no suggestions. None I should share, anyway. No one can tell you what to do or when to do it. But I hope you can quiet the voices of your family, and those of your mind, too. And hear the advice that comes from deep in your heart. And feel at peace with whatever decision you arrive at, knowing it's the right thing to do. The right thing for *you* to do."

"I know what you mean, Reverend. I've asked the good Lord for some guidance. But so far, I don't feel that's helped me get any closer to the answer—unless there's some message for me right under my nose that I can't see."

"It happens that way sometimes. Don't give up on your prayers. I'll pray for you, too."

"Thank you, Reverend. I know that you and Carolyn always have your family at the parsonage for Christmas Day, but I hope you can all stop by here and say hello at some point in the day. Whether I'm at peace with it in my heart or not, I have a feeling this could be my last Christmas here."

Reverend Ben looked sad at her statement. "Let's hope and pray for the best in this situation, for all involved. Whatever that may be," he said. "And we'd be delighted to stop by on Christmas, Sophie. We would be honored."

Sophie nodded, feeling suddenly too teary-eyed to speak. But Reverend Ben was the sort of friend who understood how you felt and what you were thinking before you even said a word. He was a blessing in their church—and in her life.

ZOEY FELT LIKE A CAT CAPTURED IN A BURLAP sack as she struggled to change her outfit in the diner's tiny restroom—exchanging her waitress uniform for black wool pants, a light blue tailored blouse, and a gray tweed blazer. Mondays were usually slow, and the lunch rush had passed, too, so few customers would come in before closing. Trudy was not on the schedule today, but James had promised to wait the tables and do his job, too, so that Zoey could slip out for an hour or two.

She certainly hoped Charlie didn't decide to run down from his office for a surprise visit and find his new manager had flown the coop. But she and James had figured out a story to cover that, too.

As Zoey emerged, she felt another bout of cold feet. How crazy was it to interview for a job that you knew you couldn't accept?

James finished taking an order from a table across the room, and headed toward her. "All set to go, I see. You look awesome, Zoey. Do you have an extra copy of your résumé?"

She nodded, battling another wave of nerves as she pulled on her jacket. "I have about ten copies. And copies of the recommendations from my professors. And two pens that write, and everything else I might need. I'm just not sure why I'm doing this," she admitted. "What's the point? Even if I get the job, I can't take it."

His gaze was sympathetic. "Think positive, Zoey. You never know what might happen. Maybe a new manager for the diner will drop out of the sky. Or maybe the diner will burn down," he added, making her laugh. "Maybe another job at the center will open later on, and you'll make such a great impression on them today, they'll call you first." He gently brushed back a strand of hair that had fallen on her cheek. "I know you're scared, and it seems like a huge effort to do this. But in the long run, you might be very happy you made the effort."

Zoey nodded and zipped up her jacket. "Thanks, Coach. I needed that. I'll try not to be too long."

"Take your time. I've got it under control here," James promised. "I was only kidding about the diner burning down."

She laughed at him. "I hope so."

He gave her one of those smiles that seemed to warm her soul. "Good luck, Zoey. Though I'm sure you don't need it. How could anyone resist you?" James leaned over and quickly kissed her. Zoey felt a thrill down to her toes and a lightness of heart that melted her worries.

On the short drive to Beverly, her mind flip-flopped between her anxiety and James's encouraging words. When she reached the center, she parked in the front, near the offices; it was a part of the building where she rarely ventured. Although she had volunteered there for almost a year, she hardly ever walked into the lobby or spoke to the receptionist, who sat at a desk near a waiting area.

"Zoey Bates. I'm here for an interview with Ms. Foster."

"Go right in, Ms. Bates, first office on the left. Ms. Foster is expecting you."

"Thank you." Zoey nodded and forced a smile. All the articles she had read online about interviews said to make sure you smile a lot, even if you don't feel like it, because smiley people are statistically more likely to be hired.

The executive offices were very modest. The door to Ms. Foster's office was open, and Zoey knocked. A woman with dark hair, streaked with gray, sat behind a desk, typing very quickly on her keyboard.

She looked up and met Zoey's glance over the edge of her red-framed glasses. "Come in, please. You must be Zoey Bates."

"Yes, I am. Nice to meet you, Ms. Foster."

"No need to be formal. You can call me Beth. Have a seat. I've seen you around the center. I understand that you've been volunteering here?"

"Yes, for almost a year. I was taking a psych class and our professor offered extra credit if we volunteered twenty hours. But I really like working with the kids, so I continued coming."

"That's great. I have a recommendation here from one of the counselors you've been working with. She's very impressed." Beth took off her glasses and leaned back in her chair. "Tell me, Zoey, why do you want to be an art therapist?"

"I've always loved drawing and painting and making collages. People say I have some talent," she added modestly. "But I don't think I want to be a professional artist and sell my work and all that. I do it for my own enjoyment and because it helps me express my feelings and figure out things. When I was younger and going through a lot of difficult times in my life—a few really dark places—making art really helped me. Now that I've taken a few psychology courses, I think it would be so great to do that as a career. To help kids who are struggling feel better about themselves and about their lives. Art can really help when kids, or even adults, aren't able to talk about what's bothering them."

Beth had been listening with a thoughtful expression. "I see. So your interest in this field comes out of your life experience. That kind of firsthand insight will help you a lot if you ever get your degree in this area."

"I'm definitely going to get my degree. Even if it takes me forever." Zoey realized too late she had totally blurted, not a good move in an interview. All the articles said that. She felt the color rise in her cheeks and she looked down at her lap.

"I hope it doesn't take that long," Beth said with a small smile. "I meant to say, that's a very positive and inspiring story."

"Thanks. But I hope you don't think I told you all that just to get the job?"

"Not at all." Beth looked down at Zoey's résumé again.

Zoey remembered she was supposed to ask

questions, too. "Can you tell me a little about the position—what I'd be doing every day?"

"I was just about to. The intern will work with me and Dr. Simpson, assisting us in screening new patients. You'll also sit in on sessions and handle some paperwork."

Zoey knew who Dr. Simpson was, though she didn't have much contact with him as a volunteer. He had a reputation for being amazing with troubled kids. She thought that she would like working with Beth, too. She seemed smart, calm, and easy to talk to—someone Zoey could learn a lot from.

They talked about the courses Zoey had taken so far and those she had scheduled for the spring. A few minutes later, Beth thanked her for coming in. "It's been a pleasure meeting you, Zoey. We're making our decision soon."

Zoey stood up and grabbed her purse, then shook Beth's hand. "Thank you for taking the time to see me today," she said, just as she recalled from her prep articles. "I look forward to hearing from you."

Beth smiled in a warm, kind way. "Thank you, Zoey. I hope to see you around the center either way."

Zoey checked her watch as she walked out to her car. She would be back in the village in fifteen minutes. She had only been gone from the diner an hour. It had all worked out.

Still, Zoey wasn't sure if she had made the right impression. Beth seemed to like her, but she also seemed like a nice person who would act interested in everyone. What did she mean by "Hope to see you around the center either way"? *That could mean she doesn't think I'll get the job,* Zoey thought.

Her head was spinning and it took her a moment to remember that even if she was offered this internship, she couldn't take it. Her father had made up his mind, and he wouldn't budge. With all the pressure he was under right now, it was a terrible time to ask him about it again.

But James had been right; the interview had been a good experience. Of course, she hoped that they chose her. But part of her hoped they chose someone else. She would feel so awful refusing the job, she didn't know if she could face it.

Chapter Ten

"SO I GUESS WE'RE NOT GOING TO THE MALL after all?" Jane stood in the doorway of Emily's office on Monday afternoon, a schoolbook tucked under her arm and a frustrated expression on her pretty face.

Emily had her hand over the telephone, several documents opened at once on her laptop, and others spread out on her desk. The office seemed dark. Had the sun gone down already? These winter days . . . She checked the time and felt a sudden panic. How had it gotten so late? Jane had been waiting almost two hours?

"I'm so sorry, honey . . . I just can't get off the phone. These documents are a complete mess." She could tell from Jane's expression that her explanation wasn't cutting it. "Let's go after dinner. I'll make something fast. Hamburgers," Emily said, suddenly inspired.

All she needed now was the meat, rolls, and everything else that went with it . . . Maybe she could text Dan and ask him to pick up some takeout?

Just like the old days, a little voice chided her. *The old days that you said were over.*

"I have a test tomorrow, Mom. I can't go tonight." Jane didn't usually sigh and pout, but she looked on the verge right now.

A voice on the phone drew her attention. "Emily? Are you still there? I didn't get the changes to page three."

"Can I call you back, Martin? In a minute, I promise." Emily ended the call with Martin Becker without giving him a chance to reply. She turned to Jane with her full attention. "I'm really sorry. They asked me to quickly look over a few documents that are going to the county executive's office. I never thought I would get stuck here all afternoon."

Not to mention for the rest of the night, Emily added silently. *Dan will love that.* But the documents outlining the SOS appeal were a mess. The group had an appointment on Friday at the county office, and all the materials for their appeal had to be hand-delivered by tomorrow noon.

Jane, of course, was not interested in any of those reasons for missing their shopping trip. Emily had promised her a new outfit for the debate on Friday, and she wanted to keep that promise. As usual, she had been walking too fine a line today.

"Let's see. How about tomorrow after school?

Or tomorrow night? You usually have Tuesdays free."

"There's a game tomorrow, Mom." Jane's tone suggested Emily should have known. "And I have a study group for the science final after that."

A game? Emily didn't see that on her phone calendar and quickly typed it in. She had already had to miss one game on the weekend and hoped she didn't miss another. The season was almost over, and Jane's team was going into a play-off round.

"I can go to the mall Wednesday if you pick me up at school. But on Thursday I have a presentation for English, so I wanted to work on that Wednesday night."

Emily sighed and put her phone down. "I'm sorry, honey. I have to be someplace on Wednesday. At another meeting," she admitted. "How about Thursday? I know you don't have a game that day."

Jane looked alarmed. "Thursday is so close. What if we don't find anything? And I still have to practice my opening statement that night."

"It won't be hard to find something nice. You look good in everything. We'll come right home, and I'll help you rehearse. You could do that debate tomorrow, Jane. It's only natural to be nervous about getting up in front of an audience, but once you get going, you'll be fine. Remember what we said about picking out a friendly face in the crowd—like me or Dad?" She was teasing a bit now, but hoped her words were reassuring.

"I know." Jane finally smiled. "But I'd rather not be shopping the night before."

Jane was more like Dan, very organized and always prepared well ahead. She had taken on none of Emily's last-minute tendencies, which was something Emily usually admired about her. Though not at the moment.

"We'll go right from school. It won't take long," Emily promised.

The phone rang and Emily checked the number. Martin Becker again. She sighed and let voice mail take the message.

Dan suddenly appeared in the doorway, peeking over Jane's head. "Hi, everybody, what's for dinner?"

He's home already? There goes my plan to have him shop.

"Nothing yet," Emily answered honestly. "Jane and I were just about to go out—"

"About two hours ago," Jane cut in.

"But I got held up. So we never made it."

"Another Lillian emergency? Did she run out of Epsom salts again?"

A silly joke, but it was actually true that her mother had once called late at night, asking Emily to run to a twenty-four-hour store for Epsom salts. She was soaking her feet in hot water for some reason and hoped Emily could bring the necessary salts before the water cooled off.

"I was asked to proofread the appeal documents that the open-space group put together. But it's a mess. And the packet has to go to the county executive tomorrow."

"So you had to revise it?"

"More like rewrite it from scratch. It's still not done. They caught us just as we were walking out the door, right, Jane?"

Jane stood with her arms crossed over her chest, looking unhappy.

Emily got up from her desk, slipping her phone in a pocket. "I'll leave this for now. Let's figure out dinner."

"I'll get the menus." Jane's tone was resigned as she headed to the kitchen for the file of take-out menus they kept handy. They hadn't used them that much lately, Emily reflected.

"Sorry about the takeout. I'm going to try the Crock-Pot again tomorrow. A chicken curry thing," she promised, knowing Dan liked spicy foods.

He was not distracted by her tactic. "Emily, you're doing it again. You know that, right?"

"I know. But this time they really ambushed me, honestly. It's just this one last push. I tried to hand it off, like you said. But I'm the only one who seems to know how to navigate this phase, and what to say to win the appeal. They've got the research about how development would stress the environment. It's enough to show cause for further study—and freeze the new zoning—but it has to be presented clearly. And they don't have much time."

"I know all that, Em. I care about preserving the village as much as anybody. But I care about having a nice Christmas, all three of us together for once, even more. So you missed a shopping trip with Janie. No big deal. I know that will work out. Meanwhile, have we done any Christmas shopping? Have we put up a tree? If it wasn't for the lights I put up outside last week, you wouldn't even know a holiday is coming around here."

"Janie's been very busy, too," Emily pointed out. "She didn't want to put up the tree until the debate was over."

"Like mother, like daughter," Dan said with a reluctant grin. "I just hope you won't be like this all through the holidays. I'm getting worried about that, no matter what you say."

"I'm sorry," she said sincerely. "I know what this looks like, but please don't worry. My part is totally and completely over this week. I'm rewriting this appeal and going with them to see the county executive on Friday, and that's it. I've already told Martin Becker and Marion Ross. And my mother," she added for good measure.

"Jane's debate is Friday, right after school."

"Dan, please. How could you think I'd possibly forget that?" She didn't mean to sound sharp, but she felt hurt. Hadn't she been the one coaching Jane's team?

Jane was in the family room, studying the take-out menus. Emily took some dishes from the cupboard and put them out on the table, though she had no idea what they would be eating.

Dan did not look reassured. "I just hope this meeting doesn't conflict with the debate."

"Absolutely not. It's starting at noon and shouldn't take more than an hour. If it drags on, I'll leave." She added napkins and silverware at each place. "I thought afterward we could get a bite to eat and then go over to Sawyers' Tree Farm. It should be early enough to put the tree up, and decorate, too."

"All right. That sounds like a good plan."

Jane walked over with the menus she'd picked out, and Emily smiled at her. "How does that sound, Jane? Do you want to put the tree up Friday night?"

"Sure. I might be totally zonked, but why not."

"We can do some baking next weekend, too. And some shopping for gifts. We have plenty of time to get ready for Christmas."

Dan gave her a helpless smile. "If you say so, Crash."

His favorite nickname—inspired by Emily's

tendency to crash every deadline—made Jane laugh. Emily laughed, too, feeling relieved. Ruffled feathers seemed smoothed over. For now.

ON THURSDAY AFTERNOON, EMILY WAS determined to be the first car in the school parking lot so she could whisk Jane off to the mall before getting stuck in the usual bus-and-parent-pickup gridlock.

She had left the house at noon with a list of errands—the usual stop at Dillard's Drugstore for Lillian and Ezra, the post office and bank, and another visit to the Bramble, to pick up an antique tea set she had spotted there as a Christmas gift for her sister.

She was walking back to her car, the china carefully packed in a box, when she spotted Charlie Bates coming out of Krueger's Hardware. Emily stopped in her tracks. Had he seen her? She hoped not. He had been so nasty and bitter the last time they met; she didn't need another dose of that. She quickly crossed the street, though her car was parked on the same side as Krueger's. She would let him pass her and double back at the corner.

But Charlie crossed the street, too. He walked quickly and waved at her, clearly trying to catch up.

Emily slowly turned to face him. Her stomach

fluttered with nerves, though she felt annoyed with herself for allowing him to intimidate her for even a second. She took a breath and raised her chin as he drew closer.

"Hello, Charlie," she greeted him calmly.

"Why, hello there, Napoleon. Enjoying life on Elba? Did you raise your army yet?"

Emily nearly laughed out loud at his greeting. "I had no idea you were a student of French history, Charlie. But you've lost me. I have no idea what you're talking about."

"So you say. Meanwhile, behind my back, you're marshaling your forces. Don't deny it. If there's anything I dislike more than a sneak, it's a liar."

Emily's back stiffened at the insult. She suddenly felt she might crush the box of china in her hands, her body grew so tense. "How dare you," she said quietly. "And how dare you blame me because your administration is just bumping along . . . and you obviously have no idea what you're doing."

She immediately felt annoyed with herself for sinking to his level. But he had gone out of his way to confront and insult her.

"Bumping along, huh? More like ambushed at every turn. You purposely stirred up that board meeting and made me a laughingstock. And now I hear you're meeting with the county executive this week. You and your anti-Bates group."

Emily didn't reply. She wasn't surprised that he knew about their appointment. He had to have some connections by now in the county seat. But she wasn't going to give him any information that he didn't have.

"I don't know what you're up to, Emily, not exactly. But I do know this—you're using this zoning debate to get back at me. Everyone knows it's just sour grapes and you're a sore loser. You're going to find out that the people want progress. That's why they picked me. You lost the election, and you're going to lose this battle, too."

Emily took a breath before she spoke. "Some people want more development in this village, and they voted for you. That's true. But once all the facts are clear and publicly known, I don't think your notion of progress will get very far." She stepped to the side and began to walk around him. "If you'll excuse me, I have to go."

"Fine words, as usual," she heard him call after her. "But you need some new hobbies, Emily, besides trying to undermine and embarrass me."

Emily tried to ignore him, but she could not resist turning once more to face him. "Good point, Charlie. You seem to have that covered all on your own."

She turned her back to him and crossed the street. If he tried to get in the final word, she didn't hear it. Dan had been right. Charlie—and probably others, as well—thought she was just taking part in this cause out of sour grapes. But the only opinion that mattered was the one she had of herself. As she gently set the box of china on the backseat, she didn't feel that good about losing her temper with Charlie. He did have a way of getting under her skin, no matter how hard she tried to keep her cool.

But after tomorrow, this entire situation will be out of your hands, she reminded herself. *Charlie might not change his idea of you. But others— people with a sense of fairness and decency—will see that you are not the ringleader or rabble-rouser he makes you out to be.*

And you are certainly not Napoleon in exile, scheming to take back your empire. The thought of that outrageous accusation finally made her smile.

"I'M DONE WITH THE UPSTAIRS, GRANDMA. I thought I'd start down here today—maybe that spare room at the back of the house? What color would you like in there?"

James was just finishing breakfast on Friday morning: his grandmother's usual hearty offering of eggs with all the trimmings, including the irresistible, freshly baked muffins. More of a Sunday breakfast, he thought, than one for a Friday morning. Still, he put another muffin on his plate, telling himself that all the farmwork he would be starting in a few weeks down in South America would get him lean and mean again.

"Plain old white is fine," Sophie answered, sitting down across from him. She looked tired and a bit distracted today. "As long as it looks clean."

"Easy enough. Does your wrist hurt, Grandma?"

"No, dear, not a bit. I think that's all healed now. Though your aunt Evelyn insists on taking me to Dr. Harding today. To follow up."

"It's a good idea," James agreed. "You don't seem yourself. Are you tired?"

She sipped her coffee, then sat back and sighed. "I didn't sleep well. Too much thinking . . . and praying. But when I woke up, I knew what I had to do."

"Do about what?"

She looked at him squarely. "About selling this place, moving out. The way your father and aunts have been after me to do. I'm going to do it. I want to stay, God knows. I'd like to pass away right upstairs in my bed, with Mac at my feet," she admitted boldly. "But I've come to see that's selfish of me. There will be no peace in the family until I agree to give up the orchard."

James felt the bottom of his stomach drop, as if he were in an elevator that had missed a floor. There had been so much talk, back and forth, in his family about this question that part of him never expected it to be resolved.

"I'm sorry, Grandma . . . This must be so hard for you. I wish you could stay here forever."

"Me, too, sweetheart." She glanced at him, her eyes glassy with tears. She forced a smile and reached over to pat his hand. "But my mind is made up, finally. That's a relief, too. It isn't what I want, but it's the right thing to do."

That was his grandmother—a woman of incredibly strong character and conscience. The quintessential mother, still making sacrifices for her children, still putting their happiness and comfort above her own. James knew if he could ever create a character on paper that was half the woman his grandmother was in real life, he'd really be doing something.

"When will you tell them?" he asked quietly.

"I'm going to tell Evelyn today. I'll take her up on her offer to have me live there. See how that works out." She glanced at him, a twinkle in her eye. James knew his grandmother and aunt did not get along all that well, and wondered what would come of that arrangement.

"Why don't you wait a few days, sit with it awhile? There's no rush, Grandma. You might change your mind," he said, knowing that was what he hoped would happen.

She laughed. "I will change my mind. That's the problem, honey. I've got to strike while the iron is hot. It's not just a whim. I know it in my heart—it's what I have to do. What the Lord has called me to do now, in my journey," she added. "That's what love is, dear. You need to see your loved ones happy and safe more than you care about yourself. Because their well-being is your happiness," she added. "When you feel that way about someone, you'll know you truly love them."

James nodded, but didn't reply. He had fallen head over heels with a few girls so far and had even thought he was in love once or twice. But he knew now that those relationships weren't real love. Certainly not the deep and lasting kind his grandmother was talking about.

"I promised your father and your aunts at Thanksgiving that I would think this question through. And I've kept my promise," she added. "So I expect, sprained wrist and all, they will let me have my last Christmas gathering here. That was the deal."

"I remember. I was sitting right there. If they argue, I'll stick up for you, Grandma."

She smiled. "I know you will. But I don't think I'll get much of a fuss once they get what they want. We don't get everything in life that we want, honey. But God knows what is best for us, and what is best for all involved, in our struggles. He has a way of working things out, if you get out of the way and let Him do His job. We usually see that later," she added. "I'm truly thankful for the years He gave me living under this roof, within these four walls. I've been truly blessed, James, since the day I arrived on this Earth, squalling my head off in that back room you're about to paint. So please, dear, don't feel sad for me." She patted his hand again. "I pray that when you reach my age and you look back, you'll feel the same peace and gratitude for your days."

His grandmother's certainty made him feel better. She did seem at peace with her decision, and he knew he had no right to talk her out of it, or even advise her to wait.

"I hope by then I have your way of understanding the world," he said. "It would sure help my writing."

Everything changes. Nothing stays the same. That was the only thing you could be certain of. His parents' divorce, growing up, and leaving home and trying to make his way in the world had taught him that already.

Still, his grandparents' house and orchard was a place that seemed eternal and unchanging, a safe haven. He had always assumed he could return to it and it would always be the same, no matter what. There were so many memories here for his entire family. So much family history, it seemed the Potter DNA had seeped into the wooden floors, and even into the apples that fell from the trees outside the kitchen window.

It would be so hard to think of this place and

know it belonged to someone else. Or even worse, to know it had been knocked down and torn up, the land filled with new houses or something even more awful.

He gazed at his grandmother, feeding bits of muffin to Mac, who sat alertly at her feet. James didn't have the heart to ask questions that probed into the future.

What did his grandmother always say? "The answers are revealed in God's time, not our own." James wasn't a big churchgoer, but he decided he would leave all of his questions and the answers to Heaven for now.

EMILY SHOULD HAVE EXPECTED THE COUNTY supervisor would make them wait. She shifted in her seat in the outer office and checked her watch again. Martin sat next to her, answering emails on his phone. Marion Ross and the group's attorney, Jack Rowland, had gotten restless and left the office in search of a drink machine.

"Does it always take this long to see him?" Martin asked.

"Yes and no. We're sort of small potatoes," she said honestly.

Twenty minutes later, an administrative assistant came out of the inner office. "Supervisor Thatcher will see you now."

William Thatcher rose from behind his desk and extended a hand. "Emily, good to see you. I read your group's letter. I understand your concern, but I don't know how the county can help. Cape Light is an incorporated village with its own laws and charter."

Pitch one, fastball, at least ninety-five miles per hour. Emily wasn't surprised. She had never met a politician willing to stick their neck out in a matter that didn't directly involve them. It was the first rule of staying electable. The group turned to her, obviously assuming she would plead their case.

"But you can, Bill. Once we explain how, I think you'll agree that the county is well within its rights to step in." She turned to introduce the others, hoping to pass the conversation to Martin and Marion. But Bill Thatcher seemed most interested and comfortable talking to her. The truth was, she was the only one able to field his questions with clear, succinct answers that pounded in the point that the county could and should step in and support their appeal.

Despite her expectation that Thatcher would not keep them long or be interested in the documents they prepared, he ended up calling in his expert on environmental impact and his zoning supervisor. Martin, Marion, and Jack looked pleased and very encouraged, but Emily watched the time pass with dread.

She closed the binder in her lap and picked up her purse. "I'm sorry, everyone. I have to go. My daughter is in a debate at the middle school. It's a big school assembly, and I have to get a good seat."

Bill Thatcher laughed. "I wonder where she gets that talent from."

Martin turned to her with an anxious look. "Can't you stay a few minutes more? I think it would be very helpful, Emily, especially if the zoning supervisor has questions."

Marion looked worried, too. "Can't you call and say you'll be a few minutes late?"

Emily knew she couldn't do that, and she had no intention of being late. But she could see that they were both worried about saying the wrong thing and obviously intimidated by the other officials coming in. Winning the environmental and zoning departments to their side today would be a huge boost.

She checked her watch again. "I guess I can stay a few more minutes. But I really need to go soon." Her group looked weak with relief.

Moments later, the environmental and zoning experts joined them. It took time to explain the situation again and more time to answer more questions. Emily stretched the five minutes she had to spare to seven and then rose from her seat.

"Sorry, I have to go. If you have any more questions for me, please get in touch. You have my phone and email, Bill." She said this quickly while backing up to the door. Her group stared back at her. *Like children left with a strange babysitter,* she thought. But she couldn't help that. *They'll be okay. You really don't have to take the world on your shoulders, Napoleon,* she told herself. *They can and will manage without you. Besides, this will be good experience for them. And a good lesson for you, too.*

She felt happy and relieved as she drove toward the middle school. She had done her part and, starting now, would concentrate on her family and the holidays. She was looking forward to picking out their Christmas tree after the debate. She had meant to take the boxes of ornaments down from the attic this morning, but that was no trouble. It was actually part of the fun, to make a human chain and hand them down and down again.

A light snow had begun to fall, and she thought how nice it would be at Sawyers' Tree Farm that night. Christmas carols would be playing, and colorful lights would be strung everywhere. The Sawyers served hot cocoa and even gave pony rides, which Jane was much too big for now, of course. But a trip to Sawyers' was a family tradition and would definitely get them all into a holiday mood.

The ride to the middle school from the Essex County offices was not long. Emily had timed it perfectly. Until she hit roadwork on the Beach Road.

"You've got to be kidding me!" she gasped, then followed the signs steering everyone around side streets in an endless detour. She checked the time on her watch. Now she was cutting it too close and was so annoyed with herself, she thought she might scream. Or cry.

Calm down. Take a breath. You're almost there. These school events never start on time. And Jane isn't the first to speak on her team. She's after Maddie and Lauren. Focus on the road and get there.

Repeating those words again and again, she soon pulled into the school lot and parked in one of the only spaces left, way at the back. She ran all the way to the building and then down the hallway. The school seemed quiet and empty. Not a good sign. She pulled open the auditorium door. The debate had already started.

Jane and her team sat on one side of the stage, behind a long table. Jane stared down at her notes. A boy from the other team stood at the podium, giving a statement. Emily was too distracted to hear what he said.

She spotted Dan in a middle row, right on the aisle. She was grateful for that and soon landed in the empty seat next to him.

"I got stuck at the meeting and hit construction on the Beach Road," she whispered. "I left myself plenty of time."

Dan didn't answer her; his gaze was fixed on

the stage. Was he angry about something? She couldn't tell.

"Did I miss much?"

"You missed Jane. She just finished."

Emily sat back in shock. She wondered for a moment if she had heard him correctly. "How could that be? She was last on her team."

"They changed the order. I don't know why. You missed her. I thought she was going to cry when she didn't see you here."

Dan was definitely angry, and Emily didn't blame him. She sat back, feeling like she might start crying herself. She bit down on her lip, feeling two inches tall.

Emily forced herself to focus on the stage and the students speaking. But it was hard to settle her emotions and get her bearings again. Jane spoke several times in rebuttal, giving excellent answers that were unrehearsed and unscripted. Emily was very proud of her, though when she glanced at Dan to share her excitement, he still wouldn't meet her gaze.

When the debate ended, Jane's team was voted the winner. Emily was glad for them but could barely enjoy the victory, she felt so guilty. She and Dan filed out of the auditorium and waited in the crowded school lobby for Jane to appear.

Maddie's mother came up to them, beaming. "The girls were wonderful, weren't they?"

"They were terrific," Dan agreed. "They worked hard."

"Yes," Emily added, forcing a smile. She was relieved when Maddie's mother walked off. Dan hadn't said a word to her since telling her that she had missed Jane's argument. She could almost feel the cold waves of anger coming off him.

Finally, Jane made her way to them, through the crowded lobby.

"You were great up there, honey. We're so proud of you," Emily began. "And I'm so—"

"Good job, Janie." Dan cut her off, something he almost never did. But he was smiling at his daughter. "You spoke very well. Your whole team was very sharp."

"Thanks." Jane didn't seem that pleased. She looked angry. Actually, Emily realized, she was seething.

Of course, she's mad at me. She has every right to be. Emily felt awful and cast around for something positive to say. "You had some great rebuttals, honey. That's even harder than giving a statement."

Jane finally looked up at her. "Which you missed, Mom."

Emily winced, feeling like the worst mother ever. "Yes, I know, honey. I'm sorry. I left plenty of time to get here, but I . . ." She sighed, her voice trailing off. "I'm so sorry. Honestly."

Jane didn't answer. She wouldn't even meet

Emily's eye. Emily felt as if she might cry, but didn't want to make it about herself. At that moment, she would have given anything to turn back the clock and make everyone at the meeting mad at her by leaving early instead of having Jane mad at her now.

"I know I messed up, but I really didn't mean to. And I did see most of it. You should be very proud," Emily added. "I bet you're hungry. Where should we eat? You pick the place. Then we'll get our tree."

Jane didn't answer. Emily could tell she was still upset and was not forgiving her so easily. At last Jane said, "Can we do the tree another night? Maddie is having the rest of the girls over to her house. Can I go there instead?"

"Sure, you can," Dan said before Emily even had a chance to respond. "We have the whole weekend to get the tree. You go have some fun."

"Great. Can you guys drop me off there on your way home?"

"Sure," Emily said weakly. She knew that Jane's eagerness to be with her friends instead of putting up the Christmas tree with them was her fault. And that Dan, who had been so set on the three of them getting ready for Christmas together, agreed to it that way felt like some kind of blow, though she suspected that he wanted Janie to have a good time with her friends instead of wading into her parents' deep-freeze zone.

• • •

AT HOME, WITHOUT A WORD, DAN STARTED cooking dinner—a mushroom and cheese omelet and a green salad. He put the news on while they ate, which he didn't usually do. Emily hated to eat with the TV on, but was grateful tonight for the distraction, especially since Dan barely spoke except to ask her to pass the pepper. After dinner, Emily offered to clean up.

"Fine with me," Dan said. "I have to work on my book. I have a chapter to finish."

Dan had another book coming out in the spring, this one about a town, not far from Cape Light, where colonial residents had disappeared quite mysteriously. People claimed the area was still haunted, and he had researched the question thoroughly.

"I can pick up Jane later. I'll text her and tell her to let me know when she's ready. I hope she has a good time with her friends," Emily added. "She needs to blow off a little steam."

Dan met her gaze. "Don't we all."

Before she could reply, he had turned and left the room.

IT WAS ABOUT ELEVEN WHEN EMILY DROVE over to Maddie's house to pick up Jane. She sent a text and waited in the driveway. Her daughter soon appeared at the door. She waved to her friends and ran down to the car, then jumped in the front seat and fastened her seat belt.

"How was the party? Did you have fun?"

Jane shrugged. "It was all right."

"What did you do? Just hang out?"

"We had this giant hero to eat, and we played a video game. Maddie's family has a humongous TV."

Jane often complained their family had the smallest TV in the universe. "I'm not sure about that, honey. But it's the smallest one we could find," Emily would always reply.

"Sounds like fun. Any boys there?" she asked in a teasing tone. She had spotted a few on the opposing team and wondered if they had been invited.

"One or two." Jane shrugged. "The girls totally outnumbered them. I don't even know why they stayed."

Emily smiled again but didn't offer any theories. "I bet you were all worn out tonight. You did a great job. Dad and I were very proud of you," she said again.

Jane glanced at her and then looked out her window. "Thanks . . . even though you missed half of it."

Emily felt a pang. "It wasn't half, not nearly. But a very important part of your presentation. I know that, honey. And there's no excuse. I did get more caught up at the meeting than I expected, and then I hit construction on the Beach Road. The detour went on forever and—I ended up being late."

Her voice trailed off. Jane was still staring out her window. Emily wondered if she was even listening.

"The meeting I had today was important. It's a situation that will affect everyone in this town for years to come. It will affect you when you're an adult, if you ever decide to live here," she added. "But I know that doesn't make up for missing your big moment in the debate."

Jane sighed. "No, it doesn't, Mom. Remember how you kept telling me that if I was nervous to look for a friendly face, like you or Dad? I did feel nervous, and I looked for you. And you weren't there. I felt so bad . . . I lost my place for a minute and my brain totally went blank. I had no idea what I was supposed to be saying, even though I'd memorized that part backward and forward. And then I felt so awful, I just wanted to run off the stage."

Emily's heart ached. Dan hadn't told her about that. She reached over in the dark and squeezed Jane's shoulder. "Honey, I'm so sorry."

Jane took a breath. She seemed determined not to cry. "I got through it. And we won, so I guess it wasn't the worst thing."

Wasn't it? Or was hearing Jane describe how

disappointed and abandoned she had felt the worst thing?

Emily felt awful, too upset and distracted to drive. She pulled over to the side of the road. Jane turned to her with a confused expression. "What's the matter? Is something wrong with the car?"

Emily shook her head and took a breath. "The car is fine. But I'm not. I need to tell you something. So please look at me while I'm talking." Jane turned, finally giving Emily her full attention, though Emily did notice a slight eye roll. "I need you to know that you are the most important person in the world to me. What you do and what you think and feel is more important than any issue or cause, or any job I've had or will ever have. Or any . . . anything. I couldn't love you more if I tried." Emily found her daughter's hand in the dark and took it in her own. "I'm sorry for what happened today. But please try to forgive me. And believe me?"

Jane stared straight ahead a moment, then looked down at their hands. "I know you love me, Mom, and I love you, too. But sometimes, I don't feel like all of that is true—that what I do and think and say is *that* important to you. You know what you always tell me . . . actions speak louder than words?"

"That's true," Emily admitted. She was aching

to put her arms around her daughter, but she was sure that if she did, Jane would stiffen, and she wasn't sure she could bear that now. "Actions do speak louder. I just have to try harder, I guess. Someday, sweetheart, you will believe me. I promise."

Chapter Eleven

SOPHIE SAT IN ONE OF THE FRONT ROWS AT church on Sunday morning. She preferred the back, but her daughter Evelyn liked it up front better on the pulpit side. Sophie had to agree that you could definitely hear Reverend Ben better; she wondered what she had been missing all these years. She also had a good view of the young family who came up to light the third candle of Advent. It was almost Christmas—only one week left.

She remembered a time when she was a young mother, too, standing there with Gus and the girls, who were just in grade school. Lifting Bart up in her arms so he could have his turn, too. It seemed like no time at all had passed since that Sunday. But, of course, decades had gone by. That's the way she felt about a lot of things lately.

Since she had made the decision to leave the orchard, she had gotten so nostalgic. Anybody would be, she knew. But she didn't like to wallow in sentiment and memories. She had always been a forward-looking person, not one to moan and groan over situations she could not alter. And she didn't want to be any different now.

She shifted in her seat, reading the bulletin. She wore her best dress today, dark red with black velvet trim at the collar. She usually saved it for Christmas Day, but today was special, too. She thought of the announcement she had to make, and her stomach fluttered with nerves. Then she asked for God's help and forced herself to focus on the service.

Reverend Ben stood at the pulpit, spreading his arms in welcome.

"Let us come together for worship," he announced, and then began with the morning prayers.

To Sophie that always meant to cast aside the cares of the material world and set your sights on Heaven for a while. On the things that really matter and will never fade or crumble or pass away with time. Give your worldly concerns to the Lord for an hour and try to see them through His eyes. How small and insignificant they are. Don't you think the power that made the moon and stars, the sun that shines and the birds that fly, can fix these worries for you? Trust in Him and let your heart be light.

When it was time for the Scripture readings, she found her reading glasses at the bottom of her purse and read along with the words that

Reverend Ben spoke aloud, from the Book of Luke, Chapter One.

" 'My soul glorifies the Lord and my spirit rejoices in God my Savior,' " Reverend Ben read aloud, " 'for He has been mindful of the humble state of His servant. From now on all generations will call me blessed, for the Mighty One has done great things for me—holy is His name' . . ."

My soul does glorify the Lord, Sophie reflected. *Even on this sad day, knowing what I have to say. Whatever He wants, I'll do,* she silently added to the verse.

When it came time for Joys and Concerns, Sophie raised her hand, and Reverend Ben called upon her first. She got to her feet.

"You can talk sitting down, Mom," Evelyn reminded her.

"That's all right. I want people to hear what I have to say." She held the edge of the pew to steady herself and lifted her chin. "I have one joy and one concern. I took a little fall last week. It was nothing at all, honestly. But I want to thank everyone for your phone calls and cards. That made me feel better a lot faster."

"We're glad to hear that, Sophie. And glad to see you back so quickly," Reverend Ben said.

"Thank you, Reverend. I have to add my concern now. Falling down did shake some sense into my old head. I've decided it's time to move in with my daughter Evelyn and her family and give up growing apples. Well, they'll still keep growing whether I'm there or not," she added with a grin. "But you all know what I mean. I won't say it was an easy decision for me," she admitted. "So I'm asking for prayers to help me through this big change in my life."

Her friends and neighbors looked back at her with surprise. Even Reverend Ben seemed surprised, though they had talked about it less than a week ago. "Of course we'll include you in our prayers, Sophie," he said. "And I'm sure many here would be happy to help you with the practical matters of moving. When the time comes."

"Thank you, Reverend. That's all I have to say, for now."

She sat down, her knees feeling suddenly watery—not the weakness of age, but her nerves giving out on her. It had taken more effort than she had expected to share the news and to show a bright face to the world.

"You did very well, Mom." Evelyn patted her shoulder.

Sophie nodded but didn't answer. Her announcement had very likely been the hardest she'd ever had to make. Next to announcing her beloved Gus had passed on. It was one thing to tell her family about her decision—and even Zoey, though she had taken the news hard. But announcing it here made it so painfully real.

The choir had begun to sing one of her favorite Christmas songs, "O Come, All Ye Faithful." She tried to join in, but her mind wandered, wondering again if she was doing the right thing. *God, please, if I've spoken too soon or I'm making a mistake, please right it for me? I feel so confused today. This is much harder than I ever thought it would be.*

EMILY, DAN, AND JANE HAD GONE TO church together and planned to spend the rest of the day putting up their Christmas tree and baking cookies.

"Should we have lunch first?" Emily asked as they got into the car. "Or go straight to Sawyers'?"

"I vote for lunch," Dan replied. "It's hard to focus if your stomach is grumbling."

"Me, too," Jane said. "At Willoughby's."

"Willoughby's sounds great," Emily replied, grateful that Jane hadn't requested the Clam Box.

Dan nodded and turned on Main Street in that direction. "It's still early. There won't be too much of a crowd. I bet we have our tree up and decorated by dinnertime," he predicted cheerfully.

"And some cookies baked," Emily added, glancing back at Jane. She felt happy and relieved that they were back on track and getting on with their holidays. Jane seemed to have forgiven her after their heart-to-heart in the car. After huffing around the house Friday night, Dan had let the topic go. He could see that she was mad enough at herself for both of them.

After a quick lunch at the bakery, they picked out a fine tree and went straight home. It took all three of them to get it standing straight and secure in the stand. Then Dan began to work on the lights, which were, as usual, tangled and missing a few bulbs.

Emily and Jane started their baking, promising Dan that they would only come out once in a while to advise on the Christmas tree lights.

"I like all white," Emily said as she measured out molasses for a gingerbread recipe. "Even though it's boring."

"All white can be pretty, but I think Dad's already strung the multicolored. I don't want to be the one to tell him to take them all off again."

"Good point," Emily agreed. It felt good to be back in an easy, happy mood with her family, especially with Jane. She had thought about that in church this morning, saying a silent prayer of thanks.

"I can't believe Mrs. Potter is selling the orchard," Jane said. "That's so sad."

"It is sad," Emily agreed. "But I suppose it's just too hard for her to live there alone and run the place. I know her children help her, but I don't think any of them are interested in taking over the business. I guess that fall scared her. She's very lucky she didn't get hurt."

"I know. But I love going there to pick apples and peaches and berries in the summer. And she used to have that big barbecue on Memorial Day every year. Remember?"

Emily measured out the baking soda and added it to the bowl. "Yes, I do. The whole town would be there. She hasn't had that sort of party for a while," she added wistfully.

"I wonder who will buy it. I hope it's someone who wants to grow apples and won't just tear all the trees down."

Emily felt a pang in her heart hearing that possibility spoken aloud. If the new zoning laws went through, Potter's Orchard would be snatched up in a heartbeat by a developer. She was sure there was a flock of them circling the town like buzzards right now, waiting for valuable property to go up for sale. But she didn't want to get into all that today. She had sworn off any discussion of that issue until at least the first of January.

The open-space group had emailed her several times over the last few days, and had also sent some text messages. But she had answered with a quick note saying she was unavailable right now and would get in touch when she had some free time.

Jane was applying her impressive volleyball muscles to mixing the butter and sugar. "You know, Mom, I was thinking, maybe Potter's Orchard is a landmark. Like Grandma's old house, Lilac Hall? Maybe someone could say it shouldn't be torn down or changed, because it's a historic site—or someone could start a petition about it?"

Dan stood in the kitchen doorway holding an armful of tangled tree lights. "I'm going to pretend I didn't hear that." He glanced from Emily to Jane and back to his wife. "Is there a virus going around this house? Is it something in the water?"

"I don't know, dear." Emily shook her head, trying not to laugh but secretly gratified by her daughter's inspiration. "That's an excellent idea, Jane. I'm not sure if the orchard would qualify, but I like the way you're thinking. Very civic-minded."

She shared a smile with her daughter, then returned to the task at hand. "Let's finish mixing this dough and put it in the fridge. While it's chilling, we can decorate."

Jane seemed happy with that plan, and Dan shot her a look of sheer relief.

C.J. HAD COME HOME FROM COLLEGE SUNDAY night, and Charlie had quickly put him to work at the Clam Box. C.J. didn't seem to mind, and even offered to close up on Tuesday night so Zoey could have the night off. Zoey had plenty left to do before Christmas, more shopping and baking with Lucy. But instead, she headed to the orchard. She had offered to help Sophie prepare for her Christmas Eve party, and there were only five days left. And the truth was, she wanted to hang out with James, too.

A few knocks on Sophie's side door caused Macintosh to sound the alarm. "Come on in," Sophie called. "The door is open."

Zoey walked into the kitchen, struck by the sight of James on a ladder, stringing Christmas lights around the room as Sophie directed from below. Christmas ornaments and an assortment of ceramic figures, tiny snow-covered houses, snow globes, and all sorts of holiday knickknacks covered every shelf and window ledge.

"That's it, honey, hang them sort of swoopy. I've got white candles for the windows and big snowflakes that hang on ribbons."

Zoey gazed around in awe. "It looks like a Christmas village in here."

"Thanks, dear. That's what I'm aiming for."

"Where did you get all this stuff? Did you buy out a Christmas store?"

"Of course not. Though I could probably open one." Sophie dropped into a kitchen chair, looking tired but pleased. "It's just piled up over the years. I've never put it all out at once, but this year, I decided to shoot the works. Most of this stuff will get passed on to whoever wants it or end up in a yard sale soon. You see anything you like, just let me know, okay?"

"Sure, Sophie. Thanks." Zoey shrugged off her khaki-green coat and forced a smile. *Anything you'd like as a remembrance or souvenir of the orchard,* Sophie meant.

Zoey felt as if her heart were on a roller coaster—her spirits boosted by the lavish, eye-popping display, then sliding down again, remembering the announcement Sophie had made at church on Sunday. Everyone had talked about it after the service, and at the diner, too. But Zoey had not seen Sophie since and could hardly believe it was true. "So, it's settled. You really are leaving here?"

"It is, dear. That fall I had was a warning, a message, I think. I'm going to heed it. I don't want to leave, heaven knows. But sometimes we have to step up and do things we don't want to do. For our own good—and for the people we love, too."

Zoey nodded. It was hard to hide her unhappiness, though she tried. "You sound as if you're okay with it. So I guess I will be, too."

"Thank you, Zoey. That's just what a dear friend should say. Isn't it, James?"

James was still on the ladder, draping the rest of the lights across the other side of the room.

Zoey could see the big dining room through the doorway, decorated just as thoroughly.

"I feel the same, Grandma. As long as you're at peace, I won't try to change your mind."

"I know it's hard to fathom, but don't feel sad for me. I've had the most wonderful life in this house, on this land. A richer, happier life than most anyone I know. I'm truly grateful for that, and for all the memories. No one can ever take that away from me."

Zoey admired her attitude. She was sure that if she was ever in Sophie's position, she wouldn't be nearly so positive or grateful.

"I wonder who will buy the place," she mused. "I hope they don't change anything." The words had barely left her mouth before Zoey regretted them. *How insensitive can you get? Sophie must be worried about the same thing, and now you've made her feel worse.*

"That's my dearest prayer now," Sophie confessed. "And my biggest regret. Those trees . . . they're like my children. I do feel as if my life's blood runs in the branches, same as my own kin. I hate to abandon them. Makes me feel like a bad mother," she confessed.

"I know, Grandma. But maybe someone will come along who wants to run the orchard." James had come down from the ladder, and he patted his grandmother's shoulder. "There are a lot of young people interested in agriculture now—

in organic farming and keeping farmland in a place like this open and undeveloped. I just saw a documentary on it a few weeks ago."

Sophie's laugh was incredulous. "It seems all the young people run off fast as they can to make a life in the city."

"It's true, Sophie," Zoey said. "I read about that, too. Look at James. He went to New York. And now he wants to work on a farm in South America."

"Good point. See, you have a young farmer right under your nose. I never thought of myself as a young agrarian type. But I guess I am," he agreed with a laugh.

James's impending departure felt like another loss, coming right on top of losing the orchard. But Zoey didn't want to dwell on that now.

"Maybe that's true. I didn't realize it was a tide among you young people."

"Do you mean a trend?" Zoey asked respectfully.

Sophie laughed. "Yes, that's what I meant, a trend. If you meet up with any of those young farmers, send them my way."

"We will, Grandma. Count on it," James promised. He glanced at Zoey. She could tell he, too, felt sad about his grandmother's decision.

"I don't know who will be celebrating Christmas here next year. Young farmers . . . old farmers. This house may even be knocked down by then," Sophie said honestly. "I want to be very careful who I sell to, but it's really in the Lord's hands. All I know is that we're going to have the best Christmas party ever, to celebrate and honor all the good times my family has known here. For three generations."

"What's going to be on the menu?" Zoey asked.

"Well . . . everything," Sophie replied with a grin. "We'll have a big punch and lots of starters. I'll make baked clams and get some raw clams, too. Your father likes that," she said to James. "The dinner will start with a corn and lobster chowder. And I'm cooking some sort of roast—beef or ham? Maybe both. Potatoes gratin and a roast goose with apple and chestnut stuffing. That's what my mother used to make every year on Christmas."

"I've never tasted roast goose. That sounds delicious," Zoey said, awed by Sophie's menu. If anyone could make all those dishes and more, it was Sophie.

"You'll have to try some. I still have her recipe. One year, she left the goose on the counter, waiting to be carved, and one of the dogs—a big hound and a real rascal—jumped up and stole it. He ran right under my brother's bed. The old wooden beds were high off the floor, and that dog crammed himself in a spot nobody could reach and gobbled up the goose in a minute flat. My mother was fit to be tied. She chased the dog with a broom. But who wanted the goose anyway, after he'd had a few bites?"

Sophie laughed at the memory, and Zoey did, too, while Mac sat at her feet, looking like he wondered what all the merriment was about.

"Macintosh wouldn't do anything like that," James said. "Would you, Mac?"

"If he could move that ladder by himself, he would. He's not that well behaved." Sophie smiled, petting the dog's head. "I hope that wherever I end up, I can take him with me," she added in a quieter tone. "I would miss his company."

Zoey felt a tug in her heart. Of course Sophie would have to take her dog when she moved. The very idea of the two being separated was unthinkable. As unthinkable as Sophie leaving the orchard.

"If you can't take Mac with you . . . well, you just won't go," Zoey said.

Sophie met her gaze and smiled wistfully, then sat back and took a sip of tea. "We will surely cross that bridge when we come to it." She set down her cup. "Right now, we have some Christmas cooking to do. Find an apron and we'll get to work. We'll start on the chowder, and maybe bake some Joe Froggers."

"Good plan. I'm down with that," James said.

Zoey was familiar with Sophie's famous chowder, but not with the baking recipe. "What are Joe Froggers?"

Sophie laughed. "You never had my Froggers? Best in New England."

"And the biggest, I bet," James added.

"If I ever had them, I didn't know what they were called."

"They're giant cookies made with spices, rum, and molasses," Sophie explained. "Crisp on the edges and soft and chewy in the middle. James knows the history. He looked it up once when he was a little boy. Always curious. Do you remember, James?"

"Absolutely. About two hundred years ago, a couple in Marblehead, Aunt Crease and Old Joe Brown, ran a tavern next to a frog pond, and they got famous for baking giant spice cookies, as big as dinner plates. They named the cookies for the big frogs in their pond. People would come from all over to drink their spirits and eat their giant Froggers. Sailors liked them, too, because they stayed chewy a long time."

"I don't make them all that big. But we'll use a coffee can for a cookie cutter."

"That sounds large enough to me." Zoey happily put on her apron, clipped up her hair, and got to work. She had come to help Sophie prepare for her party, but she was also looking forward to spending time with James. Though their shifts often overlapped at the diner, it was different seeing him outside of work. But once he finished hanging the lights, he left the kitchen, taking the ladder. Zoey realized she would be alone in the kitchen tonight with Sophie while James was decorating elsewhere. Or maybe working on his writing.

That fine. I really came to see Sophie, she told herself.

But she did feel cheered a short time later when James returned. She was at the table peeling a huge pile of potatoes for the soup. He stood by, watching her. "Better pick up some speed there. Christmas is coming."

She tried not to smile at his teasing. The pile was huge, and she had hardly made a dent. "Guys can peel potatoes, too. It's not a gender-specific activity."

He laughed. "True enough. Let's see who can peel them faster."

Zoey rolled her eyes. "Why do men have to make a competition out of everything?"

"It's a mystery to me, too," Sophie agreed.

James picked up a paring knife and grabbed a spud, losing nearly half to the scrap heap as he struggled to cut off the skin. Meanwhile, Zoey peeled the skin off hers in a smooth ribbon.

"This is harder than it looks. How did you do that?"

"Just guide the skin between your thumb and

the blade, and try to keep it thin. The goal is to get more than one French fry per potato."

"Thanks for the tip. This is definitely a marketable skill, worth learning."

"It is. Though I know you have loftier goals."

He met her gaze, his eyes dancing with amusement, but didn't reply.

They worked together awhile without talking. James improved with each try. Zoey focused on the task, all the time savoring the feeling of working with him. She felt so comfortable with James, not needing to say a word at all as they peeled their way through the pile and James forgot all about the contest.

Sophie hovered over a huge stock pot, tossing in ingredients for her chowder. She glanced over her shoulder. "It's a dull day that you don't learn something, James."

"Very true, Grandma. Zoey is always teaching me things. How to peel potatoes . . . how to stack glasses so they don't break . . . how to pack snowballs? She's a very interesting girl."

He smiled into Zoey's eyes, and she felt her breath catch—and nearly cut her thumb. *He's just being nice . . . and his usual flirtatious self. Better get a grip on the potatoes. And your imagination.*

Sophie's soup base was soon simmering, and the dough for the Froggers was mixed in big bowls. James helped for a while, then disappeared

317

into another part of the house. After a few pans of the big cookies were baked, he poked his head into the kitchen again.

"How's it going in here?"

"We've been very productive. I can check two jobs off my list, thanks to Zoey," Sophie reported.

"Then it's time for a break. Come look. I have a surprise for you." James disappeared again. Mac jumped up from his bed and trotted after him, not needing to be asked twice.

"Wonder what he's up to. I guess we should go see."

Sophie took off her apron, and Zoey did the same, then took the clip out and fluffed her hair with her fingers. She had on jeans and boots and one of her favorite sweaters—a long sapphire-blue turtleneck that brought out the color of her eyes. She was glad to see she hadn't gotten any cookie batter or soup on it.

Not that I'm trying to look especially good or anything for anyone around here . . .

She followed Sophie into the front parlor, the sound of Christmas music greeting her on the way. Some old-fashioned singer—she couldn't remember his name—singing a cheerful song called "A Holly Jolly Christmas."

Sophie cried out in delight, clapping her hands as she stood in the doorway. "Mother of Pearl! James . . . what did you do?" Zoey pressed her hands to her face and could not contain a gasp as she surveyed the scene.

The room was dimly lit, glowing with a thousand lights—swooping strands of lights on the Christmas tree and twined in pine garlands on the mantel and around the big picture window. Votive candles in colored glass holders were spread around the room, giving off a spicy scent, and in the big hearth, flames danced in a freshly laid fire.

Every music box was turned on, and ballerinas twirled, wooden soldiers marched, and ice skaters swept around a plastic pond, arm in arm. The tree itself was an utter masterpiece, every bough covered with lights and ornaments—the type of ornaments you might find in an antiques shop, Zoey noticed, all too fragile-looking to even touch, along with nostalgic touches, like pictures of Sophie's children when they were in grade school, in faded paper frames with glued-on sparkles and bows. All in all, it was the most beautiful, magnificently decorated tree Zoey had ever seen, from the golden star on top to the crèche below, carefully arranged and sheltered by the lowest pine branches.

"Did we just get transported to the North Pole?" Zoey asked.

James was delighted with their reactions. "You wanted to use all your decorations this year, Grandma. So that's what I did."

319

"And then some, I think. I forgot I even owned half of this. Every one brings back some memory." Sophie picked up the tallest nutcracker from a row of three who stood at attention on a side table. "This was Gus's favorite. He brought home this set when he was in the army, stationed in Germany."

When she looked up at them again, Zoey could see the many lights reflected in her misty eyes. Zoey glanced at James and knew he also sensed his grandmother's distress. He quickly stepped over to a side table, where he had set up an old portable record player, the type Zoey had only seen in retro shops and in old movies.

"How about some music? Did you forget you owned all these great old records, too?"

Sophie smiled again. "Records? I forgot we even owned a record player."

"I found it in the attic. And a box of Christmas albums. Have we had enough of Burl Ives yet?"

"*That's* who it is. My dad always plays those songs in the diner during Christmas. I just couldn't remember the guy's name."

Sophie looked shocked. "Burl Ives is my favorite. He does do a nice version of 'Rudolph' on that album. And 'Silver Bells.' "

"How about this one?" James put another record on the turntable and carefully moved the needle to find the track he wanted. The song "Jingle Bell Rock" suddenly filled the room.

"That's a good one, too," Sophie agreed. "You need to be our DJ on Christmas, James."

"Happy to spin some tracks for you, Grandma." He walked over and took her hand, then led her to an empty space in the parlor and coaxed her to dance.

She was at first reluctant, letting him sway around her.

"Come on, Grandma. I know you can do better than that. I saw you cut the rug with Grandpa more than a few times."

Sophie laughed, looking shy and embarrassed. "Your Grandpa loved to dance, that is true. All right. In his honor, I can do a little better. Let me just remember how . . ."

Zoey stood back, smiling so widely her face nearly hurt as she watched James and Sophie dance around the parlor to "Jingle Bell Rock."

James led his grandmother with a firm but gentle touch, and she was soon dancing along smoothly and even let him spin her once, then laughed out loud.

"You dance like a professional, Grandma. You must have taken lessons. Or danced on the stage?"

"Don't be silly," she said, breathless when the song finally ended. "That was fun. We'll do some dancing on Christmas, too."

"Don't worry. I'll get the party moving,"

James promised. "You even have Alvin and the Chipmunks."

"I was wondering about Alvin, but I didn't want to say," Zoey joked.

The phone rang in the kitchen, and Sophie headed off to answer it as the caller spoke on the answering machine. "It's Evelyn, checking up on me. Wait till I tell her I was dancing in a Christmas wonderland. She won't believe it."

Zoey turned to James. "It was very sweet of you to do this for your grandmother. She's thrilled."

He shrugged, flipping through the stack of records again. "I had fun going through all this old stuff. I'm glad the record player works. The old music really makes it."

"No doubt." Zoey watched him put another album on. "What are you playing now?"

"You tell me." He set the arm down, and all Zoey could hear at first through the old speakers was a scratchy sound. Then she heard a voice that was unmistakable and the opening bars to "Blue Christmas."

"You're a little young, I guess," he teased her. "Maybe you don't know who this is."

"Everybody knows Elvis. And I'm only three years younger than you," she reminded him.

"And years past me in some ways, I must admit." He smiled and reached out his hand. "May I have this dance?"

Zoey felt speechless and suddenly glued to

the spot. But he tugged her hand and pulled her forward, not waiting for an answer.

She fell into his arms and he smiled with quiet satisfaction, slipping one hand around her waist and tucking her other hand against his broad shoulder.

James had certainly been in good shape when he burst through the door that first snowy night. But a month of painting, carpentry, and chopping wood—not to mention carrying heavy trays of glasses and dishes around the diner—had added more muscles under his flannel shirt, Zoey noticed.

Zoey was not very adept at this type of dancing, but her feet seemed to follow his lead effortlessly as he guided her, gently and smoothly, around the small space. She smiled as he hummed along with the tune, then did a perfect Elvis imitation.

". . . Won't be the same, dear, if you're not here with me . . ."

"Pretty good. Maybe I should call you Elvis Potter instead of Harry Potter?"

He thought about it a moment. "It has a nice ring. I might use it for a pen name."

Zoey laughed. She looked up and met his gaze. He was laughing, too, but suddenly grew silent. The song had finished, and all she heard was the sound of the needle stuck on the last grooves. James didn't make any move to fix it.

"I'm glad I'm spending Christmas with you,

Zoey. You're so pretty and clever and . . . just plain . . . wonderful," he whispered.

Zoey wasn't sure what to say. She felt her heart beating so fast, she was sure he could hear it, too. Before she could reply his head dipped down and he kissed her. A sweet, questioning kiss. His hold on her tightened and she leaned into his touch, surprised at first, then kissing him back. She wasn't sure how long it lasted. But they both heard Sophie's slippers scuffing down the hallway, and Mac's quick step trailing behind her. They jumped apart just in time.

James turned toward the record player, taking off the Elvis album and slipping it back in its cardboard cover. Zoey picked up a snow globe and pretended to be studying it, though she hardly saw it in her hand. If Sophie noticed anything out of the ordinary, she didn't let on. She walked into the room talking, as if they were all still in the middle of a conversation.

"Evelyn says there's a big storm on the way. An ice storm. Everyone is running around town buying up batteries and water and groceries. I guess we should have put on the news tonight."

"I heard there might be snow," Zoey said, "but not a storm."

James peered out the window. "It's started snowing. I hadn't even noticed. It already looks icy, too. I'll drive you home, Zoey."

"Not in that old truck," Sophie cut in. "You

haven't even put the chains on. Zoey can stay over."

"Thanks, but I don't want to trouble you."

"It's no trouble. All the rooms are clean and freshly painted, thanks to James. Like a real hotel."

"Do you think it's that bad?" Zoey didn't mind spending more time with James and Sophie, but she didn't want to intrude.

"I haven't heard any plows yet. I'm not sure we will. No offense to your father," Sophie said, "but I don't think the problem with the trash and snow removal contract is completely settled yet. Evelyn doesn't seem to think so. It's another thing for her to worry about, the houses out here being snowed in. But we have a generator and plenty of food. I don't see any problem."

Zoey thought that for once the fretful Evelyn might be right. She knew that the village had made a handshake agreement and trash was being collected on a regular schedule again. But the contract was not signed, and her father still worried.

"I think you're right. If it was completely settled, we would have had a celebration at our house by now," she admitted.

It had actually been a relief to come to the orchard tonight. Lucy was trying hard to stir up Christmas spirit, but Charlie was tense and touchy and out at meetings till all hours of the night. Zoey felt bad for him, but there was no way she knew how to help.

"It's settled. You should stay." James turned to her and then back to the record player. "We have a lot more tunes to spin and Froggers to sample."

"And I was hoping for a Scrabble match," Sophie admitted.

"Perfect. But I have to warn you, I'm a master at that game," James said.

Zoey grinned. "So you say, Potter. Grab a dictionary and we'll see who's the master."

Sophie laughed. "Watch out, James. You may have met your match."

He looked surprised and intrigued. "You might be right, Grandma. I've been thinking the same thing myself."

It wasn't just his words but the way his blue gaze sought Zoey's that made her blush. She reminded herself not to take James too seriously. Even if she did believe him, where could this lead? He was off to South America in a week or two. Still, Zoey knew his disarming personality had just about melted her common sense and worn a steady path to her heart.

Chapter Twelve

CHARLIE TOSSED IN HIS SLEEP, TRYING TO catch a few more winks before the alarm went off. He had a crick in his neck and felt chilled to the bone. The mattress felt lumpy, and the quilt was barely past his knees. He punched up his pillow and quickly realized it was a wadded-up sweatshirt.

Then he remembered. He was not home in bed but stretched out on the nubby brown couch in his office, his down jacket tossed over his body as a makeshift blanket.

He sat up and rubbed his eyes, afraid to look outside, though he had been watching the storm through the night and into the early hours of the morning. He had also been talking on his phone to the fire chief, police chief, and all the town's support services until his throat was hoarse.

He walked to the window and pulled his jacket on. The heat in the building was off. He suspected the electricity was gone, too. Not a good sign, not a good sign at all.

He lifted the shade, and his heart fell. The world outside was a crystal palace—every tree, car, and building on Main Street coated with ice. Every phone and utility line hanging low with the glistening weight. He could not discern even a single tire track on the street. Or any sign that plows had passed.

Though he had called a backup list of every independent plow operator he could find, their light equipment hadn't made much of a dent. The snow was not very high, not by New England standards, but the icy coating over it had turned his village into a danger zone. He already knew from reports last night that the arctic blast had knocked down trees and tree limbs, crashing them into houses and cars. How would they even begin to clear that damage if the emergency trucks couldn't drive on the roads?

The phone rang and he answered quickly. "Village Hall, Mayor Bates."

"Charlie, it's me. Are you all right?"

The sound of Lucy's sleepy voice filled him with longing to be home, waking up with his family—and not feeling responsible for the entire village.

"I'm okay, honey. Just about to get things rolling again. I thought you were Rheinhardt," he said, mentioning the fire chief.

"I won't keep you. I know you have a lot to do. The power is off here, but at least we still have heat. Zoey stayed over at Sophie Potter's. They're all fine. Sophie even has a generator."

"Good, tell her to stay there. I'll pick her up later in the truck." Charlie felt relieved to hear Zoey was safe. The last thing he wanted was her driving on these roads. "I'm going to open the diner. At least I can set up a place for folks to get warm and get some food and coffee."

Charlie knew there was a lot more he needed to do. But that was just the way his mind worked—hot food and coffee seemed the obvious place to start.

"Good idea. How about the church? They have a generator, too. You should call Reverend Ben and see what he can do."

Charlie hadn't thought about the church, but it was a good suggestion. Maybe Reverend Ben could rally some church members and get them out shoveling?

"I'll bring the boys. We can help," Lucy added.

"Thanks, honey . . . but how will you get to town? I sent those independent plow guys out last night, but they didn't make a dent. I could have done a better job with my soup ladle."

"It's early. Maybe the sun will melt some of this down in a few hours. Just take it step-by-step. We'll get there—and take it step by step, too."

Charlie had heard the temperature would stay well below freezing today. But trust Lucy to come up with an optimistic possibility. Even walking seemed treacherous, but Charlie knew his wife would not be persuaded to stay home.

The truth was, he did want his family near him today and needed their help and company.

"Sounds like I can't change your mind. Be careful, Lucy . . . And thank you," he added quietly.

"Don't be silly, Charlie. No need to thank me. See you later."

Lucy's call had been a short respite, tamping down some of his stress. He had barely hung up before he was feeling overwhelmed again. A binder with the town's emergency plan sat open on his desk, but he didn't bother to check it again. He had memorized every word last night. Not that it had helped him much.

The roads were the problem. If only the trash and snow removal company hadn't taken such a hard line last night. They had gone back to work the past few weeks on a handshake. But the contract was not signed and now, with the ice storm, the company owner had the upper hand: If Charlie didn't agree to the terms K&B wanted, the plows would not budge.

Charlie had tried all night to persuade him, reminding the man he couldn't act without the town council's consent. But he knew this was payback for the way he had strung out the situation, bickering about the yearly increases. Now the company owner claimed he couldn't get the drivers and snowplows out unless Charlie signed on the dotted line. An insurance liability, he said. He was sorry, but it couldn't be done.

No sense calling back this morning, Charlie thought. *Though I might call later, after conferring with the council.* Right now he had to check in with Police Chief Sandborn and Fire Chief Rheinhardt. He had to mobilize every village employee and volunteer, get them out on the streets digging, and even plowing where they could. He had to open the diner and set up the warming center, and check on seniors and folks living outside of the village who were completely snowed in. He had to call Reverend Ben, who could probably help by setting up the church as another center and calling around to some of the old people. And he had to do it all right now.

Not a prayerful man by nature, Charlie closed his eyes and took a breath. *God, please help me today,* he silently prayed. *Send a few helping hands my way? And please, remind me why I ever wanted this job.*

EMILY SLIPPED OUT OF BED, CAREFUL NOT TO wake Dan. She pulled the bedroom curtain aside and blinked at the glistening shards of light. It was still very early in the morning, but the sky was clear and an icy coating reflected sharp, bright sunlight. The backyard looked beautiful— the trees and bushes, the birdbath and lawn, all coated in ice.

A beautiful disaster, Emily reflected. She could

already tell the electricity was off, and she hoped that none of their pipes were frozen. Her first thought was to check in with the heads of the fire and police departments, then rush down to Village Hall.

That's not my job anymore, she realized wistfully. *This storm is Charlie's challenge to navigate.*

Down in the kitchen, the appliances were useless. She was about to go in search of the camp stove when her cell phone rang. She was surprised to see the caller was Reverend Ben.

"Emily? Did I wake you?"

"I'm just rattling around the kitchen. It's a mess out there, isn't it? Though very beautiful."

"God's handiwork is magnificent. Though magnificently inconvenient, too. I just spoke to Charlie Bates. The Clam Box has a generator, and he's opening it up as a warming center. He asked if I would open the church, too, but I'd already thought of that."

"That's a good idea." Emily had forgotten the diner had a generator.

"He's been working hard, Emily; slept in his office last night. But this storm was particularly nasty, and there's that problem with the snow-removal company. I hope the deacons and volunteers from the congregation can help clear the town, after they've finished digging out the church."

"I'm sure they will." She glanced at her own ice-covered driveway and thought of Dan, still in bed. "It will take a while for us to dig out. But I'm sure we can get down to the church later and help, Reverend. Is that why you're calling?"

"Not exactly, though I'm grateful for your offer." Reverend Ben paused. Emily was curious now, wondering what this call was really about. "I don't mean to meddle—or any disrespect to Charlie. But I think it's fair to say he can use some help, more than I can offer. And not just shoveling—some guidance and advice from someone who has faced this situation."

Emily didn't answer. She knew that Reverend Ben must have thought long and hard before making this appeal. She didn't want to seem stubborn or spiteful, but she needed to respect some boundaries here—Charlie's and those she had set for herself and her family.

"I know you mean well, Reverend. But Charlie is the mayor now. He calls the plays today. Even if I tried to help him, I doubt he would hear me out."

"I understand. And I know it's a long shot. But if ever there was a day that he *might* listen to and even welcome your advice, this would be the one," Reverend Ben mused. " 'Blessed are the peacemakers,' Emily. And I don't need to remind you what the Scripture says about turning the other cheek?"

Emily smiled. "No, Reverend, you don't."

"The thing is, of all the people I know who love this village and everyone in it, you and Charlie are side by side at the top of the list. People need help today, Emily. It's an emergency. Charlie is smart but new at this job. You're an old hand. Maybe you two can put aside your differences and join forces? You would be a formidable team. And everyone in town would benefit."

Emily considered his words a moment. "That's good of you to say, but I'm not sure it's the right thing to do. Or even possible." She not only had Charlie's rebuff to consider but the reaction of her family. What would they say if she ran down to Village Hall today and declared herself Charlie's new deputy? She had just turned a corner with Dan and Jane. She didn't want to risk disappointing them again.

But she couldn't explain any of this to Reverend Ben, not this morning. "I appreciate your calling. I do, Reverend. But I have to think about this. It's not as simple for me as you might expect."

"I didn't think it would be. Stay safe. Please also remember, the church is open if you're looking for warmth and company."

If you don't go to the diner, he meant. Emily thanked him and ended the call.

Part of her knew she could help Charlie. But when she had tried to initiate a simple conversation with him on the street that day, he had answered with an angry, insulting rebuff. She certainly didn't need more of that.

You were giving out flyers for the open-space group, another voice reminded her. *Not the best way to win his trust.*

True. But why should I help him now? Let people see what they got when they voted for him instead of me.

It wasn't her nature to be spiteful, but Emily couldn't deny that's how she felt.

But Reverend Ben's words stuck in her head. Despite their differences, she and Charlie both loved the village and felt called to serve and protect the people who lived there.

Maybe I should go just for the sake of my friends and neighbors. Maybe there's some way I can offer some guidance without offending him?

Dan and Jane came into the kitchen together, both wearing sweatshirts over their pajamas. The heat was off, the house growing colder by the minute. Dan carried the big battery-operated radio they kept for emergencies.

"I just heard the forecast. It's an arctic blast. The ice is a real wild card. It's made a mess of everything. I just checked the street. I don't think a plow has come through yet."

Jane took a carton of milk from the fridge and sniffed. "I guess this is still good. But the fridge is off."

"There isn't much in there. I didn't get to the

market yesterday. I knew we were getting snow, but I had no idea it would be this much," Emily added, realizing they were probably among the few who had not prepared.

"Maybe we could eat cereal?" Dan pulled open a cupboard and shook a box that sounded nearly empty.

"I hear the church is open as a warming center. And the Clam Box is, too. Maybe we should go there?"

"The Clam Box? You hate that place," Dan reminded her.

"I know, but . . ." Emily met her husband's knowing gaze. She could tell he already suspected something. "Reverend Ben just called. He spoke to Charlie this morning, and he got the feeling that our new mayor could use a little advice and support. From an old hand. He suggested I offer some help."

Dan looked incredulous. "I love Reverend Ben. But does he think for a moment that plan would actually work—short of some biblical-sized miracle?"

"He seems to think Charlie is worn out and willing to listen to anyone—including me. But I don't want to go if you two don't want me to. I promised to stop jumping into causes for every little village crisis. I'm fine with keeping that promise, honestly."

Dan peered down at her. "Do you really want

to help Charlie? After everything he's said about you? I say let him sink or swim."

"That thought did cross my mind," she admitted, though not proudly. "But everyone needs advice once in a while. You gave me plenty my first term as mayor," she reminded him.

"True. But you weren't too stubborn to listen. Do you think he would even hear you out?"

"I said the same thing to Reverend Ben. But he made a good point. It's not about me and Charlie. It's about the people in this town, their well-being and safety. Families are trapped without power and are dealing with all sorts of problems. I'm willing to offer my knowledge and experience. But not if you think it's a bad idea. I guess I'm not sure what to do."

Dan gazed at her, his expression reflecting her own confusion.

"I think Mom should help Charlie," Jane said.

Emily turned to her. "You do?"

"People need you, Mom. Everyone is cold and stuck in their houses. It will be even worse tonight. You know what to do. Charlie wants to help, but I'm not sure he knows how."

Emily was touched by her daughter's understanding. "Okay, maybe I should try—if you come with me. If Dad wants to stay here, he can," she added, glancing at Dan.

"Don't be silly. Of course I'm coming. I agree

with Jane. You know what to do. You should help today, if Charlie will let you. I know what I've been saying about you keeping your nose out of town business, but this is different." He sighed. "Besides, it's hard to refuse Reverend Ben. I think he knows that, too."

Emily smiled. "Yes, I think he does."

Dan's brow furrowed. "What do you think we did with those old snowshoes? A walk into the village will be like trekking over a glacier in Iceland."

Emily shrugged. "You're always dreaming about taking adventurous vacations, dear. This will be good practice."

Dan rolled his eyes, and Jane laughed. Emily just felt glad that her family was in her corner again.

"ZOEY? IT'S DAD. YOU'RE STILL AT THE orchard, right?"

"Yep, we just finished breakfast." James was washing dishes, and Sophie was talking to Reverend Ben on her cell phone. Zoey walked into the mudroom to hear her father better. "Mom said you're opening the diner. I want to help."

"That's sweet of you, honey. I wish you were here, too. But I don't want you to drive. You wait there until the road is clear, and I'll pick you up."

"James said he'll drive me. He's going to put chains on Sophie's truck."

"That old heap? It's more dangerous than your car." Her father's voice was gruff and protective. "I know you always help me when you can, honey. I appreciate that. But you can help today by staying safe. Promise me, okay?"

"All right." Zoey felt frustrated. As much as she complained about working at the diner, this was one day she really wanted to be there with her family.

"Good girl. I'll talk to you later."

Her father ended the call, and Zoey walked back into the kitchen. James had finished washing and was drying now. She picked up a towel and helped him. "Something wrong, Zoey?"

"That was my dad. He said you shouldn't drive Sophie's truck, even with chains on the tires. He says it's too dangerous."

James reached up to hook a frying pan on the rack that hung from the ceiling. "He might be right. We haven't been outside yet. You don't look very happy at the prospect of staying here today. Tired of my company already?"

Zoey finally smiled. "It's not that," she said, avoiding a direct answer to the question. "He set up the Clam Box as a warming center. I'm sure it's crazy busy, and my father has a lot of other things he needs to do today without being shorthanded at the diner. I bet everyone blames him for the mess the storm made. Working there is the one way I can help him."

"I'd like to help, too. I'm sorry he said we shouldn't take Bella. But maybe it's for the best. It would be hard to be stuck on the Beach Road in the cold if we didn't make it."

Or worse, Zoey thought, the light truck could slide right off the road and wind up in a ditch. Or go into a spin. Her father was right. It wasn't worth the risk. Still, she wished there was some way she could get there.

Sophie returned to the kitchen and hung up the phone. She looked as if she had just heard good news. "Guess what? I've arranged with Reverend Ben to set up here as a warming center, for people who live out this way and don't have generators. We have plenty of heat, food, and water—and the best decorations in town."

James did not look surprised. He knew his grandmother well. "That's good of you, Grandma. But how are they going to get here?"

"Sam Morgan is going to drive around and pick folks up. He has a big, heavy truck with a plow on the front. Reverend Ben said he's already been to town and back. His wife, Jessica, is coming to help me and some other ladies from the church, too. If you two could just put out some folding chairs in the living room and dining room and help me with the percolators, we'll be fine."

"I'll get the chairs," James said.

"Where are the percolators?" Zoey asked.

Sophie was the only person she knew who owned two or even three giant coffeepots. Her house was as well-equipped for company as any catering hall. "I can set that up for you."

Sophie directed them, almost giddy with excitement. "They'll probably go through all the cookies we made, Zoey. But this is just as important as Christmas."

"It is," Zoey agreed. "And we can make more by then."

She set off on her job, glad to be busy.

THE CLAM BOX WAS CROWDED, AS EMILY had expected. Luckily, three seats at the counter were free, and they claimed them quickly. She recognized faces from all over town—Grace and Digger Hegman, Frank Dillard, and Vera Plante. All the members of Charlie's town council were huddled in a booth in the back. Charlie was racing in and out of the kitchen, a cell phone pressed against his ear. He didn't seem to notice them.

The chalkboard that usually posted the day's special read: FREE FOOD AND HOT DRINKS—COFFEE, TEA, HOT COCOA. SANDWICHES, SOUP, AND DESSERTS. COMPLIMENTS OF MAYOR BATES AND HIS FAMILY.

He was on the right track there. Who could refuse a hot drink today? The mere scent of the coffee was wildly distracting.

Lucy swept past with a coffeepot, surprised to

see them. "Emily, Dan . . . coffee?" she asked. They both nodded quickly. She served them and set down a hot chocolate for Jane.

"It's very generous of you to open and do all this for the town," Emily said.

"It was Charlie's idea. We'll stay open as long as people need the shelter. I just hope the soup and sandwiches hold out."

"I'm sure people are grateful just to be in a warm place," Emily replied.

"Thanks, Emily. I'll tell Charlie you said that. Charlie, look who's here, Emily and Dan." Lucy announced their presence as if the two couples were all old friends, Emily noticed. Lucy did have wonderful social skills.

Charlie looked as if he didn't want to come over and talk, but Lucy kept waving her hand. Finally, he walked the short distance from the grill. "Hello, folks. How are you faring?"

"Our heat is off, but we don't have it too bad, compared to a lot of other families," Emily said.

"Any word on getting the roads clear, Charlie?" Dan asked bluntly.

"I've been working on it, believe me." Charlie was trying to sound upbeat and in control but tension shone through. "We've got town workers out shoveling Main Street and a crew of plow operators I hired coming through. There are a lot of roads. It's going to take time."

"Of course it will. That goes without saying,"

Emily agreed. "Have you called Tom Dempsey, up in Newburyport? He might be able to help."

Charlie stared at her. She held her breath and waited, expecting an explosion.

"Dempsey?" He squinted at her. "Sure . . . I spoke to his department, to his boss. Last night."

Emily suspected he was bluffing and didn't know who she was talking about. "That's good. I'm sure he can help you, since he supervises and schedules the routes of the plow trucks for that area. Once they get their roads clear, he might send one or two down here. He did that for the village one winter a few years ago. The village will need to cover the salaries and the supplies, of course. As I'm sure you know."

Charlie nodded. "Right. We talked about that . . . He's getting back to me."

Emily nodded, feeling satisfied this slim arrow had hit its mark. "Good coffee," she said sincerely. "I know it sounds trivial, but I really missed it this morning. I can't even think straight without coffee."

"Me, neither," Charlie agreed. He folded his arms over his chest. "So . . . anyone else who might not be listed in the emergency plan? Just wondering."

Emily considered the question, thinking of county and even state officials whom she might contact at a time like this. And some at the utility company, as well. "Let's see . . . now that you mention it, there are a few . . ." She paused. "It's so noisy in here. Maybe we should talk in the kitchen?"

"It is noisy. Come on back." Charlie headed for the swinging doors, and Emily got to her feet. She glanced back at Dan, who smiled at her with fingers crossed. Emily followed Charlie into the kitchen, feeling as if she were willingly walking into a lion's den, half expecting him to bite her head off.

Charlie's cook, Tim, ladled soup in a row of bowls on a large tray while Lucy waited to carry them into the dining room. If either of them thought there was anything odd about Emily and Charlie meeting in the kitchen, they didn't show it.

"Hot soup, coming through," Lucy said lightly as she sailed by.

Emily faced Charlie and took out her cell phone, then browsed her list of contacts. "There are a few more people you might reach out to—beyond the names in the plan," she said. "Let me see if I can find them for you."

"Why aren't they in the plan? That's what I want to know."

His tone wasn't accusatory, exactly. Just frustrated. Emily would have felt the same in his shoes.

"I guess it's because there's a network of people you get to know being in the job for a long time. People I developed relationships with, who knew me and were willing to help. Not because they had to, but because we were friends and colleagues. I hope they'll help you, too. It's worth a try."

Charlie seemed satisfied with that answer but still frowned at her. "That makes sense. But why in the world do *you* want to help me? I thought you'd be pleased as punch to see me fail."

That was even a harder question to answer. "I know we don't agree on a lot of things, Charlie. But one thing we do agree on is this town and the people in it. I know you would do anything to help everyone get through this mess safely. And I feel the same."

"True enough," Charlie admitted, a little reluctantly. "Though I never thought of it that way."

"I never did, either," she answered honestly. "But maybe we should. Even if it's just for today?"

He gazed at her a moment, then handed over an order pad and a pencil. "Okay. What would you do? Who would you call? I don't know if it's sleep deprivation or what, but I guess I'm willing to hear out anyone right now."

She knew that was as close as he would ever come to a thank-you, and she began to describe how she would deal with the situation, giving Charlie ample credit for the bases he had covered. He asked a lot of questions and seemed encouraged by her suggestions. When they were finally done, he had several pages torn from the order book with names to call from Essex to Rockport, all the way down to Peabody and up to Princeton, plus a list of jobs he could delegate to his staff.

"I'd better get back to the office. You've been a big help, Emily. I can't believe it . . . but I won't forget it."

"Happy to do what I can. Is there anything else? I can oversee one of those areas for you—the warming centers or checking on the elderly?" She wasn't sure he would want her any more involved than she'd been already.

"Let's see . . . the warming centers. That's a good spot. We have one at the church and one at Potter Orchard. Sam Morgan offered his house, too, for overflow. But they're a little farther out. We need to spread the word and find more transportation. Can you handle that?"

Emily tried hard not to smile. "I think so. Thanks for the assignment," she added. "I'll check in if I have questions."

"You do that." He suddenly stuck out his hand. "I know we're usually on opposite sides of every question. I can't promise it will ever be different. But I have to say, you surprised me today. You're all right, Emily Warwick. You sure know how to take the high road."

Emily shook his hand, pleased at his compliment. "Thanks, Charlie. You surprised me today, too."

A short time later, Emily met Dan back at the lunch counter. She saw Jane across the room, sitting at a table with a group of her friends. "You were back there a long time," Dan said. "I thought Charlie might have pushed you in the freezer and thrown away the key."

"I didn't know what to expect either. But he did hear me out, and I gave him advice. I hope it helps." She took a sip of her coffee. It was cold but still tasted good. "We shook hands."

"That is big. You ought to tell Reverend Ben. He'll be pleased."

"Yes, he will," Emily agreed. "I hope you don't mind, but Charlie asked me to oversee the warming centers."

"I'm not surprised," Dan said with a smile. "What can I do to help?"

Emily was grateful for his offer and his understanding. "We need to make a ton of phone calls to start. Let's find a booth and a place to charge the phones." Luckily, she had remembered to bring the chargers.

This was not going to be easy. She didn't have any of the resources of her old office at Village Hall, but she didn't feel comfortable asking to do the job there. Even if she and Charlie had struck a truce, that was his command post and inner sanctum now.

I'm just a deputy today. Not the sheriff. And that's fine. More than fine. Just as it should be.

CHARLIE PULLED ON HIS DOWN JACKET AND gloves and worked his way through the crowd to the door. He needed to get back to Village Hall, even though he was leaving poor Lucy and the boys shorthanded. C.J. didn't seem to mind so much, but Jamie kept sending him comically desperate looks, as if no one could survive bussing so many tables.

He saw Emily and Dan in a booth, talking on their cell phones and making lists on sheets of paper most likely borrowed from schoolkids doing homework at other tables. He could barely believe Emily had come here. But the advice she had given him was golden, and he was eager to follow through.

He stepped out on to the street, wishing he could run to Village Hall, but forcing himself to tread carefully. At least there was some sand down. And his old friend Krueger was selling snow shovels and Ice Melt at half price. He stood in front of his store and waved. "Hang in there, Charlie. So far, so good," he shouted.

"Thanks, George. I'm doing my best."

A little farther down Main Street, Tucker and a few other police officers were helping shopkeepers clear the sidewalk.

"That's the way, folks. Everybody does their

part. We'll get through this. Don't worry," Charlie coached them. "Help is on the way."

"That's the spirit, Dad."

It was Zoey, standing in front of the diner. The busboy, James Potter, was with her. Part of him felt relieved to see she was safe and sound, and the other part was upset that she had not kept her promise.

"I thought you were staying at the orchard. You promised me you wouldn't take that old truck out . . . Did you drive her here?" He turned from Zoey to James, already blaming him.

"No, sir. Sam Morgan gave us a ride. He's been shuttling people in and out of town all day. He brought some neighbors to my grandmother's and said we could ride back to town with him."

"I called you, Dad. You didn't answer," Zoey explained. "I thought it would be all right. Reverend Ben thought Sam's truck was safe enough for church members."

Charlie felt foolish for losing his temper. "I guess that was okay. Right now, the diner sounds like Fenway after a home run. I must have missed the phone."

"I just want to help, Dad."

"I'm sorry. That's sweet of you, Zoey. Don't mind me. I'm tired," he admitted. "Your mother and brothers will be thrilled to see you." He glanced at James. "You here to help, too?"

"Absolutely."

"Better get in there. It's a madhouse. I'll be in my office. And thank you, honey. You're a special girl. I always said that."

"Thanks, Dad. Good luck!"

Charlie waved and concentrated on his footing again. Tiny, careful steps, one behind the other, that was the only way he could get from A to B. It seemed a metaphor for his life lately. *But at least I'm moving forward,* he reminded himself. *One slippery step at a time.*

IT WAS SOMETIME AFTER SIX THAT NIGHT when Emily called Charlie. She was at Sophie Potter's house, checking to see how many people were sheltered there and to see if Sophie needed any supplies. The house was filled, but it seemed under control, with Sophie at the stove, cooking up a storm of her own, a huge preholiday party.

"I think we've managed to get everyone who needs to be out of the cold tonight into one of the warming centers, Charlie. There's food and blankets for all, and most will have cots to sleep on, too."

"Good to know. And good job. I appreciate you stepping up." His words of gratitude were gruffly spoken. But he had thanked her, a surprising first in their relationship.

"I was glad to help. I can continue tomorrow, too," she added.

"All right, if you want to. No pressure. I'm

going to stop by the church and see how they're doing. I'm letting folks stay over at the diner, too," he added. "There's no heat at our house. Looks like I'll be there with my family tonight."

"That makes sense," Emily said.

"Where will you be tonight, you and your family?"

Was he actually concerned about her—or just curious? Concerned, Emily decided. They disagreed about a lot of things, but she knew Charlie had a good heart underneath. Very far underneath, sometimes.

"I'm going to my sister's house. She and Sam have a generator, so they offered their place as a warming center, too. But it didn't seem as if we needed another in this area. And they live a bit farther out than Sophie, so it's harder to get to."

"Very true. Though we'll see how long these centers are needed. Sophie might need a break after a day or so. Let's see how it goes. Tomorrow is another busy day. Guess I'll check in with you in the morning, Emily."

"Good idea. Talk to you then. Stay warm," she added.

"Same to you and yours," Charlie said.

Emily said good-bye and ended the call.

"Who was that?" Dan asked. He had been walking around Sophie's house, socializing with all the storm guests, but now stood nearby.

"I had to check in with Charlie. I'm going to help him tomorrow, too."

"Reporting in to the mayor?" Dan teased. "Did you ever think you'd be working for him, Em?"

Emily smiled. "I'm not working for him, I'm just a volunteer. But no, not in a million years. Goes to show, you just never know what's going to happen when you wake up in the morning."

"Very true. This morning was a perfect example of that."

A few minutes later they called Sam, and he picked them up in his truck. They stopped at their own house for sleeping bags and overnight needs and then headed over to Sam's house.

Emily knew that her mother and Ezra had been the first to arrive, rescued by Sam early that morning. She wondered how her sister's nerves were holding up, stuck in the house with their mother all day. But there were many more people in the house, Emily realized, including Molly Willoughby, her husband, Dr. Matt Harding, and their youngest daughter, Betty, as well as Jessica's younger children, Tyler and Lily. Jessica had also invited her new neighbors, a young couple who had moved into an adorable little cottage on the pond that edged Sam and Jessica's property. Emily hadn't met them before, but she recalled their last name was Quinn. Jessica often mentioned the wife, Melissa.

In the past few months, they had become good friends.

"Emily, Dan . . . give me your coats, you must be frozen." Jessica ran to the door to greet each of them with a hug. Their dog, a yellow lab mix named Sunny, followed at her heels.

"We're fine. We've been hanging around warming centers all day," Dan explained. "Grazing on coffee and donuts."

Sam had come in right behind them and laughed. "A crisis brings out the best in people. I've always said that."

"I haven't had a single donut," Emily protested. "I didn't want to spoil my appetite. I knew there would be something delicious cooking . . . Is that freshly baked bread?"

"Among other things. Molly's in the kitchen working her magic. Even I had to step aside for a while."

Jessica was a wonderful cook, but so was her sister-in-law, Molly. Emily was sure that between them, they had created a feast from whatever ingredients were at hand.

"Can I help?" Emily asked.

"Maybe later. You've been out all day working. Why don't you warm up and relax for a while? I'll make you some tea."

"I'd love that. Where's Mother?" she asked.

"She and Ezra exhausted themselves doing crossword puzzles. They worked their way through an entire book today. Now Ezra is reading, and I think she's taking a nap," Jessica reported in a quiet voice.

Emily smiled and walked into the big family room where a fire blazed in the huge stone hearth. Jessica had already started decorating for Christmas, and a row of wooden angels stood among pine boughs on the mantelpiece. Sam had carved the set for his wife during the early years of their marriage. A huge tree stood in the corner of the room, covered with lights but with no ornaments yet. At the other side of the room, in the dining area, a long table had been set for all the guests. But the room was empty now while most of the guests relaxed near the fire.

Emily spotted Ezra sitting in a chair, focused on a thick book. Matt was playing chess with Tyler, who was in middle school now and on a chess team, Emily had heard. Lily, who was six, had already pounced on Jane and persuaded her older cousin to play with her. They sat surrounded by a pile of dolls, and moments later Betty joined them.

Emily found her mother in an armchair by the fire, a book open on her lap, her head tilted back as she slept. She was about to tiptoe away when Lillian's eyes opened.

"Were you watching me while I slept? That's rather rude, Emily." She sat up straighter, smoothing her cashmere cardigan and pearls.

Not her good pearls but the single strand she called her "everyday set." *But still, only my mother would wear pearls during an ice storm,* Emily reflected wryly. She did have on a long wool skirt, thick stockings, and sturdy boots, which were some compromise with the situation.

"I wasn't staring. I was just checking to see if you were still asleep." Emily sat in the armchair on the other side of the hearth.

"I was. Until you stared me awake. Just as well. I don't know how I even fell asleep. I might as well be sitting in the middle of South Station with all the hubbub here today."

"I think it's very cozy. And calm," Emily added. "You should see the warming centers. Everyone's safe, but they're very crowded. I'm thankful we have a comfortable, private place to stay, instead."

Lillian sighed. "We could all be comfortable in our own homes if that fool mayor could do his job properly."

"Charlie has no control over the power company and how fast they can get the lines and transformers repaired, Mother. You know that."

Her mother's head tilted back with surprise. "So you're defending him now? Did you drink any free Kool-Aid at the Clam Box this morning?"

Emily had to laugh. Her mother was still very sharp for her age. Before she could answer, Molly called from the dining room, "Hey, guys, dinner is served. We have a lot of yummy food here. Please help yourselves."

"A buffet . . . I should have known." Lillian made a face as Emily helped her up from the chair and handed over her cane. Lillian had always disliked buffets; mixing all sorts of foods together on one plate was not her style. Neither was it her style not to sit and be served.

"Why don't you find a seat at the table and I'll make you a plate?" Emily offered.

Lillian nodded. "I'd appreciate that. You know what I like. None of Molly Willoughby's food, please." Her voice was very low, but she rolled her eyes. "It never agrees with me."

In the midst of this emergency, only her mother could complain about landing in one of the loveliest and most comfortable houses in the entire village and dining on food prepared by one of the most acclaimed cooks for miles around.

Emily smiled to herself as she took two plates and stepped up to the long table filled with an array of dishes—freshly baked bread, green salad, chili, a pasta dish smothered in melted cheese, and even a chicken curry.

She couldn't speak for anyone else, but she was very, very thankful to be here tonight with her family, and she said a quick, silent prayer for so many others in town tonight who were not nearly as cozy and comfortable.

She was also grateful that she'd had the chance today to help them as much as she had been able, and suddenly realized she also had Charlie to thank for that.

Chapter Thirteen

O
N FRIDAY AFTERNOON, EMILY FOUND Reverend Ben in Fellowship Hall, chatting with Claire North and her husband, Nolan Porter. Though two days had passed since they all woke up to the ice storm, Fellowship Hall was still set up as a warming center, with long tables of hot drinks and a miscellaneous, ever-changing array of food. There were some tables for eating, others for socializing, and still others where people who were shut out of offices could work, with stations to charge cell phones and computers.

There were also some cots, folded up against a wall now, but used the first and second night after the storm. Emily did not expect anyone to stay over tonight. As she supervised the centers, she kept track of the attendance at each location, even interviewing people who came and went about their situations and needs.

Charlie had appreciated her efficient reports, in his way, she reflected with a wry smile. There were fewer people passing through this center than on Wednesday and Thursday, she noticed. But she still found the number concerning.

Sophie's house had been active on Wednesday and Thursday, but her visitors had thinned out. She was also at church today, balancing a big pot of soup on a hot plate. "I cooked this last night, but I don't think I'll have enough customers to use it up today. I thought you could use it here."

"Thank you, Sophie. We can." Emily was setting out another contribution of pastries and breads from Willoughby's Bakery as Sophie disappeared into the kitchen again.

She didn't mean to eavesdrop but couldn't help overhearing the minister's conversation with Claire and Nolan.

The couple managed the Inn at Angel Island for Liza and Daniel Merritt, who lived half the year in Arizona now. Claire had lived on the island most of her life, and Nolan was a fairly new arrival. The island, a tiny jewel set in Cape Light harbor, had been hit hard by the storm. The slim land bridge connecting the island to the mainland had been washed out, and Emily had heard that at first, the only help for the island's residents had been Coast Guard boats that had arrived on Wednesday and evacuated a few elderly and sick residents.

"There were no guests staying over Tuesday night when the storm hit, luckily. Nolan and I had all we needed and then some," Claire reported.

"Except electricity," her husband added. "Still without power, but we're managing. We lost a shutter or two, but there was no major damage to the inn."

"We did feel isolated," Claire admitted. "Weeks go by when I don't set foot off the island. But it's different when you know you can't."

"I'm glad you could get back to town. It's good to see you both. Will you be back tomorrow for the Christmas Eve service?" Reverend Ben asked. "We're starting earlier than usual. We know there are still concerns about traveling, especially at night."

The older couple looked relieved. "We were going to stay over at Vera Plante's house, even though she's still without power, too," Claire said. "But that's good to know, Reverend. Thank you."

Claire and Nolan left, and Reverend Ben came over to chat with Emily. Or maybe he was just drawn by the scent of the soup? He lifted the lid and inhaled a savory aroma—a combination of rich broth, vegetables, beans, and maybe even some chicken.

"This smells delicious. What kind of soup is it?"

Emily smiled. "You'll have to ask Sophie. She just delivered it."

Sophie appeared in the pass-through window between the kitchen and the hall. "Storm soup. I toss in all the perishables I can find in the fridge. And some herbs and such. A chicken or two doesn't hurt, but you can make it fine without."

"Sounds like a once-in-a-lifetime opportunity," Reverend Ben observed. "I may have a cup for lunch. It was generous of you to bring this here, Sophie, in the midst of running your own center."

"I was just telling Emily it's slowed down out there, Reverend. I think folks are getting back to normal."

"The town has stepped up to get the roads clear and clean up the fallen trees and other debris," Emily said. "But there are still a lot of pockets in the village without power. There's nothing the town can do about that. That part is up to the utility company."

Reverend Ben nodded. "Yes, I know. I'm concerned about Christmas Eve. Even though we're holding the service at four o'clock, I'm worried about what will happen afterward. Will people go back to their cold, dark houses? That doesn't seem much like Christmas to me. I'm afraid the church can't really accommodate them here, either. Willoughby's has been very generous, and so have many church members who can cook, but I don't think we can hold a Christmas party, not on such short notice."

"I've been wondering about that, too. I thought that maybe the Clam Box would be open," Emily said. "But Lucy told me just about all their supplies are gone, and they haven't gotten any deliveries this week. Charlie is sending his cook,

Tim, to Boston today to buy what he can, but he's not sure what he'll find."

"I still have plenty in my deep freeze. And my pantry." Sophie had come out of the kitchen and set a pan of corn bread on the table, next to the soup. "I stocked up for my family Christmas party, and I tend to keep an ample supply of food on hand anyway. You'd think I still had a houseful to feed."

"You mean you'd give it to the diner or serve it here at church?" Emily asked.

Sophie looked confused. "The diner? Why would I do that?" She leaned over and nearly whispered, "I'm pretty sure that whatever I do with that food, it will be tastier than what's served at the Clam Box. No offense to Charlie Bates."

Emily knew that was true. But she still didn't understand. She could tell from Reverend Ben's expression that he was puzzled, too.

"So you want to cook it at home? And bring it here?"

Sophie shook her head again, strands of her white hair flying loose from her bun. "I want to have a Christmas party at my house and serve it all there. Clean that deep freeze right out, and the pantry. It does occur to me that I'm probably leaving there very soon, and I certainly can't take it with me, as the saying goes."

"That's most generous of you, Sophie.

Honestly." Reverend Ben hesitated, seeming overwhelmed by the offer. "But we are talking about a huge group coming into your house—more than arrived for the warming center."

"I understand, Reverend. That's the best part. I persuaded my children to let me hold our family Christmas gathering this year, and I've been thinking it would be a celebration of all the beautiful years I've spent in that house—and my entire family, before me. What better way to celebrate, and honor those years, than to open the doors and invite everyone in town to join in the party?" Her face was beaming, Emily thought, with the light of her inspiration, generosity, and loving heart. "I know I've got to leave soon, but I'd rather go out with a bang, as they say."

Reverend Ben began to look intrigued. "It's an ambitious idea, but it would give so many people the gift of Christmas who would otherwise be cold and isolated. I can't find fault with it," he admitted. "In fact, I think it might work, coming from such heartfelt, generous intentions."

"We'll all help you," Emily promised. "There are a lot of people at church who have volunteered at the warming centers and asked if there was any sort of celebration for Christmas Eve. I'm sure they'll help you and contribute dishes to your dinner, too."

"God will send plenty of helping hands. I'm not worried about that. He always does when you set out on the right path. Remember the story about the loaves and fishes?" Sophie reminded them, the note of faith in her voice pure and clear as a bell. "We just need to spread the word—to the congregation and out in the village."

"We do. There's not much time. But I'll work on that and announce it at the service, as well. Mrs. Honeyfield can make some flyers for the bulletin about the party, and directions to the orchard, too."

"I'll post flyers in town," Emily offered, thinking a Loaves and Fishes Potluck Open House Christmas Party would be the most apt description, but also wondering how many would get the joke.

"How about your children, Sophie? Maybe you should speak to them first before we get started on these plans?" Reverend Ben's tone was gentle and respectful. Emily wondered about that, too. Would Sophie's children even allow her to offer her house like this? If they did object, she definitely couldn't blame them.

Sophie sighed. "I'm not saying I plan to deceive them. But it's still my house, my deep freeze, and my doors to open to whomever I please. It won't be that way for always, but it is for now. So, I don't see any reason to ask their permission. Though I do hope they come," she added sweetly.

Reverend Ben glanced at Emily. "Fair enough.

Though we insist that you accept as many helpers as we can rally. Emily will help you figure out what you need."

"Absolutely. I'm free to talk right now if you can, Sophie."

"I am, too," Reverend Ben said. "Right after I get a bowl of that delicious soup and some corn bread."

"Help yourself, Reverend. There's more where that came from. Plenty more," Sophie promised.

EMILY COULD HARDLY REMEMBER SEEING SO many people in the sanctuary for the Christmas Eve service—or any occasion. She was very glad she had pushed herself, for once, to arrive on time with her family. Jessica and Sam had picked up her mother and Ezra and saved them seats up front. Her mother's doing, Emily guessed.

Her nephew Darrell, Jessica's oldest son, was back from Texas, where he was finishing a degree in computer science. He had always been a bright boy, interested in how things worked. He sat beside Sam, just as tall as his father now. Tyler and Lily sat between their parents, with Ezra and Lillian close to the aisle. Emily and her family sat on the other end of the pew, arriving with a few minutes to chat and catch up, though the main topic of conversation seemed to be how many people had come tonight for the service.

"I can't remember ever seeing this many—

including every Christmas Eve and Easter holiday since I was a girl," Jessica said.

"Me, neither," Sam agreed. "What a turnout. I think it's great."

Lillian glanced at them, a sour expression on her face. "Who are all these people? Not members of our congregation, I can tell you. Just riffraff. They descend for Christmas Eve, the big party night, but will disappear once the hard work starts again."

Emily shared a glance with her sister, but neither replied. There was a grain of truth to her mother's words. Some people only attended church on Christmas and maybe Easter. But did that mean they shouldn't be welcomed for these most important days? That wouldn't honor the spirit of compassion that Reverend Ben worked so hard to share with his flock. Besides, there might be potential new members here tonight. There were many who seemed familiar to her, families that had passed through the warming center in Fellowship Hall over the last few days and now were interested in what went on in the sanctuary. The thought made her smile. It seemed to her the way Christmas should be, strangers coming together, warmed and welcomed, given material comforts and nourishment, and spiritual comfort and nourishment, too.

Bright, trumpeting organ notes sounded the start of the service. Everyone turned to watch the choir march up the center aisle, with Reverend Ben walking at the very end. They were singing the processional "Joy to the World," and Emily felt a little catch in her chest. Everyone here had shared a momentous experience this week and had, by the grace of God, come through it relatively unscathed.

As her gaze followed the choir moving toward the risers, she caught sight of Charlie Bates and his family. She almost didn't recognize Charlie, who was dressed in a navy blue suit, white shirt, and bright red tie. He looked quite dignified, and Lucy looked lovely in dark blue velvet. Their boys and Zoey were also dressed in their best for the holiday. She couldn't say for sure, but she had a feeling that Charlie shared her feelings here tonight, of relief and gratitude that he had been able to help and protect people.

"Merry Christmas, everyone." Reverend Ben stood at the front of the sanctuary and greeted the congregation. "It's wonderful to see so many coming together for worship here tonight. I want to welcome everyone, most especially all our visitors. I hope you'll enjoy this service and visit us again in the new year."

He gazed out at the crowd a moment, then began the announcements. After the usual mention of monthly meetings, he looked up with a huge smile. "And I have a very special announcement to add. More of an invitation,

I'd say. But I will hand this part over to another member of our congregation . . . Sophie?"

Sophie Potter sat in the middle section, among her many relatives, who took up several rows of seats. Her grandson James, who sat next to her, gently helped her to her feet.

"After tonight's service," Sophie began, "you are all invited back to my house. Every last one of you," she added, her gaze sweeping the sanctuary. "Whether I've known you for years or we never, ever met, you are all very welcome to my house for the biggest and most wonderful Christmas party anybody in this town has ever seen. We've got plenty of food, more than enough to feed everyone in this sanctuary. But if you'd like to bring a dish, that would be fine, too. And please, don't be shy," she urged in her warm, motherly tone. "I know how many families are still stuck in cold, dark houses. That's no way to celebrate Christmas Eve, and it pains me to think of you all alone like that tonight. Come to my house and stay as long as you like. Or just drop by to say hello and grab a bite. All are welcome. I mean that sincerely. The directions are in the bulletin. But I expect you can follow a line of cars that will be leaving here tonight. The more the merrier, as they say. And you'll be doing a good deed by making an old woman very happy."

Many were softly laughing and talking quietly

about the invitation, Emily guessed. Many families had a warm house to go home to tonight and had their own plans. Her family would be going back to Jessica and Sam's, though they had all agreed to stop at Sophie's house first for a little while. Emily also wanted to make sure the town hostess with the mostest really did have all she needed for such an ambitious gathering.

"Yes, please come to Sophie's tonight," Reverend Ben repeated. "It will be wonderful to celebrate the holiday with our church family, after all we've been through."

The choir sang the introit, and Reverend Ben came down from the pulpit to call the congregation to worship and recite the opening prayers.

When it came time for Reverend Ben's sermon, the large audience sat very still and quiet. He stared down at the pages on the pulpit and shuffled them around a bit, uncommonly slow to begin. Then he looked up, blinking behind his gold-rimmed glasses, a small, gentle smile forming.

"I prepared a sermon for tonight, of course. I've been working on it for weeks, actually, based on our Advent theme of spiritual gifts. But, for some reason, I feel inspired to put these fine thoughts aside for tonight." He closed the folder that held the typed sermon and looked back up again. "I will speak from the heart—or perhaps, my soul?—part of the divine spirit that we all share.

"I have been very distracted the last few days by images of the nativity," he explained. He glanced over his shoulder, his gaze falling on the crèche that was set up on the altar. "Such a familiar scene, we don't even see it anymore. Do you know how that is? How we become blind and desensitized to sights that are so familiar? But this week, for some reason that perhaps only God knows, I looked at the scene and was struck by a new insight, a new way of seeing it. Yes, it is a symbol of the humble birth of our Lord and how he entered the world in such a modest, low way to share our humanity.

"But it is also a scene of community, cooperation, a coming together of so many diverse players in this joyful drama. Characters of high birth and low. A tradesman and his young wife, seeking a new home. A shepherd and a king. A wise man and even an angel. All from different backgrounds, with different perspectives on the world and different opinions, I'm sure. But their differences seemed suddenly trivial, eclipsed by their common experience, the awe-inspiring experience that connected them, that brought them to common ground, both literally and spiritually. The recognition and adoration of the baby Jesus.

"Can you imagine the situation that night?

Certainly, it was a crisis. Mary, forced to give birth outdoors, on a bed of straw, in a flimsy shelter alongside farm animals. Uncommonly rough, even for those days. But out of that crisis, opportunity arises. A chance for some to show their best nature, to share the experience of this young couple, not cast them aside. To aid and support this homeless family. To bring gifts and to simply respect and value them. All these very different people, brought together by the wonder of Jesus's birth. All experiencing the same revelation, the same joy in their hearts.

"I wasn't studying tonight's Scriptures when this insight came to me. I wasn't even sitting at my desk, staring into space, wondering what to say, as is often the case." His admission made many laugh.

"I was in Fellowship Hall, working in our warming center, filling the coffee percolators for the umpteenth time. Making sure everyone had enough blankets, pillows, and cell phone chargers. Surprised and grateful when the donations of food continued to come in. There were no barn animals wandering about. I don't think so, anyway," he added in a bemused tone that brought more laughter. "Only a diverse group of people, mostly strangers, brought together by an unexpected challenge, and showing their best side, their highest selves. Forgetting their differences and focusing on their common experience and the similarities deep inside.

"Finally, I thought of the beautiful, innocent baby in this scene. A baby who responds the same to the admiration of the shepherd or the king. A baby who doesn't know the difference between any of the different faces surrounding him. He reaches toward all of them with equal love. Because that is the way God has created and loves us. We are all equal in His eyes and all worthy of love, respect, and care.

"Maybe the message of the manger scene that I have overlooked for so long is simply this: In the eyes of God, our differences are infinitesimal. We are each unique, but equally wonderful, equally loved and valued. It is our challenge here, in this world, in this 'manger scene' of our own making, to see each other and treat each other just that way. To ignore the differences, the external experience, and look deeper. Down to the essential level of spirit. The way the infant looks up at each one of us, with so much love and trust.

"Sometimes we need a crisis, like a huge, destructive storm, to remind us. But the opportunities are then abundant to show care and love to each other. To express the qualities in our nature that are truly a gift from God. And we are continually reminded to look for the light that shines in each and every one of us. To feel the connection of our love for Him, and our love for each other."

The sanctuary was silent as Reverend Ben bowed his head and stepped away from the pulpit. The choir stood and began singing "It Came Upon the Midnight Clear."

Reverend Ben's sermon had put into words so many feelings Emily had experienced the past few days—but couldn't quite put her finger on at the time. He had a gift that way. She knew she would be mulling over these thoughts for a long time, well past Christmas.

WHEN THE SERVICE ENDED, ZOEY FELT AS if her family were the only people in the whole world who were not going to Sophie's house. Lucy seemed willing to go, but Charlie insisted that they have Christmas Eve on their own, just the family. He was closing the diner as a warming center and they would have their dinner there, since they still didn't have heat at home. Zoey guessed that Charlie needed a break from being in the midst of the entire village. He had barely had a minute off all week long. She could understand that, but it was hard for her to miss the party, since she had helped Sophie prepare and knew how much good food and fun Sophie was anticipating. It was going to be the party of the year, maybe even of the decade.

Across the sanctuary, she watched the Potter

clan empty out of their pew. Evelyn herded everyone to the side door, eager to beat the guests back to Sophie's house.

Zoey searched the group for James but didn't see him. Her parents and brothers were on line to wish Reverend Ben a merry Christmas, a mission that could take until New Year's Day, Zoey thought. She worked her way to a side door and stepped outside, greeted by the crisp night air and sharp, bright stars that covered the sky above the village green.

She felt alone and dispirited, not at all in a Christmas mood. She wondered how she would get through the night. She had a secret and it felt like a weight pressing on her chest. It was a secret from her parents, but she believed she was doing the right thing, keeping this from them. The mature thing. Her parents would be proud of her, if they knew. But the whole point was for them *not* to know.

She had been watching the mail the last few days—trying to be the first to the delivery before her mother or father. Which wasn't hard, since they were both out working so much. She'd received a letter yesterday, offering her the internship at the center. She had to read it a few times to make sure she understood the message. Then she felt so happy, she wanted to dance and scream. Then she remembered she couldn't take the job.

End of story. You've faced much tougher situations and disappointments, she reminded herself. *This is nothing. Besides, you knew better. It was dumb to go to the interview, knowing you could never take the job.*

She wasn't going to tell her folks and start another fight—or make them feel super guilty. And she didn't want to ruin everyone's Christmas with a big drama. Charlie was right. He had this one chance to be mayor, but she would have a lot of opportunities. She had to give him this. A special Christmas present. Even if he didn't realize it.

Someone tugged on her sleeve and she turned to see James, his face inches from her own. "Hey. I've been looking all over for you. I thought you left."

"Just slipped out to wait for my folks. It was so crowded in there. I thought you left with your family."

"I escaped the iron grip of Aunt Evelyn. It's all hands on deck, but I think they can manage without me for a little while. Are you coming to the orchard tonight? I hope so," he added. His blue eyes sparkled, as bright as any of the stars.

Zoey shook her head. "I'm sorry . . . I don't think I can. We're having Christmas Eve at the diner. There's still no power in our house. I don't think I'll be able to make it out there."

James looked surprised and disappointed. "Maybe later? I think the party will go on awhile. I can pick you up," he offered. "Maybe your whole family will come. They know they're invited, right?"

"Yes. And I'll remind them, but I think my dad wants to just lay low tonight. He's burned out from dealing with the storm and talking to everyone in town all week."

"I get it." James nodded, sounding sympathetic. He took her hand and caught her gaze. "It won't be the same without you. I was hoping we could dance to another Elvis song," he added. "Maybe you'll be able to slip away. I'll hope for the best, as my grandmother always says."

"I will, too," she promised, though she wasn't sure she could muster much hopeful energy tonight.

James leaned over and kissed her cheek. She felt happy again and wished she could go with him to Sophie's at that very moment.

They both heard his father calling from the parking lot, "James, where are you? We're leaving."

He gave her hand a quick squeeze, then vanished into the darkness. When she turned, Lucy was standing on the church steps, waving to her. "Zoey? We're going to the diner now. Dad is bringing the car around."

Zoey shook her head. "It's okay, I'll walk." Her

hands dug in her pockets as she headed across the green toward Main Street.

It was going to be the longest Christmas Eve of her life.

IT HAD SEEMED AN ODD IDEA TO HER TO spend Christmas Eve at the diner, but once the rest of her family got there, it didn't seem odd at all. Her mother had set up a small Christmas tree on one of the tables and their presents were stashed underneath. Her father disappeared into the kitchen and returned wearing a Santa cap. He set out some tasty snacks on the counter and carried around a tray of glasses filled with his famous Christmas punch. He had turned on Christmas music and sang along as he passed out the cranberry potion.

"I bet you don't know who this is singing," Charlie said.

Zoey took a sip of punch—mainly cranberry juice and ginger ale, but it was tasty. "Bet I do. Burl Ives."

Charlie looked surprised. "Very good. Best Christmas album ever."

"It's Sophie's favorite, too," she said, though she wasn't sure he heard her.

"Is this box for me? Is this the video game I asked for?" Jamie stood near the tree, shaking the gifts.

Lucy took the box from his hands. "We'll see.

We're not opening gifts yet. We have to eat dinner."

"What's for dinner? I'm starving." C.J. had worn a tie and jacket and his good wool pants to church, but now he yanked off the neckwear and draped his jacket over a chair. "Can I turn on the TV?"

"No, sir," Charlie replied. "No TV on Christmas."

"Thank heaven," Lucy said with a sigh. A big table in the center of the room was covered with a red tablecloth and set for five. She added a centerpiece of pine and holly and two diner candles. "See, it's just as nice as home."

It really wasn't, but Zoey appreciated her mother's effort to make it so. And her father's. It was certainly better than their cold, dark house. Even candles and a fire in the hearth couldn't dispel the shadows these last few nights.

"I think it's fun," Zoey said, determined to at least act cheerful. "The table looks very pretty. Can I help you with the food?"

Lucy had folded green napkins into little hat shapes and paused at the table to prop one up. "Thanks, dear. It's all ready. I made a roast and mashed potatoes."

Jamie took a seat and tucked the cloth napkin into his collar. He also wore his best clothes: a navy blue blazer, a white dress shirt, and a red tie. Zoey thought he looked like a miniature banker or lawyer. He enjoyed dressing up and didn't rip his tie off nearly as fast as C.J. always did.

"Church was so long," Jamie said. "All the singing made me hungry."

"Singing can't make you hungry, dummy." C.J. sat down and shook his head.

"Don't call your brother names, please?" her father said.

Her mother carried in the roast, and Zoey carried the side dishes. "I loved the singing," Lucy said. "That was the best part. I hope we can sing some carols later, before we open the presents."

Her brothers groaned together, making Zoey laugh. When they finally settled down, her mother asked everyone to bow their heads and said grace.

"Well said, Lucy. Thank you for that prayer. And for this delicious dinner. What a feast."

"Thank you, Charlie. Enjoy, everyone."

Zoey passed the serving plates around and filled her own dish. The meal did look good, but she couldn't help but wonder what they were eating at Sophie's house right now.

"Did you see how many people were headed for the orchard?" Lucy was obviously thinking in the same direction. "It looked like a car parade heading out of the church parking lot. I'll bet half the town will be there."

"At least they have someplace to go. I can do

without a big crowd tonight, everyone asking me when the roads will be clear and the power back on. I just want to relax and enjoy Christmas."

"I understand," Lucy said. "It's been a long week, and a very hard one."

So much for hoping, Zoey thought.

"I bet they're having fun." Jamie pushed a string bean around his plate. "All the kids in my class are there."

"Another reason to steer clear," her father said. "The noise must be deafening."

"It's a big house. People will spread out," Zoey said.

Lucy tilted her head to one side. "A big party can be fun. It's very good of Sophie to open her home for people who still don't have power or any way to cook a dinner. But we have everything we need. It's much cozier here."

"I agree. This is the perfect place for us to celebrate Christmas." Charlie smiled and gazed around the table. "Merry Christmas, everyone. Now, let's eat up so we can get to those presents."

A short time later, they were sitting by the tree and Charlie was passing out the gifts. Zoey was surprised when she opened a big box and found a pair of high boots that she had really wanted. "How did you know I wanted these, Mom?"

"I saw you eyeing them in the store when you thought I wasn't looking. I have my ways, you know."

Zoey felt touched by her thoughtfulness. She got some other great gifts, too—clothes that she had wanted and some books and art supplies. And it felt good watching her parents and brothers open the gifts she had chosen for them. She had bought Lucy a pair of comfort clogs for the hospital; she was on her feet so much at work. And Zoey had found a fancier, less practical gift for her, too.

"Oh, Zoey . . . this is beautiful." Lucy unfolded the flowered scarf Zoey had chosen and wrapped it around her shoulders. "Don't I look elegant?"

"You always look just right to me," Charlie answered. "But those flowers do look nice with your eyes and your dress."

Her mother seemed pleased and kept the scarf on. It did go well with her blue dress. She put her arm around Zoey's shoulders and gave her a hug. "I love it, honey."

When it was Charlie's turn to open his present, he tore off the wrapping, then carefully lifted the box cover. "Well . . . I'll be. I thought I was getting a pair of earmuffs."

"It's a desk set, Dad, for your office in Village Hall. I thought the mayor should have something special."

"This is special, all right." Charlie seemed impressed, even a bit awed, as he examined each piece of the fancy leather set—a desk blotter, a pencil holder, a note holder, and even a pricey pen and pencil set. "This looks expensive, Zoey. I think you overdid it."

"Do you like it?"

"I'll say. It belongs on a judge's desk. No, the president of the United States," he corrected himself. "You were way too extravagant—"

"You need that, Dad. Besides, you gave me a big raise. I could afford it," she added with a grin. "There's something else for your office. On the bottom of the box. Do you see it?"

He dug through the box again and came up with the last tissue-wrapped packet. He tore off the paper and smiled at the family portrait Zoey had framed for him.

"That's perfect, honey. Just what I need to give me a boost when things get rough down there."

"Things are going better now," Lucy assured him. "You did a lot the last few days to get us back to normal. People are grateful."

"After a shaky start," Charlie agreed.

Zoey was about to agree. She, too, had heard some good reviews of her father's performance as mayor the last few days. But before she could comment, her cell phone buzzed. She pulled it out from her pocket and found a text message from James:

Haven't given up on you. I can pick you up. My dad's car, not the truck. I know your father hates Bella.

When she looked up, she found her parents watching her. "Everything okay?" Lucy asked.

"It's James. He wants me to come to the orchard. Can I go? He said he can pick me up with his father's car."

Her parents exchanged looks. Charlie sighed. "I don't know. Christmas Eve is a time to be with your family."

"That's true," Lucy agreed. "But Zoey helped a lot with the party preparations, and she is close to Sophie. It's probably the last time Sophie will have a big get-together in that house."

Zoey's phone buzzed again with a text:

Everyone in town is here. They're all asking about your dad. They want him to come. I'm not just saying that to get you here . . .

Charlie leaned close, as if sensing his name had been mentioned. "What's he saying now?"

"He said everyone in town is there, and everyone is wondering if we're coming. They're asking for you, Dad. They want you to come."

"Me? Why would they want to see me?" he scoffed, but Zoey could tell he felt good about that report.

"Because you're the mayor, dear, and we've all just muddled our way through a big ordeal, and now folks are relieved and celebrating," Lucy replied.

"Can we go, Dad?" C.J. asked. "My friend Mike just texted me, too. He says it's awesome."

"I guess I've been outvoted," Charlie said, but he seemed pleased. "Let's clean up a bit and get our coats on."

CARS LINED THE NARROW LANE THAT LED TO Sophie's house. Luckily, a car parked close to the house was pulling away, and Charlie quickly claimed the spot. "You'd think it was the county fair in there," he mumbled.

"At least we don't have far to walk," Lucy said, balancing the large bowl of Christmas pudding she had made for their family's dessert.

"I'll carry that. You take my arm, Lucy," her father said gallantly.

Her mother had packed up the desserts she had prepared—a big Christmas trifle and an orange spice Bundt cake. Zoey carried the cake and followed them. The front door was open, and guests streamed in and out, many also carrying trays of food and gifts.

They stepped into a scene of light, music, and laughter. Zoey had never seen Sophie's house so active or filled with so many people— children and their young parents, old people, and everyone in between. The most well-to-do people in town were there, like Lillian and Ezra Elliot, and the most humble, like Grace Hegman and her father, Digger. She saw Reverend Ben and his family, including his daughter, Rachel, her husband, and his grandchildren. She even saw Santa—a guest in a full Santa suit—with a flock of kids buzzing around him as he gave out small toys and candy.

Sam and Jessica Morgan, along with their family, were there. Even though they had power in their house, Sophie had insisted that they come. Zoey even saw Tim, and Trudy with her husband, though Zoey hardly recognized her coworker out of her waitressing uniform.

She carried the cake back to the kitchen and found Sophie in the center of a flock of women busily keeping the party running—washing at the sink, putting food in the oven, and taking other dishes out to the many tables set up around the house.

Sophie suddenly noticed she was there and called out to her. "Zoey, I'm so glad you could come. Merry Christmas, sweetheart." She pulled Zoey close, and Zoey hugged her back.

"My mom made this cake, orange spice."

"Looks delicious."

"Can I help you with anything?"

Sophie shook her head. "Absolutely not. You did more than your share already, young lady. You go enjoy yourself. I'll be out in a minute."

Zoey slipped out of the kitchen and looked

around for James. There were candles everywhere and fireplaces glowed, shedding a warm, flickering light throughout the house. The amazing decorations that James had arranged had not gone to waste, Zoey realized. It was almost as if James had guessed there would be a spectacular party here, deserving such a grand display.

Long tables, covered with bright tablecloths, seemed to bend under the weight of all the many platters, with Sophie's roast goose front and center. There were spicy scented baked hams and roast turkeys, with all possible side dishes, along with an array of casseroles and tempting entrées the many guests had contributed. Even though Zoey had already eaten with her family, she felt her mouth water at the sight. *This is the closest thing I'll ever see to a medieval feast,* she thought.

In one corner of the front parlor, Grace Hegman played Christmas songs on the piano. Other guests, including Emily Warwick and her husband, Dan Forbes, had gathered around to sing along.

Among the familiar faces of church members and townspeople, Zoey spotted the Potter clan— James's father, his aunts, and all his cousins. She had never met his older sister, Miranda, but Zoey recognized her from photos. She had come up from North Carolina with her family and stood near the Christmas tree, balancing a baby on her hip.

Every time Zoey turned around, she saw Santa Claus again. A tall, lean Santa, she noticed, despite the padding under his suit. She caught his eye and realized it was James. The beard and suit had fooled her, but he could never disguise those eyes.

"Excuse me, Santa, but your reindeer are blocking the driveway," she said.

"Thank you, miss. I'd better be going, anyway. But I do have one more present to give out . . ." He searched inside the bag and came up with two small packets. "Do you know anyone named . . . Zoey?"

Zoey felt herself blush. "I think I do . . . and I think she has a gift for you, too."

"For me? How thoughtful. Why don't you find this Zoey and tell her to meet me outside on the porch?"

"That's a good idea. I'll give her the message right away."

Zoey grabbed her coat from the pile on a bench in the foyer and found the gift she brought for James, which she had left under the tree. When she stepped out on the porch, it was suddenly quiet. She could still hear the voices and music from inside, but the sounds seemed muffled and distant.

She watched the party through a window for a

moment, as if watching a movie with the sound turned very low. Sophie had emerged from the kitchen, though she still wore her apron. She moved around the parlor, talking a few minutes with each of her guests. She no sooner started one conversation than some other guest walked over and hugged her hello, or thanked her for opening her doors—and heart—in such a grand way. Little children ran up to her, asking permission to attack the cookies and cakes or wondering when the gifts would be opened. Piles of presents sat under the tree. Zoey had left one there for Sophie, a present she had asked for, in a way.

Even Lillian Warwick, sitting in a high-backed chair by the fire, looked remarkably content, one hand clasping Ezra's as he stood by her side. Sophie looked happiest of all, absolutely glowing with an inner light of love and contentment. This night was surely all she had hoped for.

Zoey felt someone standing nearby, and James stepped out of the shadows. The only thing left of his costume was the red gift sack. He had exchanged the red suit and white beard for a fisherman knit sweater and jeans, along with his handsome, beardless face and heart-stopping smile.

"Santa sent me. He had to go," he greeted her.

"It's getting late. He has a lot of ground to cover," Zoey replied, remembering James would be leaving for distant points on the globe himself soon. Another thing she didn't want to think about now.

"You looked lost in some deep thoughts out here. I bet you missed seeing his sleigh fly off the roof."

"I did," she admitted. "I was looking in at the party. There are so many people here. And your grandmother has some connection to each of them, either family or friends, neighbors or members of our church. She's like an apple tree," Zoey decided. "Her roots to this place go so deep. It's hard to believe she'll ever leave here."

James laughed and brushed her hair from her cheek with his warm hand. "You sound like the writer now. But I know what you mean. I can't quite get my head around the idea that our family is giving up this place. I'm not sure it's really hit her, either. I'm just happy she got her wish— to hold this big party for her last Christmas here."

"Me, too. But I bet Sophie isn't surprised by how amazing it is. She'll just say something like, 'That's God's way. You hand Him your troubles, and He figures things out better than you ever can.' "

"You nailed it. That's *exactly* what she said, just this afternoon, when we were setting up the tables and chairs."

Zoey laughed with him but also felt a twinge of envy. Sophie's faith was so strong. Zoey did pray from time to time, and did have faith, but not nearly as much.

James pulled a paper gift bag out from Santa's red sack. "Getting back to Santa, I promised him I would give you these." He handed her the two tissue-covered packets, and Zoey felt suddenly shy, handing over his box.

"What is this?" He shook it and listened, reminding Zoey of Jamie. "You open yours first," he said.

"All right." Zoey took a breath and opened the smaller packet first. Inside, she found a slim silver bracelet. It had some writing on it and she brought it closer to the window in order to read the inscription. *She believed she could, so she did.* The words touched her heart. She looked back at him, feeling tongue-tied.

"I saw it in a shop in town. It reminded me of you. Even if you don't get that internship this winter, I know you're going to do great things in your life, Zoey. You're just that kind of person."

"Thank you . . . that means a lot to me. That you would say that," she said quietly.

"Open the other one," he coaxed her.

Zoey had forgotten there even was another gift. This packet was about the same size but a bit lighter. She pulled off the paper and found what looked like a leather wallet. Not a wallet exactly, more of a small black leather book cover, stamped with gold writing. She opened it, but didn't see anything inside.

"It's a cover." He seemed amused at her confusion. "For your passport."

"Thanks," she said politely. "I don't have a passport, but I guess I should get one someday."

"I think you should get one right away. You'll need it to visit me. Maybe over spring break?"

The reassurance that he wanted to continue their relationship after he left should have made her happy. But Zoey's heart fell with the sudden reminder of his departure. Soon, James would be thousands of miles away. "Spring break? Maybe . . ."

If I quit school and manage the diner full-time. And if my parents both get head injuries. Even if I had the airfare, does James really think my dad will let me go to South America to see him?

But she knew he meant well and didn't want to sound snide. Especially not tonight. She forced a smile. "I should have a passport. You're right. I'll get one right after Christmas," she promised. "Want to open your present now?"

"I thought you'd never ask." His package was a bit bigger and heavier. He tore off the paper and uncovered two books. One was a novel, the other a blank book with a black leather cover for his writing.

He picked up the blank book first and smoothed his hand over the cover. "This is beautiful. It's almost too good to write in. I'm used to the shabby notebooks I pick up in the market."

"I thought you could use something special for your trip."

"This is special, all right. Thank you." He picked up the novel next and read the title with reverence, "*On the Road.* This is great. I love this book. How did you know I love Jack Kerouac?"

Zoey shrugged. "Maybe because you carry the paperback around with you constantly and study it the way Sophie reads her Bible? The guy in the bookstore said this is a new edition. It's got a copy of his original manuscript. He typed it on long strips of paper and taped it together?"

She didn't totally understand, but when the book had caught her eye, the bookseller explained that Kerouac had typed the novel on eight strips of tracing paper and taped it together to make a scroll. This new edition reproduced the first, unedited manuscript.

"Wow . . . I really wanted this. I heard about it, but I didn't realize it was out yet." James eagerly flipped through the pages, then stopped to read her inscription.

Zoey knew it by heart.

> To James—
> I know this is a writer you admire. I'm sure that one day, I'll be seeing your

books in a big display just like this one. I hope you find a lot of interesting stories to tell in your travels. Good luck and happy landings!

—Zoey

He looked up at her, his eyes glowing with emotion. "Thank you, Zoey. These are the best Christmas gifts I've gotten in a long time. Since . . . I can't remember when."

Zoey smiled. She was so pleased that he liked the presents she had chosen. Before she could say a word, he pulled her close and gave her a long, tight hug. "Merry Christmas," he whispered in her hair.

"Merry Christmas, James," she whispered back.

He pulled back a bit and kissed her. A long, sweet kiss that made her rise on tiptoe and hold him close again. Their embrace felt as though they were moving to a new place in their relationship, even closer and more trusting. But at the same time, Zoey sensed a note in their kiss that was bittersweet, the beginning of a farewell that was certain to come.

James stepped back but still held her hands. "I really hope you come and visit me. I'm definitely going to Peru. I got an email back from the organization and the farm owner there yesterday. He offered me a job and I accepted."

Zoey felt stunned, even though she had expected this news almost from the first day they met. "Great. Congrats." She tried to sound cheerful and wondered if she was pulling it off. "When do you leave?"

"That's the bad part. Very soon. The day after New Year's."

"Monday, January second," she said. She felt as if someone had knocked the wind out of her—hollow and aching inside.

"That's right." He nodded, looking as if he wondered how she knew the calendar so well.

Zoey knew the date because that was the same day her internship was supposed to start. "That's soon," she said. Nine days away.

"Yes, it is." He sighed. "But I don't want to turn it down or ask for a delay. It's a good spot and I might lose it."

"Sure. You need to take it. That was your plan. It's all worked out." He looked grateful for her understanding. Zoey did understand, and yet she suddenly felt distant from him. She knew that he cared for her—but apparently not that much if he could leave here so easily.

Lucy had been right, after all. Zoey had been foolish to get so involved with him. To think it was fine to fall for him, knowing this was only a brief stopover in his travels.

"I had some news this week, too," she said suddenly. "I got the internship."

She hadn't told anyone and hadn't even planned to tell James. But it had suddenly spurted out. Maybe she wanted him to know interesting things were happening in her life, too?

"Wow, that's great. I knew they would pick you." He hugged her close a moment and stepped back. "When do you start?"

Zoey slid her glance away from his. "I don't start, actually. I still can't take it."

"Did your parents say that?" His tone was protective, as if he wanted to argue with her parents on her behalf.

"You're the only one who knows. I don't want to put them in that spot right now. My father just had the worst week of his life." Somewhat of an exaggeration, but not much. "I know he still needs me to manage the diner, and I don't mind so much now. It's only a few weeks. I can stick it out."

James sighed. "You're very noble, on top of all your other wonderful qualities. I don't think I'd be nearly as selfless."

Zoey didn't bother to debate. She didn't think so, either.

"I think it's wonderful that you love your family so much. I really do," James continued. "But what about your own life—your own goals? You're not a child anymore. You don't have to do what they say. The sooner you realize that, the better for you. Honestly, I'm just telling you from experience."

His well-meaning advice made her angry. She didn't need James Potter to tell her that she had her own life. What did he know about her life, anyway?

"I'm not doing this because my parents say I have to. Or even because I'm afraid they'll be angry and we'll argue. I'm doing it because I love them, James. I want to help my father. He worked very hard to be mayor. That's all he's ever wanted. You don't live here, so you don't get that part. He has this one chance to do it right. I want to give that to him, if I can. I certainly don't want to make it harder for him."

James stepped back, his expression serious. "You're right. I don't live here. I probably shouldn't butt in. But maybe I see things clearer because I don't have all that baggage in the way. It's a waste that you got this opportunity and you can't take it. What would your father do if you broke your leg or something? He would have to figure it out. I think you should go for it, Zoey, and not worry about what your parents say."

Zoey sighed and stared back at him. "Easy for you to say. You do whatever you like. You say you want to travel and write, but I think you just want to get away from your father. Run off to Peru. Good idea. Good for you," she nearly shouted. "I really don't need your advice. You don't understand my life at all."

James looked upset, and Zoey knew she had probably gone too far. But she couldn't help it. James suddenly seemed different to her. Not the caring, sensitive guy she had thought he was.

"I'm sorry," he said quickly. "I don't know how we got into this." He reached for her hand, but she pulled away and headed for the door, suddenly chilled.

She turned and met his glance one last time, her heart feeling as if it had just cracked open. "I'm sorry, James. I . . . can't do this. I don't do good-bye very well. I guess that's something else you don't really know about me."

She felt bad for unloading on him. And sorry now that she let herself get so involved with him in the first place. What she said was true. She didn't do good-bye very well, though she'd had more practice than most people.

She walked into the house through the side door, leaving James out on the porch with his thoughts. The party was thinning, but everyone was still so distracted, no one noticed her slip back in. She left her coat in the mudroom and took a moment to compose herself. Was she crying? She hoped not. She ran a tissue under her eyes and dabbed her nose.

She pulled off the bracelet James had given her

and tucked it in her pocket. She would stick it in the back of a drawer when she got home. Maybe take it out someday, when thinking about James didn't hurt anymore.

Maybe when I'm old as Sophie, she decided.

Chapter Fourteen

Y OU'RE UP EARLY, GRANDMA. I THOUGHT you'd be tired from the party."

"I'm fine. Never felt better." Sophie turned from the sink to find James in the kitchen doorway, with bedhead and a day's growth of beard shadowing his lean cheeks. He sure looked tired—and not in a very good mood for Christmas Day.

"Merry Christmas, James."

"Merry Christmas, Grandma. I'm glad you got your Christmas wish," he added. "Was the party all you'd hoped for?"

"Was it ever. And then some." She shook her head in disbelief. "There's not even much cleaning up to do. Everyone pitched in before they left. But I do want to get a few things in order. A few more folks from church are coming by soon to help and take away all those folding chairs and tables we borrowed from Fellowship Hall."

"I can help with that." James sipped his coffee, staring into space again.

Sophie had rarely seen anyone so glum on

Christmas and wondered what was going on. "There are still a few gifts to open. Why don't we do that later?" she suggested.

"Sure. Whenever you like."

"I already opened the gift Zoey left for me. A large-print Bible. Just what I wanted. Remember when I fell on the steps and was going on about it?"

James nodded, barely smiling. "I do. That was thoughtful of her."

"It was. As usual. I got her a little something, too. Maybe she can stop by this afternoon and open it."

"I think she's busy with her family."

Something in his tone piqued Sophie's radar—a hint of friction between them? But she didn't feel comfortable asking questions. Young people had to work things out for themselves. *What was meant to be, will be,* she reminded herself.

"Well, I'm sure to see her before the New Year. Before you go," she added, thinking of the plans James had made for his departure. "Did you tell her about Peru?"

"I told her last night. She was happy for me," he said in the same flat tone.

Sophie wondered now if that was it. It only made sense. Of course, Zoey was disappointed to see him go. And he felt bad, too. Anyone with eyes in their head could see how the two got on.

It was a shame, but they were headed in different directions right now.

The good Lord did have a way of bringing people back together who belonged together, she knew that as well. Best to just let this settle, like a bottle of cream, and see what rises to the top.

"I'm going to put the extra dishes away in the china closet. You get a bite to eat for yourself," she told him.

"I'm not that hungry right now. Guess I overdid it at the party. I'll take Mac for a walk if you don't need me right now."

Macintosh loved to be outside, in any kind of weather, though Sophie could not recall the last time anyone had taken the dog for an official walk. He was an independent old hound who walked himself. But she could see that James was restless and a bit dispirited. She thought fresh air would do him good.

"Good idea. He'll follow you. But take some treats in your pocket in case he goes chasing a rabbit or some other critter."

The dog knew he was being talked about and jumped up from his bed. He ran to James and put both paws on the young man's knees, staring up with an imploring look.

"Okay, buddy. You're on. Let me get my coat and gloves."

Sophie was already in the dining room, working on her dishes, when she heard them leave. She returned to the kitchen a short time later and stood drying another stack of dishes that needed to be stored.

A knock sounded on the side door and she checked the time. Church volunteers already? It seemed too early for that. She opened the door to find her new neighbors, Melissa and Tom Quinn, a young couple who had moved into the area a few months ago. She had seen them last night at the party.

"Merry Christmas, Sophie. I hope we're not disturbing you?"

"Not at all, come on in. I was just cleaning up a bit."

"I heard people talking about that last night, and we came to help. Tom brought you some firewood," Melissa said, turning to her husband.

"You must have used at least a cord last night," Tom said. "We have plenty. I'll stack it on your porch later."

"Thank you so much. That's very generous of you. I was wondering what my son would say when he saw how low that pile is," she added with a laugh. "Take off your coats. Would you like some coffee or tea? I was just about to sit down a minute."

Melissa took off her coat and reached into her big leather bag. She handed Sophie a parcel wrapped in a cloth. "The wood is sort of a Christmas present. This is, too."

Sophie unwrapped the cloth and found a beautiful handmade bowl with a dark blue glaze.

"Isn't this beautiful? I love the color. It's perfect for my kitchen," she added, feeling a tight spot in her heart, wondering how long she would even have her own kitchen. But the girl could not have known that. She meant only good.

"Melissa made it. She's a potter," Tom said proudly.

"Are you? My granddaughter Miranda is an artist, a jewelry maker. She used to have a studio right out there in the barn."

Melissa glanced at Tom. "Yes, we know. We were talking to her last night."

"She told us that you're planning on selling your property, the house and the orchard?"

Sophie nodded. "Yes, I am. I have to. It's gotten too much for me, and my children have been after me awhile to go. The orchard especially is hard to manage at my age . . . though it never felt like work," she added. "I grew up here. I was born right in this house, and I've lived here ever since."

Melissa smiled sympathetically. "That must make it even harder."

"It does," Sophie said. "Or it will, once I sell and go. My children are going to put the place up right after the New Year. I don't know how long I'll stay after that. My grandson James has been here the last few weeks, but he's leaving in a few days, too."

"You can't live alone here, is that it?" Tom asked.

"I'd stay until I died in my bed," Sophie said honestly. "But I have to see common sense, too. I can't stay all alone anymore. The winters are too long and hard. I suppose I could find a companion of some kind. But my kids say, just let it go. So . . . here we are."

She looked up at the young couple, realizing she had been lost in her own worries and probably rambling. "I'm sorry, I didn't mean to bore you with my troubles. So, tell me about yourselves. Your aunt left you a little cottage down the road, Melissa?" she recalled. "On the pond near the Morgan property?"

"That's the one. We need to make some improvements, but it's very comfortable, for now," Melissa said. "Tom grew up in Vermont, and I grew up in the Berkshires. We met in college and lived in Portland awhile. But we both wanted to move back to a more rural place."

"Cape Light is perfect for you, then," Sophie said.

"Almost," Tom agreed. "Right now, we're looking for a piece of land to cultivate. I studied agriculture. I've been working on organic farms, and I'm ready to start my own."

"Good for you. You know, my grandson was

just telling me there are a lot of young people interested in farming again. I didn't really believe him . . . but here you are."

"Yes, here we are." Melissa smiled at her.

Sophie suddenly understood the reason for their visit. Aside from the lovely Christmas gifts.

"Do you think you'd be interested in selling just your property, Sophie—the orchard and outbuildings?" Tom asked.

"We don't really need the house. We're not sure we can afford the property with the house, too," Melissa said honestly.

"Or maybe you would consider leasing the land to us, and we would cultivate it? I would keep the orchard," he said quickly. "Though I'd turn it green."

Sophie's head was spinning. Were these young folks sitting at her kitchen table—who suddenly looked like angels to her, complete with halos and wings—really offering to buy the orchard, to keep her trees and take good care of them? To even let her keep living in the house if she liked? She pressed her hand to her chest. She could barely breathe.

Melissa looked at her with alarm. "Sophie, are you all right?" Melissa jumped up from her chair, looking ready to administer first aid or call 911.

Sophie caught her breath and laughed. "I'm perfectly fine, dear. I'm just so happy, I don't know whether to laugh or cry. You can't know what this means to me, to hear you say you'd like to buy the orchard and keep growing apples. And I can stay in this house, too." She shook her head. She was crying now and took a tissue from her pocket to dry her tears. "You can't know. It's an absolute . . . miracle," she said finally.

Melissa reached over and touched Sophie's hand. "You'd be helping us, too," she said. "We've been looking for months for the right place. We know you probably have to talk this over with your family. We don't want to create any problems for you, or any trouble. But this place is just perfect for us. It would mean the world to us if we could work this out."

"It's our dream come true," Tom said.

Sophie lifted her head and smiled at him. "I know . . . that's what makes it perfect. Now that you two have found your way here, I feel certain in my heart that it *will* work out."

Sophie heard the side door open and then Mac's paws clicking on the wooden floor. He raced into the kitchen, straight to his water bowl, where he lapped furiously. James soon followed, his cheeks red from the cold and his hair wind tossed. Or maybe he hadn't combed it yet. He had taken a shower but he had not shaved, Sophie noticed. Was he growing a beard for Peru?

"This is my grandson James," Sophie said. "Maybe you've already met?"

"Yes, last night when he bore a strange resemblance to Santa." Tom stood up and offered James his hand. "Nice to see you, James. Merry Christmas."

"Merry Christmas," James said to both of them. He turned to Sophie. "Your dog took me for quite a hike, Grandma. I checked the trees. It doesn't look like the storm did any damage. But some of the wire supports on the new row of Granny Smith saplings were loose. I can fix that for you before I go."

"You sound like you know your way around an orchard," Tom said.

"A little. I used to stay here for a few weeks every summer. My grandpa would always have us in the orchard, helping him. We used to call it Apple Camp."

Melissa laughed. "What a good idea! I'm sure a lot of eco-minded parents would sign their children up for that camp."

Sophie laughed, too. "You'll have to jot that down. It's always nice to figure out a few ways to bring in some extra money. I kept bees and had a cutting garden, too. We had a little shed on the road that sold fresh flowers, honey, fruit, and my pies and preserves."

James looked confused. He turned to Tom. "Are you thinking of opening up an orchard around here?"

"Yes, they are," Sophie answered. "You remember those young farmers you were telling me about? Well, here they are. Melissa and Tom want to buy my property and keep the trees and grow vegetables on the land, too. Isn't that amazing news?"

James looked stunned. He slowly smiled. "That is amazing. I know what I said, but—"

"You didn't really believe it," she finished for him. "Well, I did. All things are possible with God, James."

"I guess so, Grandma. This is certainly proof."

Someone knocked on the door, then pushed it open. "It's just me, Sophie," Sam Morgan called out. "We're here to pick up the tables and chairs. We'll start with the stack on the porch."

James rose and pulled his jacket on. "I'll help them."

"We will, too," Melissa said as she and Tom got up to follow. She turned to Sophie for a moment. "We'll talk more about the details. Can we call you tomorrow? Or maybe you'd like us to deal with a realtor?"

"You can deal with me," Sophie said quickly. "I'm still the owner here." She was reminding herself as well, she realized. She didn't need Bart and some real estate broker raising all sorts of objections and hurdles for these young people. *We'll get our ducks in order first,* she decided. *Then I'll tell them.*

I trust you to iron out the practical details of all this, Lord, she added, offering a silent prayer.

410

You've taken me this far; I know you won't let me down now.

SOPHIE WAS THANKFUL THAT IN THE DAYS after Christmas, none of her children mentioned putting her house up for sale, or any of the heavy issues that had hovered over their holidays. Maybe they had agreed among themselves to give her a few days' grace—to simply savor the success of her Christmas party and recuperate from that event.

Or maybe they were all too busy with their own lives.

Whatever the reason, she was thankful. The days between Christmas and New Year's Eve provided just enough time for her to talk over the sale and terms with Melissa and Tom. And enough time for them to get their finances in order and even get a preapproval from the bank for a mortgage.

She still hadn't quite figured out how to share the news with her family when Bart called on Thursday night. "I was thinking of coming up tomorrow," Bart said. "I want to say good-bye to James before he leaves for Peru."

James was leaving Monday. It was getting close. But Sophie had a feeling Bart had other business on his mind as well.

"That would be fine, Bart. I'll tell him you're coming. I'll make a nice lunch," she added.

Once they had hung up, Sophie wished her son would come that very night. She felt suddenly on edge and wanted to get the conversation over with, though she felt it would be best to tell all three of the children at once.

God, give me strength. I'm leaving this in your hands. I'll do whatever pleases you, she promised.

She felt even more nervous the next day as she prepared for her son's visit. Her hands trembled, and she dropped a cup as she carried it to the table. Luckily, it was empty and didn't break.

James jumped up from his chair and picked it up for her. "Are you all right, Grandma?" He had been lost in his thoughts, writing in his book, but now carefully helped her into a chair.

I might ask you the same, she nearly replied. He had been moping around the house the last few days, ever since Christmas Eve.

Maybe having second thoughts about his trip? Or maybe it was something going on with Zoey? Zoey had stopped by for a few minutes the day after Christmas, but James had been out and she hadn't asked after him.

"I'm fine, dear. Just some nerves about seeing your father. He and your aunts have been quiet as mice lately about selling the house. But I have a feeling that's why he's really coming."

"You haven't told them about Melissa and Tom?"

"Not yet. I want to tell them all at once. And I needed a few days to work things out with the Quinns. We haven't put anything in writing yet, but we agreed on a price. I think it's a fair one, and I hope your father agrees."

"It sounds serious."

"It is. I gave them my word. They have the means to buy this place and a letter from the bank to prove it. But I expect a landslide of objections from your father and your aunts."

"I do, too," James said. "But I'm in your corner, Grandma. I think this is a great solution for you. I hope they can see that."

"I do, too, dear." She patted his arm.

The doorbell rang. Sophie looked at James. Only strangers rang her doorbell. "I'll get it," James offered.

"No, let me." Sophie took off her apron and smoothed her dark red dress. Mac trotted after her, barking along the way. She pulled the door open and was surprised to see Fran Tulley.

The Tulleys had not come to her party. Power had been restored to their street, and Sophie had heard in church that Fran and Tucker had a houseful, with their married children home for Christmas.

Sophie was not sure why Fran would be all the way out here today, but thought it might be some church business. Along with her purse, Fran had a pile of folders tucked under one arm.

"Nice to see you, Fran. Did you have a good holiday?"

"It was wonderful. My son and daughter-in-law are still here. I wasn't going to work at all this week, but I told Bart I could spare some time today."

Sophie was confused now. "Bart asked you to come here?"

"Yes, he said to come around noon. He told me you're ready to list the property, and he wants me to work up an asking price." Fran looked surprised and embarrassed. "Are you sure he didn't tell you? We've all been so busy with the storm and the holiday, it's easy to forget things."

Sophie paused and counted to three before answering. It was so easy to tell old people they had forgotten something. *Did I do that, too, when I was younger?*

"Maybe that's what happened. *Bart* must have forgotten to tell me he asked you here," she said mildly. She noticed another car turn onto the property and recognized her son's blue sedan. "Here he comes now. No harm done. We'll work this out." She ushered Fran inside and shut the door. "Bart will be a while. He drives up that lane very slowly."

"It is bumpy. You really need to pave it," Fran said as she followed Sophie into the kitchen.

Sophie caught her grandson's eye and smiled. "People say that. I guess we'll see."

Fran took off her coat and quickly set up shop at the kitchen table, with a notebook computer, folders that said BOWMAN REAL ESTATE, and a long yellow pad.

Bart soon came through the side door without knocking. He stamped some snow off his feet and called out from the mudroom, "I'm here, Mother. Is Fran here yet? I'm sorry, I forgot to tell you she was coming."

Sophie glanced at Fran. "That's all right. I guessed something like that must have happened."

Bart walked in and kissed her cheek, then greeted Fran and James. Her grandson had begun setting out the lunch she had made, fixings for sandwiches and salads.

But Bart didn't seem interested in eating. "I thought it would be a good idea to let Fran look over the property while I'm here. We need to get started with the listing."

"Yes, dear, I understand. Let's all have a bite first. No need to rush, is there?"

Fran glanced at Bart, then back at Sophie. "I've already had some lunch, but I wouldn't mind coffee."

"Coming up." James was at the stove and served coffee all around.

Sophie sat down at the head of the table and waited for James to return. "Let's say a little blessing over the meal." Her guests bowed their heads and joined hands. "Dear Lord, thank you for a wonderful Christmas. As you can see, we're still enjoying your bounty and the leftovers. Please watch over all of us in the new year and keep James safe in his travels. Most of all, please keep us mindful of your word. Help us trust in you with all our hearts and lean not on our own understanding. In all our ways help us submit to you, and know that you will make our paths straight."

Sophie lifted her head and smiled. She glanced at her son. She knew he had faith, but her open way of expressing her own made him uneasy at times. He cleared his throat and looked down at the table. "Very nice blessing, Mother."

"Thanks, son. The words just came to me. That's the way it is sometimes. Try some of that Virginia ham, it's very tasty. And there's turkey, too."

She passed her son a platter and then passed a bowl of potato salad to Fran, who had decided she was hungry after all. "What a pretty bowl," Fran said.

"A Christmas gift from a new friend, Melissa Quinn. She and her husband, Tom, just moved in down the road. That old cottage on the pond, near the Morgan property?"

"I know the one. It was passed on in a family trust," Fran replied.

"That's right," Sophie said. Mac started barking and ran to the side door before they heard a knock. Bart was about to bite into the sandwich he'd built for himself, but paused. "Must be Evelyn. I told her I'd be here."

Sophie was not surprised. Her son had planned an ambush, but she was well prepared.

"I'll get it, Grandma," James said.

"You sit. I'll see who's there." She glanced out the kitchen window as she headed to the mudroom, happy to see the Quinns' green truck parked behind Bart's car.

Lord, if I'm doing the wrong thing, I'm sure you'll let me know pretty quickly, she silently prayed. Then she pulled open the door and welcomed the young couple in.

"I hope we're not here too early," Tom said.

"You said noon, but we thought you might want to visit with your son awhile," Melissa added.

Sophie helped them off with their coats and herded them toward the kitchen. "Right on time. We were just sitting down for lunch."

The curious stares of Fran and Bart greeted Sophie and her guests as they walked in. "This is my son, Bart Potter, and Fran Tulley, a friend from church," she explained, not wanting to scare them.

Fran looked surprised at that introduction, but didn't contradict her. "This is Melissa and Tom Quinn, my new neighbors. We were just talking about you. Fran was admiring that bowl you gave me," Sophie explained.

The Quinns stood beside her, looking a bit uneasy. Bart jumped up and offered his hand. Sophie had taught her children good manners, and he had not forgotten.

"Have a seat, you two. Have a bite to eat. Get them some coffee or tea, James," Sophie told her grandson as she sat. She would have done it herself, but she didn't dare leave the couple alone with Bart and Fran.

Bart glanced at his mother curiously, as if to say, "We have family business to discuss. Why in the world did you invite them here?"

Sophie ignored his dark looks. Fran looked confused, too. "So . . . how do you like Cape Light? Have you been in the cottage very long?" Fran asked politely.

"We came in September," Melissa said. "We like it very much."

"The cottage suits them fine," Sophie jumped in. "But they've been looking for some property to cultivate. Tom's studied organic farming, and he likes the idea of apples," she added. "So we talked about them buying this place, and we've come to an agreement."

Fran sat back in her seat, looking the most surprised. She turned to Bart. Bart looked surprised as well, but Sophie could tell from the grim set of his mouth he had been expecting her to toss up some obstacle to his reasonable, well-meaning plan.

"A deal to buy the orchard? Well . . . I guess we can consider all offers," he said in a smooth tone. "Once Fran works up the figures. But we were hoping for a buyer who would take the house and land. It will be harder to sell the pieces separately."

Tom seemed about to speak, but Sophie held up her hand. "That's just it—why it works so well for me and why I've given my word to them." She caught her son's eye with a look he knew well. "If the orchard is taken care of, I see no reason why I can't stay on in the house. I plan to find a nice companion who will live here and help around the house, as needed."

Bart shook his head. "Mother, we've been through all this. You promised us," he reminded her.

"I did," Sophie agreed. "But that was when I thought I couldn't burden you and your sisters with worrying about me living here all alone and taking care of the property, too. It seemed selfish to put that responsibility on you, along with worrying about my well-being. But now these young people have appeared out of the blue. They love the trees and will take good care of them. That was part of my prayers, too."

"It would be easy to divide the house and property," Fran said. "I've already looked into that question." She searched through her folders and flipped one open.

Bart glanced in her direction and back at his mother. "That still doesn't solve the question of you staying here."

"It does for me, son. Don't you see? With these lovely people taking over the orchard, it's a sign that I am meant to stay. My dearest prayer is to spend the rest of my days—be it one or one thousand—right under this roof. There's nothing wrong with me but old age, thank the Lord. With a companion, I'll be fine. I'm going to try. No matter what you or your sisters say."

Bart looked about to object again and just shook his head.

He turned to Tom Quinn. "I don't know what sort of agreement you have with my mother. But, as you can see, the issue is more complicated than she's told you."

"I think we've struck a fair price, sir, if that's what you're worried about." Tom also had a folder of papers with him and handed it across the table to Bart.

"Here's a list of recent sales of comparable properties," Tom said.

"And we have a letter from our banker there, too. There shouldn't be any problem with a mortgage," Melissa added.

James had been so quiet that Sophie had almost forgotten he was there. He suddenly jumped up in his chair. "Dad, I think we should go outside with Tom and Melissa and walk the property. They have a lot of great ideas for the orchard and the land. We can show them the equipment in the apple shed and talk about the sale of that as well."

Bart looked up at his son, seeming surprised at the idea. "All right. I could use a breath of fresh air." He got up from his chair and looked back at his plate. "Save my lunch, Mother. I barely got to eat a bite."

Sophie nodded. "Take your time. It will be right here."

"I think I'll be going, too," Fran said. "It doesn't look like you need my help after all."

"I'm sorry to take you out of your way today, Fran. As you can see, this is all new to me," Bart apologized.

Fran shrugged. "All's well that ends well." She smiled at Sophie as she pulled on her coat. "I couldn't quite imagine you leaving this place, either," she confessed. "You're like a village landmark or something by now. I mean that in the nicest way."

"That's a very nice compliment, Fran." Sophie laughed. "Maybe I should get a bronze plaque and wear it around my neck. Then my children would stop pestering me."

Fran laughed and hugged her good-bye. "Thanks for the lunch. I can find my way to the door. Happy New Year, everyone!" she called back.

"Happy New Year, Fran," Sophie answered, feeling that her own prospects for the new year were ever so much brighter.

As Fran left from the front door, Bart, James, and the Quinns left from the side of the house. Sophie ran to the kitchen window to watch them begin a tour of the property.

James was such a clever boy. That inspiration had come from Heaven above, actually, she corrected herself. Either way, she was sure that some time with Tom and Melissa would convince her son they were the perfect people to take over the Potter land. Bart acted as if he didn't care who bought the place, but she knew, deep down, he felt an attachment to the orchard and his family home—when he was able to silence the very practical, businesslike voice inside him.

Just as the group emerged from the barn, she saw Evelyn's car pull up. Sophie was relieved to see Bart summon her over and introduce her to the Quinns. She had not been looking forward to explaining it all to Evelyn while the others were out.

"Thanks again, Lord. It's going along beautifully," Sophie said as she watched from the window, washing up a few dishes.

A while later, the group came back inside. Sophie had fresh hot tea and coffee and a platter of cake and cookies ready. Sweets did tend to help people act and speak sweeter to each other, she had found.

"Did you have a good walk?" she asked as they came in.

"We did," Bart replied. "We had a good talk, too. There are some more details to work out, of course. But I'm tending to agree with you, Mother. I think the Quinns are good buyers for the property." He glanced at his sister. "What do you say, Evelyn?"

Evelyn shrugged. "I trust the business details to you, Bart. But I'm happy to see the orchard go to a family who will keep it running. I know that means the world to Mother."

Sophie didn't reply. Her heart felt too full of gratitude, and her eyes felt watery, too. "Thank you both. I knew that once you got to know Melissa and Tom, you would understand that I was doing the right thing."

"In that respect," Bart agreed, not yet letting her off the hook for the living-alone idea. "The conversation is not entirely over, Mother."

"No, it isn't," Evelyn agreed.

"We can see you have more to talk about, and we don't want to intrude," Tom said. He offered his hand to Bart and then to Evelyn. "Please call me soon to iron out the rest of the agreement."

"I will, Tom. Good to meet you," Bart said.

Good-byes were exchanged all around, and the Quinns showed themselves to the door. James went outside with them. "I'm going to close up the barn and find Mac. He's been out long enough, too."

"Good idea. Thanks, honey." Sophie faced her children and took a steadying breath. Neither of them had sat at the table yet, and she didn't want to, either. Best to have this out on her two feet, she decided.

"Bart told me you plan to stay in the house," Evelyn said.

"With a live-in companion," Sophie cut in. "I can find one easily—"

Evelyn held up her hand, like a crossing guard directing traffic, and Sophie's heart fell. "That may not solve our problem. You had James here with you, and yet you managed to fall."

"That could happen at your house as well," Sophie pointed out reasonably. "Even if you put me in a wheelchair, there's no guarantee I'll never take a spill. But I aim to hire a professional, someone who's been trained to care for an old woman like me."

Evelyn and Bart exchanged a glance. "Bart and I talked it over outside," Evelyn said at last. "If you hire a professional caregiver, and if you agree to follow some basic safety guidelines, we're willing to try it . . . for six months," she added.

"We'll be keeping a close eye on you. No driving or cleaning out gutters, and no climbing ladders of any kind," Bart reminded her. "If there's the least reason for concern, we'll have to revisit this question."

"And we get to meet and approve of the person you hire to live here. Before you give your solemn word again, Mother," Evelyn added.

Sophie felt her cheeks grow warm. She had acted behind their backs with the Quinns, it was true. But she believed the Lord forgave her for that. As Fran had said, all's well that ends well.

"Of course you'll help interview my companion. I had no intention of doing it without you," she promised. She suddenly felt light, almost giddy with happiness. "So it's all settled? I can stay in my house—me and Mac?"

"Yes, it's settled," Bart said gruffly. "Amen to that."

"Amen," Evelyn echoed. "I'll call Una. She's been burning up my cell phone line."

"Yes, call your sister. Give her the good news. You're very good children, and I love you all dearly. I don't tell you enough," she added.

Evelyn and Bart glanced at each other and laughed.

"I would never say that," Bart replied, patting his mother's shoulder. "But we do deserve a little special credit today."

She agreed with that. And she was sure the good Lord did, too.

Thank you for bringing them both around to my point of view, she said silently. *Thank you for this happy day and all its blessings.*

Chapter Fifteen

O N NEW YEAR'S EVE, THE DINER CLOSED at three o'clock. It wouldn't open again until Monday. Christmas and New Year's Day were practically the only days of the year Charlie closed entirely.

Zoey watched the clock. It had been a very slow and boring day, even though Saturdays were usually busy. She had spent most of the time at a table in the back, figuring out her schedule for the next semester. She was working with just her mother and father, but there had been hardly any customers all day. She had harbored some crazy fantasy James would stop in to say good-bye, though part of her knew it was best if she didn't see him at all.

They hadn't been in touch since Christmas Eve. She had managed to avoid his work shifts; it wasn't that hard, since she made up the schedules. He was leaving on Monday, so she really ought to stop thinking about him now.

Still, she wondered what he was doing tonight to bring in the New Year. Packing, probably? That wouldn't take too long. Everything he owned fit in a backpack. Her friend Laurel was having some people from school over, and Zoey had promised to go there. Better than staying all alone in her room while her parents had company downstairs. She would only sit around moping about James—and might even give in to the ever-present urge to text or call him.

And the point of that would be? It's not like he's going to come back from Peru and see me on weekends, she reminded herself. *Maybe some-day I'll write him a letter.* Though she doubted she would ever work up the nerve to do that, either.

"Three o'clock, on the nose," Lucy announced. She had the broom and dustpan out to sweep up. "Flip the sign and see what your father's up to, will you, honey? I need to get home and get ready for my company."

As eager to leave as her mom, Zoey ran back into the kitchen. Charlie had it well under control. "You go help your mother. Remind her to shut off the ice maker."

"All clear in the kitchen. Dad said to shut off the ice maker. I can do it," Zoey announced as she walked out again.

Lucy didn't answer. Zoey looked around for her and found her at the back of the diner, standing next to the table where Zoey's laptop and books were spread out. Lucy looked up from a sheet of paper she was reading and stared at her.

"Zoey, what is this?"

Zoey walked closer and glanced at the paper her mother held out to her.

"How did you find that? Did you go through my things?" Zoey said, feeling suddenly and totally upset.

"I found it on the floor, under your chair. You got that internship and you didn't even tell us?"

Zoey stepped back. She nodded, a lump in her throat. "I went on the interview a few weeks ago. For the experience," she added. "I never thought I'd get it."

Her mother shook her head. "I'm not mad at you for that part. But why didn't you tell us you were chosen? This is a big honor, honey. Why did you keep it a secret?"

"I knew I couldn't take it. I already promised Dad I'd work here over winter break. He was going through so much with the storm, I didn't want to make more problems for everybody. So I thanked them and said it wasn't going to work out."

Lucy stared at her, her eyes wide and glassy. She let out a long breath. "You just sit here. Don't move until I say," she warned.

Zoey sat down. She knew her mother was going to tell her father. But there was nothing she could do.

Lucy marched to the kitchen and pushed open the door. "Charlie? Come out here."

"I'm almost done, Lucy. I'll be right out."

"Come out here now. We need you," her mother insisted.

She heard her father grumble and the squeak of his kitchen shoes as he hurried out to the dining room. "What is it—that ice maker leaking again?"

Lucy held out the letter. "Remember that internship Zoey wanted? Look at this. They chose her, out of everyone who applied."

Her father took the letter and read it quickly, then looked back at her mother. "When did this happen?"

"I don't know. Ask Zoey. She says she already turned it down, because she promised you she would work here."

Charlie stared at her. "Zoey . . . you didn't, did you?"

Zoey nodded. "I sent an email yesterday. I said I was very honored and grateful, but I had to help with a family situation. I didn't want to bother you, Dad," she explained. "You were dealing with so much in town with the storm. I promised I'd help you. I didn't want to go back on my word."

"You did that for me?"

Zoey just nodded. "I want to help you, Dad."

He shook his head and cleared his throat. "Honey, that's just about the nicest thing I ever heard. I feel awful about this—"

"See? That's just what I mean," Zoey interrupted. "I didn't want you to feel bad. That's why I didn't tell you."

"Well, now we know," Lucy said gently. "I don't think it's any accident I found that letter, either."

"Your mother's right. You take this job. It's important, and a lot better use of your time than working here. I see that now. I'll figure it out," Charlie promised.

"Besides, I changed my schedule at the hospital for January. I'm working more nights and can help here during the daytime," Lucy added.

"And I'll find someone else to fill in," Charlie promised. "For goodness' sake, if I can dig this town out after the storm, practically single-handed, I can figure this out, too."

"But I already turned it down." Zoey couldn't hide her frustration. "They probably gave the spot to someone else by now."

Charlie pulled out his cell phone, pushed his glasses on, and started dialing the center, reading the phone number off the very fine print on the letter. "I'll call them right now and tell them your plans changed."

Lucy checked her watch. "Do you think the place is still open?"

Zoey knew it was. There were plenty of parents who had to work a full day on Saturday, even if it was New Year's Eve.

"If it's closed, we can leave a message. Maybe they didn't fill the spot. And if they did, maybe they'll take you, too," her father said. "Never hurts to ask."

Zoey heard the line ring and felt mortified. She couldn't let her father speak for her, as if she were an immature high school kid. She snatched the phone away, then walked as far as possible from her parents.

Beth Foster, the woman who had interviewed her, answered. Zoey quickly explained why she was calling.

Ms. Foster heard her out and took a moment before she replied. "We did offer the placement to another candidate, Zoey. But I was very sorry that you couldn't accept. I think, under the circumstances, we can take two interns this winter. Why don't you come in on Monday and we'll figure it out? There's an orientation from nine to three."

"Thank you so much. I'll be there. Thank you, Beth." She turned to her parents, who both looked very nervous, waiting to hear the answer.

"Ms. Foster told me to come in on Monday. They might be able to use two interns."

Charlie walked over and hugged her. "What did I tell you? Persistence wins the day."

Of course her father would have a corny motto to mark the occasion. Not quite her story, but Zoey didn't argue. She was too happy.

Lucy hugged her, too. "I'm glad I grabbed the broom today. Please don't keep things from us, honey. Even if you think it's for our own good?" She stood back and caught Zoey's eye. "We're certainly not perfect parents, but we always want the best for you. Please trust in that. We love you so much."

"I know," Zoey said, hugging her back. "It's totally mutual."

"I'M GLAD WE GOT HERE EARLY. NOT A SEAT left in the house." Emily's mother had to shout to be heard above the din in Village Hall. She gazed around at the standing-room-only crowd with an astonished expression. "Quite a turnout for the day after New Year's. I hope Bates can keep things under control. Though I doubt he's learned his lesson."

"Never mind Bates. I hope the crowd bodes well for our side," Ezra said.

"I do, too. But it's hard to say," Emily answered honestly.

She had expected high attendance at this meeting, the first of the new year. The open-space group had been working hard to encourage their members to make their voices heard tonight. Their opponents had apparently done the same.

Charlie and the council entered through a side door and took seats at the long table in the front of the room. Emily noticed that Charlie had his gavel handy again.

"Welcome, everyone," he began. "Thanks for coming out tonight. It's another cold one out there, but at least we all have our heat on, and we can put that ski underwear away for a while. That storm does make you grateful for the little things." A few people laughed, including Ezra, earning a sharp look from Lillian.

"First up on the agenda tonight, the proposal for new zoning. Town residents will have the opportunity to vote this law onto the books at a special election . . ."

He paused to put on his reading glasses and glanced down at a binder that was open on the table in front of him. Emily recognized it— the town bylaws. At least the bylaws would be handy when the open-space group made their move. She spotted Martin Becker sitting on the edge of his chair, a sheaf of papers in his lap, looking like a tiger about to spring on his prey.

"The bylaws state that a special election can be called by a majority of the council within forty-five days of the motion passing." Charlie looked up at the audience. "I open the floor to comments. But I'm warning all of you, if it gets disorderly in here, the council will vote. Whether you all had your say or not."

"He's a megalomaniac," Lillian muttered. "He's going to force this through, no matter how many people object."

"Calm down, Mother. Let's just listen." Lillian knew the open-space group had come with a plan to derail their opposition, but Emily had not divulged the details to her—or to anyone, except for Dan. It was vital that their plan did not get out and give the zoning group a chance to counter it.

George Krueger was the first at the microphone. "The residents of Cape Light want closure on this question. We need to put it to a vote, the sooner the better. I say the council votes on the motion and we set a date for the village to vote."

Fran Tulley was the next in line. "I agree with George. Most of us voted you in on this question, Charlie. We'd like to see you move along with your promises and vision for the village."

Her mother made a huffing sound. "Of course she would say that. She's just seeing dollar signs, all those big properties on the Beach Road broken up and sold to builders."

Ezra shook his head. "Doesn't look good for our side. Oh dear, what a night."

Emily felt bad, seeing him so distressed, but Martin Becker was next at the microphone. She touched Ezra's arm. "Look, it's Martin. Don't worry. He's got something up his sleeve."

"Well, it better be good," Lillian whispered back.

"Mayor Bates, town council members, I'm speaking for the residents who oppose new zoning laws, those who joined the open-space group and signed the petitions we've presented to you."

"We know who you are, Marty," Charlie said. "Just get on with it. We don't have all night."

"All right. Here's a letter from the county, signed by the county executive, the county zoning supervisor, and the county's supervisor of environmental impact." Martin held the letter up, displaying the bold stamp of the county on the letterhead. "I won't bother to read it aloud, but it's an order to the town council to freeze this question for twenty-four months so that a full review by an independent group can be conducted."

"What do they think they're going to review?" George Krueger interrupted.

"They'll be looking at the effects of the new zoning proposal on the area's infrastructure and environment, and particularly the impact on wildlife and the local ecosystem."

Charlie looked dumbfounded. Then his eyes narrowed. "That's a lot of official signatures, Marty. Congratulations. But what does the county have to do with our business? We're an incorporated village. We run our own show here."

"I understand," Martin said. "However, there is a bylaw in our village constitution that supports this action. I have a copy of that as well. In fact, an attorney at the county supervisor's office has also written a letter explaining that this is fully within their powers."

Emily watched Charlie's confident expression melt. He stood up and held out his hand. "Can I see that, please?"

"Of course. I have copies for each of you." Martin walked up to the table and handed out the letter. He turned to the audience.

"We also have copies for residents. If anyone would like one, please raise your hand."

Every hand in the room went up, and the noise level suddenly rose. "Ho, ho! Way to go, Marty!" Ezra laughed and slapped his knee. "What a brilliant maneuver!"

Lillian gave Emily a squinty stare. "A well-intentioned man. But I see the handiwork of a master here. This is your doing, Emily, isn't it?"

"I knew about it, but I couldn't tell anyone, Mother. Sorry."

"From the sound of it, you not only knew, you were the one who cooked this up. What does Martin Becker know of village bylaws?"

Emily smiled but didn't reply. "Look, the mayor is ready to speak. Let's be quiet."

Charlie had been in a huddle with the council

437

members, their hands covering their microphones as they frantically whispered to each other. Carl Nelson, the village attorney, began searching the bylaws.

While Martin handed out information packets to the audience, Art Hecht walked up to the microphone. He waved his copy of the letter from the county.

"This is a load of baloney. It's our town, and we can do what we want without a bunch of county bureaucrats butting into our business." He looked up at Charlie and the town council. "Are you really going to give in to this without a fight?"

Charlie had returned to his seat, his back ramrod straight, his expression grim. He banged his gavel for the first time that evening.

"I understand you're upset, Art. But let's tone it down a notch. Carl Nelson has just looked over the letter and checked the bylaws up here. It appears that this action is within the rights of the county, and our village must abide by this directive."

"You're kidding, right?" someone else shouted out.

Carl, the town attorney, leaned forward to speak. "This is not a request we can argue or fight. Not without the village taking the county to court, where we would probably lose and spend a great deal of money and also tie up this question for much longer than twenty-four months. The bylaws are very clear. I advise the town to comply."

"I agree with Carl," Charlie said. "And so does the rest of the council. We accept these documents into the minutes. The proposal for new zoning is tabled for twenty-four months, for a period of review, as so directed in this letter."

Charlie tapped his gavel. It wasn't exactly a bang, Emily noticed. She watched him shake his head, then scan the audience, his eyes finally finding her. She stared back at him and shrugged.

To her surprise, he smiled. It was the smile one would grant a worthy opponent across a battlefield. Emily smiled back.

"Twenty-four months? That's just enough time for a new mayor to come in," someone shouted out.

"You never know what's going to happen, fellas. This is politics," Charlie said. He cleared his throat and checked the agenda. "On to the next item. The town has finally signed a contract with K&B Carting . . ."

"That is enough time for a new mayor to come in. Or an oldie but goodie," Lillian murmured.

"Not a chance, Mother," Emily replied, though she did feel very happy and relieved to see the plan had worked.

"You say that now. But you've saved the

village from certain disaster. From complete extinction, actually. Word will get out. They'll want you back, mark my words."

Word would get out if her mother had anything to do with it. But Emily had no time to get into this conversation again.

"I've got to go, Mother. Jessica and Sam will take you home. They're sitting across the room. We've already arranged it."

"Yes, I noticed them there. All right, you run along. Your work is done here."

"Good show, Emily. You should be very proud," Ezra added in a hushed tone. Emily touched his arm and thanked him as she slipped out of her seat and headed for an exit at the back of the room.

Once outside, she walked quickly down Main Street and met Dan and Jane at the Beanery.

"Did we win, Mom?" Jane greeted her.

"Yes, honey. *This* time, I think we did. I think the entire village won, for years to come."

"Someday, even Charlie will agree with that," Dan said.

"You never know. Stranger things have happened," Emily replied.

"Well, we're very proud of you, Jane and I," Dan said, glancing at his daughter. "I know I put up a fuss when you started to help that group, but I can see now it was very important and your help made all the difference."

"Thank you, honey. That's nice of you to say. But I know why you felt upset, both of you. I promise not to get carried away on any more causes. Honestly."

Dan took her hand. "But that's just the point, Emily. That's who you are. I was wrong to ask you to change totally. I know you're still trying to figure things out, to find your way after being mayor for so long. But we wouldn't want you any different."

"He's right, Mom," Jane agreed. "You wouldn't be you."

Emily suddenly felt as if she might cry. "I don't want to be mayor again, so you don't have to worry about that. But I probably will be drawn to causes and issues from time to time. I guess I can't help that," she admitted.

"As long as it's occasional, I won't object. And as long as it doesn't interfere with any vacation plans." Dan checked his watch. "Which reminds me, we'd better get moving, or we'll miss the talk."

Emily linked her arm in his as they left the café. Jane trailed alongside, toting a knapsack of schoolbooks and her laptop. They were headed for the library, where Emily and Dan were going to attend a presentation on ecotourism, to help plan their trip, and Jane was going to work on a research project.

Emily felt lighthearted, as if a load had been

lifted. She was not only happy about the outcome of the zoning question but also relieved to put aside politics and focus on her family. They needed her love and attention as much as the village of Cape Light did. Even more.

No matter what her mother said, or how much she goaded or stroked Emily's ego, Emily was sure she would never want to be mayor again. But she could see now that she still wanted to serve and help. She always would. It was part of her DNA. These sideline efforts would never be the same as "running the show," as Charlie liked to say. But Emily thought now they might even be better.

ON THE TUESDAY AFTER NEW YEAR'S, ZOEY woke up and realized that James was gone. He had taken off for his new life in South America. Well, at least she, too, had a sort-of-new life, working at the center. It was a relief to be out of the diner, which just reminded her of him. She felt an aching emptiness deep inside—and regretted that she had not gotten in touch after their argument.

But he never made a move to get in touch with you, she reminded herself as she finally got out of bed. *Which probably means he didn't want any big farewell scene, either. Maybe this is the best way for both of us. Sophie must be wondering what happened, but she probably understands.*

Zoey didn't need to be at the center until noon, and Sophie had left a message on her cell phone Sunday, saying she had big news to share and asking Zoey to stop by sometime.

Zoey decided to stop at the orchard on her way to Beverly. She had been avoiding James since Christmas Eve, and the result was that she had also avoided her dear friend. Sophie needed her support now more than ever, with her move coming up. And Zoey planned to be there for her—now that the coast was finally clear to visit.

Zoey hadn't even told Sophie yet about the internship. She could hardly wait to see her friend's reaction.

She pulled up the bumpy private road and parked at the side of the house, behind Bella. She had just gotten out of her car when Mac raced out of the barn, barking and wagging his tail. Zoey expected to see Sophie follow. And saw James instead.

She felt shock and something else—something that was a lot like happiness. But she quickly covered over both reactions with what she hoped was a neutral expression.

"Hey, Zoey. Are you all right? You look a little pale. Like you just saw a ghost."

She lifted her chin, determined to keep her composure and not look as if she cared so much. *It's just as well to run into him,* she decided. *It's probably better to say good-bye and take this chance to talk things out, if we can.*

"I'm just surprised to see you. Weren't you supposed to leave yesterday?"

"Well, my plans changed. I got an offer to work on a different farm." He came closer and stood with his hands in the pockets of his jacket, his blue gaze fixed on her in a way she found unnerving.

"Is this another farm in Peru? Or that one in Chile you were talking about?"

"Actually, it's right here, in New England. It's not exactly a farm yet. It's an orchard, but new people are taking over, and they want to grow vegetables and herbs, and increase the honey production, too."

Zoey didn't understand at first. Then she thought he had to be teasing her. She squinted up at him. "You mean, *this* orchard?"

"I do." He looked as if he wanted to laugh but was trying hard not to.

"How can that be? Did Sophie find a buyer already? I didn't even know she put it up for sale. But she left me a message that she had some big news."

"It's big news, all right. You know my grandma. She has her own way of doing things. She found this young couple, the Quinns. They live down the road, and they just happened to be shopping around for an orchard." James laughed and shook his head. "But she's keeping the house, and she's going to stay here. With a live-in companion. And I'm going to stay here, too."

"You are?" Zoey's eyes grew wide. She blinked, not knowing if she wanted to laugh or cry.

"The Quinns offered me a job. And I decided to take it."

Zoey was so amazed by that news, she could hardly breathe. She looked out at the trees, then back at James. "I don't understand. Are you sure this is what you really want? Traveling around and having new experiences . . . that was your dream. I didn't mean to belittle it, either, when we had that fight. I said a lot of mean things on Christmas Eve. Things I wish I could take back now. I'm so sorry—"

"I'm sorry, too, Zoey." He met her gaze with a solemn look. "I should have gotten in touch with you and apologized. But I had some real thinking to do."

"Me, too." She had to summon her courage for what came next. "I'd be lying if I said I wasn't glad to hear that you're staying, James. But you had your heart set on traveling. I don't understand what's made you change your mind. I'd hate to think it was anything I said."

"No, not at all. But getting to know you has made me see a lot of things differently. There's plenty to write about right here, right under my nose. And I still want to visit all those places someday. But I know now it wouldn't be any fun without you, Zoey. My heart was set on traveling. But now it's set on you—stuck on you, I'd have to say. What do you think?"

Zoey felt her heart melt. He actually looked nervous, waiting for her answer. She reached up and looped her arms around his neck. "I think that traveling together to Peru, or anywhere with you, is an excellent plan. And I'm thinking it's going to be a really great new year. Which I didn't think at all a few days ago."

He smiled and pulled her close. "I feel the same about that, too. Happy New Year, Zoey."

"Happy New Year," she whispered back, knowing that she had never meant it more.

Their lips met in a deep, warm kiss. Zoey was swept away on a wave of joy and a feeling of connection and belonging to someone that she had never quite known before. When they finally parted, she noticed that James's eyes looked glossy and bright. Was he about to cry, too? She was sure a few tears of happiness had slipped from her eyes. They stared at each other and laughed.

"Let's walk a little. I'll show you some of the changes the Quinns want to make."

James put his arm around her shoulders,

and she wound her arm around his waist. They headed toward the rows of apple trees, their steps timed perfectly together. Zoey knew she would remember this day for the rest of her life. She had never been quite so blissfully happy.

SOPHIE WATCHED THEM WALK INTO THE orchard and sighed. It was a relief to see James and Zoey make up. James had been a basket case ever since Christmas Eve. She'd had to bite her tongue a few times to avoid saying, "Just call her up. Talk it out."

But she didn't want to meddle. Though she did leave that message to get Zoey over here and get it over with. That wasn't meddling, exactly. Just stirring the pot.

They're both strong willed. But meant to be, she decided. *I wasn't worried, not really.*

She gazed out the window again and saw them in the distance now. Just a young couple, holding hands as they walked through the orchard. She saw herself and Gus. *We must have looked just like that, walking that same path, way back when. Everything comes full circle, doesn't it?* She closed her eyes, her gratitude for all that had come to pass these past few days welling up inside.

Thanks again, Lord, for all your help. For making everything that seemed so wrong turn out

447

right. Much better than I could ever expect, or imagine.

I'll be right here when you need me. Until then, I'll enjoy the peace and joy in my heart. And the miracles you send every day in my world.

Center Point Large Print
600 Brooks Road / PO Box 1
Thorndike, ME 04986-0001 USA

(207) 568-3717

US & Canada:
1 800 929-9108
www.centerpointlargeprint.com